The tale of monstrous horror that began in *Beastmaker* continues in *Beaststalker*. . . .

The young woman saw a ripple on the green hillside. It's just a squirrel, she decided. Until she heard the loud rustling of leaves. Until she looked at the figure ten feet away. She looked but could not—would not—comprehend. It looked something like a man. A hairy man cloaked in long, thick sorrel fur. He—it—was muscular but hunched at the shoulders and bent at the waist. The chest was a patch of black on the reddish fur. The paws, long, strong and furry, looked more like hands, claws like brass stilettos extending an inch beyond the fingertips. The head was draped with a black lion's mane, framing the deep-set eyes, flattened nose and the muzzle elongated like a baboon's. But this was no man, no lion, no baboon. This was a monster, a *beast*. . . . Shrieking, she began to run. She felt something stab her in the back, felt her flesh ripping off as she hit the ground, enveloped by a horrible scent and green darkness. . . .

Also by James V. Smith, Jr.

BEASTMAKER

BEASTSTALKER

JAMES V. SMITH, JR.

A DELL BOOK

Published by
Dell Publishing
a division of
The Bantam Doubleday Dell Publishing Group, Inc.
666 Fifth Avenue
New York, New York 10103

ISBN: 0-440-20172-1

Printed in the United States of America

Published simultaneously in Canada

November 1988

10 9 8 7 6 5 4 3 2 1

KRI

My thanks again to Bob and Lori. And to the Horseman, for his help with maps and shared recollections of majestic Montana. And to Colonel Herb Spier, Indiana National Guard, the quintessential jet jock, for teaching me the rudiments of air-to-air combat.

Eric, Cassie, Joel—
don't walk in the woods alone.

PROLOGUE
1

The copper mongrel found the remains, two weeks old and sun-dried to strings and ooze. Raccoons and opossums had left little but the bones and the rancid oils easing into the earth. And, yes, the stench was left behind too, hanging in the air like an invisible cloud. So the mongrel rolled in the body sludge, squirming on his back, wearing the earnest grin of a dog absorbed in the instinctual duty of carrying the scent back to the pack.

"RUSTY," came the shriek.

The dog twirled to its belly and skulked from the chaotic mob of bugs toward the ten-year-old ankles of the girl.

"Mazey, what's wrong?" asked the boy, pushing a leafy bush aside.

"Oh, yuk," she said, stuffing fingers up her nostrils. "Rusty's been rolling around in dead stuff."

Dead stuff. Patches of fur, tufts of pet fuzz. Broken, greasy cat bones. Dog bones. And some bones of the very raccoons and opossums that had scavenged here. All were mixed together in a small-animal graveyard. It seemed as if the pets and wild animals had migrated here to die. And there was one wide, deep spot of body oil. Bigger bones. Not of a pet. Not of a varmint, but horribly smelly nonetheless. The boy and girl were repulsed by their own pet.

"God, he stinks," said the boy. "Let's get out of here. Bugs are crawling in his fur and everything."

They burst from the bushes below the low bluff. The dog recovered from its shame and joined the game, tagging along. Its yapping spurred them on.

Free of the stifling air, the pair now squealed at the dirty dog, which didn't recognize their flight as a snub, rather than a game. Between breathless laughing and shouts at their pet, they called to each other.

"You have to give him a bath, Kyle," Mazey yelled.

"Nuh-uh."

"It's your daw-og."

"Bullshit, Mazey."

"Ahhhm, I'm telling you cursed."

"I'm so sure."

In the chilly, damp shadows a pair of fevered, pained eyes fluttered open, startled by the children's shrieking. Instantly, the eyes narrowed, focusing in the direction of the sound, *the* spot. Prey. The ambush spot had been visited by prey. The fevered eyes had missed seeing. And the ears heard too late for a stalk. But the hunter instinctively knew it was not too late for a kill. The sound of shrieking grew louder, louder. The hunter gathered itself for the attack.

They crossed an open glade by a pond and clattered across a wooden footbridge that spanned the gully below the dam.

"God," shrieked the girl. "I can still smell him. Rusty, get away."

But Rusty was nowhere near enough to be still offending their young noses. He had stopped to shed his maggots with a roll in the grass. He now lagged far behind, loping toward the footbridge to catch up. The children had a hundred yards head start on him.

The startled hunter coiled for a chase, a short dash to bring the pair of children down. Then to drag them into his lair. Then . . .

As the ambusher sprang, it lost footing and sprawled in the mud. In a second it had gathered itself for another lunge, but they were past, the opportunity lost.

Another kill was delivering itself, though.

The hunter could hear the approach of a panting dog.

The pet hit the planks of the bridge and the new stink. He drew up, dog nails scritching to a halt, leaving white skid marks in the treated pine.

His dirty copper fur bristled from shoulders to feathery tail. Rusty, nose to the pine, growled through the slots between the planks.

An answer to his challenge rose up in the form of a powerful puff of stench and a low growl, deep and labored. From the dankness of the marsh grass beneath the footbridge came sounds of movement—swishing grass, sucking mud. The taut breathing hissed as if beckoning—indeed, daring.

The copper dog trembled. Confused, he looked up the hill at the backs of the two children disappearing toward the red brick houses that were the officers quarters. He cocked his head and yapped at the pine. Pure bravado, for he was losing his nerve. He looked up. Then down. Then he decided. He yelped for the children to wait. Too late. They were out of sight. He bunched to take off, to follow, to leave this overpowering presence behind . . .

. . . when the planks beneath him erupted.

Kyle and Mazey Lee ran up the rear stoop of the two-story house and slammed the screen door before ever looking back for the dog. Now they giggled breathlessly, squealing at the memory of that awful smell, arguing about who would have to wash the dog —this for the benefit of their mother.

But Nancy Lee would have none of it. She plucked the telephone handpiece from her ear.

"You two be quiet."

"But, Maw-um," shrieked Mazey, "Kyle has to give Rusty a bath."

"What? Listen, I'm on the phone. Go outside."

"But Maw-um . . ."

Kyle interrupted. "Rusty's been rolling in dead stuff and he stinks like crazy, Mom."

Nancy Lee stretched the phone cord to its limit and looked over their heads out the screen, mother's sensitive nostrils dilated to pick up any trace of untoward odors.

"Rusty's not even around here. You two get outside. We'll talk about this when I'm off the phone."

Brother and sister peeked outside. Not seeing or smelling their pet, they crept out like a pair of cat burglars, trying to avoid attracting the dog's attention.

2

They had backtracked and were now standing ten yards from the footbridge. Her straight black hair shining in the sun, Mazey pressed close to her brother's shoulder. A few years earlier, she might have held his hand.

"I'm cold," she said, and shuddered as if to prove it.

"How can you be cold on a day like this?"

It was early fall, just at the point where school had begun and leaves hinted at turning. The sky wore the blue of postcards—too blue to be real.

She didn't answer, but neither did she mock him for the gooseflesh she saw on his clammy arm.

They were gawking at the hole in the footbridge.

"Let's go home and tell Mom. She can call Dad at work."

"For what? To tell him Rusty rolled in dead stuff and ran away to hide so we couldn't give him a bath?" The boy looked around to confirm that everything but the hole in the footbridge was normal. It was. There was the golf course not a quarter mile away. Swishing traffic plied the roads nearby. This was the middle of the afternoon at a quiet army fort in Indiana where soldiers trained on typewriters and computer keyboards rather than in tanks and helicopters. Just as his dad always said. Just before he called it the boringest spot on earth.

"There's no reason to be afraid," Kyle announced. "Rusty fell through the bridge and we better check to see if he's hurt." He leaned forward, waiting for his sister to hold him back, to counsel caution. She did not.

* * *

The hunter waited. The prey would come. The prey always came to him. The dogs and cats had gone to their graveyard in answer to the powerful fragrance of their dead predecessors. And, as the hunter had recently discovered, a child often came right after a pet.

They would come to him.

The boy's hair—light and airy, blond and flyaway—lifted in the breezes like fluff from a cottonwood tree. To Mazey, it looked as if fear had made his hair stand on end.

"Come on," he said, stifling a shudder. They advanced toward the first planks of the bridge and once again they were assaulted by the horrible smell.

"Why didn't *we* fall through?" she whispered. "We went over it first."

He showed his growing impatience with her. "Because it wasn't broken then, stupid."

"But how did it . . ."

He shushed her and led the way out on the boards.

He wore tennis shoes, which padded on the pine. Her hard flats trip-trapped on the boards. He knelt near the hole and picked up a swatch of copper fur.

She leaned on the bridge railing and looked over the side. "Look, there's bits of Rusty's hair floating on the pond."

"Sure enough, he did fall through . . . yaaagh." He shook the fur off his fingers.

"What's wrong? Kyle-Lee. Oh, you, you're just trying to scare me."

"No," he insisted. "No." He swallowed hard and shuddered, no longer able to stifle his fear. "Blood. There was blood on that fur."

"Cut it out, Kyle, or I'm telling Mom . . ."

Below, the water splashed a little, accompanied by a thucking of mud.

"Let's get out of here," she said.

"It could be Rusty. He could be hurt . . . *Rusty.*"

The boy knelt on all fours and gaped into the dimness below.

A low growl rose through the hole. The growl ended in a hiss.

"Rusty?" he whined, tensing to bolt.

"You made that noise, Kyle. I'm leaving. I'm telling Mom you're trying to scare me." She backed away from the hole.

He turned toward her to protest her leaving or to ridicule her or maybe even to curse her. But he uttered no sound other than a wheezing croak as a dagger-tipped paw flicked out of the hole in the bridge and closed on his throat.

She saw her brother's eyes go wide and then keep on widening, bulging from their sockets, his face reddening, lips blueing. The paw grasped the fine throat and punctured it, releasing blood and air and a rattling as of dry leaves in October.

She flew off the bridge and ran for the second time that day breathlessly up the hill toward home. Once she looked back and saw nothing but her brother's leg protruding from the footbridge. The leg kicked against the wood, the heel hammering on the planks. But she could hear nothing besides her own frantic breathing, and she kept running toward the back of her house, feeling first a whimper, then a scream rising from her chest. When she plowed into her mother at the back-door of their quarters, the screams burst loose.

3

Although it was afternoon in Washington, D.C., all the shades in the office were pulled down, darkening the room so effectively, it might have been night.

The hulk of Rodney Gerlach leaned into the circle of light cast by his desk lamp. The soft glow failed to ease the harshness of his features. He looked gray, rough, and hard, like granite freshly blasted from a quarry. His crew-cut hair stood erect, a brush of dirty pig-bristles, dull after the mud has dried and flaked off. Pockmarks, deep pores, and gray beard-stubble accentuated his coarseness. Even his suit was gray, rough-woven, dull. But his eyes shone. Cold and unyielding? Yes. Dull? Never.

At the perimeter of light in front of the walnut desk a pair of legs rose into the darkness. The legs were trousered in blue pinstripe but were unmistakably locked into the military position of attention, heels touching, toes pointed out at forty-five degrees. One knee twitched.

Gerlach sat hunched over his hands, fingers thick and rounded, practically nailless, like bratwursts. Smoke seemed to be coming out his ears.

Finally he raised his head, revealing the fat stub of a cigar banked in the corner of his mouth. The gray cheeks caved in a little. The cigar glowed. A yellowish cloud leaked from the thick lips as he exhaled a low growl.

His eyes locked onto the figure standing before him.

One twitching pinstriped knee jerked into a heavy quiver.

Gerlach snickered. He sneered upward into the

darkness. All he could see were two crescents of light glaring off spectacle lenses.

"Another incident, you say?" His voiced rasped, and his eyes glared. He knew what the reaction would be. And the corner of his upper lip lifted as the knees trembled even more.

"Yes, sir."

"Another child?"

"And a dog. More dogs and cats have . . ."

Gerlach snorted. "A dog," he muttered. "That's important, you think?"

"Sir . . . nossir . . . I was just articulating a thorough, accurate, and . . ."

"Fuck a bunch of dogs, Gates. You say there was a disappearance from the Michigan group?"

"Yes, sir. John R. Bertrand. A sergeant major. As you already know, he was reportedly on convalescent leave from an illness and didn't report in. . . . We've now been apprised he's been missing for a week."

"And how many does that leave outside our . . . control?"

"Well, over the last two years, eight disappearances have transpired—in Washington State, Louisiana, Montana, Idaho, and one in British Columbia, Canada."

"Where the fuck they going? Who's taking them?"

"Sir, I'm unwitting . . ."

"It's rhetorical, Gates," he snapped. "It's got to be either the Russians or . . . or that damned dead researcher has left us another one of his goddamned legacies."

There was a lengthy silence as Gerlach clamped his teeth on the cigar. He felt his grasp slipping on the smoldering anger that kept everybody in his command

under control. He bit down harder on the cigar until
his jaws ached. Before his temper reached critical
mass, the pain in his jaws and temples restored his
anger to a manageable level. Back under control, he
took a deep breath.

"Right, Gates. Don't leave anything out. I *do* want
you to be . . . thorough."

Gates exhaled in relief. And he *was* thorough. He
told all that had been learned and surmised of the hap-
penings at Fort Benjamin Harrison, Indiana. Gerlach
did not interrupt the half-hour briefing.

When the report was done, Gerlach grunted. "So.
How many of the Michigan group and family are still
around?"

"Three, sir—four if you count Larson."

"I count her. A decision, Edward . . . I've reached
a decision. Call a Yankee priority. Take them."

"But a Yankee, sir? Next to a war-footing alert, that's
the most . . ."

"Edward?" Gerlach said, with extraordinary gentle-
ness.

"Sir?" The very mildness in manner shook Gates
anew.

"Who am I? What's my title?"

The confused aide stuttered as he said, "Why, you're
the president of The Corporation, sir. . . ."

"And what does The Corporation do, my friend?"

To Gerlach, the aide looked as if he might break into
tears, and that made the president happier than he'd
been all day.

"Sir . . . uh, The Corporation is the nation's domestic security agency . . . uh, we . . . it's an off-
the-books, plausibly deniable organization that con-
ducts intelligence activities against . . . uh, enemies

of the state unbeknownst to them and others within the boundaries . . ."

Gerlach slammed a meaty fist on his desk and growled menacingly, "So why are you lecturing me on what a goddamned Yankee priority is, Edward?"

Gates stood rooted, speechless, trembling.

Gerlach repeated his order. "Call a Yankee. Take them."

"C-c-capture them, sir?"

"No." Gerlach sneered, mocking his aide. "K-k-kill them. Everybody in the Michigan group. No more cloak-and-dagger shit. No finesse. No nothing. Just kill the whole fucking lot of them."

There was silence, and the tremorous knee pulsated faster.

Gerlach's eyes narrowed. "Well, what's the fucking problem, Gates? Get it off your chest before you piss your pants or something."

"Sir, do you mean to . . . have Payne affected by the same kind of . . . transaction as the others?"

Gerlach practically shouted. "Isn't that what I just said?"

Gates talked fast.

"Yes, sir. But what about his threats to disclose our mandate . . . to expose us . . . his so-called insurance? What about the packages set to be mailed off to the press and Congress in just such an eventuality?"

"You've told me we've made progress on tying up those loose ends, Gates. You haven't been exaggerating those reports, have you?"

Gates recoiled and went on talking, his voice near breaking. "No, sir. We're ninety-nine percent positive of our monitoring efforts. But we can never be abso-*lute*ly certain . . . sir."

"Take the chance."

"Sir . . ."

Gerlach finally erupted. One paw drew itself into a club and smashed the walnut plain of the desk, setting the lamp to tap-dancing.

"Cowards . . . I'm surrounded by fucking cowards and fucking politicians. Nobody ever gets perfect certainty in this business, Gates. It's war, you dickhead. I want that . . . monster found and captured or killed and I want its carcass put in a body bag and taken to the mountain for analysis. I want Payne killed. . . ."

Gerlach paused as an idea struck him and he did not shout when he spoke again.

"No." He contradicted himself. "Kill Larson. And the others—uh, and Jacobs and Bertrand's wife. And anybody else who gets in the way. Got that? Anybody who asks too many questions or even remotely seems to be getting in the way."

"Yes, sir." Now Gates's voice trembled as well as his knee.

"But don't kill Payne. I want him taken to the lab on the mountain. I want him analyzed, examined, whatever is necessary to get to the bottom of this. Kill the others, but not Payne. Take him alive. Catch him. . . . We can always kill him later . . . after we've found out about the . . . insurance policies, as you call them."

"Yessir. Uh, sir . . ."

"What is it, Edward?"

"There's a substantial risk that a number of people at this Fort Harrison will be investigating the disappearance of the sergeant major, uh, Bertrand, and the girl last week and the killing of the boy today . . . and those pets," he added.

"Don't we have some of our best people in Indiana? Didn't I just order Barnaby down there?"

"Yessir. In fact we have him and several other points of contact near enough to Indianapolis to be effectual."

"Well, put them on alert. I'll personally talk to Barnaby. Anybody snooping might have to be killed. Did we direct the secretary to get Kirk out of there?"

"Yessir, as soon as that girl disappeared, I told the secretary of defense to get Kirk reassigned."

Gerlach smirked. "How'd he take it."

"He . . . resisted. He objected to receiving orders from us, sir."

"He's a coward . . . a politician *and* a coward . . . but he *did* send the order to pull Kirk?"

"He promised he'd personally write the SSU order. Naturally, I already had a workable draft with me. He signed it. I . . . don't know if he'll go to the President to request intervention . . ."

"Hell, he ain't got the guts to go to Big Guy. As if the Man would even want to listen to a story like this . . . kids, pets, soldiers, disappearing, all because of some shit stirred up in the sixties by his own government . . . genetic weapons shit."

Gerlach's mind began wandering. He pulled back to the present dilemma. "Kirk," he said. "We can't have anybody with his background too close to what might happen. So either we get him out of there with that SSU . . . or we kill him too."

"Yessir."

Gerlach narrowed his eyes against the glow from the lamp.

"And anybody who loses his nerve, Gates. I want him killed too."

"Yessir."

Gerlach purred sarcastically. "Dismissed, Edward."

The pinstriped legs buckled as they tried to turn. The man almost went down.

"Edward?"

"Sir?" Gates looked back over his shoulder.

Gerlach spoke as if thinking aloud to himself. "Not rhetorically this time—are the Russians behind these disappearances from the Michigan Group, do you think?"

"I'm unwitting of any Soviet involvement, sir."

"Goddammit, I'm asking what you THINK, not what you're WITTING of. Is there a Russian in the woodpile?"

"I . . . think . . . at this point in time . . . no."

Gerlach leaned over and spat into his trash can. Then he straightened and spoke low and gravelly. "They better be, Edward. I can handle a Russian. But . . ." He went speechless.

Gates swallowed a dry gulp.

"Dismissed."

Gerlach smirked, watching the figure tack unsteadily across the silver carpet. With his knee, he pressed a button inside the desk well, releasing a latch.

When the three-hundred pound hatch chunked shut, he peeled the hot stub from his lips and stamped it out in an ashtray. He folded his meaty paws together, clutching them to stifle the trembling he felt in the bratwursts.

He sat muttering strings of four-letter words and a four-word sentence over and over. "They fucking better be."

He snatched the telephone from its cradle to talk to Barnaby, the only agent besides himself he could *really* trust.

"And four great beasts came up. . . .
The first was like a lion . . . and it was
lifted up from the earth, and made to
stand upon the feet as a man, and a man's
heart was given to it."
—The Book of Daniel, 7:3–4

BOOK I

AT THE HANDS OF
BEASTS

1

Fort Benjamin Harrison, Indiana.

The post that time and the army forgot. It was destined to be so. Nobody but scholars and a few Hoosiers can remember a single achievement of its namesake president, let alone distinguish between William Henry, whose fort is in Montana, and Benjamin.

About the time of the Civil War, stuffy Indianapolis citizens scratched the fort's obscurity into the sands of time. When the Union Army proposed converting an arsenal at the edge of town into a permanent garrison, alarmed Hoosiers demanded the troops be billeted a minimum of fifteen miles away to protect the ladies from unruly bluecoat soldiers believed to be as threatening as the distant Confederate rebels. So the Army procured farmland to the northeast and let its soldiers sleep forever after in the bucolic setting.

Now Indianapolis's Fifty-sixth Street peters out on Fort Harrison. And the honor of Hoosier ladies still benefits from the Civil War legacy of their concerned ancestors. The fort is garrisoned with more civil servants than soldiers. Most of the soldiers who do go there are students at the genteel schools of computer science, administration, finance, reenlistment, stenography, and public affairs, which draws a few sailors, Marines, airmen, and coasties as well. The major occupation—or preoccupation

—of the fort's leadership is playing soldier. It's as if the cadre of officers and noncoms assigned there must struggle to keep their identity in the profession of arms. They resist being forgotten by the system. They do this by marching the troops, briefcases and steno pads at the ready, to the cadence of airborne songs, their formations transparent imitations of spirited, disciplined paratroopers in step. They send clerks to the only firing range on post (other than the skeet club and police pistol-range), which is so small, M-16 ammunition cannot even be fired there—rifles must be fixed with an inner chamber .22 caliber device. They send trainees on so-called field training exercises, though the maneuver area is so small, the troops sleep on cots in large tents. The cadre guide them on tours to point out examples of field fortifications and foxholes they will never have to build or dig—or even see again.

Officers in the combat arms: infantry, armor, artillery, and aviation, regard this charade as a sham within a sham. They dread assignment to Fort Harrison as an exile from the mainstream. They spend their time reminiscing about "real army" assignments and combat and action. Like comic-strip generals, they call their contacts in the Pentagon and try to attract attention to their inconsequential achievements. Anything but to be forgotten.

All in all, Fort Benjamin Harrison emits the air of a tiny, sleepy military post converted into a large, sleepy veterans hospital, its patients over-flowing with war stories.

In fact the post headquarters once was a hospital. But on this day in the command suite of offices, once the psychiatric ward, the drowsy leadership of Fort Harrison awakened with a fury.

* * *

Major Grayson Kirk felt his guts twanging with anxiety as he ran for the general's office. Although the news had him agitated, Kirk wore the proper somber mask as he stepped up to the chief of staff's desk. His breath came in short bursts, as if he'd grown short-winded from the run down from his office. But even at thirty-six, Kirk was as well-conditioned from daily running and swimming as his mended body, pinned and knitted bones and scarred flesh, would allow. It was good condition, not great, for the six-foot-three lanky frame.

Kirk leveled his voice, controlling the shortness of breath caused by anxiety.

"Sir, the general wants to see me about . . ."

"I know what the general wants, Major," said Colonel Arthur E. Keating without troubling to disguise his dislike. He flicked his hand at the wall. "Go stand over there with the rest of the staff until we're assembled and invited in."

Kirk's dark eyes glanced where Keating indicated. No sense in provoking the chief's hair-trigger hatred for him. He saw the others seated in chairs against the wall. He nodded at them in turn.

Lieutenant Colonel Michael Duda, the provost marshal, ignored him in favor of sternly studying the carpet's weave. Duda had big problems, Kirk knew. A child had been missing for more than two weeks and Duda hadn't produced the first practical clue to her disappearance.

Sitting beside Duda was Howie Ferrin, chief of CID, the Criminal Investigation Division. Sids wore civvies, so it wasn't always easy for Kirk to tell ranks, but he could always pick out Sids from real civilians—much as their unmarked cars stood out from most cars on the road. Sids always drove the cheapest low-bid government motor-

pool cars: one-color, blackwalls, vinyl bench-seats, no car-
pets, straight stick on the column, no air, no radio—not
even AM. The Sids likewise failed at looking nongovern-
mental. They cultivated sideburns longer than regulation
and wore scruffy mustaches they always seemed to be
licking, when not even the greasers among civilians wore
sideburns anymore. Sids stood out just like their cars. But
their clothes *really* made them stand out.

Kirk hid a smile as he surveyed Ferrin, who wore
brown polyester trousers that brushed the carpet at the
heels of his black service dress-shoes. Kirk had noticed
Sids always wore either their military-issue shoes . . . or
else they wore the same thick crepe-soled shoes cops everywhere favored. Ferrin wore a rayon shirt behind a
muddy paisley tie strategically selected to go with all the
polyester suits he owned. Ferrin also wore a facial mask
of disinterest. He didn't acknowledge Kirk's existence.
He opened the plastic briefcase Sids always carry and
pretended to study its contents, the portable radio, the
fresh legal pads, thirty or so pencils, pens, and china
markers. Ferrin adjusted a dog-eared notebook, sliding it
to hide a crushed package of peanut butter-and-cheese
crackers.

Kirk's smile broke into the open. He looked away, right
into the face of the next man.

Colonel Martin Grier smiled back at Kirk and issued a
guarded word of greeting. Blood and guts couldn't completely darken the hospital commander's day. Quite the
contrary, they might have brightened it, Kirk knew.

Lieutenant Colonel Constance Gail flexed her cheek
muscles at him to reveal the perfect results of orthodontia
and her best imitation smile. Gail was the staff judge advocate, the post's chief legal eagle, the military's version
of an attorney general. She had a few problems too, Kirk

mused. Chief among them were her looks. In fact, she was downright pretty. And her name. Who could take seriously a senior military officer with dimples and a name like Connie?

Kirk had fantasies about her. Not that he'd ever make a pass at her. She had proved so hardass in only the three short weeks she'd been at the fort that the word among the troops was, she wore platinum panties. In his fantasies there was always the doubt she'd even respond to him, that he'd be worthy of her. He certainly harbored no illusions about his own looks. Even if he *could* soften his bitter, dark eyes, his face was too round, too weathered from squinting. Once it had made for a nice smile, wide and dimpled, but now there were scars only clumsily hidden by army cosmetic surgeons. Now his left cheek pulled up shorter than the right, giving him a crooked self-conscious smile and a half wink every time he was truly amused or happy. But even the most innocent smile made him look cocky, wiseacre, even wiseass. He'd had many an ass-chewing for giving the look to Keating. He'd had many an obscenity uttered at him by women miscalculating his intentions.

So he didn't smile much, especially around the chief— even without the wiseacre look, Kirk could be a wiseass. Keating seemed able to bring that out of him.

And his ears were too big to suit him. Although most people didn't notice them, he was self-conscious about them, especially each time he had a military haircut. So he got fewer haircuts than his superiors liked—resulting in his getting more ass-chewings from the chief than anybody else on the staff.

All in all, his appearance caused him a lot of trouble.

Kirk had guessed the makeup of the small segment of staff who would be invited to this strategy session. The only surprise was himself. He knew Keating disliked him, distrusted him, dismissed him. The hatred came not only for his marginal military bearing. Keating also treated him as a lightweight because of his assignment here as a public affairs puke. Keating hated public affairs officers because they were members of the general's personal staff and could technically bypass the chief of staff. Keating had intimidated the other members of the personal staff, but not the wiseacre. That made Keating hate him all the more.

Kirk found a place to stand against the wall. He passed up a spot on the couch beside Colonel Connie. He imagined he had enough problems without being distracted by the nearness and scent of her—she always wore something musky, something that intoxicated him. He needed to be alert. And her beauty stimulated his emotions and hormones, dulling his intellect.

So he concentrated on the ugly Keating and felt much sharper.

He knew why Keating disliked him. Chiefs of staff were supposed to hate everybody but the general they served. They were *especially* hateful of helicopter pilots, whose flight suits never looked even remotely crisp and military—starch diminished flame retardance—and whose flight pay gave them the same monthly pay as chiefs of staff, who—everybody knew, for chrissake—were far more important. Worse, Kirk drew the pay although he didn't fly much anymore—too many bones pinned together; too much flesh spliced, stapled, and grafted together from the pieces collected at a remote landing zone acknowledged to be inside Vietnam's borders but known by a few to be deep inside Laos.

That he retained flying status at all was just a formality based on his promise that he wouldn't really get into combat or experimental cockpits anymore. In return they would overlook medical conditions that would demand a disability retirement in most soldiers. They would let him hang around in training commands and exiles such as the public affairs assignment at sleepy Fort Harrison, where he'd been for the past two years. Oh, and yes, he would have to consent to having his file combed and preened and sanitized until it looked as if he'd had a bland, uninteresting career devoid of those years of intelligence forays into places whose names could never be mentioned.

Deal?

Does this mean a dead-end career? As in public-affairs-officer-dead-end career?

Either that or the disability retirement. Deal or not?

Deal.

I should have taken the disability, Kirk often thought. It wasn't easy being disliked, distrusted, and dismissed. Public affairs weenie. Damn.

But Kirk had General Ford to thank for saving his career and for taking much of the humdrum out of his new job. The general loved to fly—didn't have wings but loved to get his hands on the stick. When he heard about Kirk's medical board, he intervened, making him his personal pilot, getting him a seat in the Public Affairs Officer Course at the Defense Information School. They had developed a closer relationship than what usually existed between a general and one of his subordinates. In the cockpit, the general permitted the major to be much more informal. They usually left the crew chief on the ground so they could talk in private. In fact, they had become near-friends. Naturally Keating spotted the relationship and despised Kirk all the more for it. He interpreted it as presumptuousness on Kirk's part and he'd begun referring to him as "the general's fair-haired boy."

General Ford saved his career, Kirk reflected. Trouble was, Ford's rescue consigned him to a life as a government flack. And kept him at sleepy Fort Harrison. So Keating could fuck with him.

Never was that more apparent than two weeks ago when Carolyn Dean disappeared. All that remained was a pretty, buck-toothed thirteen-year-old, one-inch tall face self-consciously staring out from a school snapshot. Her parents insisted she wouldn't have run away. Kirk had recommended the fort release her photo and vitals to the press, engaging their help while time was so critical to finding the missing child. No, said the chief at that meeting. No press, no fuss, no investigations. Kirk argued. Keating smugly took a vote, his eyes pinning each staff officer before taking roll. Howie the Sid had stammered his agreement with the chief before going into a coughing fit. Duda, the fort's top-dog lawman, silently yielded to Keating's four-eyed stare, though a provost marshal should have known better than to paper over a possible crime.

All eyes had looked to the commander, Harry X. Ford, Major General. Ford blinked rapidly. Nobody had told him, Kirk mused. Hey, General, you might have to make a decision, God love ya.

Ford squinted in the steely-eyed manner he'd seen in the war movies. "I defer to the chief of staff," he had growled, making his dodge sound like a command.

Keating widened his eyes at Kirk. "No press, Major."

Kirk had taken a big chance. He took his case over Keating's head directly to the general. "Sir, this isn't some kind of embarrassment to the command that we should sweep under the rug. It isn't like the case of Sergeant Major Bertrand going AWOL a couple weeks ago. This is a little girl . . . lost . . . maybe kidnapped . . . hell, maybe she *is* a runaway, but this kind of thing in the papers isn't going to make the fort look bad. We . . ."

"Goddammit, Major . . ." blurted Keating.

Ford raised his palm to the chief. Perhaps he didn't understand the implications of the defense budget and Gramm-Rudman-Hollings, or press relations, but he knew insubordination when he heard it. And insubordination—even from fair-haired boys—he would not tolerate.

"Major Kirk, when I came up in the army, we had respect for a decision once made. We knew we were allowed an opinion when asked, but when the boss made up his mind, we saluted smartly and stepped out."

Kirk stifled an urge to spit. "Sir . . ."

"KIRK."

Ford raised another palm at Keating, who'd leaned forward at the edge of his chair like a sprinter in the starting blocks.

"That will be all, Major." And don't ever try to take advantage of our cockpit relationship again, added the look that accompanied the general's words.

And Kirk had saluted smartly and stepped out. Keating's horseshoe-tapped heels had clip-clopped after to chew a little more ass.

"KIRK."

It was Keating again. In the here and now. This time to blast him out of reverie to enter the office of Harry X. Ford with the others.

Kirk wondered why. His own sources had told him of the discovery of two bodies. One, a decomposed corpse, had been found in the woods not a half mile from headquarters. He guessed Carolyn Dean, the thirteen-year-old. Why would they want the public affairs officer around for the discussion of how to handle the matter? If they didn't want Kirk to publicly acknowledge a runaway, certainly he—like the press, a virtual enemy of the army—couldn't be trusted with the discovery of two corpses. His source said a second child had also been found—at the pond. Kirk assumed a drowning. For a drowning, he could probably issue a release, he mused.

Inside the office, Ford posed beside his raised desk, hands on hips. For crying out loud, he was wearing a pearl-handled, nickel-plated .45. Come *on*, General, Kirk thought. Who do you think you are? General George C. Scott?

When the others had selected spots in front of easy chairs, Kirk took up the position of attention before a leftover wooden seat near the general's desk.

"Be seated, gentlemen," Ford said, without regard for the striking Lieutenant Colonel Gail, whose honey hair was pulled back into a knot at the base of her skull, whose porcelain complexion and Windex-blue eyes immediately eliminated her from the ranks of gentlemen. Ford nodded at Keating and stepped up to the eight-inch platform on which his desk stood, and took his chair. The others sat.

"Gentlemen—and lady—we have an enormous problem," Keating began.

Atop the platform, the general's head jerked imperceptibly at the discovery of a woman in the room. Kirk bit down on the inside of his cheeks to suppress a laugh. The shorter muscles inside the left cheek gave him less to bite on there.

Keating's eyes pinned him, catching him in another of those wiseass smiles, the only kind his facial musculature would allow. Keating blinked, breaking contact, sparing him a reprimand until later, and continued. "The Dean girl was found today. Her decomposed body was lying in the woods less than a mile from here."

Kirk looked for some kind of contemptuous sneer from Keating, body language saying that all the press releases in the world wouldn't have helped find her or prevent her death. But Keating seemed shaken. Two dark patches of perspiration had crawled from beneath his armpits to the pockets of his shirt. To Kirk, Keating himself was the contemptible one. For all the army's infatuation with fitness and health, Keating carried forty excess pounds on his stout frame. And he constantly had a cigarette going. Even in the general's office he dragged on a filter between ragged breaths and halting sentences. Kirk dredged up the word "loathe" from deep within his vocabulary. If Keating hated him, certainly he loathed Keating.

As Kirk daydreamed his idle contempt, Keating talked. A windbag. Like a daytime soap, he thought, you could ignore half his monologue, tuning in now and then and never miss the essence—if there *was* any essence.

But no. What was this fat slob saying? NO. The dependent son of one of the staff also found today? Dead? *Not* a drowning? Mutilated? Kyle Lee found dead? Kyle? Not "Kit" Lee. Not Nancy and Noble's son, you lying son of a bitch.

Kirk jerked erect in the chair, forgetting for the moment how his mended bones and joints always locked up and resisted movement. Duda reported his part in the discovery.

"When I arrived on the scene, nothing was disturbed— the ambulance people and the military police were gagging and vomiting. Nothing could be done for the boy. I picked up . . . his leg was wedged in the planks of the footbridge . . . and it was detached . . . torn off. The boy's body was disemboweled. Torn apart. . . . Even I . . ."

Duda had turned the color of flour paste at the recollection. His stomach visibly lurched as it must have at the scene.

Major General Harry X. Ford gaped. All the war movies in the world couldn't have prepared him for this. He looked helplessly at Keating, who could do no more than relay the look to Colonel Grier, the hospital commander.

To himself, Kirk kept denying it could be Kit Lee, the son of his friend Noble—the kid he always sat next to at dinner when Nancy and Noble invited him over to try to match him up with some eligible woman they had found at church or PTA. He had to get out of this room. To get to a phone. No, to run over to the Lees. To hear them say it was a lie, at least a mistake.

Grier perked up as if to give credence to the lie. "I personally assisted in the preliminary autopsy. Er . . . uh, the results are incomplete as of now."

"What the fuck does that mean?" growled Keating.

"Er . . . incomplete. The report is incomplete, and er . . . the body is . . . incomplete. Parts are missing. I sent a couple corpsmen back to the scene of the . . . accident to search for more parts of the anatomy. I'll have more to tell later when they . . ."

General Ford's jaw lengthened. "Parts? What parts?"

"You know, sir . . . parts . . . I'd rather complete the inventory for you when the pathologist—"

"What parts, Doc? What parts are missing right now, right this fucking minute?"

Kirk thought the very words as urgently as Keating was uttering them.

Grier shifted in his chair. "The heart and liver. . . ."

"Get on with it, Martin, we have to know what you've found."

". . . the left side of the face . . . the neck . . . the viscera had been scattered. . . . Like I said, the heart and liver—they seem to have been torn out . . . or . . . well, no, not that."

The wet patches on Keating's shirt were about to join below the pockets where his paunch pulled against his buttons.

Keating scraped his steel-cleated heels on the tile. He whispered, "Or what?"

Grier choked on the word. "Consumed. Possibly consumed . . . I don't know . . . maybe, maybe not. But probably not."

The general's gaping mouth formed the word silently.

Kirk felt his own insides being torn apart.

"Eaten?" Keating asked in disbelief.

Ferrin, the CID agent, made his first contribution of the day. The Sid nodded dumbly, adding striking detail to the inarticulate doctor's findings.

"I seen the teeth marks, General. That boy's leg was bit clean off. I seen a dog attack once and I know . . . but this was not from no dog. Chunks outta his torso like a . . . shark or sumpin . . . crunched a hunk outta that boy's face like you'd take a bite outta a apple . . . mouth musta been . . ."—He held his wrists together and meshed and unmeshed his fingers as if they were giant imaginary teeth in giant imaginary jaws—"I never seen nothin like it. . . ."

Duda had been there with Ferrin. Eaten was the right word. He confirmed the findings by remembering, by running from the office, gagging.

* * *

Below the pond and the footbridge, the trickle of water ran beside the road in a deep trench with stone walls rising five feet in places. The thing had followed the bed, hunched over and bent as if every joint ached, stopping and crouching into a huge fur ball whenever a car passed. In fact, the beast lived in feverish, cruel pain. Its pain drove it to kill, either from the chaotic aching inside its head or from the insatiable appetite that manifested itself as piercing hunger pains. Pain drove every instinct. The pain of sunlight confined the animal to the night and the dark places. The painful sound of sirens drove it from its latest kill to move along the road.

Once past the golf course, it had slipped into the edge of the wood line to avoid the openness of the small-arms range. It had negotiated one asphalt road, dropping to all fours, bounding awkwardly across, stumbling past a gravel path. There it found the bicycles, the human scent on the bikes still strong. The rage in its head and the pains in its stomach tore at him. Simultaneously, he felt another rage—this one in his genitalia. The three rages threatened to tear this animal apart. Yet they were the only forces driving, holding it together . . . these three forces of hatred.

The pair of ten-speeds had been hidden in the deep underbrush of broad leaves and ferns. The thing sniffed around angrily, as if offended—no, infuriated—and began creeping low among the ferns in the direction the scent led him. The farther uphill it crept, the lower it crouched, until it writhed upward on its belly, propelled by hatred.

Below the crest of the hill, the sergeant first class touched the woman's hand and pulled off his sweatshirt. She followed his lead and pulled hers off too. He was an instructor in the computer science school. She was a private first class and his student.

He draped his sweatshirt over a damp log and sat down on it, pulling her to him. She helped him unsnap the brassiere. She tossed it off.

He tasted the salt on her belly.

She pushed his head lower and smiled at both the magic of his tongue and the setting they had chosen. She gazed around at their world of green. Sunlight filtered through the canopy of walnuts, oaks, maples, and hickory trees; and the fragile green undergrowth reflected the emerald glow back toward the sky. She stood waist-deep in green, bathed in the serene green shade, and clutched the ears of the sergeant. As her eyes rolled skyward, she saw a green ripple on the green slope below.

A ghost at the edge of her vision, she decided. All her attention began to focus on the parts of her body beneath the surface of the green sea.

Until she heard the rustling of leaves.

Until she looked at the figure ten feet away.

She looked but could not—would not—comprehend.

It seemed something like a man. A hairy man cloaked in sorrel fur. He—it—was muscular but hunched at the shoulders and bent at the waist. The fur was long and thick, but the musculature of a man showed through. The chest was a patch of black on the reddish fur. The head was draped with a black lion's-mane framing the features: deep-set eyes, flattened nose, muzzle elongated like a baboon's. But this was no man, no lion, no baboon. This was a monster, a beast, a chimera . . . a . . . Her mind raced, searching for the right word that would help her comprehend, but . . .

. . . then it moved . . .

. . . and her mind stopped searching.

She flinched as the thing advanced.

The sergeant took her reaction as encouragement. He grasped her shorts and lowered them to her knees.

She screamed and lurched away, ripping her nails into his left ear, throwing him backward off the log.

Lying on his back in the mattress of green, the sergeant first class shrieked a curse at her for the sudden change of mind, sudden acquisition of morals, sudden whatever. He touched his ear and found it bloody. His passion died at the sight.

Then he died at the hands of the beast.

Literally.

They were long, strong and furry, more hands than paws. The claws, like brass stilettos, extended an inch beyond the fingertips.

The animal-man-thing plunged the nails into the sergeant's white belly. The fingers followed. Then the wrists. Up to the elbows.

The beast heaved backward. The dying body bowed upward, following, leaping off the ground. The claws came out of the body with the heart still spurting, fragments of the lungs big as frothing red sponges.

It slung the body parts skyward and dove back into the grab bag of the chest. Mercifully, the sergeant had already died.

The private had fallen on her back. She couldn't get up because of the shorts at her knees. She rolled and tore at them and finally got to her feet, running uphill.

Instantly she knew that was wrong. She knew they had come from below. She didn't know what lay over the crest of the hill. She knew she must turn and run downhill. She didn't know what had happened to the sergeant, but she knew it was not good. She could see the wildly rippling undergrowth. She saw that the leaves were being painted with red, greasy paint and she knew it was blood. She knew she must get back to the bikes and the road. She didn't know if she could make it. She knew the branches were slapping at her bare chest and she knew she would be scratched, maybe even scarred. She felt something grabbing at her and she didn't know whether it was the undergrowth or that . . . that thing. She knew she would cry. But she knew it must not be now, for that might attract that . . . monster. She knew the road was just ahead. She heard the sound of a car passing. Now, maybe a scream . . . she felt something stab her in the back. She knew. Couldn't hold the scream as her breath escaped her. Felt first her shorts, then her flesh ripping off as she hit the ground enveloped by a horrible scent and green darkness. She knew she was being killed.

Then she knew nothing.

Not even the vibrating drone of the Huey could soothe Grayson Kirk. He tried to let it. The pedals tickled his feet as he pressed too hard, picking up the tiny high-freq vibes that came through from somewhere along the tail-rotor drive. The one-to-one vertical from main rotor blades not tracking tried to jog him down to a lower level of tension. Screams, whistles, whines, and roars blended into a white tornado of noise to dull his senses. And the greenhouse window above his head let the sun through to bake him dull. To no avail. All the distractions of flight in the helicopter could do no more than drive his consciousness inward to a focused spot, a dot at the center of his body—perhaps the soul—where Kirk could concentrate on how much he was disturbed and hurting for his friends, Noble and Nancy Lee.

Testimony at the staff meeting had reproduced the sketch of the afternoon's horror and Kirk couldn't keep it from vividly replaying on the theater screen of his mind: Nancy had called the military police and had gone back to the bridge with her hysterical daughter; police, ambulance, and fire truck—already rolling en route to one of their incessant drills—had simply been diverted. They had arrived as the mother had begun to stagger toward the lifeless leg protruding from the boards; the provost marshal ordered somebody to restrain the screaming mother; he pulled on the leg, and finding no resistance of body weight, had fallen on his butt, brandishing the limb and setting off renewed hysteria and waves of nausea and anguish.

The anguish infected the staff gathering. Even Keating had lost his nasty edge, Kirk noticed, forgetting for a moment he was an asshole. Ferrin, the CID master of the obvious, allowed as to how the investigation was ongoing. Duda, his color not improved a whit, had returned to the room after vomiting, wiping his mouth with a sleeve. The hospital commander added more gore to the details. Colonel Connie Gail and Kirk simply sat stunned.

Only Harry X. Ford, more a paper-shuffling general than a field leader or an intellect, in Kirk's opinion, seemed to have the presence of mind to suggest the august body of the fort's leadership should develop a course of action.

"We need to develop a course of action," Ford had said gently yet authoritatively. "We need to decide what sort of person or animal is responsible for these deaths, if they're related. I want a search plan executed today. I want some advice on how to guarantee the safety of the remainder of our soldiers and dependents. I want a report drafted for higher-ups. And what about civilian authorities in Lawrence and Indianapolis? And the press—what about them? Answers, please."

Keating finally opened his mouth.

But he was cut off in mid-inhalation by Colonel Connie. "I say no press and no civil authorities. And nothing to the residents of Fort Harrison."

Ford addressed his perpetually heavy eyelids to Kirk, who couldn't contain his astonishment, his expression saying "Why the hell not?"

He remembered himself. "Why not, ma'am?"

"Later. Right now the legal ramifications are enormous. But nothing will compare to the panic you'd set loose on this fort if you started a Chinese fire drill. You'd just generate mystery and hysteria. That would be exacerbated by introduction of civilian law enforcement, FBI included. And the press would stir it all up till we'd have frenzy on our hands."

Bullshit, thought Kirk. His face repeated the thought as his eyes went from flat to glittering black. But he nipped his lip and said, "I must disagree. We have the apparent murders of two children. And we have the disappearance of Bertrand, a goddamned . . . a sergeant major, and we don't know yet whether he's another victim or the killer or AWOL or even related to all this. We've kept everything silent so far and it's gotten us nowhere. . . ."

"Whose side you on, Kirk?" Keating slipped back into his asshole role in time to dress down the major.

Kirk suggested getting the situation out in the open.

Keating demanded to know what the hell for.

Kirk offered suppression of rumor, cooperation of press and police, safety of soldiers, openness in government, constitutional obligations. . . .

"Horseshit," Keating interrupted.

"What if the press got hold of an anonymous news tip?" Kirk said. "Wouldn't that make us look like we were covering up?"

"Is that a veiled threat, Major? Like maybe you'd be calling in the news tip?"

"I don't like my loyalty questioned, Colonel."

In uncharacteristically harsh language, Ford told them to shut the fuck up. The room went silent for a minute of verbal stalemate, although the body language shouted threats, retribution, hatred, and obscenities back and forth.

Finally Colonel Connie raised her porcelain chin. General Ford nodded at her to speak. Calmly, she repeated her stand. As she spoke, her upper lip tended to lift into a lawyer's sneer. The minutest of twitches flung the sneer in Kirk's direction.

Just when—for the first time in years—he thought he might be willing to offer to buy her a drink and show his vulnerable side to a woman, she was going to repulse him.

Okay, bitch, Kirk irrationally threatened with a cocky raised eyebrow and wiseass grin, you may be losing your last chance to screw a pilot.

The Sid, preferring shadows, in which he could hide his bungling, opted for a total news blackout.

The provost marshal dashed out to call down the toilet bowl for Ralph again.

Colonel (Doctor) Hospital Commander Martin Grier scratched his nuts.

And Harry X. Ford, his moment of leadership fleeting, went dumb-ass. He told Keating he'd be in his Huey. He ordered Kirk to take him flying so he could pull his thoughts together.

Officially, the matter was in Keating's hands.

What a sham. What a shame. Nobody had a damned word of concern for the families of the murdered children. Shit. Kirk had asked if he could visit the Lees before they went flying. Ford hesitated. Keating filled the pause with his observations that the helicopter was parked and waiting on the command pad, that Kirk was a staff officer and a command pilot and not a goddamned chaplain, and that there would be plenty of time to pay respects after the general released the major. Emphasis first on general, then on major. Shit, shit, shit.

Still he tried to let the helicopter's vibrations soothe him. They would not. Could not.

Grace Lee. Called Mazey, the name originating with Noble Lee, her father. From the hymn "Amazing Grace." Shortened to Mazey.

She was ten going on eighty since the horrid death of her brother, Kyle, called Kit by Daddy, who could never just use people's right names. The grief confused her. She didn't want to play, didn't even want to see her friends, didn't return the affections of mom or dad. All she could do was go outside to sit on the curb alone and gaze down at the bridge below there at the pond. All she could feel was the horrible emptiness inside from the loss of her dog, Rusty, and her brother, Kyle. She cried silently.

Already they had repaired the footbridge. But the new planks just called attention to the spot.

Mazey did not care much to play down there or anywhere. Ever again. She didn't seem to feel anything anymore.

In fact she hardly felt the bumper of the racing sedan as it jumped the curb and smashed into her. And she didn't feel it dragging her apart as she rolled and scraped between the curb and chassis. She simply didn't have time to care about being killed by a hit-and-run driver.

A stroke of pure damned luck, thought Barnaby, when

the rattling beneath the car stopped. In the rearview mirror, a bloody bundle of rags lay in the gutter.

And Barnaby laughed, hoping Kirk would be as easy.

"Penny for your thoughts, Grayson."

"You'd court-martial me, General."

"You have to learn to relax. Flying. Now that's relaxation, boy."

Kirk smiled weakly. Inside the battered body was anything but a boy. He was a bored, tired, broken, and mended man older than his years. Nope. Add angry and sick at heart to broken and tired. He'd rather have been with the Lee family, if only for a moment, to relieve them of their grief. Or to have them relieve him of his. His smile felt pasted on.

Ford acknowledged the smile just as falsely and then grew serious.

"Son, there is much more to this business than meets the eye."

Kirk opened his mouth. When joyriding in the command UH-1H, Ford had always given him liberties. Now was the time to speak his mind about the arrogance of Keating that might lead to a public affairs disaster in the handling of the murders.

But Ford wasn't giving liberties today. "Don't interrupt, son. Not now. I'm disturbed by ominous . . . communications I've received lately. I brought you up here to talk. Somebody wants you reassigned. . . ."

"Keating, naturally."

Ford shot him a glance that shouted, "Goddammit, I said no interruptions. Major, you're getting as bad as Keating himself."

"Sorry, General." And he truly was sorry for becoming as noticeably obnoxious as his nemesis.

"Washington has sent orders for you. They're effective immediately. You must leave tomorrow."

Kirk's jaw sagged.

"No, it's not what you think. Keating doesn't know a thing—I had to personally sign for the message from the signal center."

Kirk's eyes narrowed.

"No, don't blame the chief. Keating's not even involved through back channels. This came from the highest level in the Pentagon—directly from the secretary of defense . . . personal from the secretary to me . . . personal and urgent . . . Secretary Sends Urgently. I've known four-stars who've gone through thirty years and not gotten one of those. And now—because of you—I get my first."

Kirk blinked. Not that again. They promised he'd never be asked to participate in programs like that. If he healed . . . if he debriefed satisfactorily . . . if he would agree to a nice, quiet retirement on active duty until the actual retirement rolled around. Once they had called him out to fly some experimental equipment on a Huey, but that was short-lived. They sent him back to the ennui of everyday staff life. But at least they promised to leave him alone. And now . . . goddammit, not the SSU message.

Ford whispered into his mike, "Why are you mixed up in this Secretary Sends Urgently message traffic? It can't possibly be related to this other stuff—these disappearances, these killings. Can it?"

Déjà vu sent Kirk into a spasm of short breaths. His chest tightened. His arm jerked involuntarily on the cyclic. The Huey leaped upward a hundred feet.

Ford took the controls away. "Get a grip on yourself, Kirk. Jeesuz H. You're really a lot more than a public affairs flack, aren't you? What kind of shit have you been into before?"

Kirk remembered how to regain his composure. He put on his blank face and looked into the general's eyes.

"You can't say, can you?" said the general, declaring more than asking.

Kirk blinked noncommittally. His mind was elsewhere —many different elsewheres. There were the jungle elsewheres, the night rendezvous in the black foliage. There were the city elsewheres, the blacked-out landings with muffled engines and blades in elsewhere Asian capitals; the important Asian bodies snatched, the important Asian bodies interrogated, the important Asian bodies escaping from helicopters 2,000 feet above the South China Sea, and in a couple of notable instances, above the Tonkin Gulf. Then there were the Washington elsewheres, at a dozen nameless motels with dozens of nameless men and women contacts. The training elsewheres: Panamanian jungles, Louisiana swamps, Nevada deserts, California language institutes, Virginia "methods courses." All thanks to SSU's. Many of them. The memory of every one of those elsewheres still had the power to ignite prickly skin all over his body, to kick-start his pulse, to flutter the heart, to clutch the lungs, to ejaculate the sweat glands.

"Shit, I've been flying with a spook," said the general. He was studying Kirk's face, reappraising the pilot-public affairs officer-veteran-soldier in the light of this newly revealed dark side.

But Kirk wasn't paying attention. His mind had departed for an elsewhere. The fiery elsewhere in the middle of nowhere where six men lay stretched out, waiting to be picked up, looking combat-ready in the half-lit moon even though the black smiles on their throats had been cut there by enemy blades. And where an enemy force with automatic rifles lay waiting in ambush for a Huey crew to land unsuspectingly. A string of tracers had splattered the twin-engine Huey like a fire hose. In the cockpit, the copilot jerked around in his straps, a maniac gone mad from being tickled by giant hands, hands that punctured his thorax. The elsewhere mentality of aiming the crashing Huey down the hosing tracer-fire and the insanity of the I'm-taking-you-zip-assholes-with-me declaration as the flames pooled over the men chained to the gun.

Ford jerked the helicopter around. He wore a mask of pain. *He's feeling betrayed,* thought Kirk. *Well, screw you, General. I can tell you about betrayal. I could if SSU would let me, that is. I can't. I wouldn't. I don't owe you anything anyhow. But goddammit, I know all there is to know about betrayal.*

Kirk remembered the elsewhere of a hospital. For three years, including convalescence. The elsewhere of a mind fevered any and every time it thought about it.

So fuck you, General.

"Fuck me," said the general.

Kirk did a double take.

"Jeesuz H. Keerist, Kirk, look at that."

Kirk looked. Ford was pointing between his knees past the pedals through the chin bubble in the floor of the cockpit. Kirk looked between his own feet. Below lay the skeet range with its open ground. And across the road stretched a walnut plantation, undergrowth climbing halfway up the ten-year-old trees. Its regular crisscross pattern reminded him of the Michelin plantations in Vietnam. There was . . . a sorrel pony with a black mane. No, a man dressed in a reddish gorilla suit . . . something weird . . . a pitiful skit being played out by some poor actor below . . . in a bizarre gorilla suit.

Kirk froze.

The actor grew bigger as the Huey descended.

Kirk shook his head to clear it, pulling his attention from the apparition below, and propelling himself into action. He flipped to the military police channel on the FM tactical radios and called for the Papa-Mike, the Provost Marshal, to report to Charlie-Golf, the commanding general, right away at the walnut plantation. As the acknowledgment was coming through his earphones, Kirk's heart jumped as the . . . thing below grew bigger and plainer.

He remembered a similar final approach path he'd taken in a fiery jungle. He glanced at Ford. Target fixation. He was flying the Huey right into the ground, where that . . . beast was now turning and grimacing savagely at them.

He wrested the controls from the general and drew the cyclic back between his thighs, quickly but gently so as to avoid dipping the tail rotor into the hard, brittle walnut branches below. He pulled in the collective with his left hand, adding left pedal for trim, glancing at the N1 power gauge to ensure there would be no overtorque and at the rotor tach to guard against rotor overspeed. The plummeting helicopter dipped its skids into a trough of foliage.

Kirk pulled more power and gripped the transmit trigger on the cyclic, hollering out Maydays. He saw the rotor rpm dropping, felt the sluggishness in the controls, saw the torque meter register in the red. The helicopter's tail flicked right, a violent, unnatural twitch that felt like a horse shying.

Probably a tail-rotor strike, Kirk thought, possible momentary stoppage and gearbox damage.

Christ, what a time to crash! Not here. Not now. Not when something down there . . .

The general shouted something about a monster. Or was it an observation that they were crashing?

The general may have been a lousy pilot but he knew a crash when he saw one, felt one, was in one.

Walnut spears tore at the fuselage.

The tail flicked right again.

Tail-rotor failure imminent, Kirk knew. He'd felt this before. The only things missing were the bullets, the engine failure, the fire. Maybe later they'd have the fire.

Open ground lay to the right. He could pull up, slide over, chop throttle, autorotate at low level. An easy maneuver practiced a hundred times in one of those special flying schools he'd attended elsewhere. It would be easy unless the failure came above the trees while pulling power, aggravating the spin that would follow.

Where the hell was that beast? That . . . monster? Could he avoid the crash, the trees, and *it* too?

No. None of them.

The Huey settled yet another foot into the trees.

He decided to sacrifice the aircraft to save their lives. He aligned the craft in one of the furrows of foliage. He twisted the throttle to idle stop, held the collective, dropped right pedal to the floor. The Huey, its guts pulled out, sighed, settled. An enormous hand jerked the tail, and the fuselage twisted, hitting the walnuts. One of the gearboxes had failed, Kirk knew by the sound and feel. He'd made the right guess. The trees held the fuselage straight. Near the ground, as the blades began screwing into the leaves, he pulled the remainder of his pitch, hauling the collective clear up under his left armpit to bleed off as much inertia as possible from the blades.

Blades sheared branches. Branches and broken tree

trunks impaled the tail boom and the cabin. One main rotor blade snapped half off and whirled through the plantation like a weed cutter. The unbalanced remainder of the rotor and hub jerked the cockpit from side to side until it tore out the transmission in a wrenching, metal-rending crash.

Kirk cut the fuel and electrical switches just as the Huey hit the ground and bounced with a final shriek of walnut fingernails on metal.

Ford sat cursing and sputtering.

Kirk yelled at him to unstrap. He'd seen JP4 and magnesium combine to barbecue human flesh before.

The helicopter rolled against a tree trunk. The walnut held it at forty-five degrees. The smell of hot metal and cold tree blood—a combination like a panful of sawdust left to sauté on the burner—stung Kirk's nose.

He felt panic rising in his chest. This was too much like a midnight crash he'd been in before. The smells and sounds sent his memory plummeting down into the agonizing depths. He'd screamed then. In pain, in fear, in anger, in desperation. He'd cried then. He knew, just *knew*, he was being killed, that he would die anonymously and unacknowledged in Laos. As he had died, he uttered what was to be his last word, an embarrassing capitulation to desperation and futility, a disgusted "fuck."

But this time he fought off the panic. He freed himself from his lap and shoulder harness, tore off his helmet, and fell toward the general, who had stopped yelling profanities.

"Sorry," he said from habit. "Get free, General. You need help?"

The general didn't answer. He was conscious but dumbfounded, staring out the windshield, a trickle of blood coursing down his cheek.

"Come *on*, General, get free. Here, let me." Kirk pulled at the latch and threw the general's belts off.

The general sat unmoved.

"That thing," he whispered.

Kirk remembered that *thing* he'd forgotten about for a couple of seconds. That *thing* could be more lethal than the crash. He tried to swivel in his seat and struggled to get a look at something besides the ground just outside the general's door below.

The general choked, as if on his own spit. Kirk saw him trembling. The man must be in shock, he thought.

Kirk drew back a hand to slap him to his senses.

The general's hand came up clutched around his .45 caliber nickel-plated, pearl-handled automatic.

Kirk stared down the cycloptic black eye. "I . . . really wasn't going to hit you, General."

The general roared an unintelligible command and smashed Kirk's head aside with the pistol.

Kirk fell back into the pilot's seat, stunned more by the general's vehemence than the force of the blow.

The general fired his automatic.

The pistol exploded, deafening him. Kirk ducked away. The man had gone mad, Kirk thought. He peeked. No, Ford wasn't crazy. He aimed the pistol at the windshield.

"General . . ."

The pistol bucked in the general's fist, deafening Kirk again.

The monster roared and tore through the quarter-inch safety glass of the windshield as if it were a thin sheet of ice, filling the cockpit with its putrid stench and an exploding shower of glass crystals and the guttural scream, not stopping until it had buried its claws in the general's chest and torn out two fistsful of ribs as it pulled the rag-doll corpse out the windshield, doubling the body backward, literally breaking it in two.

All was silent. All was unreal. Kirk shook his head, expecting to wake up from a dream. A curtain of red clouded his left eye. He wiped it away and found blood oozing from a lump where the automatic had connected with his forehead. No dream. All this was real.

And all was not silent. In the distance came the whoop of a siren. Duda. Or maybe an ambulance.

All was *anything* but silent. Kirk heard smacking and slurping sounds. The sound grew louder, either because Kirk had begun to pay attention to it or because the beast had become more voracious. Bones snapped. Kirk could deduce the meaning of those sounds. It was too real, too real to be believed. Harry X. Ford, major general, U.S. Army, had sacrificed himself in saving Kirk's life. Now he had served himself up as the entree, stalling so Kirk could . . . Could what? Escape? Fight? Wait and hope the siren would scare that thing off?

Yeah, right.

A part of him went automatically to work. He must not move too abruptly, must not attract attention. He turned slowly in his seat. The line of sight past his knees allowed him to see a reddish patch of fur with bunching muscles beneath. He moved a knee. Less than six feet away beneath the nose of the chopper, a black mane bobbed up and down. The mane was framed in red. The beast was burrowing into the chest cavity of poor, pathetic, dumb old Harry X. Ford. He watched great bloody teeth bite down and heard the crunch of human bones and cartilage.

Kirk fought his stomach down.

He looked for a weapon . . . maybe the fire extinguisher . . . yeah, right again. A glint of mirrored metal from the copilot's seat. The automatic. Goddamned considerate of the general to drop the pistol.

Kirk reached across the console, trying not to move his feet, which were only a yard away from that red fur with only the chin bubble between.

His arm wasn't long enough.

He held his breath and rolled over on his chest to gain another inch of reach.

Finally.

He could touch it. He fought back the wild impulse to grab and start shooting wildly. The late Harry X. Ford had already taken a stab at that tactic. With one finger he hooked over the slide near the front sight. Pulled it closer. Froze.

Where were those sounds, the signature of the beast?

The siren was louder. Had it drowned out the slurps? Or had the thing slunk away. He dared not roll back for a peek.

The wildness in his chest won over his self-control. He snatched at the pistol and leapt for the space between the Huey's armored seats . . .

. . . just as the hairy red arms dove through the shattered, bloodied windshield fragments where Ford's body had exited.

As he fell into the back and rolled, Kirk caught a glimpse of the seat webbing being shredded where his hand and the pistol had just been.

The stench hit him again, this time mixed with the earthy fragrance of human gore—he'd smelled that time and again in Vietnam. Only the tightening of every body muscle and an enormous burst of adrenaline kept him from vomiting.

He couldn't stand up on the cocked deck of the cabin. He kept sliding down to the lower side, which opened to the ground. Reason told him he didn't want to meet this beast on the ground. He scratched and scrambled to the skyward-most cabin door opening, pulling on the passenger seats for leverage.

Grunting and growling sounds came from the front. Kirk chanced a glance. The thing began climbing through the shattered windshield and was nearly into the cockpit. It threw out its arms, those hairy paws and those claws, grabbing for a better grip on the pedestal console.

Kirk hung by his left arm and aimed the pistol into the face only a couple of feet away. The screaming face, forehead dented deeply into a concave, the brow heavy, the eyes sunken, the forehead smashed. The cheeks and jaw were huge, bone crushers in an extended muzzle. The teeth. *The teeth.* The teeth were . . . oversized human teeth, three times as long as normal size, dark and burnished like rails after a freight train has passed by—the canines maybe four or five times larger than normal, like gorilla fangs—but longer, more like those of a lion or tiger. The eyes. The damned eyes are blue, Kirk thought. Blue, red-rimmed, fevered and fiercely intent on . . . on what, he did not know. There was no doubt this ferocious apparition was about to squirt through the hole and tear him apart, but those eyes were not full of hatred. They were expressing something else.

The blade sight covered the bridge between the blue eyes.

The hand trembled.

The beast did not struggle. It stopped roaring and made a clicking, choking sound, as if murmuring or clearing its throat.

Kirk had killed before. In combat. What the hell was keeping him now? he asked himself. Wasn't this combat? No. Something was wrong, he answered. But what?

He saw a spurting wound in the crook of the beast's neck. Ford had hit an artery. The thing was dying, maybe was already dead.

Kirk lowered the pistol—he wouldn't have to kill after all if this thing died by itself right there. . . .

The thing lunged with a splitting roar and fell into the cockpit. Kirk fired on reflex and saw a squirting puff of dust rise from the lower back. A shriek filled the cabin.

The thing tumbled over the seat and slid down the cabin floor to the ground below Kirk's dangling feet.

He pulled his knees up as it swiped at him.

He climbed skyward.

It followed. Its spinal column must be shattered, he saw. Its legs dragged behind as it pulled itself upward.

The siren had arrived at the edge of the trees. Kirk heard Duda shout. No matter. Nobody could save him but himself.

He aimed between the blue eyes.

Again the animal stopped struggling.

Kirk hesitated.

The beast bunched its arms to pull up on the seats.

Kirk fired.

The beast's head flew back and rebounded forward against the cabin floor. There came an agonizing howl, the painful screeching of nails drawn across a chalkboard as the animal's brassy claws raked the cabin floor. It was a death wail, Kirk knew. He relaxed, letting his aching legs dangle.

Duda yelled for the general. There followed the crashing of brush.

"Here, Colonel. In the Huey."

The animal came to life and went for Kirk blindly. Literally blindly, for its eyes had collapsed into a hole in the center of its face. It caught his boot and twisted. Its teeth gnashed, searching for a crushing bite.

It was Kirk's turn to howl. He pointed the pistol and fired at every part of the beast not in line of fire with his foot. New, weak geysers of blood sprouted from the animal's head and neck with each shot. He fired until his gun was empty. Finally the beast fell into a heap on the ground.

He stuck the pistol into the calf pocket of his flight suit and began lowering himself slowly toward the ground. From the front of the aircraft he heard a moan and the sounds of retching. Apparently, the hair-trigger stomach of Duda had found the remains of the late Major General Harry X. Ford. What a day the guy was having.

Kirk let himself down. His ankle throbbed. He couldn't see down his body to the damage and was reluctant to try looking. When the foot touched the ground, it gave way and he fell, rolling away from the animal. He felt his foot swelling, filling the inside of the boot, and he dared not take it off. He crawled from beneath the Huey's wreckage, dragging the foot.

Martin Grier. Through medical school they called him Ichabod after the Washington Irving character. He preferred what his mother had called him: lean. He knew what he looked like—from the side, with nose and chin and Adam's apple, knees and feet jutting forward, he looked like a zagging line.

But now he was somebody. A doctor. And an army colonel. Because he allowed the army to pay for the last years of med school when his own funds ran dry, he was a doctor. And because he was a doctor with a debt to repay to the army, he was a colonel. After only a few years of average practice at medicine and exceptional performance at administration, they had made him a hospital commander.

Big deal. What did all that matter? Now that somebody was trying to kill him.

That's what he'd been telling the FBI over the telephone. He tried to convince Lieutenant Colonel Connie Gail.

"Look," he sputtered, "You see how the people at that meeting in the general's office keep turning up dead or missing? You heard the radio call about the general's helicopter crash. Kirk was on that helicopter too. I tell you, this is too thorough for it to be an accident."

Connie Gail greeted his conclusion with dismay—as did the FBI. Grier made another phone call while she was there, insisting on protection. The FBI resisted. He argued they were only jealous of his superior deduction at the connection between the deaths and disappearances and the meeting in Ford's office.

Coincidence, the agent said.

"Bullshit," he shouted. "I'm right."

And he was.

They found him dead, the needle still in his arm, a massive dose of pure morphine in his body.

Officially, they called it an accidentally fatal substance-abuse incident. Whether the death was the suicide of a fringe paranoiac or a murder, the FBI couldn't be certain.

If you can't decide, the agent in charge ordered, just play it in low key until you have some hard evidence—emphasis on hard.

Lieutenant Colonel Connie Gail had indeed laughed at the yammerings of Colonel Grier about some sort of conspiracy to kill all the leadership of the fort. But it was an uneasy laugh.

His near hysteria made her nervous. So she had left him and rushed back to her own office across post.

There she'd found messages. Messages from agents. Agents of the FBI. What had Grier done? Had he tattled his story all over the state? What if he'd dragged her name into this?

She returned the phone calls tentatively. A stern voice told her that Grier had been found dead. Murdered.

She insisted she'd just left him. Alive, she emphasized. Dammit.

The agent told her to stay put. The FBI would come out to pick her up immediately and place her under protection as a possible witness.

To what? she demanded nervously.

But the agent instructed her not to answer her doors or phone until they arrived.

How would she know it was them?

Answer only for the person who used the code word *Lurker*, she was told.

But what . . . ?

The FBI agent hung up.

She locked her office door and paced back and forth. She stared at the phone. Suddenly she didn't know about anything. For instance, was that really an FBI number she'd called. She checked in the phone directory. Yes, the FBI number checked out. But her telephone could just as easily be bugged by somebody else.

Lurker. The very word made her shudder. Lurker, indeed. What if this FBI man was part of the murder plan? Otherwise, how could they have found the body of Grier, whom she'd left only minutes before? *Or* what if she was a suspect instead of a witness? She knew people in Washington she might get *real* protection from. But now the thought of using the phone frightened her. Anybody could be listening.

Suddenly she felt adrift. And vulnerable. She decided she couldn't answer the door for anybody—whether they used the code word or not. And she couldn't be here when they came. No. She would talk to the FBI on *her* terms, but first to somebody in government she knew and trusted. And, she decided, a voice at the end of the phone wasn't enough to persuade her to do otherwise.

If only there was enough time.

She used the back entrance of the Staff Judge Advocate building and crossed the alley behind the fire station. As she pushed through a stand of bushes, taking a covered path to the headquarters parking lot where she'd left her car, she heard the squealing tires of speeding cars. Somebody had come for her—the FBI or erstwhile FBI?

She paused at the bank of the creek that fed the pond near where that boy had died. Was this a mistake? she asked herself. Should she be going back to meet those people? Would she now be sought as a fugitive? She compared that fate to what might happen if she gave herself up to somebody who didn't want to protect her after all.

The decision made, she plunged into the creek up to her knees and stumbled up the opposite bank. When she heard shouting from inside the SJA building, she began to run toward her car. A strange, giddy feeling rose up in her chest, part excitement, part fear. And she found she relished the feeling.

Duda and Ferrin watched Kirk being loaded into the ambulance. They thought it fortuitous that one should happen by with another patient. When the ambulance began pulling away, Duda looked to Ferrin for help.

"You know, Howie," he said, "I hate being in charge

when I don't know what to do. All I want to do is crawl into a damned hole and go to sleep and wake up to find this is all over, that it's been some kind of mistake, a dream."

Ever the clever one, Ferrin grunted his assent.

"What could have done that to the general? You think the crash? Getting thrown through the windshield? Could that have gutted him out like that?"

Ferrin wagged his head.

"Kirk kept telling us to look under the chopper. Let's see what he was babbling about."

Ferrin led the way through the grass on his knees, making a tunnel. He found the scent first, gagging and fetid. He held his breath until he matched the sight to the smell. He backed out hurriedly. He felt himself backing into Duda. Then, before he could even turn, he heard Duda choking again. Cripes, even before he could see that . . . that monster under there. What a weak stomach for a cop.

Duda lay behind him. Ferrin sneered and blew the odor from his nostrils. Cripes, the guy must have fainted this time. Impatiently, he crawled backward over the provost marshal, his face buried in the grass.

He muttered a curse and reached to roll over the powder puff cop, to revive him, maybe even to send him down the tunnel to really get a face full. The lieutenant colonel's body rolled over. But not the head. The one had been nearly severed from the other.

Ferrin drew a deep breath to curse as a hand grasped his hair, and he felt a hot paper cut across his neck. His exhalation came, not as a curse but as a ragged hiss through the slit in his neck, followed by a cough as blood poured down his trachea and esophagus.

Always the weak, silent type, Howie Ferrin, Chief Warrant Officer, top Sid hand at sleepy old Fort Harrison, had no more breaths or grunts left in his body to protest the unfairness. It was Duda who wanted to go to sleep and forget all this, not he, Ferrin. It was his final thought.

Barnaby drew the knife blade through the dirt to dry it. Two more down. That left Kirk. Clean up this mess. Then take care of Kirk . . . that was the imperative.

The helicopter was already listing heavily to its right, the side where the fuel cap was located. It required only that the cap be unlatched and taken off. Then a walnut twig to hold open the one-way valve. Jet fuel sloshed over the stack of bodies that had been dragged beneath the Huey. Then a highway emergency flare. The fuel would get hot enough to ignite the aircraft skin and soon the other light metals would catch fire and burn white hot. The hardwoods would help the fire along and keep the fire trucks at bay. The bodies would be ash, perhaps no more than a mixed cluster of teeth. Cleansing fire. Ashes to ashes.

Kirk had been surprised at how quickly the ambulance had arrived. The ambulance driver had said they were passing by with another patient, a suicide victim. He pointed inside at the mountain of a body covered by a snowy sheet.

Long-dormant instincts inside Kirk began to reawaken. Something was wrong here, but what?

The driver helped his assistant roll the body to the ambulance floor, making room for Kirk.

Kirk resisted riding with a cadaver.

The driver insisted.

That body. An authentic corpse. It finally convinced him to set aside his suspicions. He told himself he was no longer in the spook business. He needed to get back to garrison, to find somebody he could trust, somebody to talk to about this business with the monster and the general.

Even ignoring his instincts, he resisted climbing in with a dead body. That they dumped it unceremoniously to the floor was no consolation at all. It lay on its side, and they rearranged the sheet over the shoes. Kirk saw there were horseshoe taps on the heels and then shook off the odd feeling, thinking the oddity was to be noticing things like that. Fresh blankets and sheets were unfolded for him.

Kirk refused to be strapped to the cot. The huskier of the two, an ape dressed in white, demanded it be done, citing regulations. Kirk understood regulations. He'd had to deal with them often enough himself. Rather than give this dope trouble about rules he had no control over, he finally consented to one belt across the thighs.

The ambulance bounded across the meadow near the walnut grove, found a gravel path, and turned left onto the asphalt. Kirk was transfixed by the mound of bouncing flesh on the floor beside him, its back to him. He was bothered by it. He grimaced at it and at the ape who was fidgeting above the corpse's head.

As the ambulance had rocked into its left turn, the sheet slid off the shoulder, revealing the back of a wrinkled, fatty neck and a neat, round, draining hole at the base of the military whitewall haircut.

Suicide, hell!

Those horseshoe taps belonged to Keating, always clicking around the headquarters like some cavalryman, sounding more like a cav man's horse, acting more like a horse's ass.

And that fat horse's ass under that sheet could belong to nobody but Keating.

Jesus. And the turn to the hospital was right, not left. Kirk bolted upright.

"My ankle," he groaned. He rubbed his calf and ankle, slid a hand into the calf pocket and grasped the .45.

The ape brandished a syringe. "An injection," he ordered. "To kill the pain."

With one hand, Kirk ejected the empty clip in order to let the slide forward. He spun and aimed the pistol low, aware that he must not let the ape see the empty slot where the clip had been.

"Get back or I'll blow your balls off." He knew the effect that visual remark would have.

The ape hesitated, an automatic male reaction, dropping a hand to his crotch. The determined expression dissolved from his face.

Kirk fumbled with the belt across his thighs.

"Put that needle down and back off."

The ape's jaws knotted.

Kirk saw the programmed determination and knew that stiff training had begun to take control of the man's emotions. Kirk needed the bluff of a lifetime.

"Move, asshole. If you know anything about me at all, you know I've got the capacity to kill. Better yet, to leave you transsexed. Ever been shot by a .45 slug? I have. It's like having somebody run you through with a blunt spear."

The man laid the syringe on the cot.

"Better. Now back off."

Kirk still fumbled with the belt. Dammit. It wouldn't come loose. He looked forward and met the eyes of the driver staring in the rearview.

"Pull this thing over and stop. This ride's over for me."

Kirk waved the pistol for emphasis. He kept tearing at the belt fastener until finally it began to loosen.

The eyes in the mirror brightened. The driver shouted. "No clip . . . the gun's empty. Jump the bastard."

The ape coiled.

Kirk drew back his right to throw a punch.

The driver, perhaps to help his buddy, hit the brakes.

Tires yelped. So did the ape as he leaped, but the van had braked—So he flew toward the front of the van instead of at Kirk. Keating, also unrestrained, shot forward and rolled over onto the ape. The ambulance kept rolling up the road at an idle speed toward Fall Creek bridge, where the creek formed the north boundary of the fort.

Finally, Kirk freed his thighs and he tumbled off the cot. The driver twisted out of his seat and began pulling his shirt up. The ape beneath Keating produced a 9mm semiautomatic.

Kirk threw Ford's pistol at the driver, now kneeling between the front seats.

The .45 caught the man on the forehead.

Kirk ducked as a shot spanged into the roof of the ambulance.

The driver fell backward under the dash, his shoulder mashing the accelerator to the floor.

The ambulance lurched forward.

Keating rolled down the other ape and knocked away the hand holding the 9 millimeter.

Another shot went awry, this time into the floor.

On all fours, Kirk's hand fell on the syringe. He snatched it up and dived over Keating, his fist clutching the dart of the needle, aiming it like a bayonet. First the needle, then the syringe, then Kirk's thumb drove through the ape's eye into the skull.

Kirk grunted in revulsion and wiped off his thumb. He

had no time to get queasy. He wrenched the 9 millimeter from the ham of a hand and aimed forward. But the driver was already out cold.

Through the windshield, Kirk saw the abutment of Fall Creek Bridge attacking the van. He slid his newly acquired pistol into his calf pocket and grimaced at the pain shooting through his ankle. For a few moments he had forgotten the injury, but now the pain reasserted itself with a vengeance.

He hunkered down behind Keating and asked for the god in charge of assholes to do him just one more favor today: to cushion the impact of this impending crash.

In quick succession . . .

. . . The ambulance plowed into the concrete pillar.

. . . The ape plowed into the back of the driver's seat.

. . . Keating plowed into the ape.

. . . Kirk hit the soft cushion of Keating's fat gut.

. . . Then they were all churned like corn seeds in an air popper as the van flew up and over the abutment toward the creek.

His vision was blacked out before they hit water, but he could hear the splash and feel the impact. And then, pinned beneath one or more heavy bodies, he could feel icy water swirling around his thighs. As they had done before during drinking binges, his lips tingled. Inside his head the constellation began to spin like a showing at a planetarium. The inclination was there. To escape this vale of tears, all he had to do was relax. He would sleep. Nevermore to be bothered with army bullshit or pain or monsters or the mystery of why somebody non-Asian kept trying to kill him. Nevermore. All he had to do was let his consciousness slip. The water crept up his chest. Cold way to go, drowning. The chill and the idea revived him, and his breath quickened. But the dead weight insisted he reconsider. To die or not. No, not this way. He fought the water gurgling over his mouth and would have screamed except he was afraid of inhaling.

His last thought was of the blue eyes of that monster and the pleading expression in those eyes. How could a man-eater who'd just been chowing down on the general be wearing anything but a savage face? And where did this thing that looked like Bigfoot come from?

Keating rolled over and pushed his head under.

His last thought, the last word running through his mind, was a repeat of another last word in a previous life, a previous death.

Fuck.

2

The sun had snagged itself for a minute or two on a rocky peak, inflaming the rock into molten, glowing lava, giving a oxyacetylene-cut edge to the ragged shoulders of the summit. In another minute, the fire would cool. A shadow would race across the alpine lake and darken the glacial valley, literally just a scooped-out place among the Continental Divide's lesser mountains in Montana's Great Bear Wilderness. The sky would stay light for another hour, even as the valley changed, the pines darkening to deep shades of jade before going furry black, the tamaracks staying golden until the last. The red and rust and gray of the higher mountainsides, too savage to bear growth less hardy than lichens, would fade to black as well. Here the big sky of Montana was delimited by peaks and ridges and evergreens, everywhere shrinking the horizon.

Only Marion Lake's eighty-acre surface would resist the curtain of darkness. For as long as the sky held light, Marion would reflect it. When the color of the sky deepened to midnight-blue, Marion would too. Like a precious jewel, it would catch every glimmer of brightness and dimness and bend it, reflect it, enrich it, as it shot the rays back toward the heavens.

On the west edge of Marion, where the snowcaps drizzled into the lake via a wending ankle-deep, ankle-freezing creek, a fire feebly held back the darkness and chill with a reddish yellow glow that occupied all of one cubic yard of the millions of yards in the valley's thin atmosphere here at an altitude of 7,100 feet.

A man leaned into that cubic yard to soak up what warmth he could before the valley siphoned it off and chilled it.

A woman stepped up behind him and draped a wool army blanket across his shuddering shoulders. Her face reflected his pain in the fire's glow.

"That's it, Mark. Tomorrow we're out of here. I've got to get you to a doctor." She used his real name. Mark Payne himself had used it for thirty-three years of his life. That is, until two years ago when he had to give it up forever and take on another identity. When he'd disappeared, he had become somebody else, giving up his name and past, surrendering something of his soul as well.

But no more. He wanted his old name back. If he were dying—and Christ, nothing could hurt this bad and *not* be fatal—he wanted to be Mark Payne again. And he wanted her to be PJ again, Pamela Jane Larson Payne. Not Jane Welch. Bullshit on that. He wanted to die with his name on.

He gazed deeply into the simmering coals, letting the radiated heat soothe his aching face. Probably, he thought, his gums and jaws and even his teeth were throbbing from clenching against the chills. No, that was an evasion. His face had hurt for months. He was grateful for the army blanket. The chill had seeped into his back, which was away from the fire. What you need in the mountains is a triangle of fires so you can sit in the middle and never get . . . Stop . . . He fought off the obsession with warmth. It was the delirium, the fever, the disintegration of the mental faculties accompanying the racking body pains . . . the facial aches invading every joint, bone, and muscle . . . the inflammation, the blackouts he'd had since joining the army in the sixties, the crawling skin of the last year. God, this is how his father died, isn't it? This must be—go on and say it—this must be . . . cancer. Except for the itch, it's the same set of symptoms his father had. . . . It had killed his father, so would it . . . Stop . . . there you go again, he insisted, carrying on a half-delirious argument with himself. He had done so all day.

Still, he thought, a triangle of fires *was* a distress signal. And if he were not a distressed, pathetic excuse for a . . .

PJ touched his shoulder, and he convulsed.

"Sorry," she said, seating herself beside him on the log.

"No need to be sorry. I was daydreaming."

"Let me get the air mattress from the tent. You sleep by the fire. I'll tend it."

"You pamper me as if I were your child."

She smiled into his face, her green eyes more fiery than the fire itself. The smile said she loved him. His face softened a moment and returned the sentiment.

Then pain tightened his face again, accenting the scars. There was the white line, bright enough to be a chalk mark, on his cheek. There was the crescent cut by a .44 slug into the edge of one ear. There were other, more savage reminders under his shirt, rumpled traces of burns and ragged reminders of slashes. The history of his pain-wracked body was written in the scars and aches and fevers and who knows what given him by one quasi-government organization called The Corporation. His adult life had been shaped by it, his hatred stoked by it.

Now he knew he was dying, in part killed by that organization. He would give in to his wife, go to the doctors and get confirmation of what he already knew. Then he would drop his insurance policies in the mail. He would go down. But he would take them with him. Bastards.

Suddenly his hunched body stiffened erect. He twisted and gazed across the shimmering lake, concentric ripples everywhere, the azure mirror disturbed by feeding fish.

She didn't ask. She turned the opposite way from him by reflex. To watch for an attack from his back. For more than two years they had lived this way. Supposedly, they had been guaranteed safety. They even had the insurance, twelve copies of a research journal, an agent's confession, and an explanatory letter that would be triggered by fail-safe devices to go into the mails—items that exposed the enormity of crimes a government could stoop to. There was proof of government-endorsed high crime of domestic spying and officially approved murders. And they had proof of the immorality of drug experiments on U.S. citizens and soldiers. And there was the horror of genetic research on producing monsters. And there was . . .

. . . A frightening noise rattling among the mountains.

He cast his head from side to side, trying to pinpoint the direction of the droning sound.

He and PJ had talked about their fears, their paranoia. He insisted they were right to be wary. The memory of their victimization was still too fresh. The visions of horrible deaths and ruined lives too vivid. He had argued that the moment would come. It was preordained that they would not die of old age.

Trouble was, the moment seemed to come every day in some form, insignificant or otherwise. The backfire of a car ripped them with an instant of terror and minutes of aftermath until the adrenaline subsided. The face of a stranger seen twice in a day was reason enough to leave a town.

The droning increased in intensity.

The mountains echoed the unnatural sound, as if trying to shrug it off, reject it from the wilderness.

He knew the sound. So did she. They both had been army helicopter pilots two years ago, he a senior captain, she a warrant officer.

"There," he said, his arm shooting out from beneath the blanket to point.

A light helicopter emerged into the high valley from the east, the direction of Essex and the Izaak Walton Hotel, where the Paynes had a room under their assumed name, Welch. The army called it an OH-58, a Kiowa—usually naming helicopters after Indians, an ironic, belated concession to the Frontier's vanquished tribes. In civil aviation it was known as the Bell Jet Ranger.

At first it flew high enough to be illuminated red-orange by the sun's dying rays. Payne watched it descend into the bowl of darkness. It hugged the south edge of the lake a mile away and flew a gentle clockwise arc.

He stood up, placing himself between the craft and the fire. PJ stood beside him and took a corner of the blanket. They had long since quit questioning each other's precautions. Though there had never been an incident since the tidal wave of killings and attempted killings two years ago, one always indulged the fears of the other.

They stretched the blanket out to wall off the fire's glow from the helicopter.

"Too late," he said.

The Kiowa tightened its turn and climbed out of the valley, reversing its direction.

She spoke hopefully: "A sightseer? A joyrider? Maybe the forest service—"

"No."

They stood watching the aircraft disappear over the

same spot it had come from on the ragged edge of the blackened trees to the east.

"It was searching, systematically going around the lake. I shouldn't have blocked the fire. Or else I should have blocked it as soon as we heard the sound. That tipped them off that we saw them, dammit—that we feared them." His anger clearly came in part from the forced admission to that fear.

"Maybe they're just keeping tabs on us," she offered.

He dropped the blanket to the ground. "No. They know there's only one practical way up here. They wanted to pinpoint us. Somebody will be coming."

"Why wouldn't they just wait till we started down the trail?" she asked, a note of desperation slipping into her voice.

"I don't know. I just know they didn't follow us into the Bob Marshall Wilderness or through Banff when we were up there. They didn't want us two days ago at the hotel. They could have taken us then. Now they want us. They want us badly enough to take a risk as obvious as a helicopter recon. Something must have happened."

"We have the insurance—"

"We're cut off from ten copies of the insurance, PJ. We can't start notifying our people from a place this isolated. And our two copies are useless here."

"But the fail-safe copies—If we're not back, they'll be sent out—"

"Yes, but the fail-safe alert won't trigger for thirty days. Maybe they've tracked down all our people. Maybe they've already gotten those copies. Maybe that's why they could afford to be so reckless as to fly up here."

She was not necessarily convinced, but enough so that she knew to err in favor of caution. "What do we do?"

"We move."

She spoke into the darkness of the pine forest to the west. "Are you strong enough to go over the top?" she asked. "No, of course not," she answered herself.

"That's one of the things they'll expect," he added.

"We'll never get by them. The trail down to Essex is too narrow. At night we'd never have a chance."

"You're right. But they won't be satisfied waiting below. By now there's a squad of goons hiking up the trail this way. They'll split up and take the footpaths around the lake." He tossed a couple of damp pieces of kindling on the fire, sending a shower of golden sparks upward. He looked at her as if expecting her to persuade him he'd been talking nonsense.

She stood hugging her own arms, gazing intently into the fire.

He leaned into the nylon tent, then leaned back out, dragging two belts. He handed her the holster with a small automatic. He swung open the cylinder of a .357, found it fully loaded, and snapped it shut.

He ducked back inside and withdrew the waterproof pack, the pack with two inner packages wrapped and sealed against water for these two years. They were the last two insurance policies they could be sure of, the photocopies of a research log full of descriptions of horrid experiments and results that could only be called beasts. And there was evidence of the killings: names, dates, and places provided with an affidavit from a former agent of The Corporation. The affidavit named names still in government, politicians and bureaucrats, places where figurative skeletons and real bodies were buried. And the affidavit described in detail the planned use of genetic weapons more horrible than those biological weapons condemned by the press and the Congress. The materials inside that pack would explode into public view with an impact that would make Watergate and Iran-Contra seem like fairy-tale memories from childhood.

He said, "Strap on every weapon you can. Every knife, hatchet, ammo clip, every pointed stick you can lay your hands on. I'm going to prop up these sleeping bags to make them look occupied."

"Stay and fight? You want to make a stand here against them? Mark, they'll be on guard. They saw you block the fire—you said so yourself. They'll never buy it that we'd stay here and sleep. They're too smart."

For the first time in days, he smiled. The light of the fire glowing at him from below made his haggard expression ghoulish.

"You're right. They're too smart for their own good. And we're going to shove their smarts right up their asses."

Payne shuddered, feeling exposed and cold on top of the huge boulder where they lay. But chilly as it was, the temperature didn't wholly explain his trembling. This time it was not the pain. It was the anticipation. His enemies were making some kind of move. He had always known they would come. The former agent who'd had an attack of conscience before he died had told him of The Corporation, its mission of domestic surveillance, and, when necessary, intervention, a euphemism for acts as cruel as murder or even crueler. Payne knew the men would come. It had taken some time for them to unravel the labyrinth he and PJ had left behind, but they *had* come.

At last, he thought.

He welcomed the reckoning.

PJ shrugged the pack onto her shoulders and followed him around the lake to the boulder, just as she had followed him around Texas in an earlier battle in their war, as *she* had begun following him from one haven to another around the country.

"If—where should these packages be sent? I mean—"

"I know what you mean," he said. "God, it was so stupid of me to insist we come here. I couldn't have been stupider than to take us away from civilization, from phones and post offices."

"Mark—"

"Never mind, Peej. Too late to worry. If you should get out—if I get out—send one package to Beard, the sheriff. Send the other to Ken and Maggie."

"Mark. My god, Ken and Maggie Poole might get—"

"I know, PJ. But what can I do? This—Corporation has to be destroyed. We should have sacrificed ourselves to do it already. Our safety has been so thin—so in vain."

"And Beard wouldn't help you—"

"He's a sheriff. He's sworn to uphold—"

Mark stopped there. How could he persuade her when he didn't even have a very strong conviction himself. Beard was so full of vengeance two years ago, he'd tried to commit murder, tried to kill Mark himself. He fingered the crescent cut into the edge of his ear, the hole from a bullet intended for the center of his face.

He'd have to send out those last two packages in hopes that one of them or the ten already positioned two years ago would get through to the intended recipients: people who could or should want to do something about the lawlessness of The Corporation he'd discovered and unmasked.

"Mark," she whispered. "What about Grayson Kirk? You always used to talk about him. Couldn't we just send one to him? He's at Fort Harrison, isn't he? I know a family there. I could—"

"No. He used to be some kind of intelligence agent himself. For all we know, he's connected with them."

"Mark."

"No, PJ. We can't take the chance. Kirk could be part of the group. He's probably even a more dangerous bet than Beard."

He put a hand on her mouth. It was time they kept quiet anyhow. And he had better take a few minutes to review the reasoning that got them there to the top of a rock in the middle of the Montana mountains.

The north side of the lake offered the cover of trees, hiding the trail. There a million caves of darkness tunneled amidst the undergrowth off the path. There lay a thousand logs to cuddle against, a hundred shallow divots to huddle in, now that the roots of huge pines had been yanked up. In contrast, the south side yielded almost no cover at all. The gravelly boulder-strewn slopes of the mountains dropped right down into the water's edge and continued into the depths of the lake. The path meandered nakedly beside the cool water, sometimes dipping right into the lake. Two people could hide in perhaps a dozen places.

He had chosen the south side, the naked side.

He had reasoned and counter-reasoned and counter-counter-reasoned, trying to creep into the darkest reaches of his mind to duplicate the depths of their depravity.

He reasoned they understood the impossibility of escaping over the west ridges at night. The best anybody could hope for would be to hide below the timberline and find the trail at first light. So they would put a landing party on the ridges by helicopter in the morning. Nobody could traverse those bare trails above the trees without being spotted. And just five miles to the west over that ridge, Hungry Horse Reservoir formed a barrier more than fifty miles long.

Next he reasoned they would have to send a party in to flush him out of hiding. It might take time, but it could be done. They would simply turn the hikers and campers and fishermen away from the lake, isolating it—tell them about a marauding grizzly or something. Then they would systematically search the bowl below the tree line and above the lake. Actually, it would require two parties, one along the north side and one along the south path. If the Paynes moved at night, it would have to be on the trails.

The easy, obvious way would be to send the primary search party along the south trail. Even the dimmest of lights from the heavens would at least illuminate the edge of the lake. A full squad could walk fairly quickly and quietly—stealth would not be all *that* important. They had the numbers and time—all the advantages. *But*, he counter-reasoned, the very darkness and difficulty of the north path, a kind of tunnel through the trees, would be an advantage to those who knew how to leverage the most from every competitive edge. A small party could advance with flashlights blazing, without the pretense of stealth, daring the Paynes to spring an ambush so follow-on forces could envelop them. *Or*, the prey might stand and fight somewhere at the site of a ruse or fortified area. *Or*, they might be driven around the south trail into an ambush set by The Corporation's soldiers.

Or, the whole thing was a cruel trick of his increasingly paranoid personality. Nobody would come. Nobody was interested in them except the night clerk at the hotel, wondering whether they'd skipped out without paying. The helicopter had been a Forest Service fire patrol—or even a joyride. Nobody cared.

Fine, he reasoned. Then the worst of it would be a miserably sleepless night spent atop a rugged boulder that simply would not yield a single hollow to the bony parts of his body.

He had thrown together a couple of surprises at the camp and had laid a heavy log in the fire to keep it hot with coals for a long time. They had raced silently along the south trail around and between boulders bigger than M-1 tanks and many times as heavy. In places they had to grasp the sparse brush to keep from slipping down the steep bank into the water.

Finally, they had scrambled as far as he dared. He didn't want to run into the enemy dashing along the trail from the opposite direction if the enemy had out-counter-counter-reasoned him. He had chosen this very spot two days before, when they had hiked past it to select their campsite—in the last two years he had cultivated a habit of choosing strategic spots everywhere he went. Like an extraordinarily defensive driver who views every other driver as somebody out to cause an accident, he anticipated every possibility of offense and defense. His was a chess game with moves many times more numerous, unbounded by two colors, six ranks, thirty-two pieces, and sixty-four squares.

Usually.

Now his mind began rattling off the ever shrinking walls of panic inside his skull. Now he began the fearful process of finding fault in his reasoning and counter-reasoning.

This time, he'd failed PJ and himself.

This time he'd put himself into a hopeless position, like trying to start a chess game with the handicap of losing half his pieces and being able to play only on one color.

He'd chosen a spot among a jumble of boulders big as

shanties. Farther up the slope, giant boulders perched, wedged and balanced against each other as if put there by some giant hand. Closer to the peaks, sheer cliffs blocked any practical night escape. Below them lapped the glacial green waters of Marion Lake.

He'd chosen a boulder that loomed out over the lake, hovering above the water. Daylight would have exposed them. The flat, slanting top of the rock resembled a sloping pitched roof. And only darkness hid them from the western side of the trail. He'd left their butts hanging out to dry, left them swinging in the wind. Totally abandoned. . . .

NO.

He fought for self-control.

He must not surrender his reason.

No, he reasoned.

Anybody passing through would be looking upslope and to the other side of the heap of rock for danger.

And if he had outreasoned them, he and PJ could slip off the boulder before light and find a crevice above to hide in. He and PJ would climb up the most rugged of slopes, the least likely of escape routes. At worst, they could fight it out from the natural fortress of stone above. If he'd not been so weak, so close to one of those increasingly frequent, increasingly painful blackouts, he'd have begun climbing already. If he'd felt strong enough to fight, he'd have picked a better spot. If, if, if . . .

God, how the imagination could run away.

All this without the first concrete clue that a soul in the world knew or cared a whit about the Payne couple—known as the Welch couple—who insanely planned to spend their night on a rock exposed to the damp, chilly alpine elements while their fire a quarter mile away burned a little brighter, now more yellow than orange, and their sleeping bags sat uselessly, two mounds of down propped up on bushes without bodies inside to warm.

PJ moved closer to him, to soak up some of his chill, to impart some of her warmth. She leaned to his ear.

"You sleep," she whispered. "I'll watch for a couple hours."

But he was already unconscious, exhausted by the effort of their walk, dazed by another of his blackouts.

Two Martian-like sets of eyes stared at the figures just outside the perimeter of the fire.

"Shit," muttered one of the Martians to himself. He pulled off his headgear, the infrared binoculars he had worn strapped to his head for nearly an hour, and tapped his fellow invader on the shoulder. He motioned for them to hunker down behind the deadfall so they could whisper into each other's ears and so they could rub their heads to restore circulation to the scalp.

He was Pearson. At least that was his latest identity. It would change after this operation. With luck, tomorrow. He pulled a transmitter from his sportsman's vest. Three rapid, short pushes on the silent transmit button. Two longs. Repeat. To the receiver about half a mile away the bursts would sound like interruptions of silence in the rushing torrent of squelch noise.

Pearson and the second man had started out in the dark more than an hour ago with two sets of infrared binos. They went staggering up the north trail to the upper end of the lake toward the defiantly glowing campfire. The pair walked as quickly as possible; infrared torches, invisible to the naked eye, lighting the way. Gradually they adjusted to the lack of depth perception through the binos, and they stumbled and cursed much less often by the time they'd closed on the fire.

A second pair of men waited with white lights for Pearson's signal. They were to be decoys. They would blaze away with powerful flashlights, carelessly following the first team's stealthy steps. When the quarry, the Paynes, reacted to the white lights, Pearson's team was to surprise them, capturing them alive—at least capturing the man alive. A third set of binos and a Starlight scope went with a trio of men along the south trail. They would proceed slowly, their artificial night-eyes looking for the pair of former army officers skulking along the lake. The orders demanded they capture at least one of their prey alive. Interrogators needed somebody for drug-induced conversation. The matter of the insurance policies. The Corporation had to be sure they had rooted out all of them.

Pearson knew more about Payne than the others did. As mission leader he had to. He would be making split-second decisions in the field, and it was imperative that he understood his man. Payne, like any hunted animal, would be dangerous. He must suspect the danger he was in. He most likely would be desperate, even suicidal. Unconfirmed reports indicated Payne had taken ill—so make that a hunted, *wounded* animal. But his weakness was the woman, Pearson reasoned. He must find a way to use her against him. If she were to die, then Payne would be impossible to bring home alive for questioning—he'd fight to the death.

He reasoned Payne would have suspected the helicopter. He asked that it not be used. But the director from Washington had insisted. If he's up there; find the son of a bitch first. You'll never sneak up on him, the raspy telephone voice of Gerlach had said.

Right, Pearson argued, but why not just let him come down the trail to us?

And what if he goes over the top and comes back another way?

Shit, he's not superman, Pearson had argued.

Gerlach had exploded at the casual insubordination, cursing and raving until Pearson had to hold the telephone away from his ear.

Now, squatting behind the deadfall, he wagged his head to rid it of the memory of Gerlach's rage.

Pearson looked eastward, back across the lake toward the logjam, where the lake fed a white-water creek dropping down the slope toward the Izaak Walton Lodge. Why did people 2,000 miles away think they could run an operation at night in the mountains?

And where the hell were the white lights?

Impatiently, he mashed the button on his radio transmitter, repeating the sequence: three shorts, two longs, repeat.

There.

Two white torch beams stabbed into the darkness and lashed across the east end of the lake. The torches glimmered and bounded, starting out without hesitation along the trail through the trees on the north trail. The drive had begun.

He turned toward the fire, where the two mounds hulked at the edge of the camp. He waited for the Paynes to discover the lights and move. He had reasoned Payne had not doused the fire because he would lay a trap of his own. Payne had been in combat before—in Texas two years ago as well as in Vietnam before that. If trapped, as he must know he was, he would fight like a cornered rat. That's why Pearson and his teammate had crept slowly along the last quarter-mile, their depths of vision skewed by the binoculars. Finally they had arrived near the campsite. The naked eye could barely see the outlines of the crouching Paynes. The binoculars cleared up the outline. But the fire was too bright. It kept washing out the image in a sea of green phosphorescence.

After a minute, the mounds had not moved.

The other man, a brute with a sloping forehead, tapped his elbow.

Pearson leaned in and whispered, "I don't know . . . either they're asleep or . . . dummies."

Payne had outreasoned him. By now the figures should have noticed the lights and moved. Amateurs would have been jabbering and moving about the fire.

Pearson's pulse quickened. Think. Now what? Were the figures too cool to be believed? Were they going to sit silently in ambush for the hour or so it would take for the torches to arrive? Or had Pearson marched right on by the Paynes, who might be hiding in the forest at the lake's edge? Would they wait for the white lights to go by as well?

Would he try the south trail?

Would he slip down to the east end?

Either of the last alternatives would be fine.

He'd sent one trio of men to sweep the south trail.

Another trio was lurking at the head of the trail for the contingency of Payne's trying to slip past the patrols. Pearson had all the contingencies covered.

He had Payne bottled up in this valley.

"Don't I?" he asked himself.

Or was Payne hidden deeper in the woods, waiting for somebody to attack the camp? Was he on the other side of this very deadfall?

Or . . . were those two mounds by the fire really the Paynes sleeping?

Pearson smiled. God, he loved combat. It was the excitement of an uncertain outcome as much as anything else. Combat was better than sex—as long as he won.

He still had all bets covered. It *was* possible that the IR approach had gone undetected, that Payne and his wife had gone to sleep. He and his companion might launch an assault of their own. He hunkered down and motioned, pointing first at his companion, then to the huddled figure on the left. Then he pointed at himself and the figure on the right.

Pearson crouched, pistol in firing position, behind the log. He waited for his brutish mate to nod. Then he grunted and raised his pistol. They stood up and dashed in opposite directions around the deadfall, rushing the camp.

Pearson grabbed the sleeping bag and yanked. It flew into the air without resistance. He cursed. Already he knew he'd been tricked. Yet he aimed at the second sleeping-bag dummy. The brute yanked it halfheartedly.

Pearson saw the glimmer of a nylon monofilament going taut as the down-draped branch toppled. He saw the two-pound white brick being jerked into the coals by the fishing line.

He yelped, and they both ran, diving over the deadfall, hugging the logs away from the fire.

They did not see or hear the brick of C-4 explosive flame up and hiss as it burned blue and orange, gradually enveloping the blasting cap embedded in the composition.

"Duck," growled Pearson.

The brute may have looked stupid, but he needed no urging to duck. He had already flattened and begun burrowing under the gray knotty log.

* * *

PJ stiffened when she saw the dancing white flashlights at the east end of the lake, beams and reflections playing across the water. Before she could even touch his shoulder, Payne sat upright.

For him, the sight of those lights confirmed and validated all the paranoia of the past two years. At once he felt relieved for all the old anxieties and deeply disturbed at a new set.

"Why so obvious?" he murmured. "What are they up to?"

"Could it be a bunch of kids on a night hike or something?" she asked, hopefully.

All their questions were answered with the explosion at their vacated campsite.

An orange ball of flame flashed at the valley, sending up a fountain of embers. The sight was followed by the sound, a crackling explosion that penetrated the body through the chest as well as the ears. The violence of the noise was doubled in intensity by the steep bowl of mountains and from its unnaturalness in this alpine setting.

Immediately the sound rattled around the walls of the valley and escaped to the heavens.

The white flashlight beams stopped traveling to flicker crazily into the trees and out across the lake.

The campfire disappeared.

A few loose stones rattled down the slopes above and splashed into the water below.

Squirrels and day birds awakened and squawked their protests.

A booming echo returned as rolling thunder from some distant mountain, then another echo from a more distant mountain, then another and another, each fainter than the last, rattling and rolling softer and softer until all grew silent again.

So, reasoned Payne, they had outreasoned him and had sneaked up on the campsite. But he had out-counter-reasoned them. Two of the four blocks of explosive he had lugged around for the last year had come in handy. He had even wondered whether the blasting caps would still function. And he'd wondered whether he'd truly begun to go mad as his anxieties continued to grow without anything concrete to nurture them. He still had a pound brick of C-4 beside him on the rock. And PJ had another pound, its cap, igniter, and short fuse tucked awkwardly into the waistband of her trousers. So. Call the first round a draw.

In a fifty-foot radius of the campfire, little fires had sprung up all over. Payne could see them blossoming. He didn't think the timber was dry enough to catch in a big way. And there was no breeze. But he could hope. If a fire could get going strong enough to draw the forest service . . .

Across the lake, the white flashlights had begun dancing again, even more deliberately dashing toward the west shore. Payne knew better than to be concerned about them—they were obviously a diversion. He lay scanning the blackness along the south shore where the trail wended toward them. There had been no sight or sound from that direction, confirming that somebody was almost certainly coming from there. Possibly their enemy had used some kind of night-vision devices, starlight gatherers, or IR. Maybe he and PJ had already been spotted sitting up startled at the explosion. He patted the pack on his wife's backpack, gently pressing her into the top of the stone block. She, needing no urging, seemed to be absorbed into the stone.

* * *

Pearson knew he'd blown it, literally and figuratively. Momentarily, he was beside himself with rage. All the trouble of having night goggles flown in. The surreptitious approach. Splitting into three teams. The enveloping movement. Damn. A bona fide circle jerk. So this is how Custer felt. Goddamned Gerlach would kill him. Literally, not figuratively.

No need. He might have to do the right thing and kill himself. Or die of embarrassment. One way or another, Gerlach would have his ass.

There he was: Mission Leader on The Corporation's most active, most critical operation—stomping out little forest fires like Smokey the fucking bear.

He'd shouted into his radio for the white flashlight team, the decoys, to hustle their asses up to the campsite. No need for stealth now. Payne and the woman probably had laid up halfway up the mountain, rolling around in the brush laughing.

At first Pearson and the brute had just crept around the camp's perimeter, pistols at the ready, gingerly stepping on embers. Then, as the little blazes flourished, throwing them onto a lighted stage, they ducked and feinted, kicking at the hundred fires. Finally, as the little fires grew together into a couple of dozen bonfires bathing the end of the lake in light, threatening to ignite the entire valley, they holstered their pistols and stomped all over until their trouser cuffs caught fire.

Pearson shrieked an obscenity. It seemed to clear his head. He began thinking more rationally. He spoke his thoughts as they came. "Either they're going to get burned out or we are. By morning this place will be swarming with firefighters. We'd better give this up and start building a new plan."

"What about headquarters?" asked his brutish companion.

Pearson gulped. He knew the Payne stories, the failures of four previous agents, even The Corporation's once-top agent. All failures. All dead. Goddamned Payne. He hoped the bastard *could* be captured alive. He'd like to work a little persuasion on him. Then he'd ask for permission to do the killing. Never before had he wanted so desperately to kill.

A pine tree exploded into flames, becoming a fifty-foot sparkler. The heat drove Pearson and his companion away from the campsite. They moved toward the south so they would not be trapped in the brush.

He looked out across the lake. The steep slopes surrounding had begun to take shape orangely in the glow of the fire—now a pair of bona fide forest fires growing together into one huge blaze. He could even make out the huge individual boulders at several places along the shore. The party with the lights would have to turn back. The forest on the north side would soon be a wall of fire. Maybe it wasn't so bad. Maybe Payne and the woman were up the slope and would be caught in the blaze. No. It was crazy for him to be hoping for an act of God to do his work for him.

He jammed his radio up against his lips and ordered the team on the north shore—those with the white lights—to get their asses up to him in the next two minutes or head back before they became trapped in a fire. He ordered the team on the exposed south shore to sweep the trail westward, using as much caution as possible. He forbade them the use of white lights. He had to outreason his prey. Maybe he could still catch Payne at being too tricky for his own good.

* * *

Payne first saw the trio as orange-lit figures flitting one by one around a gravel slide on the trail toward them on their own side of the lake, the south side. It gave him some satisfaction that he had been right about the direction of the main threat. But the sight of the main threat materializing diminished that satisfaction altogether. These men were pros. They kept a distance of twenty to thirty yards from one to the other to avoid being taken out in a single fusillade. The point man moved forward as the trailing men crouched and scanned up the slope, looking over the barrels of rifles. When the point stopped and crouched, the other two moved forward. The lead man was carrying a carbine, and on his belt was a pistol and a lunchbox-size case, probably IR binoculars and an IR flashlight. The second man's rifle was an M16 equipped with an enormous scope, a Starlight scope, Payne guessed, capable of intensifying the ambient night-light for sniping in the dark. Both IR and Starlight were now useless in the valley's glow because the brightness washed out their viewing surfaces. The third man was carrying a machine pistol or a submachine gun. He looked back on the trail frequently. A professional group. They would be hard to outreason. But he had to try. They were still about a hundred yards away. Time to plan would be short.

PJ gripped his bicep and signed for some relief. Unconsciously, he had been pressing her harder and harder into the top of the stone even as he raised his own head to get a view.

He relaxed.

What could he count on?

He could depend on his and PJ's safety for the moment. They were perched higher than the trail by twenty feet.

The top of the boulder leaned out toward the lake. And fortunately it tipped away from the advancing men. If any part of their outlines was visible at all to the trio, the backlighting of the forest fire would simply silhouette it as an irregularity atop the stone.

The point man would tip his hand in less than a minute. How he handled a similar, smaller cluster of boulders fifty yards away would be the clue. There the trail also passed between rocks, with one boulder—smaller than the one they were lying on—also leaning out over the lake and tipping toward the forest fire.

A minute later Payne had his answer. The point man stuck his pistol out of the dark space between boulders and came out crouching—sweeping his gaze uphill where the most likely danger would be, where the ambush would be swift and fatal if sprung. The point man drifted out of sight as the trail dipped into a tiny inlet. The second man stepped out of the boulder cluster with the M-16. He also swept the slope with his rifle. A little later Payne could make out the submachine gun and two arms weaving out of the darkness. The glow of the forest fire transformed the figures into wavering shapes, orange holographs that faded in and out of focus. Payne had to blink to convince himself he wasn't dreaming.

What he had seen so far gave him hope. Maybe they could survive this after all. The trio looked everywhere but into the water and up to the tops of the exposed boulders. Maybe they would pass. As he thought it, wished it, the point man rounded the last bend in the trail before Payne's hideaway. And he and his wife were committed to their—his, really—course of action.

Slowly he lowered his head. Almost breathlessly he whispered instructions for her to watch toward the fire. He would continue to look where he had been. Once again, as he had been so often in the past two years, he felt aware of just how much he cared for this woman with the green eyes, the blond hair, the passionate, loving character—more character than he would ever have. She had saved him from his perpetual adolescence, his drinking, his carousing. She had saved him from himself. And because of her binding herself to him, she had strapped on his woes as if they were her own. Now she lay prone in the middle of a burning valley, being hunted like an animal for no other reason than that she had met him and had fallen in love with him, a terminally troubled, continually ill fugitive.

He felt so inadequate. For the past six months he had been deteriorating continually. He remembered his father's cancer, sickness and surgery and chemotherapy. The old man's hopes and prayers that had gone on and off for years until not even he, the most desperate hoper and pray-er, could manage to cling to life. Payne knew he was dying. Just as his father had known it about himself. And he had taken that same dying trek into the wilderness. Like some aged elephant on the way to the graveyard, he had plodded weakly on in this last journey into the mountains he loved. Knowing that he would soon be incapacitated. First the head rushes. Then the years of blackouts. Then the episodes of crawling skin, aching joints, especially the throbbing in the face, the irregularity, the headaches, the excruciating toothaches. Until the blackouts grew longer, and the periods of recovery became shorter and less frequent. He knew no medical miracle was going to save him, even if he should get out of his present predicament. Something terrible and permanent had taken possession of his body—if not his soul. Something had been killing him for years . . . something in the drugs he'd been injected with against his knowledge, let alone his will. The job of those drugs was almost done. He knew he would now die. He had wished only that he could go without endangering or hurting the only love of his life.

Fat chance. Now that he had placed her in a no-win spot. He had taken the position nearest the direction he guessed the danger would come from. But now his plan was to let that danger pass, putting her in harm's way. What a stupid, inconsiderate jerk I am, he thought.

He squeezed his eyes shut to wring out the self-pity, allowing himself to concentrate on the present situation. He needed strength. Now. He opened his eyes and slowly raised his head.

His left eye flinched. Only twenty yards away, the point man was advancing quickly toward the boulders. So close. Payne could even make out the determined, set jaw, as if the man expected a hailstorm of gunfire any second. The man's eyes swept forward, then upslope, then repeated the circuit. Payne cringed as the eyes swung over his own gaze. The man did not see them. He was too much concerned about the potential of dangers from upslope.

As the point man disappeared below his line of sight, Payne ducked a little lower. He tapped PJ to alert her but he dared not turn and risk exposing them with a movement.

A snap of gravel told him the man was passing beneath the boulder. PJ stiffed against his touch. He gripped his .357. Slowly he lifted his left eye again.

The second man was approaching. No problem. Even more so than the first, this guy concentrated his senses upslope.

Payne turned his attention to the third man, who had

slipped out from between the smaller cluster of boulders. He, too, devoted his search to the hillside.

Suddenly the trail man crouched.

Had he seen them?

No.

He was pivoting to his rear. He scanned the tops of the smaller boulders, sighting over the barrel of his short gun. Then he stood up and walked briskly out of sight along the inlet.

Payne turned his head to survey the possibilities of discovery from PJ's direction. What he saw enraged him—at himself. He had screwed up.

The pair of forest fires had grown into a single spectacular conflagration, climbing up the north and west valley walls. He and PJ might as well have been sunning themselves nude by daylight, so naked did he feel. For, though they could not have been seen atop the rock in the dark, they would be in plain sight in the light of the fire—like nude sunbathers on their pitched roof. The point man emerged, moving into his field of view. Seconds later, he disappeared around a finger of a slope running down to the water. But if he had turned as the trail man had turned . . .

Payne's fevered mind raced. The second man marched into view. Payne brought up his pistol and laid his arm across PJ's neck, the front sight along the man's spine. But as the brightness of the fire increased, the men had stepped up the urgency of their pace. Almost without stopping, this one passed around the bend. Payne's pistol arm rose and fell gently with PJ's breathing.

Payne's racing mind could come up with nothing better than what he was doing. They couldn't climb down— he didn't even dare to look up too quickly to get a fix on the trail man—because he could not even guess where he might be.

Best to take a chance he wouldn't look back and discover them. And in case the enemy soldier did turn . . .

In less than a minute, the back of the trail man's head offered itself to the muzzle of the .357 magnum. He was twenty feet lower but not ten feet away laterally.

And suddenly Payne stopped hoping for the best.

He knew what to expect in the next seconds. The man would turn. He would spot them. Then . . .

His mind groped ahead, searching for courses of action for the seconds after that. Any straw to grasp. Could they hold out against the pair that would return a few seconds later? Should they even try? Should they jump down and try running down the trail to the east before the two men returned? Would there be some sort of ambush on the trail down to the lodge?

Before he could pick from the possibilities, before he could sort and evaluate, before he could even select blindly a stupid idea for an eventuality a minute away, the trail man crouched below the sight blade of Payne's pistol and spun toward them, compressing all potentialities into the present moment.

Payne dipped the muzzle of the pistol and found the head, putting it atop the blade of the front sight.

PJ saw. She stiffened, holding her breath so he could steady his aim.

Payne didn't wait for the head and shoulders to complete their pivot. There was no hope. Not with the brightness, not with only twenty—

. . . his pistol erupted—the intention was already there, the finger had taken out the slack, and then a straw's worth of pressure more, not even a conscious physical act but merely the willingness to yield to the necessity.

The head exploded like a melon. The man didn't even know what had killed him.

But Payne knew.

The Corporation killed him. It had turned Payne from a semiproductive soldier and sometimes drunken carouser into a pathetic paranoid killer, his mind and body deteriorating since the experimental drugs had been injected into his body in basic training.

And the man's own efficiency had killed him. If only he'd been careless just this once. If only he'd marched on without turning. IF, if, if . . .

Just thinking about it had wasted precious seconds. They still lay exposed to the direction of the fire.

Payne knelt and pulled the igniter on his C-4 block. He stood and tossed it as hard as he could toward the bend where the men would appear. Maybe they'd screw up once more and stick their faces into view at the right moment. . . . There he was, hoping again when he should be acting.

"Come on," he shouted. They had a few seconds before the explosion, he knew. He started counting as he began climbing down the side, away from the bomb he'd thrown. He grabbed her and started pulling.

"Careful," she shouted. "You'll kill us both."

"Four . . . five . . . PJ, what the hell are you doing? Come *on*. We got ten seconds tops."

"My leg . . . it's asleep . . . the circulation . . . help me. . . ."

She crawled unsteadily to the side.

He tried to hold her even as he braced himself.

Two heads, silhouettes of bowling balls, came into view along the line of the slope.

Seven.

He brought his pistol around and fired twice. They ducked. If he could make them stay down long enough for her to climb or fall off that goddamned rock. If, if, if . . .

Eight.

He felt a warm shower. Heard the pop of a rifle. Thought of the stupid little retort: IF, IF, IF, a snotty battalion commander had once shouted at him; If a frog had wings, it wouldn't bump its fucking ass every time it jumped, Lieutenant.

Nine.

She fell flat on the boulder as if exhausted.

He screamed her name. The warm shower . . . it was her blood.

Ten.

His answer was a volley of gunfire. The bullets snapped by overhead and spanged angrily off the rock. He heard her gasp in pain.

Eleven . . . twelve . . . where the HELL . . .

Then the explosion.

The heat slapped his face; stung his eyes; blinded him; blew him off the side of the boulder.

Pearson had decided the pair with flashlights on the north trail would never make it through the flames. He radioed them a terse message to retrace their steps all the way around the lake and follow the party on the south trail.

Just as he'd finished his jumbled order, the two men ran out of the wall of flames, their clothes smoking. One of the men ran up, shaking his radio. "Did you just call? Couldn't hear you for the fire. What did you want?"

Pearson smirked sardonically. It figured. He couldn't even make a wrong call properly. "Never mind," he said. "Let's start around the south side until we meet up with the others."

Half an hour later, he saw the point man approaching from three hundred yards up the trail next to the lake. A crushing sight. That meant Payne had given them the slip. He tried for a second to imagine how Gerlach would take the news. Then he decided he'd rather not imagine.

Pearson's capacity to hope returned when a single gunshot from ahead cracked through the muffled roar of the fire climbing the hill behind them. It could only be Payne springing his own ambush, choosing to fight rather than flee. Combat. God, there was hope after all.

Pearson and his crew broke into a run along the footpath. The point man and his companion had flattened out on a gravel slide. Where was the third man in that party? And who was doing all the shooting? Pearson looked up the slope. Nothing but those giant boulders strewn up and down the mountainside.

Next the pair of men started shooting—not upslope but nearly level. He followed the aim of their arms and saw the boulder. A figure lay there. Yes, he could make it out. Then he guessed that the third man had discovered Payne . . . or had been ambushed by him . . . and now . . .

. . . the gravel slide in front of his men blew up in their faces. The bodies like bits of tossed salad—one in a giant horizontal backflip, the other as a folded corpse— were launched into the lake.

He and his men hesitated. Then they broke into a run. Payne mustn't get away. Better to run into an ambush and be shot to pieces than to face Gerlach's wrath in failure.

* * *

Payne felt himself falling for an hour or so. Felt the icy water slap him back to consciousness. His pistol was gone. For a second or so he searched among the stones at the water's edge. Then he cursed himself. What he cared about was not in the water but atop that goddamned rock.

He climbed, his hands wet, slippery, numb. For the moment there was no danger. Surely the pair of Corporation men had taken a snootful of stone to hell with themselves.

His head came up over the edge, expecting to find her as he had left her, sprawled, dead. But no, she had folded herself into a fetal position. She was hugging her chest with one arm, pulling at her stomach with the other hand.

"PJ."

"Go, Mark. Go and save yourself."

"Are you crazy? You've been watching too many movies. Come on, I can help you down. We have time to make a run now."

He lifted himself as if climbing out of a pool.

She rolled over to her knees.

Even in shadow he could see her shirtfront glisten. He knew it wasn't water.

She heaved at her belly and pulled out the C-4 block. He could smell her blood. Something inside him began to unravel. It wasn't just this. Or even the pain. It was more.

He loved her . . . was losing her . . . was losing himself. A trickle coursed across his lips.

His blood? Or hers? He tasted it. He couldn't tell whose it was. No matter. Wave after wave of pressure built up inside him. His chest and head were about to explode.

"Go, Mark," she pleaded.

Go? He couldn't even move, could only feel his blood

heat past the boiling point, as if it were about to split the seams of his skin, his skull.

He heard himself screaming at her but couldn't make out the words that tumbled like soggy cotton balls from his paralyzed mouth.

She leaned toward him and kissed him.

He gargled at her and reached, horrified to see her fear of him, mortified to see her pulling away from him, stupefied as she placed her wet palm on his face and shoved him back.

Something inside him exploded.

As he fell for the second time, he screamed the word, NOOOooooo-o-o-o, long and cord-wrenching. And now he tasted her blood on his lips as he hit the water. Whatever had burst in his chest and head had set him aflame. He'd felt the heated panic of battle before, but this was not it. This was severe, mindless, painful panic. This came as a belly flop into a vat of hot oil, not cooled in the least by his icy plunge into the glacial lake.

He climbed, flailing, from the water, up the steep bank, clawing, scratching, screeching. White flashlight beams stabbed his way. But he did not care. He could not have defined composure, let alone regain it.

A shadowy figure, wrapped by white light, stood up defiantly atop the rock.

"No," he shouted, alarmed.

Half a dozen shots cut loose at once. Miraculously, she was not hit.

She sank to one knee and fired her own pistol twice.

"No."

He heard the snap of an igniter.

"PeeJaaaaay," he wailed.

More shots.

She drew back her arm to throw the C-4.

She crumpled, dropping the explosive over the side onto the trail.

"No." He snapped.

Stunned, his head buzzing in rage, he took off, running down the trail away from her. Away from the imminent explosion. Away from The Corporation's men. Away. He knew it was wrong to be running. But then, he had no weapon. Away. And, too, there was that pound of explosives about to go off. And PJ had been shot down a second time. Away, away. He . . . stopped and asked himself where the hell he was running to. Away where? He knew volumes about what he was running from, but where the hell to? The only thing that had ever mattered to him was behind.

He stopped and turned as the C-4 went off, further scrambling his ability to reason.

The blast sent him staggering backward a step. But PJ had dropped the bomb into the crack between boulders, and the rocks took the full force of the detonation.

The forest fire half a mile away formed the backdrop for the slow-motion action of silhouettes.

The boulder he'd just lain on, the one that still held PJ, pivoted toward the lake, rocking slowly toward the water as a cloud of smoke and dust rose from beneath the base where the trail passed. The heart of the cloud was black, but at the edges, where the wall of fire showed through from behind, the smoke turned yellow. For a second, the stone poised on its fulcrum, balanced, undecided about its momentum.

Then it decided.

Painstakingly it rolled toward Marion Lake.

As it did, a bundle of laundry flopped across the top of the black outline.

The stone tipped, picking up speed.

A scream rose from Payne's chest. It came out a roar. He felt a chest not his own tighten and expel every molecule of air through his throat. The sound was not his own. The unfamiliarity and volume of it even surprised him. He no longer felt as if he were in hot oil . . . for now the hot oil was *in* him, coursing through his veins and arteries, deep-frying his brain.

The laundry bundle of PJ's body flew off the rock, arms and legs flailing, and splashed feebly into the lake.

Payne felt something inside his head explode hotly. He heard the roaring again, and a fraction of a second later again realized it had come from him.

Yet he could not move. He was rooted to the spot, helplessly watching, screaming, roaring, as the boulder eased heavily into the lake, erasing the insignificant ripple PJ had made as she went under.

As if a keystone had been plucked free of the jumble, the entire slope began to move. At first it slumped, sliding into the space vacated by the huge boulder. That movement set loose half a dozen rocks as big as cars. They rolled and bounded down the face of the mountain, shooting sparks and foaming golden, backlit clouds. Whereas the largest boulder had majestically sunk like a giant hippo submerging, these rocks dashed down the hillside and plunged and splashed into the lake like frolicking boys on a summer day.

In seconds, the show ended. The mountain had slid. In a couple of minutes the aura of the golden cloud of dust would have thinned to nothing. Tomorrow, nobody would pay attention to the repositioned stones. In a couple of years, wild-game animals and outdoor people would have marked the place with a new segment of foot trails. Nobody would ever know what had happened to form the arrangement of boulders.

Except Payne.

He would know.

He would never forget the scene so permanently burned into his memory in the illumination of the forest fire.

Sudden grief had burned a mental picture of that woman under that pile of mountain beneath the lake.

Still he hadn't moved. He stood feeling his own senses vanish even as he knew the last of her life must be seeping from PJ. He felt his skin burning, itching. He felt his brain smoking. He felt the synapses in every neuron of his body misfiring, setting muscles to twitching. His heart pounded like an irregular piston seconds before the engine explodes.

His life was over. He did not have to reason or think or even feel the truth of that. It was an objective fact. All that remained was the formality of body immobility and brain death.

He took a step tentatively. It was a test to see if all the enormous power of his urge to kill could be mobilized to unroot him from his present spot.

The foot responded.

And he attacked toward the still-smoking rubble, thinking he would be killed, hoping he would be killed, knowing that he would kill as well.

Pearson saw an entirely different view of the events. In the first place, the fire lit the scene, providing so much more detail. The golden stones and figure danced lightly, almost floated, into the water.

He felt a twinge of disappointment when the woman disappeared beneath the water and jumble of stone. That meant they would absolutely have to deal with Payne— now that the woman was dead, they were automatically under orders to take him alive. Pearson knew Payne's history. He would be tough to find, tough to subdue, tough to break.

He gave his orders, and his remaining three men spread out, each picking the best way possible over the gravel slide and new arrangement of stone blocks.

Before the first of them had crested the newly formed slope of rocks and gravel, Pearson knew he was at least partly wrong. Payne wouldn't be hard to find at all.

He prided himself on being tough, but the screams curdled Pearson's blood. First came a yelp of surprise, followed by a wail of pain. Pearson looked over in time to Payne—a wild man, unshaven, hair flying, clothes torn—leaping and roaring at the brute who'd originally been Pearson's teammate in stalking the campfire.

It looked as if their faces might collide, but at the last second Payne tucked his chin and directed his forehead into the brute's nose as if it were a soccer ball. Both men went down amid stones the size of odd-shaped cinder blocks.

Pearson heard bones crunch as his man's back met the rocks. The brute grunted, expelled air, wilted, head lolling back, blood gushing from mouth and nose. Payne shook the rag doll by the throat, spraying the blood around, mainly on himself.

Pearson himself yelped, shouting into his radio again, ordering the men posted on the trail below to get their asses up here to help with this capture. For a second he wondered if three more were going to be enough. He shouted into his radio, insisting they run all the way. He wondered if he should call for more men from the outposts along Hungry Horse Reservoir over the ridges to the west.

Clearly, Payne had gone mad. Pearson could see he

didn't seem to care about his own safety; didn't even look for the others closing in, stumbling over the ankle-breaking stones toward him. He directed all his fury at the latest dead man, who could no longer harm him. Seemingly enraged all the more by the lack of resistance from the lifeless brute, Payne picked up a bowling ball of a rock and raised it over the body.

"Freeze."

It was a second agent, a stubby Irishman. Pearson circled away from the idiot. Such a command would only work with somebody rational enough to be fearful. Payne would simply have a new victim to attack. Pearson didn't want to be anywhere near the Irishman when his bluff was called.

But Payne did freeze—for a moment.

Then he turned, the boulder still raised over his head. The agent crouched in a sitting-supported firing position.

Payne launched the rock.

The Irishman rolled away from the flying stone.

But not away from the flying Payne.

Pearson saw Payne, mindless of the man's flailing pistol, begin pounding the agent on the head with both fists. The Irishman yelled for help, and Pearson and a third agent, a black giant, closed in cautiously. The giant carried a shotgun.

He leaped and swung the shotgun barrel downward. It glanced off the back of Payne's head, stunning him. But in a second of panic or rage, the Irishman disregarded his orders and fired his pistol at Payne's face.

With the explosion, Payne's head flicked away.

Pearson had closed enough to see a rip appear in Payne's scalp. But that wasn't the only damage done by the bullet.

The black agent flew backward, shotgun clattering

among the rocks, both hands clutching his face where the Irishman's bullet had struck him after passing through Payne's hair.

Pearson saw Payne's hands close on the Irishman's throat. The powerful fists seemed to be kneading dough, so deeply did they clutch the neck.

The man's eyes bulged in supplication toward Pearson, now also closing in on Payne from behind. As he lay dying, he kept trying to bring his pistol around, kept trying to disobey orders, kept sticking the gun at Payne's face, kept trying to kill him.

Payne seemed willing to let himself be killed. He didn't struggle for the gun. He just kept kneading the broken throat.

Pearson reached around and took the agent's hand, prying the pistol away. No matter. The man had already died. Pearson had never understood the Irishman—always so prone to kill first and answer for it later.

Payne continued to work over the corpse like a terrier worrying a dead rat.

Pearson stared in awe. He calmly holstered his pistol and stuck the Irishman's into his belt. He searched and found a hefty yet manageable stone. He raised it and brought it down against Payne's skull hopefully—hoping the force of the blow would not kill his man.

Pearson's hope was rewarded.

He felt an excruciating pain at the front of his pants.

The bloodied, battered wildman had turned his throat-crushing grip on Pearson and now had both fists ratcheting down hard on his nuts.

Pearson could not believe. Could not believe the way his lungs tried to crowd themselves right out of his body, filling his chest with gorge. Could not believe the power in those hands on his genitals. Could not believe the ferocity of the man beneath him, pulling him down by his crotch. Could not believe his own madness.

But now at least he finally understood the Irishman.

Against orders, risking Gerlach's wrath, reduced to saving his own existence at the risk of everything else, he yanked the Irishman's pistol from his belt, stuck it between Payne's bloodied teeth in that wide-open, roaring mouth, and pulled the trigger.

"And behold another beast . . . and they said thus unto it, Arise, devour much flesh."

—The Book of Daniel, 7:5

BOOK II

FROM THE MOUTHS OF BEASTS

1

Grayson Kirk was flying again, in Death Valley. Again and again and again.

The first time he took on the valley one-on-one was for real, in 1976. Exercise Bold Eagle. Or was it Bald Eagle? Or was it 1975? Hell, what's the difference? he would think after every dream. Then, in his sleep, he would take off again at the north end of the canyon.

The flight begins with a pinnacle takeoff from the edge of a high bluff above the asphalt ribbon of black. Things at the north end of Death Valley look pretty ordinary. About like the rest of this region of California and adjacent Nevada. Dirty desolation. About as inviting as if some jerk had dumped countless giant ashtrays on one of those tan pool-table covers—after tearing and rumpling the fabric.

Pinnacle takeoff. Slide forward, dragging the ground. Then, as the craft settles at translational lift speed, add a touch of power and lift off a few inches. Approach the edge of nothingness as fast and low as possible.

As the earth dives away, you're supposed to maintain altitude, gaining airspeed until it's safe to climb out. That's what you're supposed to do, but there's no fun in that. The thing to do is drop out the bottom, following the terrain, getting as close to the slope as possible, gaining airspeed, losing altitude. It's almost as wild as running full tilt downhill, except it's controlled, and probably safer—unless the engine quits.

The altitude above ground varies from ten feet on down. And when the altimeter is set properly, it shows the craft is flying below sea level. The feeling is one of awe to think that if somehow the sea were allowed to equalize all at once, a two-hundred-foot wall of water would crash down on the Huey.

The flight down Death Valley at 120 knots and single-digit altitude in February requires every faculty. The valley floor undulates, here a wind-blown dune, there a deadfall. It might have snowed the night before and dirty little drifts might have collected. In other places, streams the color of coffee lightened with low-fat milk might run together and percolate back and forth along the valley floor, having no place to go but shallow pools that will soon disappear after nourishing the sparse vegetation, reworking the landscape, and freshening the pastels.

Kirk's flight was a test of some electronics gear and noise-suppression package designed to allow helicopters undetected access to forbidden areas in hostile, friendly, and even neutral countries.

The officer giving the oral debriefing was an engineer. And an arrogant one at that.

The equipment worked satisfactorily aboard the Huey, Major Kirk. Your compartmentalized segment of the experiment is now complete, he had said. The technology will be put aboard more advanced helicopters flown by engineers. As you know, the Huey and Vietnam tactics are obsolete. This is not to suggest that you . . . are obsolete. Well, you know you have our everlasting gratitude.

The chief memory for Kirk was not the slur, not the wonder of the electronic wizardry that allowed him to navigate undetected across Nellis Air Force base's gun-

nery ranges and radars to Tonopah low level, down
Death Valley, through Fort Irwin's maneuver area with
dozens of helicopters and troop units, through the
orchard of space dishes, including the centerpiece Gold-
stone Antenna, across the mountains and right through
the heart of China Lake's Naval Air Station with its secret flying corridors and state-of-the-art radar technology
—where only a low-level B-52 crew saw him as they
crossed paths, the B-52 flying a hundred feet below the
Huey—to a landing beside a classified hangar at ul-
trasecret Edwards Air Force Base, there finally to be de-
tected only by an alert driver of a snack truck trying to
pedal his coffee and doughnuts.

No, the chief memory was the flight down Death Valley. The colors, the scenery, the monument, the vegetation. His copilot whispered his regret at not bringing a
camera. Kirk snorted at that. No camera could record this
flight like the body's senses. No flight had awed him more
than that one. It was fitting that it was to be his last spook
flight for the intelligence agencies. He would be set aside
for the younger generation, those with the advanced engineering degrees. But he would always have that memory.

Pinnacle takeoff. Slide forward, dragging the ground.
Reach translational lift speed before lifting off.

Approach the edge of nothingness as fast and low as
possible.

Down the slope.

Down the valley.

The Iowa police searched frantically for E. Gardner
Jacobs. They called him Jake in the many prisons he'd
lived in from juvie detention centers as a kid, to military
stockades in his short stint as a soldier, to the big house,
where he went shortly after his dishonorable discharge.

Jake, a small-time career criminal—thief, burglar, drunk, pimp—had been missing for days. He'd gotten his wish . . . he'd finally made it to the big time. For now he was being hunted as a killer. They said he'd snapped, though those who knew him said he merely was up to his old shit again. They had taken him out of the general prison population anyway, after he'd gone nuts in the mess hall and started a brawl. Beaten and bloodied and still raging furiously, he'd been carted off to the dispensary. They had locked him in a padded cell. He'd worsened.

They took him out for a shrink's consultation. He'd overpowered his guards—probably with one or more accomplices, it was said. Actually, he didn't overpower his guards as much as kill them, leaving their bodies along an Iowa state road.

The authorities issued a bulletin on Jake. He had risen in notoriety so fast—they wanted him dead or alive.

So it was a cautious pair of county deputies responding to a report of somebody seen staggering across a golden soy bean field between parcels of ripened corn. They found a set of deep, irregular tracks in the soft black earth. The tracks meandered through the waist-deep golden soy crop and into the corn, which was tall enough to shut out the sunlight.

The deputies advanced into the rustling cornrows with pistols drawn.

This animal was well suited to the cornfield's special qualities. Lying just inside the first rows, it could watch the approach of the two men. Then it could quickly travel between the files of corn to gain some distance. And although the visibility of his pursuers extended a quarter mile both ways when they looked down the narrow channels, they could see only six feet across the grain of the rows. Dashing across a few rows gave the beast another channel to travel in. So in only a minute he'd put a hundred yards between himself and the wary officers.

Suddenly the beast stopped and began burrowing. Beneath the crust, the earth was soft, dark, and rich. Its claws ripped and tore and dirt flew into a mound, as if some giant badger had begun digging after a prairie dog family.

In only two minutes more the beast had dug itself a hole big enough to hide in, or big enough for its own huge grave, if need be.

The deputies argued about calling for backup. One insisted they do it to be on the safe side. The other pointed out they hadn't yet confirmed that the sighting might be anything but a drunk or hobo on the move.

So they followed the deep tracks awhile, quickly picking up a pattern of travel—the dashes down the rows, the zigs and zags across the grain of the field, then another dash.

One argued they should run after their quarry. The other cursed that idea roundly, pointing out that the obviously clever nature of this pattern practically eliminated the theory of a drunk wandering around on a toot.

He suggested they begin just running across the rows, looking both ways until they spotted their quarry. The plan passed on an immediate vote. The two lawmen began crashing through the corn. In less than fifty feet they saw it.

They stood pointing at the dark mound a hundred yards away, mostly obscured by golden fronds. But it was clear enough for them to discern the earth had been freshly turned.

One of the deputies radioed for backup, his voice trembling into the handset. He reported they had possibly found the suspect, E. Gardner "Jake" Jacobs. The second deputy gave the first an evil eye, clearly saying with his look that they had no such proof. But he didn't protest the call for backup. Something was out of the ordinary here. And his ragged breathing gave unmistakable outlet to his fear.

They each took a row and advanced on the dark mound. Each pointed the way with his pistol. Deliberately, they moved in, seeing the mound take shape. Keeping abreast of each other, they moved through the corn.

At ten feet from the mound, the first stopped, then the other. They looked at each other through a window in the wall of corn fronds and shrugged their faces at each other. Then they did what cops always do.

"Police officers. Freeze," shouted the first.

"You're covered," shouted the other. "Come out or we'll shoot."

Nothing.

They could not see into the hole, for the mound was in the way at this distance.

The first pulled out his radio and reported the situation.

The second stepped forward.

The first reported they had found Jake.

The second hesitated to give the first time to catch up.

Together they poked their pistols over the mound, pointing down into the hole.

Their faces dropped.

They cursed. And lowered their weapons and their guards.

The hole was empty.

But not for long.

For a second, each thought the dry sound of crashing corn was made by the other. Then each realized the other had not moved. In the next second each thought they had found Jake.

And in their last seconds they realized they had found something entirely different.

When the backup deputies arrived, they found the patrol car locked and idling at the edge of the gravel road. They found three sets of tracks in the soft black soil, which they followed into the cornfield, where they found signs of a struggle at the hole. They found the roots of the corn both watered and fertilized in blood that had soaked to a depth of a foot in one rich place under the torn throat of a corpse. They found parts of the other in the deep, dank hole. But they did not find all of either of the deputies.

The lawmen didn't know what to do. For lack of a better course of action, they issued an updated bulletin on Jake. Now he was wanted for the murder of four cops. Forget the alive part. They wanted him dead.

The gray hulk of Gerlach filled up with air and smoke as he sucked clouds of yellow from around his head.

Gates, his secretary, waited, trying to keep his own nose from wrinkling at the pungent odor of the cigar.

Gerlach exhaled slowly. The yellow smoke had turned blue, having had the worst particles filtered out by the lungs of the chairman of The Corporation. He logrolled the cigar to the left of his mouth, where the corner pooched downward even more than the right. When the cigar had sunk into the groove there, Gerlach spoke gruffly.

"So. Edward. What's the story in Iowa?"

Gates tossed down a written report and summarized its contents. "Another beast," he said. "The authorities are denying anything but that a fugitive has gone berserk. But we've confirmed it's another one."

Gerlach shook his head in disbelief. "In Iowa? Now that's a definite change in the pattern. You check on that. And get somebody down there to intervene soon as the cops come up with the thing."

Gates scribbled a note to himself.

Gerlach continued. "What do you have on the Fort Harrison stuff and the Michigan group?"

Gates told him. He began hesitantly, for not all the news was good. But Gerlach listened intently, forgoing the impatient grunts and scowls he lavished on the routine, boring reports he usually received. This news was consequential, and Gates began to appreciate the seriousness of the matter as his boss leaned forward, squinting at every scrap of information, written or spoken.

At the conclusion of the report, Gerlach sighed heavily. "As far as we know, then, Edward, we have taken out everybody who might either have been an eyewitness or a recipient of a copy of that insurance policy of Payne's?"

"Yessir."

"Payne taken care of?"

"Yessir."

"Payne's wife dead?"

"Yessir."

"Body found and disposed of?"

"Well, no, sir, but Pearson saw her buried under an avalanche—and that lake is a hundred forty-five feet deep."

"Goddamned you're so . . . exact, Edward. Wonderful."

Gates let down his guard and smiled.

Gerlach snarled in contempt. "You tell the stupid bastards not to assume she's dead until they've found her body. I want you to assume the worst, the goddamnedest awfulest worst. Understand?"

Gates cleared his throat. "Yessir."

"Get a team back up there and find her body. Then we'll *know* she was buried under an avalanche in a hundred-forty-five-foot-deep lake."

"Yessir."

"All the command group at Fort Harrison taken care of?"

"Yessir."

"The only other problems being Kirk and the woman colonel?"

"Yessir. And Jacobs."

Gerlach kicked back and dropped his heels on his desk. He sucked on the cigar, stoking its coal to bright red through the gray ash.

"Kirk," he said. "Kirk . . . he's our fucking problem. Tell me what you know about Kirk and his past."

When Gates finished nearly an hour later, Gerlach sat up and smiled viciously.

"You did a good study on Kirk, Edward—only one thing you missed. I used to be his boss . . . well, I was just a voice on the telephone and the radio to him. Did you find any connections between Payne and Kirk?"

Gates shrugged. "Classmates and friends from flight school. Nothing more. No basic-training connections. No Officer Candidate School."

"Still. I want you to tell the people in Indiana not to finish Kirk until we know for sure about this sunken body of Payne's wife. We wait until we're sure she didn't send one of those research logs to him. We keep surveillance on him."

"Yessir."

"Kirk . . . when we finally do have the liberty to finish Kirk, I think we'll just about have this entire business wrapped up, Edward, my man. Let's put a couple more agents on him until we get the word from the search team at that lake in Montana. Kirk is not your ordinary army buffoon, Gates. He's a dangerous one—trained in methods I personally developed. We'll need to keep close tabs on him until it's time to move in on him. How's Pearson? Can we put him on this, or is his pecker too sore?"

Gates blushed. "Mister Pearson is convalescing, but we've ordered him here to the complex for a debriefing. He may have to be medically retired, sir."

"Too fucking bad. Guess Pearson would say Nathan Hale was right."

"Sir?"

"I regret I only have one dick to lay down for my country."

Kirk flew down the slope, down the valley.

Again.

And again.

Down the slope.

A woman's cool hand on his forehead.

Down the valley.

The rich fragrance of expensive perfume mingled with the sweetness of woman scents.

He awoke thinking he had died.

The blue eyes and porcelain skin of Lieutenant Colonel Connie Gail hovered above his own face. He felt a powerful urge to pull her down for a kiss. Then he felt his nakedness between soft, perfumed sheets. A momentary surge of blood to his genitals. A quick, hot wave of embarrassment.

Yes, he was dead, and this was heaven. But why did he have the aching lump on his head? You weren't supposed to have pain in heaven. Were you?

"Ma'am?" he mumbled, his voice croaking.

"Major Kirk. Thank God. I didn't know how seriously you might be injured. I couldn't take you to a hospital without their alerting . . . whoever it is that's trying to harm us."

He remembered the ambulance, remembered backward to the creek, the ambulance, those men, the monster, the Huey crash, the murders.

"What? How did I get out of the ambulance?"

"I pulled you out."

"How?" He noticed for the first time a redness on her left cheekbone and a swelling above her eyebrow.

"Well, I didn't actually pull you out. You did that yourself somehow. You floated up. I swam out and pulled you to the bank. It was hell getting you into my car." She fingered her injuries again. "I banged my face."

"Where am I?" Kirk sat up in the bed. Obviously it was her bedroom.

"My apartment. Your . . . uh, clothes are in the dryer. If you're well enough, we've got to move. I've packed the car."

His embarrassment forgotten in the rush of questions that came to his head, Kirk searched her face for answers.

"Move? What in God's name is happening?"

She shrugged. "Maybe later we can figure it out. Right now we should be leaving, Major Kirk. I'll get your flight suit. That will do for now, but you'll have to be getting some less conspicuous clothing until we can get the proper authorities to straighten out this mess for us."

She was beautiful. He watched her profile as she talked. She had left her hair in damp ringlets. Her makeup had washed off, leaving her cheeks shiny, her lips pink. She actually looked younger with no powder or eyeliner or lipstick. Or maybe because she'd let her hair out of the severe bun at the base of her neck. Oh, she didn't look all that young—not a damned teenager, he thought—she must be near forty. Yet she was not like those scores of women he'd met in the clubs, twenty-five-year-olds who plastered so much shit on their faces. *They* looked forty. She looked five years younger. A mature thirty-five. That was more his style . . . shit, what was he thinking? Grow up, he told himself. He knew he needed to learn to care about women for more than their ability to share sensual pleasures. Maybe she'd be the one to straighten out his libido . . . to teach him the meaning of love . . . to . . . nah. Get real, he told himself.

Imagine. She had swum out into Fall Creek and pulled his butt out of the water. She had undressed him—he shuddered at the idea—and dried out his clothes.

"What happened to you after the meeting?" he asked, half rhetorically.

She stopped at the bedroom door and talked. Her composure had to have come from her training as a lawyer. She remained unruffled as she told him of Martin Grier's theory about the deaths, about Grier's death soon after. She mentioned the FBI, her uncertainty, her run through the creek to her car.

She talked about driving off post, using the back road, past the smoke of the burning helicopter. She'd run up behind an ambulance. As she'd tried to pass it, the ambulance had speeded up and collided with the Fall Creek Bridge, flown up, and tumbled into the water. She had been in panic, fearful for her own safety, and would have left the scene, except that she'd looked back and seen a body float free—his body.

"Well, the rest is the brief history that brings us up to the present," she said.

Kirk kept his silence, trying to sort out the insanity of the day, the bravery of this beauty.

"Do you know what all this means?" she asked.

He squinted at her, trying to force the cobwebs from his head, focusing his thoughts to keep up with her. He didn't know the first thing about what all this meant.

"I . . . uh . . . what?" he said.

"It means," she said, "that Ford and Keating and Grier are dead. And somebody tried to kill us too . . . maybe Martin was right."

"No. . . . Howie Ferrin and Duda . . . they were at that meeting too."

She shook her head slowly.

"Yes," he insisted. "They put me in the ambulance."

"They died in the helicopter fire. I heard it on the news while you were out cold. There's no more keeping the press under control at Fort Ben's retirement home. They're all over the place."

"But how? They were alive when I . . ."

"Fire. The radio said they died in the fire of the helicopter crash."

"But there was no fire. . . ."

Now Kirk knew he had lost his competitive edge. And he used to be such an artful cynic in those days of playing the intelligence game and the counterintell game, one day a terrorist, next day an anti-terrorist, day after a counter-terrorist, spook, counterspook. Until you couldn't tell the players anymore, program or no. So the only thing left worth saving was your sanity. And that was possible only with a healthy dose of cynicism, sarcasm, and a black sense of humor. Here a couple of brick walls had fallen on him, yet not till Colonel Connie told him of the helicopter burning in a fire that could only have been set to kill Duda and Ferrin and to destroy evidence did he realize the intrigue surrounding them. He'd forgotten how naive he could be, how dull he'd grown in the absence of exercising his specialized training.

"Is this all you have to tell me?" he asked, his voice tinged with irony.

She smiled, reflecting the irony with a curl of the corner of her mouth.

"No. There's more, lots worse."

"I don't believe that. What could be worse?"

"They're after us. The FBI hasn't exactly put out a bulletin naming us as suspects in the killing of all those people. But I think they're after us just the same. I know people in the FBI. I know how they operate. Those people who came after me . . . they most definitely were *not* FBI."

They looked into each other's eyes for a long moment.

"You don't seem surprised," she said.

"I'm not." He wasn't. It hadn't taken him more than a few moments to shrug off his naiveté, to toss off the burden of those brick walls. He pulled back a dark shroud inside his mind, revealing ruthless memories, memories that both haunted and excited him. Though the machine of intrigue and counterintrigue had grown rusty, it still functioned.

He saw her watching him. And he saw her shudder. There might have been the beginnings of tears in her eyes.

When the woman spoke, her voice quavered. "I just realized I don't even know what to do next."

So much for old hard-ass Connie. She was human and a

woman after all. For a second he wondered about the platinum panties. Then he forced his mind back to the present danger.

"We'll be all right now," he assured her. And because his long-buried instincts seemed to have come back to him in a rush, he believed he could now take control. At least that was what he told her.

She left him and came back with his Nomex flight suit. Then she left him alone to dress. He dressed quickly but awkwardly in the warm one-piece. The blows to his head, first from General Ford, then inside the bouncing ambulance, had left him dizzy. Or maybe he was just generally confused. What did Colonel Connie mean when she'd said that somebody was trying to harm *us?* And *we've* got to move? How did *she* suddenly get involved? He thought he'd be better off sending her to some kind of safe haven, taking this situation on alone. He sat for a few minutes after dressing. He needed to collect himself.

Gates approached Gerlach's desk.

"Edward, my man, you have a certain spring in your step. You look to be the bearer of good news."

Gates smiled.

"Yessir. We've found the Payne woman."

Gerlach took a rare turn smiling. He pulled on a desk drawer and withdrew an eight-inch cigar.

"Dead?" he said. The cigar penetrated the sphincter Gerlach made with his mouth, burying half its length.

The smile on Gates's mouth slipped a little. "No, but we have her completely under wraps."

The cigar squirted out. Gerlach's eyes narrowed.

"And she never left the isolation of the lake, right?" The urgency in his question was barely hidden.

"Well, no, sir. . . ."

"Good." Gerlach puffed himself up, reversed the cigar, and wet down the dry half the same way, licking and slurping at it, blackening it with spit.

"Well, sir . . . I mean, no, that isn't exactly right. She never left the mountains, but she did make it back down the trail. We found her in a car wreck beside a highway through the mountains."

"Damn." Gerlach's word might as well have been belched from the mouth of a cannon, so galvanizing an effect did it have on Gates. "Goddamn sonofabitch. You people are so incompetent."

He stood up behind his desk.

"Did anybody find any copies of the log in her possession? Did anybody check the hotel mailbox? Are there any buses or trains through there that might have taken a package or letter from her? Could anybody have driven out of the mountains and mailed it for her?"

Every question was snapped off a little sharper. Each one was like the crack of a whiplash cutting a vicious nick in Gates, who had suddenly become the bearer of bad news rather than good.

Gates looked at Gerlach's hand. The cigar, an expensive Havana variety imported by agents from another agency, was crushed in his fist. It was an angry omen.

"We . . . they found no evidence of any more research journals . . . and they did check the mails with negative . . ."

Gerlach had begun whispering, creating an even more ominous effect than the shouting.

"Start her on the drugs. Find out if she had time to mail anything—a letter or one of those research journals. Were there any calls made from any phone in that area to anybody of influence, anybody in the country? Find out. See if any journal could have been mailed. Find out where they went. Get them. Or kill the addressees."

The last word was simply a hiss.

Gates stood nodding, although Gerlach had stopped speaking.

"Edward," Gerlach said gently.

"Sir?"

"Move your ass."

When Gates had gone, he lit another cigar, sucking deeply on the fragrant first embers, hoping to inhale a moment's relaxation from the nicotine.

Impossible. Impossible to relax when so many people made so many mistakes. He'd do this himself if he didn't have to be the boss. He wished he had more agents like Kirk. Kirk absorbed every detail of training, yes, but he was more than just well-trained. He'd had that instinct for anticipating trouble, for planning for every possibility, every contingency. He could play the mind games necessary to excel at this trade. Nobody ever surprised Kirk because he'd always traveled the territory over and over in his mind. Payne, the amateur, had demonstrated a similar quality, a natural instinct for being able to anticipate and countermove. If Payne had been trained in addition to having such natural tendencies, he'd probably still be roaming free and there'd be even more dead Corporation bodies decomposing in the valley of that Montana lake.

Only one other agent Gerlach had ever trained displayed the kind of raw talent of Payne and the rare talent of Kirk. Barnaby. Barnaby had it all. Superior training and mentoring. Currency in all the arts of The Corporation. And all the right instincts. He thanked the stars that he'd had the foresight to send Barnaby to Indiana before all this bullshit had broken out. He pulled deeply on his cigar again and again. Finally. The thought of Barnaby's competence and the acrid smoke of the red-hot cigar coal began to soothe him.

There was nobody else he trusted—except himself, of course. One more pratfall by his protégés would mean only one course of action left to Gerlach—he'd have to un-ass Washington and go settle this damned problem himself.

Jay F.W. Pearson couldn't get comfortable. Not emotionally, which embarrassed him. Not professionally, which frightened him. Not physically, which kept him shifting in his first-class seat on the flight from Washington to Indianapolis.

His nuts hurt. That goddamned Payne had hurt him seriously, must have ruptured one of his balls. He refused treatment, not as much a self-imposed penance as a last-ditch effort to keep himself from being retired or worse by his employer, The Corporation, which did not tolerate incompetence. Six men lost to Payne and his wife. Pearson and the trio who arrived late to the scene of carnage had wired the six by the necks and ankles to rocks before sending them to the bottom of the frigid lake. They would have to be recovered later—probably by night divers—and flown out. Fortunately, the cold waters of Marion would preserve them well enough until after the firefighters had done their job on the blaze that was scooping all life out of the valley of Marion Lake.

His nuts had hurt so bad, he was barely able to drag Payne's body through the icy water to the pontoon-equipped helicopter. The only comfort he'd had was the numbness of his nuts in Marion—that and when he duplicated the remedy in the bathtub of a hotel overlooking the

Potomac, using five buckets of ice and an hour's soaking to reduce the throb to a manageable ache.

Bad as that was, it was even worse that he'd lost control and shot Payne. Lost control of his emotions. Disobeyed orders. If Payne died, Pearson knew he was as good as done himself.

That on top of losing six good soldiers—hand-picked by Pearson, in fact—in attempting to capture one damned woman and an invalid civilian. It was enough to end his career in The Corporation. End his life maybe.

So he refused medical attention and begged Gerlach to let him go out alone after Kirk, the other glitch in the works, the last detail to be cleaned up now that Payne and his wife had been put away.

Gerlach had consented sardonically, laughing at Pearson's pain, laughing at his volunteerism as if there had been no choice in the first place—and apparently expecting him to fail. He must have been sure of it. He ordered Pearson to work with two agents.

Pearson protested.

Gerlach insisted—at the bottom of his lungs, rasping such a threatening whisper to Pearson that he knew he could not refuse the offer of two more good men. He knew they would be under orders from Gerlach to prevent the Numb Nuts, as Gerlach already had called him, as he knew he would forever be known, from screwing up another mission. Like it or not, he would be on the case with another agent, Keeney. Gerlach had placed a third agent, Barnaby, in charge and had other agents to use on demand. Pearson bristled that he'd not be in command. But Gerlach had simply bitten down on his cigar, forcing its tip up. And he'd glared into Pearson's eyes. Pearson broke eye contact meekly. Barnaby was in charge . . . period. His acceptance of that fact was a matter of life and death . . . Pearson's. The mission was clearly what men and women in the trade called a "one-way job": He could not come back from it alive unless Kirk was taken dead.

Pearson seethed at the flight attendant for badgering him to tighten up his lap belt. If she only knew how high up into the abdomen a pair of crushed nuts could ache. He seethed at the pilot for the roughness of the approach into Indianapolis. And he seethed at Gerlach, the Numb Nuts monicker, and Barnaby and Keeney. He'd not met the pair. Didn't even know whether they were on the flight with him.

Gerlach's orders were simple and direct. He was to meet Keeney in a Union Station bar. They were to partner up. Barnaby would work alone, taking orders directly from Gerlach, reporting directly to his man, relaying orders to Pearson through Washington. Barnaby was one of the superagents. He didn't deal with scum like him and Keeney, except in an emergency. They would only meet each other if the proper classified ad were placed in *USA Today* with instructions only the trio could decipher.

Pearson also felt an enormous frustration with the first mission Gerlach gave them in Indianapolis. Pay a visit to Bertrand's wife, he'd ordered. Pick up any useful materials—whatever that meant—and leave her the victim of a senseless crime.

Pearson seethed at the unknown Barnaby and Keeney. Pearson seethed at Payne, Larson, Kirk, and Connie Gail. Of all of them, only Kirk could he do something about. He had permission to kill Kirk as soon as Payne's wife was broken and the books were recovered.

And, by God, he'd do it with relish.

They had stopped off at a shopping mall to buy him some casual clothing, cheap but less conspicuous than an army flight suit. Now they sat deep in the least boisterous corner of the boisterous bar. She gazed thoughtfully into the foaming iced Margarita for a while, then looked up, catching him staring at her.

He looked away from her, feeling self-conscious for his plentiful scars and ears, uncomfortable less because of the difference in rank than because of the enormous appearance gap between them. He picked at the hair on his temples, trying to make it bridge the gap between head and ear. He began trying to remember how he looked before the scars and surgery. She interrupted his reminiscences.

"I've never been a fugitive," she said.

He seemed momentarily confused. "Well, I haven't either, Counselor . . . I mean . . . well, I don't mean to sound defensive. I guess if I *have* to be a fugitive, it's nice to be on the lam with a lawyer."

"Lucky for you, Major."

For a second they locked glances, trying to read in each other's eyes the meaning between the spoken lines. Then both looked away at once.

"To be honest, Colonel, I'm not sure what we should be doing next. Do you have any ideas?"

"We could begin by using names besides major and colonel, which could blow our cover. Besides, I'd feel more comfortable."

Kirk seemed surprised at her willingness to lower the barriers of formality.

"Connie, then?" he asked.

"No. Make it my other name. Just call me Gail. That will keep us from being too obvious, and you won't have to feel self-conscious about first-naming a lieutenant colonel."

His stomach sank. He really had wanted to first-name her. "Fair enough. Call me Kirk, then, and we'll be even."

Other than nearly crying this afternoon, her blush was the closest thing to genuine emotion Kirk had yet seen in her. He stared into his beer, fighting back the prickly heat of his own blush. It was embarrassing. He'd found her pretty many times in the few weeks he'd known her—at least sexy. But now maybe it was the beer, the dimness, the civilian clothes, the honey hair cascading down to her shoulders—or maybe it was just the rush that danger gave him, a feeling he'd forgotten or at least had learned to dislike in his memory—but damned if he didn't feel it coming back in the form of a devil-may-care attitude that transformed her from pretty to beautiful and from attractive to ravishing. He remembered the words of a country tune: "I'm just a drink away from loving you."

"What are you smiling about?" she demanded in a hushed voice.

"Nothing. You don't have to whisper.

"Kirk," she said, making the word sound not a bit like a first name, "I don't know what this business is all about, but it seems we're in it together. I guess we'll be able to . . . to endure each other until my legal contacts can straighten out the misunderstanding that's at the bottom of it all. But I'd feel better if I knew just one thing."

"Oh, yeah?" His face lit up with a blush of his own, surprised at her confidence, stung by her brusqueness. She'd certainly recovered from the shaky, vulnerable female who nearly bawled in the car a couple of hours ago. "What's that, Gail?" He did his best to make her name sound like a last name, wringing all the disrespect he could from a civil question.

"You're not at the bottom of something really criminal, are you? You're not the object of this manhunt because you've done something illegal like drug dealing, are you? I mean, before I trust you, I think I have the right to know whether I'm a hostage or an accomplice or providing aid to a fugitive or something, don't I?"

A flush of anger burned his cheeks. "That's more than just one thing, Gail. And you're beginning to sound like the public defender assigned to Richard Speck."

"Jesus, Kirk, can't you just answer the question so we can get on with some kind of strategy?"

This was such a disappointment to him. He'd had this fantasy, this idea, that they would somehow fall in . . . well, fall in like, at least. But clearly the tone and bitterness pointed in another direction. He didn't help with his retort.

"If you think I'm mixed up in something, Gail, you just get your tail up and march it out of here. This thing will be a whole lot easier for me to manage on my own without . . ." He had the decency to hold his tongue.

"Go on," she challenged, "finish it."

"You're so damned clever, Counselor, you finish it."

"You meant to say it would be easier to manage without dragging a woman along."

"Bullshit. You're not as smart as you think. That isn't what I was going to say at all."

She glared at him, her eyes darkening and narrowing to gunmetal-blue slits. "You were too. You were going to say dragging a bitch along—your wiseass smile said it for you."

"Wrong again." His wiseass smile became a wiseass sneer. "Dragging a platinum-assed bitch along." Instantly he wished he hadn't said it.

Her eyes filled with hatred. With a visible effort she held her own counterstrike response.

They sat silently for a long time, sipping half earnestly at their drinks, glancing anywhere but into one another's eyes, ordering a sandwich apiece to pick at.

Finally, she sighed. "Okay, so you're not the criminal here, just one of the victims. We're both being victimized. It would be—will be—in our best interests to drop the hostilities and cooperate. Agreed?"

"Agreed. And I'm sorry I used that language . . . those words."

"Why don't we just leave now?" She shoved her chair back.

"The phone call."

She raised an eyebrow.

"We didn't just come here on a date, Gail. We're waiting for a friend of mine, somebody who will help us get a line on this mess."

A look of astonishment erased her expression of disdain. "You mean we're not just going to flee? You mean we're going to try to solve these murders and unravel this mess?"

"You sound like somebody on one of those righteous TV lawyer shows. The truth is simply this: Somebody is trying to kill me. There's no romance in that, no glory, no nothing. I'm going to . . . I, not you . . . I am going to find out who and try to get them first."

He couldn't believe the way he was talking—like some righteous TV detective himself. Amazing the way she brought out the worst in him. And after such a brief acquaintance.

"And what about me?" The tinge of vulnerability, the *proper* tinge of vulnerability, had crept back into the tone of her voice. Finally she had discovered her place, he thought.

"*You* are going to stay out of my way."

She swallowed and shrank back into her chair. And again he felt ashamed. He hadn't always been such an arrogant pig. Had he? No. Really only with her. Other women he respected, and they respected him. But something in the chemistry between them . . . she definitely brought out the worst, he thought.

A silent half hour later, Kirk was occupying himself by watching an obnoxious drunk at the bar. Connie Gail invested her energy in ignoring the drunk as well as Kirk.

The drunk would not be ignored. He was dressed in greasy blue jeans and a checked shirt. A Ralston cap sat cocked on his head. But wearing a wardrobe out of place in a yuppie bar wasn't enough for him. He stepped up to the table. "Pretty lady, how are we this evening?" He stood oscillating like a sapling in a breeze. Then he remembered to tip his hat, revealing a flattop haircut underneath.

"*We* were fine until now."

"Would the pretty lady care to dance?" He held the hat suspended over his brush-cut.

"No. And certainly not with you, bozo."

The drunk pursed his lips and nodded, his eyes fixed on the ceiling. He dropped the hat crookedly on his head.

He drawled, "Then I reckon a blowjob is out of the question."

She gasped and looked up into his victorious leer. Her eyes flicked a glance at Kirk.

The drunk practically spat into Kirk's face. "Or maybe you're the one in this place who gives out the blowjobs."

Kirk remained impassive. He drained his beer and spoke so low the drunk had to lean down to hear. "Maybe you and I could go outside and talk about it."

The drunk snorted and straightened his Ralston.

He turned and walked toward the door. Connie Gail opened her mouth and half rose from her chair. Kirk held up a palm and followed the staggering man out the door alone. The bar patrons gaped and began murmuring to themselves. A few men began sidling to the doorway to satisfy their curiosities.

But within a minute Kirk was back, brushing off his cheap off-the-rack sports coat that was too generous around the middle.

There was an audible sigh among the small crowd that had seen them leave, a certain pride among the health-and-fitness-conscious yuppie set that one of their own had dispatched such an obviously Hoosier soybean farmer so handily.

The waitress arrived with a trayful of drinks set up by various admirers around the house.

Kirk took one and waved it at half a dozen pair of expectant eyes waiting for the acknowledgment.

Connie Gail interrupted. "But if you left that man lying out there . . . The police will come. Don't you think that's a little risky?"

He looked at his watch. "You're right. Better get moving now."

Outside, they walked across the mall parking-lot toward their rental car. Suddenly, a pair of tires screeched ahead of them, and a pair of headlights on high beam spotted them. Even so, in the glare of the mall lights they could see the red of the Ralston cap swaying in the cab of the pickup aimed at them.

Kirk stood rooted to the spot.

She grabbed his elbow and tugged.

He faced the pair of oncoming lights.

She dived and rolled between two parked cars.

The pickup squealed to a stop, its bumper nudging Kirk's knees.

Kirk leaned down and peered at Connie Gail, who had

come up catlike, planting her feet like a runner in the starting blocks.

"Rolling around on the asphalt is kind of hard on the wardrobe. C'mon, say hello to the Chicken Man."

He held open the door of the pickup. The man in the Ralston cap had sobered up; had stopped leering; had become suddenly friendly.

"Hey," he said, "I'm Alva J. McClean. You can call me Chicken Man. Or Jud, if that's more to yer liking. Me and Grayson has been together forever. Pleased to make your acquaintance, ma'am."

She stopped brushing her clothes. As the truth set slowly in her mind like the sun at dusk, her features hardened.

"Get in, please," said Kirk.

Her eyes glittered.

"Ma'am . . ." said McClean, pulling on the bill of his Ralston.

"You bastards."

Kirk could feel the tiny shower of spit as she spoke one syllable at a time through her teeth.

"You-dir-ty-bas-tards."

Kirk took her by the elbow. "Get in, Colonel."

She jerked her elbow away.

Kirk's own features hardened. "Dammit, Gail, I'm sorry. Now slide your ass into that pickup seat, or Jud and I will leave you here."

She glared at him. She moved, stepping up into the cab, but never dropping the glare.

They drove in silence. McClean made a couple of attempts to start up conversation. Once he referred to the irony of her being a colonel and he a Kentucky chicken rancher. She looked at him in disgust. So it and all his other icebreakers withered into the whine of the tires until he gave up the effort.

Finally she spoke, hard and flat.

"The car."

"It's the last link to us. It will turn up and be returned soon enough."

"But my luggage," she said. "I have some pretty expensive clothes—don't give me those looks, you morons, just because you never owned anything more expensive than army uniforms or . . . or dungarees. I know clothes aren't as important as our safety, but this isn't exactly a case of one or the . . ."

She followed Jud McClean's pointing thumb and looked into the truck bed at her bag. She turned back to the front and stared straight down the road into the path the headlight beams cut into the night. For the third time, she called them bastards, this time under her breath.

"Look, Gail. I didn't have time for explanations back there."

"Baloney."

"Okay, I had time. It's not good practice to blabber"—his tone became conciliatory—"but I should have told you."

"Look, Major . . ."

"Kirk."

"Don't give me that bullshit—Major. You just listen. As long as we're in this together. As long as I'm a lieutenant colonel and you're a major. As long as I pulled your unconscious butt from Fall Creek. As long as people are chasing both of us, I need to know. I want to know what's going on from here on out."

"Okay. I promise. Kirk, right?"

"Gail."

"Call me Chicken Man," said McClean, beaming beneath the bill of his Ralston.

She cocked her head at him. She barely concealed a look of contempt that intimated she'd just as soon kill him for the cheap trick he and Kirk had played.

McClean leaned around her. "I don't think the colonel likes the Chicken Man, Grayson."

Even she had to smile at the understatement.

The tensions reduced, Kirk capsulized the gist of the events at the nightclub. He explained sheepishly that he and McClean had agreed over the phone that they would meet in the bathroom or outside and transfer the baggage. McClean chimed in to brag that the fight scene was his last-minute idea. He complimented Kirk for playing along so well. Connie Gail just grimaced and flapped her hand to make Kirk go on with the story.

He took the visual cue. McClean had been Kirk's crew chief for nearly two years in Vietnam. McClean had pulled him from a crash in an enemy-held zone. Together they'd evaded patrols for two weeks. That was about the size of it. They had kept in touch through the years in the way soldiers always say they will but usually do not. They had spent many a night tossing back bottled long-necked Sterlings in Louisville clubs or just out back of McClean's place upwind of the chicken sheds after dark.

She flapped her hand.

That's about all there was to tell, Kirk said. Except that now Jud would put them up for a while and run the public errands so the two of them could stay out of sight.

"Which brings us to the present circumstances," said Gail. Her temperament had evened out entirely. "What precisely must we do to make progress? Which progress is eminently preferable to giving up the initiative to our enemy while we sit around fecklessly."

McClean, wide-eyed, mouthed the word "fecklessly" and gazed in mock astonishment at Kirk.

"By way of explanation, Jud, Gail is a lawyer." To her, he said, "I've got some old friends in and out of army intelligence. Some of them are in Defense, some CIA, some pretty high up by now, I'd imagine. I also know a senator—a Vietnam veteran. My idea is to call and put ourselves under somebody's protection at a safe house, you know, guarded and all. . . ."

"I thought you wanted to avoid the passive, to take the initiative," she protested.

"I do. But there's not a lot we can do alone. Best way to get a feeling for the climate is to relay our suspicions of a conspiracy in all those deaths, to get somebody to call off the law, the Sids and the FBI. If we can get under the protective mantle of another agency, at least law enforcement can be called off."

"But if we give ourselves up . . ."

"I didn't say we'd give up. I said we'd tell them we wanted to, that we don't feel safe, that we suspect a conspiracy, that we want a few ironclad guarantees—for instance, that we won't be shot on sight—as so-called escapees. If we get no more than the manhunt called off while details for surrender are worked out, that will be a victory."

She relaxed. "And I can call some of my friends in Military Justice. They can work on the same angle. We don't want them to declare us AWOL. We want them to help clear the decks for our safe passage into the custody of authorities." She brightened and explained to their driver: "The way these things work, Chicken Man, the more agencies we get involved in the process, the greater the entanglements and jealousies. Consequently, the more time, the more freedom of movement, we'll have."

He nodded knowingly and glanced askance at Kirk. "I been there, ma'am. I been in government and I been working with Agriculture, y'know. Yeah, I been there."

Martha Bertrand lay terrified. She had lain that way every night since her husband had disappeared. The army had been properly concerned about her husband. They knew a sergeant major wouldn't just go AWOL. The major—Grayson Kirk was his name—had been especially concerned. So much so, she had given him her best color portrait of Command Sergeant Major John Bertrand, taken on the day of his graduation from the Sergeants Major Academy. Kirk had promised to use the photograph to help find John. He said he would have it copied to black and white, distribute it to the Indianapolis papers, run it in the *Harrison Post,* hand it out to police and the noncom associations. Then he said he would return it in mint condition. Kirk had done none of those things. And when she had phoned to ask when she might get it back, he said he would personally bring it back—there was some trouble with "officials," as he put it, in publishing and passing around the photo—but he would return the original that very day.

And he had returned it personally. He had stayed, seeing her need to be comforted. He had taken time to talk. She had shown him the photo album documenting her husband's career from basic training through every school, through every promotion—each milestone marked by a new photo. He nodded politely. She knew he was not really interested, but just being kind. That was fine with her. But when his gaze landed on one particular page of the album, his interest suddenly showed a genuine spark. Bertrand had marked his basic-training photo. Bright blue foil stars, the type schoolteachers use, had been pasted onto the chests of a dozen men in the photograph—a couple of black men, a handful of white men . . . one with white hair. Kirk had asked about that because he recognized a friend of his in the photo. Private Mark Payne had gone on to OCS, he said, and had been in the same flight school class as Kirk. And now Payne wore one of those blue stars on his chest. Why? Kirk had asked. But she had not known why her husband had marked them so. Or why he had circled their names at the bottom of the photograph. Or why he'd become so depressed every time he delved back into the distant memories from basic training.

Kirk had asked to borrow the photograph so he could call a friend at the Pentagon to look up the names, to find similarities between the men decorated with blue stars. Why? she had asked. No reason, he had said. But she found a new concern—that Kirk might be some kind of military police detective trying to implicate her husband in some kind of wrongdoing. She said as much.

And he had assured her such was not the case. So she had given him the photograph.

At this very moment, though, Martha was not at all concerned about Kirk or the basic-training photo or even her husband. She was concerned about herself.

She had heard a snap. She recognized the sound. John used to cut glass to frame the tiny watercolors she collected at amateur art fairs. The snap was the sound of a fracture shooting randomly across a pane of glass.

She lay paralyzed by fear, waiting for the next sound.

It came. The brushing of a window sliding up its channels.

She picked up her telephone but found it silent.

She waited for footsteps in the hall.

They came.

The door.

Soundlessly, a shaft of light grew across the wall of her bedroom.

"Please don't hurt me," she whimpered.

Pearson obliged. He struck her hard on the temple with his blackjack, and she was unconscious after only a moment of deeply concentrated pain. The second man, Keeney, rummaged through her dresser and withdrew a stocking. He stretched it and tied it viciously around her lax throat. He watched, transfixed as the face began blackening and blueing, the deeper arterial blood still pumping to the head and face but the surface venal blood trapped above the nylon knot.

Pearson ordered Keeney to rape her. Keeney protested. Pearson growled an angry obscenity, imitating Gerlach. Keeney obliged to the best of his ability, but his best was a halfhearted attempt.

While he was thus occupied, Pearson scattered the contents of Martha's purse and began tearing the house apart.

They left with a box of inexpensive jewelry and seemingly useless papers and books—including the album of John Bertrand's photographically documented career.

They left in a hurry, for the night still held an abundance of work for them.

As they drove north on Interstate 65 toward Chicago, Kirk pointed at the corner of the windshield. McClean took the exit. Kirk pointed again and Kirk used the phone at the service station. She sat in the cab. McClean returned to the pickup with sodas, Kirk with a sickly, pained expression. He refused the soft drink. McClean shrugged and began chugging it down,

Kirk nodded to him, and McClean headed the pickup south, back toward Indianapolis.

She turned to Kirk, "What was the phone call about?"

McClean replied, "He don't wanna be bothered about it, ma'am."

Her angry tone flickered up like a flame from embers. "Can't *he* talk? He *said* he wouldn't hold back any details from me."

"Noble Lee," said Kirk, shaking himself as if stirring back to a temporal level of consciousness. "I called my friend Noble Lee. To offer my sympathy for the death of his son. And to leave an innocent trace of ourselves by calling from a phone on the road north to Chicago."

"And?" she prompted.

McClean huffed as if to say: Why don't you wait and see, woman?

She tossed McClean a hateful glance. "And what?" she insisted from Kirk.

"And he told me his daughter had been killed as well."

"My god," she gasped. "I . . . I'm sorry. How?"

"Hit-and-run driver."

"What a horrible coincidence . . . or do you think it was murder?"

"No goddamned coincidence," said Kirk between his teeth. "The somebitch drove clear up on the curb to get her. He dragged her under the car a hundred feet. Never slowed down at all. Even Noble, poor goddamned naive Noble, knows it wasn't an accident. He's getting his wife and himself the hell away from Fort Ben tomorrow."

"What kind of man would . . . Who *are* these people?" she whispered rhetorically.

"And now I've endangered Noble."

"What? How? How could an innocent phone call . . . ?"

McClean jumped into the Ping-Pong match of the conversation as if to spare Kirk the pain of saying it. "The phone call from Grayson. From what Grayson says, somehow those two children seen something they wan't supposed to. Maybe the parents were safe, maybe not. Not now, for sure. Anybody who gets a phone call from Grayson, anybody who meets Grayson"—he looked at his companions—"anybody riding around in the cab of a ram-tough pickup with Grayson . . . is going to get his ass killed . . . *and*, pardon my French, *her* ass killed too."

"But why?"

Kirk whispered a question in answer. "I wonder . . . could those deaths have anything to do with that . . . that monster . . . ?"

"What monster?" She and McClean asked at once.

Kirk decided it was pointless to hold back any longer. No point in worrying about his own embarrassment about telling such an incredible story. Maybe if they had heard something on the newscasts about monster remains being found in the aftermath of the crash. Maybe he was dreaming. Maybe . . .

"What monster, dammit? Grayson, you ain't holding back on your old buddy, are you?"

He told them. The telling of those events inside the helicopter and matching what he knew about General Ford's death to the corpse of Kyle Lee didn't reduce his own incredulity. Talking aloud actually made the realities he'd seen even less believable to himself. He tried to sum up.

"Unbelievable as it seems, it must have been that beast that caused the deaths. The kids must have seen it. Everybody connected with those deaths, investigating them and all, is dead. Everybody who's seen the beast I saw at the

helicopter . . . is dead. Now I may be endangering anybody I contact. Noble may be next."

"A little melodramatic, wouldn't you say?"

They glared at her in unison.

Kirk spoke in a controlled voice, but he was unable to
keep the urgency from his tone. "We *have* to believe Noble Lee is in trouble. If we're wrong, no harm done. If
we're right, I might be able to save his life—his and
Nancy's." He smacked his lips in disgust. "Though I
doubt she wants to be saved after what happened to her
children."

"What can you do? Why couldn't we just call the police?"

"And what? Tell them a story about monsters and drag-
ons?"

They rode in silence for a long time along rural Indiana
roads, meeting little traffic. Though it was only nine P.M.,
most of the farms were dark.

"Grayson," she finally said.

He looked into her eyes.

"Kirk," she said. It sounded like a first name. "I meant
Kirk. You're right, of course. We have to help the Lees.
What else can we do?"

He smiled weakly at her. She returned the smile wanly.
Maybe she wasn't such a bitch after all.

He left them at a Speedway motel and drove toward
the fort across town. He left orders to avoid using the
telephone, any telephone, so nobody would be the wiser
about their latest shift in travel directions. She wanted to
know where the hell he thought he was going, what the
hell he was doing, and why the hell she was being left out.

"Why not just call Noble Lee?" she said.

"That might just speed up a decision to kill him and

Nancy. . . . I already told you their line is probably tapped."

Further than that, he would not argue, saying he didn't have time for explanations.

She called him a few names.

He said he was going to talk to Noble Lee, to advise him of the danger he might be in. He said he'd be back by midnight.

She called him a few more names.

He left. As he drove, he recognized the hopelessness of hoping there'd ever be any kind of relationship between them. Funny. The thought of that implausibility made him sad. For a while there this evening, he had toyed with a fantasy. It wasn't a particularly rare fantasy; he often had it about women that were untouchable. Just for a moment he would wonder what life would be like with a forbidden woman—a friend's wife, or a woman passing by him on the interstate, or a woman on-screen or in an ad, or even a nun—he once saw himself as somebody who could save one of the nuns in his grade school from the cloistered life—or as in this case, a woman officer who outranked him. In a bar or almost anyplace, he could strike up a conversation with an approachable woman— even hit on her. But these other women were untouchables, and he could only fancy how things might be because of the barriers that kept him from hitting on them. And so often he found after a night of passion that he didn't want the touchables. He wanted the untouchables. Or so he thought. And she was as untouchable as they came. The chemistry between them could only be described as volatile hatred.

For a while tonight, he thought she might be lowering those barriers, making herself reachable. And he wanted to reach to her. But no, her momentary soft spot had hardened. She was going to be the colonel, and he was going to have to be the major. And that made him feel sad, even pathetic, maybe even sorry for himself.

The big, tough, macho war-hero-pilot-agent-commando had nobody to love. And nobody loved him. Poor, poor Grayson Kirk. He recognized the ache behind his nose. He didn't cry of course. He hadn't cried for . . . he didn't know how long. He'd never cry. But he often had had that ache. Feeling sorry for himself.

Kirk parked the pickup in a troop lot next to a barracks. It was the least conspicuous place. Soldiers—men and women—loitered in the parking lot, meeting, greeting, farewelling, kissing desperately, as if shipping off to war instead of merely getting in ahead of midnight bed check.

He pinched his nose hard to ward off the ache. He needed to turn off his emotions for what lay ahead. Noble Lee very likely was being watched by somebody waiting for him, Kirk knew. Getting emotional would be the worst thing that could happen to him now. Feelings would only get in the way.

He pulled down hard on the brim of the cap he'd borrowed from McClean and strode toward the golf lodge, a favorite troop hangout.

He limped a little, his ankle still stiff from the twisting that monster had given it. But it had loosened up by the time he passed by the housing area where Noble Lee lived with his wife, the last of his family.

The pistol felt heavy and uncomfortable stuck into the front of his pants. For the dozenth time he adjusted his shirttail as if hiding an erection instead of the automatic. Once weapons had been his appendages. When he put them aside, he felt like an amputee. But now, years later, the pistol felt as awkward as a new prosthesis.

Several couples walking toward the barracks passed him. They seemed glued together, though the early-fall night air was uncharacteristically hot and thick. Leaning as if to support each other, they ignored him. And he gave them the barest of glances as his eyes swept around beneath the bill of the cap, looking for anything out of place.

The sidewalk passed by Lee's street within a hundred feet of his quarters. The residential street led nowhere, just circled behind and turned into a narrow alley. Only residents used it.

He saw Lee's lights were all on. He couldn't decide whether he should view that as bad or good.

The door of the club opened in his face, startling him. He was met by a swarm of young drunks on the way out —and by visible clouds of cigarette smoke and invisible clouds of the sweet-sick stench of spilled beer, and hundreds of decibels of rock music, shouting, and giggling.

Feeling vulnerable, he sucked his gut in, trying to envelop the bulk of the automatic. He pushed through the crowd to get inside, took off the cap, jammed his hands into his jeans, and joined the group outside, retracing the route he'd just taken. At six-three, it wasn't easy to look inconspicuous—his head stuck out above all the other heads. So he slumped a little.

There were eight men—boys really—and six girls. He stuck to the back of the mob as if he were part of it. There was only one direction for the mob to flow—eastward, back toward the barracks—and he hoped they wouldn't do anything characteristic of teen mobs; that is, he hoped they wouldn't do the unpredictable.

The mob did fine by Kirk's standards. Until they got to the alley that ran behind Lee's. Then the biggest of the boys, a muscular specimen with brush-cut hair, held out his arms, halting the group.

"Wait," he ordered.

The girls giggled, the other boys cursed him without fervor—he was too big to curse seriously.

Brush-cut pushed through the mob toward Kirk, who tensed, readying to cut the boy down with a knee to the nuts if necessary.

But brush-cut brushed by, barely acknowledging Kirk's existence. His attention was fixed on a bush. He unzipped and sighed excessively to the giggling approval and suggestive remarks of the mob.

Kirk thanked brush-cut silently for the display, the rush of water, the extra minute to study the darkness in the alley. He looked for cover, for ambush sites.

Brush-cut belched wetly and zipped up.

Kirk took over his spot at the bush and pretended to urinate as well.

For the mob, the novelty had worn off. It moved off, leaving him alone in the shadows of Fort Harrison's VIP guesthouse.

Minutes later, Kirk lay on his belly, pressed into the crisp shadow of the car shelter across the alley from Lee's backdoor. A security light high on a utility pole lit up the alley and backs of the houses. He fought off the inclination to just walk around the front and ring the bell. He had seen nothing out of place. The lights were still blazing inside, but the death of two family members probably accounted for that. Maybe lights to ward off loneliness. He doubted if the Lees could sleep, even this close to midnight.

Only the memory of earlier cautions in his life kept him pressed into the gravel beside the shelter. Something told him to wait beyond the limit of safety his eyes prescribed.

So he decided to wait longer. He would use the time to find a way to approach Noble Lee, who didn't know he was coming. How would he tell the man he and Nancy were in danger? For that matter, how would he make them set aside their grief even to care about being in danger?

Another silent five minutes passed. Kirk braced his hands on the ground beside his chest so he could push himself up.

Pearson clapped the handpiece into its hook in the pay phone outside the barracks.

"Hot damn," he muttered, muffling his voice but not his smile. He had reported his readiness to move in on the Lees—the standard procedure in nonemergency killings was to call headquarters to see if an eleventh-hour stay had been granted.

Great news. All kinds of it.

There had been no stay. He and Keeney could stage the double suicide Pearson suggested. The field boss, Barnaby, had approved it and corporate headquarters had given a final blessing. And he had to find an envelope addressed to Kirk. And if there was none, to wait and check the mail until it arrived, most likely in tomorrow's mail.

Kirk, the woman army officer, and a second man had been spotted returning toward Indianapolis. They had been located at a Speedway motel.

But the good part, the smiley part, was Gerlach's report of what the phone tappers had heard. They had listened to Kirk talking to Lee, and there was reason to believe he would make personal contact. So Barnaby had approved an immediate kill-on-sight order to reduce Kirk if he should come this way from Speedway. Barnaby would clean up "other loose ends," the headquarters contact said. Barnaby would coordinate the movement of another team on the Speedway motel to "clean up the situation there." Pearson knew that meant the woman and the man with the pickup would soon be finished. Kirk would be coming to the fort in that pickup. Pearson repeated the truck's license number over and over, embedding it in his memory.

Pearson had never met Barnaby, and maybe never would, but already he decided he liked working for the man. He was decisive, direct, and brutal. Pearson especially admired brutality in a boss.

He walked back toward the Lee quarters as quickly as he could without attracting attention. Still smiling, he reached into his jacket pocket and squeezed twice on his radio button to alert Keeney he was coming.

Kirk heard the two snaps. The sound came from barely a foot away, from the other side of the wall, from inside the car shelter. He had risen to the front-leaning rest position, as if for pushups, when the sound froze him.

He lowered himself. Slowly. He cringed, fearful a joint might crack or a piece of gravel might rattle or a twig might rasp against the boards of the shelter.

Once down, he rolled left onto his side and pulled the 9 millimeter from his pants. His pubic bone throbbed in relief.

Immediately he was back in Vietnam. Cracking squelch or snapping the silence on a radio was the way of communicating with ambush patrols and outposts that couldn't dare to speak or even whisper at night.

Kirk knew he was in hostile territory.

If he had stood up, brushed himself clean, walked into the light across that alley . . .

He strained to hear into the garage.

Nothing.

He rose to his knees and looked around him. He shuddered at the thought of so many hiding places. He also took a moment to curse himself for not taking this mission seriously enough. There was no round in the chamber of the automatic. If he had to use it now, he'd first have to jack the slide once. No way to move metal over metal now without giving himself away. Not if his enemy was close enough for him to hear hostile snaps from tiny speakers at reduced volume.

If that's what it was.

Did I really hear it? he asked himself.

Bullshit, he answered. No time to be second-guessing. He had dug down involuntarily into his war-conditioned reactions when he heard the sounds. He could consciously doubt himself about other matters, but those reactions had to be trusted.

He leaned an ear next to the wall without touching it.

Nothing—he heard absolutely nothing except the white noise inside his own ears.

He closed his eyes, held his breath, and increased his concentration on hearing.

Still nothing.

No, there . . . the sound of a wheeze or a nasal whistle. Or the twittering of a mockingbird. Or the whisper of an insect, or even a tiny wheeze in his own chest. Which was it?

A distant shouting-match broke out from the direction of the barracks. It kept up so Kirk's near hearing was neutralized. He opened his eyes.

He dared not wait.

The pair of snaps meant something. If somebody was simply making a radio check, no problem. If somebody had signaled the party in the car shelter to move, he would have done it by now. If somebody was coming . . .

It had to be that—a prearranged signal of an approach.

Kirk knew he had to act. He ran down the options instantly. Sneaking around would be observed by bad guys and good guys alike as suspicious. Even openly walking down an alley would be noticed in this neighborhood where everybody probably knew his neighbors. And the bad guys would be on point instantly for any intruder, *any* movement. If he were to gain any advantages, they weren't likely to come from any surreptitious act.

He pointed his pistol at the wall.

Pearson could barely restrain himself from running down the alley, though his aching, swollen balls were restraint enough. It had occurred to him that Kirk could already be on the way over, might even be inside the house. Keeney didn't know to expect Kirk. Pearson expected Kirk to be cautious. He knew the spook background, the special training—although he regarded that Vietnam stuff as primitive by modern standards. Kirk would definitely be on guard and dangerous. The only question was whether Kirk could sneak by Keeney before he got back.

Pearson's question was answered by a gunshot and a shout. He heard the *bisst* of two silenced shots in reply.

Christ, Kirk had fired first . . . but at least Keeney had survived to shoot back.

Pearson broke into a hobbling run, moving onto the grass to muffle the sound of his approach.

Not that it mattered. Along the alley, backlights

snapped on. He heard questions being shouted into the night through open windows. He might be challenged by some dumbass major or colonel with a pistol any minute. Goddammit, every one of the bastards in this kind of profession was probably armed to the teeth.

Piss on it.

"Police," he shouted down the alley. "This is a police matter. Please stay inside—KEENEY, where are you? Where the fuck *is* he?"

Kirk fired a bullet into the front-door lock, smashing it. He then shouldered the door open and burst into the Lee house, shouting:

"Noble, it's Grayson Kirk. Nancy, Noble, where are you?"

His plan had been simplicity itself, a characteristic that always seemed to work for him. He had stood up outside the car shelter, jacked a 9-millimeter round into the chamber, fired into the garage—elapsed time, a second or so. And he had run away. Past the next car shelter, across the alley, between houses—stopping to pry two bricks from a flower-bed edge and hurl them through windows of different houses—and to the front of his friend's quarters. Maybe fifteen seconds more gone.

The seconds counted, every one.

The pair of silenced slugs slapping back at him through the shelter wall told him he hadn't hit the enemy. It didn't matter. He needed to make noise, to arouse the neighborhood, to get the residents to make the necessary calls to military police for him—he wouldn't have time for that, once inside. He would have to herd his friends into the basement or upstairs and stand guard until the area was crawling with cops and angry neighbors. From

there . . . well, he decided to play it by ear if he succeeded till then.

He knew the house. In a happier time, he had eaten
dinner in the dining room to the right. Past it was the
kitchen on the alley side of the house. In front of him
were the stairs. To the left the living room and past it a
sun room, two walls of windows looking to the side and
the alley again. He decided the lights were to his advantage. Once he had his friends protected, nobody could
sneak in.

He shouted left and right.

No answer.

He decided on the bedrooms and bounded up four
stairs before he heard Noble's slurring voice from below.
It drew a curse from under his breath.

"Noble," he shouted, "get down on the floor."

"What?" It was Nancy this time.

"Shit," Kirk shouted, "both of you get down on the
floor."

He rounded the corner and saw them standing in the
doorway to the sun-room. They stood propping each
other up, their eyes reddened and swollen, too dazed to
know the difference between danger and the insanity of
their friend, Grayson Kirk.

Kirk dropped to his knees as if to demonstrate. He held
out his hands in supplication, the pistol gripped in the
right fist. He waved at them as if he were a third-base
coach trying to get his runner to slide under the tag.

He shouted loud and angry enough to hurt his throat.
"Hit the fucking deck, goddammit, somebody's out there
with a fucking gun."

That did it. Their knees buckled and they went forward.

"No," shouted Kirk. "NO-O-O-oooo fucking wa-a-a-y."

Suddenly he was crying, desperately shedding tears of grief and frustration even as he shouted, the cords and veins in his neck straining to break free.

There had been the tinkling of glass, the slapping against the wall behind him, the pair of dazed expressions turning to pained, the splatters of blood first on their faces, then on his.

Kirk rolled and came up on an elbow, firing, still emitting an anguished groan, until one by one the three lights in the room had shattered.

He crawled to the pair of bodies and sobbed at what he saw.

Nancy was finally out of her misery of losing two children in a day. In the dim light from the entry, Kirk saw a ragged, spurting exit hole above her left eye, the flyaway hair she'd willed to Kit moved with every whisper of the air he disturbed in the room.

Noble Lee coughed, choking in his own blood. Kirk saw the pulse dying in weaker and weaker spurts from a gaping flap of open-neck flesh. Lee raised a hand. Kirk stretched out to clasp it. The hand fell on the table, blooding a thin manila envelope. The envelope fell off with the hand clutching it.

"Grayson," came the weak voice gurgling through the torn throat.

"Yes, Noble, what?" He leaned in to hear.

"This came for you," were the last words Noble Lee uttered. His head fell on his hand, and a gush of his blood spilled onto the manila.

A stunned Kirk stared in shock.

It wasn't just blood or death. He had seen those before, not enough so he didn't care, but enough not to be shocked. He had even heard last words before, dramatic ones like "Tell my wife I love her" and "Kiss my new baby for me when you get home." Even "Kiss my wife," which he did, and "Give my ol' lady a good screwing for me," which he didn't, but had shared a bittersweet last laugh over.

But "This came for you"?

He grabbed his friend's hair and shook more blood from the wound. "Jesus, Noble. Jesus H. Christ, not like this."

The only response was the squishing of air escaping the wounded throat.

A yelping siren closed in. More sirens sounded off in the distance. People milled around outside. He could hear them shouting back and forth, women taking inventories of their families, men asking loud questions and giving equally loud answers about what had been happening. The disturbance he'd started had brought the police. And now he—already a fugitive—was trapped at the scene of a double murder. Try explaining that, he thought, clearing the grief from his mind and body—the ache this time coming not from feeling sorry for himself.

Flashing lights strobed through the room, lighting up the tears welling in Kirk's eyes.

A man shouted for silence outside.

Kirk raised up onto his knees and saw a swarm approach the police car. A pimpled youngster, confused and probably even afraid, stepped out, hitched up his pistol belt, and demanded to know what had happened. A dozen people tried to answer the young cop, who couldn't have been much past twenty, Kirk guessed.

The kid tried to gain control of himself and the crowd.

Kirk stood up, then knelt again. He would have left the stupid, damned envelope, except that as he rose to his feet he recognized the name emerging from under the blood puddle on the manila: Payne. The partially obscured return address read: Emerg————ark Payne.

Emergency . . . something . . . from Mark Payne.

He tucked in his shirt and jammed the envelope under his belt, the wet side toward his belly. He had no choice, for he had concocted a dumb but simple plan from somewhere inside his subconscious, and the sight of blood would give him away. He jammed his automatic into his rear pocket, replacing McClean's baseball cap on his head.

Outside he could hear the kid cop asking if anybody had been inside.

Kirk wiped his tears and ran to the front door, pulling the brim down over his brow, hoping the shadow would hide the distinctive scars and wiseacre look from somebody who might know him in the crowd.

"I have," he shouted.

The kid pulled a .45.

The crowd oohed collectively and dispersed, clearing a line of fire between Kirk and the MP as if this were a scene from a western movie.

"I came through the back," Kirk yelled, holding up his palms. "You better call a doctor and get in here. I think they shot each other in a domestic . . . or else it's a double suicide."

"Oh, my God," shrieked a woman. "Nancy. They've just lost their children. It's the Lee family. Suicide. Oh, my God."

The crowd pressed toward the door.

The cop knew he had to take charge.

"This is a crime scene," he squawked. "You can't go in there."

"You better get in here," Kirk ordered in the voice of a commissioned officer. "There's people been killed and you have a job to do."

The kid responded. He waved his .45.

"You, sir, better get out of that house. It's a crime scene."

Kirk obliged, slipping down to the edge of the crowd.

The kid went inside, leading with his pistol, ordering his partner to stand at the door and keep people away from the scene.

In less than a minute he was out vomiting.

More sirens arrived, an ambulance, more police cars, two fire trucks.

The kid finished spitting up.

"Hey," he said, suddenly coming to his senses, "where's that guy that came outta the house?"

Heads began pivoting everywhere in the crowd.

Somebody mumbled, "You know, that guy looked like that major, you know, Kirk? You know, the guy the FBI's looking for."

Emergency cars streamed toward the Lee house, and pedestrians followed, homing in on the array of flashing lights and growing crowd. The curious left their barracks, in small groups of the bravest and most inquisitive at first. Then larger and larger groups followed, streaming across the ballfield and PT areas. Groups leaned outside the windows of barracks and gathered in parking lots.

Kirk just watched. There was no need to hide. The crowds gave him his anonymity. He jumped up to sit and watch on a PT platform, where tomorrow a drill sergeant would stand and shout. He ignored the police and crowds. His attention was on McClean's pickup parked among other cars in the barracks lot. The first question was, Could he get to it without trouble? He decided he could. That would be the easy part.

The hard part was the answer to the question Was anybody staking out the Dodge?

Nobody seemed to be around but curious soldiers. The most practical of them had already begun moving back inside to sleep before tomorrow's hardships of defending the country in steno class and whatever.

A pizza truck pulled up to the barracks and the driver ran inside carrying pizzas stacked up to his chin.

Except for the riot of strobing lights behind him, everything looked normal.

Kirk jumped down from the stand. The best time to leave would be in the middle of the confusion, he knew, when he was least conspicuous and before the military police satisfied their curiosity at the crime scene and started sweeping for the stranger who'd been inside the Lee house.

He joined a group moving toward the barracks. They were yammering excitedly about murder and fear.

Ahead, a car moved slowly by, easing into the parking lot. All traffic was rolling slowly, the drivers careful of pedestrians aimlessly milling about, so Kirk paid it only a first glance. He kept searching the dark areas for somebody staking out the pickup.

As he closed on the Dodge, he began searching between the cars. He dropped behind his group and knelt to fake tying a shoe, then looked beneath the cars.

Nothing.

Yes . . .

. . . something.

Suddenly he was aware of a change.

It was barely perceptible.

The slow-moving car had slowed yet another fraction behind McClean's pickup.

Kirk veered between two parked and rusted cars.

Another change.

The slow mover picked up speed and left the lot slightly faster than it had gone in. On the street, it turned right and cruised out of sight.

He listened.

There. He heard it roar away. Tires squealed as it turned again. Circling.

Already somebody had recognized the pickup and was onto him. He cursed to himself, asking obscene questions he had no answers to. The only thing he knew for sure was that they'd be back in seconds to keep a closer eye on McClean's pickup. He couldn't take off in it. He'd have to use an alternative means of getting off this fort again.

He slid into the cab of the idling pizza truck, put it in gear, and followed the route of the suspicious car. The street in front of the barracks was empty except for a lone sedan parked along the curb across the street. It was the car that had driven through the parking lot. They would be afoot and on the lot side by now, watching the pickup, he reasoned. And this was their car.

He stopped the pizza truck in the street, putting it between the car and the barracks. Bingo! The car was idling. Locked but idling.

In minutes a frantic pizza delivery boy would be going all over, shouting about his stolen truck. They would know who'd done it and be on the lookout for him again. They'd soon be running back here to their car.

As long as they'd be tracking down a known vehicle, he might as well make it as well known as possible.

Kirk shut off the pickup and dropped the keys down a storm drain. It took only a second to bash a hole through the driver's window with the 9 millimeter and enlarge it for his hand.

The aroma of the pizza reminded him how hungry he was. He went back to the truck and took three.

He cruised down the street before turning the headlights on. But already he had stuffed a whole slice of pepperoni and sausage into his face. He smiled for two reasons: one, because he was so damned clever; two, because he liked pepperoni.

It troubled him that such professionals were out to kill him. Still, he couldn't wait to tell McClean how he'd gotten the pizzas.

Suddenly he choked. Suddenly he realized that in the excitement of eluding the military police and his pursuers here, the death of a pair of friends seemed so trivialized—almost forgotten—in the moments that he had reverted to the behavior he had displayed in Vietnam. His friends had been murdered. Their very blood had spattered him. And all he could think about was bragging to a drinking buddy about how goddamned tricky he was. What had he come to? he asked himself. He gagged and spat the mouthful of pizza out the window. What the hell had he come to?

An hour later he'd become even more grim, gripping the wheel of the stolen car, racing to the Speedway motel, where he'd left Colonel Connie and Jud McClean, where the desk wouldn't answer his frantic phone calls.

Now he understood so much more, the monster, the murders.

He'd been driving I-465, the loop around Indianapolis. The smell of pizza had grown nauseating, so he rolled the window down and littered the freeway with pizza. He then slipped the envelope out of his shirt. He'd seen again that it was addressed to him in care of Noble Lee. And he saw that partial return address again: Emerg————ark Payne.

He had slipped a thumb under the flap near the dried blood. He poured out the contents of the packet into the swirling breezes in the car. A letter and some photocopied notes—they looked like entries in a diary. The pages of a letter fluttered as he tried to read. A woman, PJ Payne—Mark's wife—had written the letter, desperate, long, rambling, frantic. In it she told him Mark Payne had been killed. This letter was a matter of life, the first page told him. And it was a matter of death.

The letter apologized for exposing him to danger, possibly his own death. If he hadn't already experienced a number of attempts at that, he might have found the letter a hysterical, melodramatic fantasy concocted by a paranoiac. But he believed. He knew he had to get off the road and study this letter. He'd become something of a paranoiac himself in the last few hours.

Kirk found an exit with a fast-food stop and a booth with a little privacy. He read it all, studied it. In the stark fluorescent light of the hamburger joint, it seemed too unreal to be believed. If not for the constant reminder of the blood on the envelope, the enduring anchor to reality, this might have been some kind of fantastic joke, some kind of science fiction dream. Drug tests? Monsters? Who could believe such stuff?

He could. He'd seen such a monster—and he could feel the wound it had given him every time he moved his ankle just so. He believed. He understood. But understanding only made him feel worse.

Bertrand. His photo album. Bertrand and Mark Payne had been in the same basic-training platoon. They were both destined for Officer Candidate School. Both thought they'd become ill from a virus in basic. Bertrand dropped out, stayed enlisted, rose to sergeant major. Payne stayed commissioned. PJ's letter explained why the BCT photo had the stars on so many men in it. They identified the men who had been subject to drug testing—presumably intelligence-enhancing drugs. Now those men had been disappearing for years. Bertrand had kept track of the men who'd vanished, had kept track of them with the blue stars. Until he'd disappeared himself.

But why? Kirk asked himself. Why were they disappearing?

And Mark Payne's brother-in-law. He had been creating modern Frankenstein monsters. Recombinant DNA? What the hell was that? Monsters he understood. But DNA? He'd have to get a look at the copies of the research logs. He'd have to track them down and see for himself. Later. PJ Payne told him in a last wobbly paragraph where he might look to find one or both of the last two copies of the logs.

Texas.

He'd have to travel to Texas to fully understand the contents of this frantic letter.

He looked at his watch. After two. He had decided to call the motel room so the others wouldn't worry. And maybe they would have some ideas about what to do next.

No answer.

He wondered why the desk clerk wouldn't answer the phone. Clerk asleep? No clerk after midnight? No clerk after No Vacancy? Every idea he came up with seemed perfectly reasonable. So why did he feel so jittery?

It was after two when he cruised the darkened sedan into the rear of the service station adjacent to the motel. On foot, he took the dark way to their room, through the alley behind. Passing the office, he saw the sign and relaxed a little—NO CLERK AFTER 1:00 A.M. He chalked it up as one of the hazards of vacationing in no-frills motels.

There was nothing suspicious in the alley or motel parking lot.

Nothing suspicious in the well-lighted front walkway to his room.

He walked nonchalantly with his hands in his pockets, the right gripping the pistol. But he was anything but nonchalant. All of his physical and mental faculties were focused on the environment of the motel. It mildly surprised him that even though he'd been out of combat so long his senses could become so sharply honed so quickly. He credited it to the urgent tone of PJ Payne's letter.

Nothing suspicious as he slid in the key. He pushed open the door and padded into the room. Then it hit him. His hand touched the light switch just as the numbing fragrance of human gore mugged his senses.

Even as the light came on, he dove to the carpet and rolled, coming up sweeping the room, the automatic held in both hands.

The pistol came to rest on the lifeless, drenched body of Jud McClean.

Kirk forced the gun on another sweep of the room— toward the bathroom door, back to the front door.

But he wasn't as sharp as he'd thought.

He couldn't take his eyes from his dead friend sitting up in bed, the lifeless, glazed eyes gaping open, mouth gaping in a silent scream, throat opened in another silent gape.

Kirk swept the room with the gun again and he backed up against the wall, alternately covering the bathroom door and the front door.

But still he couldn't take his eyes from Jud McClean,

though he knew his staring merely branded a vision of horror into his memory.

McClean's stocking feet made a ridiculously neat V. One sock had a hole in the tip, allowing a ridiculous big toe to stick through. His shirtfront was reddened; had begun darkening to black—a bib of blood.

Kirk saw the reason for the bulging, drying eyes—a hole in the Chicken Man's temple. Incongruously, he hoped the shot had come before the knife.

His stomach lurched, and he knew he would be sick if he didn't look away. It wasn't the sight or scent of the blood. It was that another of his friends, the third friend he'd seen killed in hours . . .

. . . Connie. Gail. Where was she? Was she the fourth?

The bathroom door had been slid shut—it rode on rails into a pocket in the wall to open. A slit of light escaped from beneath it.

Kirk stood up and moved toward the door, creeping like some matinee Indian in the forest.

Suddenly he felt another presence and lurched into the wall, bringing the gun to the spot by the bed. He tensed, barely able to prevent himself from firing as his vision took in and processed the sight . . . the sight of a man lying face up, two more eyes open but unseeing. Kirk's heart seemed to be crashing from one wall of his chest to the other, rebounding like a pinball. He'd almost shot a dead man. He'd almost given away his tentative control of this situation.

He swept the gun around the room again to reassure himself that he hadn't missed something else. Jud still sat grinning, and Kirk's stomach lurched again. Were it not for his high state of anxiety, he was sure he'd be vomiting, cramped, crying, completely out of control of himself and the precarious circumstances. But he kept thinking about

Connie Gail too. She was something of a bitch. And she kept rebuffing his attempts to be decent, kept bringing out the worst in him. But he cared about her.

He reached for the finger hole that served as a handle to the sliding door. Gail. He was worried about Gail, afraid he might not find her, more fearful he would find a bloody corpse in the tub. But he held back from touching the door hole.

He picked up a ladder-back chair and crouched for leverage. Struggling with it at arm's length, he lodged a leg into the hole on the third try.

His inclination was to relax. Somebody should have opened fire by now at the clumsy attempt at rattling the door on its tracks. He wanted to shove into the bathroom and find Gail alive, though he knew that would never be.

So he had to fight those inclinations. They were tendencies that would kill him.

He shoved the door open, hoping to find nothing.

A shot answered him, shattering splinters through the cheap paneling where his head would be if he were standing. He threw the chair into the opening. Another shot tore off more splinters high and right.

He swung his automatic, lunging, dropping to his knees before the door, realizing this meant Colonel Connie was dead—dead too—like Jud and Nancy and Noble and Kyle and Mazey and Payne—Mark Payne, one of the best friends he'd ever had through their short flight-school and war acquaintance before he, Kirk, had gone into the spook business.

He was angry, sad, hateful, as the pistol came around. He saw blood spatters drying on the bathroom tiles. He saw the fat sausage of a silencer on the pistol's muzzle, the eye of the sausage gaping at a spot above his head. He saw the figure cringing in the tub, the fearful eyes wide, the mouth open in a scream as he covered the face with his own pistol and pulled the trigger, saw the gun leap from the hand, the tile shatter behind the head as he jerked the shot away at the last instant, sparing the life of the bloodied, horrified Colonel Connie Gail.

2

Mark Payne was disappointed to discover himself alive, if alive was what it was.

He knew enough to realize he was rising like a gas bubble in a swamp. His state of consciousness had been mushy for days. He'd risen half a dozen times before, but this was different.

Before, doctors worked over a vaguely familiar body below him, probing into the mouth, cutting down deep in his throat, sewing deeply, rolling over the body, working on the back of the neck.

Before, the doctors responded to the urgent tones sounded by the machinery hooked to the body, injecting enormous needles into the chest of the figure below until Mark sank down into the figure. Another time, he rose from the body when only the machines were on guard, only a nurse asleep in a chair beside the bed of the vaguely familiar figure. This time he nearly escaped from the body. But they wheeled in a cart and machinery with paddle terminals—just as on television—and restarted the heart, capturing him again.

A third time, he resisted the needle's effect, ignored the shocking paddles—didn't even feel them—just watched the body as they tried to jump-start it and failed. He felt he would be free until they cut into the chest of the figure below; sawed through his sternum like a rack of ribs;

pried open a gaping hole, lifted up the heart; massaged it; injected it; gave it a gentler but more direct, more persuasive, shock.

Again he'd been trapped, sucked back into that broken, unfamiliar shell he no longer wanted to inhabit.

He felt the staples, stainless-steel claws clutching his split sternum. He felt every stitch of the needles and thread. He knew pain, he knew imprisonment. They had trapped his spirit inside that aching chest that no longer really belonged to him.

He wondered why. They had expended so much effort trying to kill him. They had killed PJ, the only thing that had kept him going these past two years, the only connection to reality he'd ever had, the only reason for caring.

Why bother now to bring him back to life?

It must have been days since he felt himself coming into consciousness, though, because he became more aware of the pain in his chest and throat. Because he felt his anger rising. They had spent so much time trying to kill him since those days in Texas. Why save his life now? Goddammit.

He felt himself being loaded into the back of a van. He was barely conscious and didn't have to fake anything. Belts strapped him to the cot or stretcher or whatever it was, but he couldn't have resisted anyhow.

The drive was a long and rough one.

Mark felt every sway in the road; saw the day turn to night, then to day again; tasted the dust seeping into the van. The air grew colder, the road rougher.

The road began to pound him back to the level of consciousness he hadn't experienced since that night on Marion Lake. He hated it. His throat hurt horribly, his chest throbbed with every bump in the road and with every beat of his heart.

He needed a drink of water badly. And he was hungry. Thirst and hunger—the body's signals that it wanted to go on living. God, he hated consciousness, hated living without PJ.

The van began climbing a steep, gravelly slope—he felt himself sliding toward the back of the van. He felt the switchbacks and the dust. He felt the air chilling, smelling of pine. Although his eyes were blindfolded, he knew they were in the mountains. Why? Why were they taking him back to the mountains?

The throbs in his chest sped up; began to hurt more exquisitely. Was it possible to hurt more than this?

Finally the van stopped.

He felt himself being transferred.

A helicopter. He smelled the pungency of JP-4 and hydraulic fluid. The engine started and he knew it was an OH-58 by the urgent, flimsy whine of the starter and the rushing explosion when turbine speed and temperature were hot enough for the throttle to be twisted open to flight idle, dumping atomized fuel into the heated igniter chambers with compressed air.

It was a short flight. The helicopter landed at a higher altitude. Mark could tell it by the popping in his ears before landing. There was no reversal of the pressure and no prolonged descent.

Mark lay as limp as he could while men's hands checked his belts and handled the gurney.

The helicopter took off, leaving him in a blast of Arctic air that refreshed rather than chilled him.

He heard gates opening and closing, heard and felt the crunching of gravel beneath the feet of the men carrying him. A set of hinges squealed, letting out a heavy stench that almost made Mark try to sit up against the belts. Then the gurney was rolling across a smooth floor.

He recognized that fetid odor. But from where?

The men cursed under their breaths as the smell grew stronger.

Mark's throat tightened, an involuntary spasm that hurt so bad, tears welled in his eyes.

The gurney stopped rolling.

A door opened, and he was rolled ahead.

The door slammed. He heard a bolt being slid home. Then a padlock. The men were gone.

He found he could move. He slipped an arm free of the belts and stripped away the blindfold.

A light burned red into his eyelids.

He opened his eyes.

He found himself lying in a sally port, the enclosure between locked doors leading from one cell block to another.

A prison.

Alone.

No.

That smell, deep and stifling, told him of other presences.

The sounds of movement—heavy breathing and groaning—confirmed the presences.

Somewhere in the distance an electric motor hummed to life. Then he heard a succession of locks snapping open. The gate leading into the darkness slid open.

He turned his head on the cot. The stiffness in his throat resisted the movement, stinging him.

The darkness began to move, taking shape as hulking figures, brown and black. Two monsters advanced into the light toward him. No, three figures . . . all beasts.

For a second he struggled against the belts.

Something tore in his throat, something from the wound or surgery. It felt as if he'd been shot all over again, that he'd been stabbed in the wounds. His chest pounded, ready to burst apart the staples and stitches. A hiss uttered from his lips and dissipated as a gurgle. He tasted his own fresh blood, warm and rust-flavored.

The odor from the beasts took his breath away. He felt the pain subsiding with his consciousness.

Why the hell would The Corporation go through all the trouble to save his life just to have him torn apart? Damn. He wished he could get his hands on one of the tormentors who'd done this to him. He struggled against the straps on his arms and felt one give.

God, they'd kept him alive for this?

The beasts drew back.

Mark prepared to fight to the death.

What the hell, he decided. This is what he wanted. Surely the next life would not be so painful as this. And there was no life worth living here without PJ.

And even the pain was subsiding as he lost consciousness from the exertion and excitement.

His lips grew numb, tingly. The edges of his vision closed in as the beasts leaned over his body, fangs bared, growling.

His vision shrank to a pinpoint and flicked off. His consciousness lingered a moment at the two areas of pain—in his chest and in his throat. Then the pain died. The sounds of grunting faded to miles away. Even the stench seemed as if it might disappear.

He willed himself to smile. At last he would have peace, he would know about PJ, maybe they would be together.

In the twilight of his consciousness, he knew the feeling of a smile was there, though it was in his spirit and not on his face. He felt the first happiness since . . . he didn't know when.

He thought of PJ's green eyes.

And then, mercifully—before the beasts had even touched him—he was gone.

Kirk watched in wonder that the facade of Colonel Connie had broken down, shaken loose by trembling shoulders, washed away by her tears. So she was human after all.

In her uniform and in character as the fort's chief lawyer, she had seemed more like some kind of legal computer incapable of feelings—unless snottiness was a feeling.

Now she cried. And she bled from the angry slice that ran nearly the whole length of her right forearm, the wound he had put there. She was a bleeding, broken, vulnerable, beautiful—human being. A woman.

Well, with her face contorted in pain and anguish, a new shiny knot growing on her right cheekbone, the swollen corner of her mouth, the blood seeping down her chin, her tousled hair, maybe she wasn't exactly beautiful at the moment. But with her newly found humanity, she would be more striking, more beautiful, than ever.

He stepped into the bathroom.

She cringed, pulling away to the corner of the bathtub.

"It's me . . . Kirk," he said.

"I thought . . ." She met his eyes and she sobbed.

He shook his head and shrugged, indicating the obvious.

"They're gone," he said. He looked back toward the bedroom. Jud McClean's ridiculous big toe still stuck through his sock. The horror there was still reality. His stomach cramped violently, making Kirk very dizzy. He leaned back on the counter to steady himself.

"How many . . . ?" he asked.

"Two. . . . Jud . . . he stepped out . . . for cigarettes. It happened so fast. When he came back, they shoved him in the door . . . and pushed me down. Jud fought like a—he cut the one before . . . they were tying him up and cutting him. . . . Oh, God, Kirk, I've never seen so much blood . . . and I've never . . . Kirk, I shot a man—the one by the bed. I mean I killed him. And I shot the other one too. . . . He . . ."

Kirk saw she was losing it.

"Easy, Gail. Take it easy." Good advice, but he was feeling ill at ease himself, right at the edge of getting sick. The sight of blood had never been something to make him queasy. But all this blood tonight had come from people he cared about, maybe even people he loved.

She shuddered violently. "They punched me. They were going to kill me too. I . . . grabbed a gun off the bed and . . . just started shooting . . . and killed one. I think I wounded the other before he got away. . . . I thought you . . . I thought you were him . . . coming back for me."

He shrugged again. Then he shook himself. He needed to regain control of himself so he could prevent her from going hysterical on him. She'd begun repeating herself. She was babbling.

"Your arm." He pointed. She cradled her right arm in her left hand. The blood had begun draining down her left forearm too, dripping from both elbows. "I'm sorry," he said. "I thought you were one of them too."

"I'm sorry," she said. "I thought . . ."

"Yeah. We both made a mistake. Now forget it, Gail. You better let me wrap that up in a towel until I get you to a doctor."

"No." She wagged her head. "It's not serious. . . . I

was a nurse before I decided to try something less . . . stereotypical."

Of course, thought Kirk. He could see her returning to character. The sickness inside him surged ahead of his momentary relief that he'd not shot her. And ahead of the mistaken impression that she was a fragile woman.

He handed her a bath towel and watched it soak through scarlet even as she wrapped it around her forearm. He bent over for the dropped gun, suddenly feeling ill.

He sat on the toilet and put his head down to restore the circulation to his head. He needed to regain his equilibrium, his senses. He needed to think. How had he gotten mixed up in all this murder, all these monsters? So suddenly. How did all these things go so wrong . . . ? *No*, thinking like that was unproductive. It was *not* that something was wrong here, but that he needed a solution to make things right. Better he be concocting answers to all the questions. All the shots would bring police. He couldn't answer all the questions that would be asked. And he'd never find any solutions from a jail cell.

"The shooting," he said. "Cops . . . we have to get . . . uh . . . The firing . . . Why aren't they already here?"

She bent down and brandished the pistol with its silencer.

"Right," he said.

She stepped from the tub and touched his head.

"You all right?"

"We've got to get out of here," he said.

"What about Noble Lee?"

"Dead." His stomach cramped at the remembrance of Noble and Nancy's dying. His every vision was of death.

"Nancy too," he said, sighing heavily. "I suppose Mark Payne too."

Her eyes narrowed at him. "Who?"

"You wouldn't know him. A friend of mine. Noble gave me a letter. . . ." The thought moved him to action.

He shot to his feet. "Come on, we've got to get out of here. I found out what we're dealing with, who we're dealing with. I read about a research journal and some other papers that explain that monster I saw and probably some others."

"Research journal? What research journal? What are you talking about, Kirk?"

"Later. I'll tell you later, when we go get it."

"Get it? You're talking in riddles."

"Patience, Gail. I don't have it. I read about the journal in a letter from PJ Payne. I saw a couple of its pages. People are being killed for it."

She stuck the pistol in her belt and adjusted the towel on her arm. Her color had become gray, making her look all the more pathetic. Scared, Kirk thought. Finally human.

"Where are we going?" She whispered.

"We'll find a clinic where you can get stitched up. Tell the doc we ran off the road—that you, uh, put your arm through the windshield."

"Then what?"

"Then we hit the road to Texas."

"Texas? To get this . . . journal?"

He nodded. "Texas. Where all this monster bullshit and killing began."

She shook her head—bewildered at the new information, he thought. She might even be going into shock.

Kirk darkened the motel room and peeked outside. Nothing moved in the parking lot. No traffic moved on the nearby streets either. He shivered at the knowledge that two dead bodies were lying in the darkened room.

"Gail," he said, turning.

She groaned as his elbow touched the blood-soaked towel.

"I'm sorry," he moaned in sympathy. In the darkness, she leaned against him and pressed her cheek against his chest. He took it as a sign of forgiveness.

"The car is behind that service station. I'll go get it. You stay inside until I pull up to the door. Then you come out."

She nodded against his chest. He inhaled the sweetness of her hair and bit his lip to stop himself from actually kissing her head.

He stepped away from her and cracked the door, letting the neon and mercury light of night spill into the room. Nothing stirred outside. All his attention went ahead of him as he stepped out, his hand grasping the pistol in his belt.

He heard the click of a heel behind him and whirled to order her back into the room.

What he saw immobilized him for a second.

Her eyes and mouth were wide open in that expression that preceded a scream. He read it instantly, but the second he lost in turning would be among his last. He'd been careless. He would die for it, he knew.

He tried diving and rolling.

As he was going down, yanking at the pistol, he saw the shadow of the man between the cars. He even caught a glimpse of the pistol tracking the leap he'd made. His own gun wouldn't come free of his waistband. He was done. The sound of the pistol spitting through its silencer was no surprise at all. He'd screwed himself.

He felt the kick in his lower abdomen. The slug in the gut doubled him up.

His breath wouldn't come.

A second shot would nail him before he could straighten up and pull the pistol.

But the second shot did not come from the assassin.

Instead, the spitting of a silenced pistol came from behind him.

Finally, Kirk had his 9-millimeter out and pointing at the man between the cars.

No need. For now the assassin crumpled.

"Kirk," came the groaning plea of Connie Gail, "please speak to me."

"I'm okay," he said, his struggle for breath belying his words. He felt around his belt for blood. He found none. He ripped at the front of his pants and stuck a finger through the bullet hole in the denim. He frantically pushed at the tender spot above his pubic bone. But he'd been spared.

He gazed in wonder at the pistol that that been stuck for those extra seconds in his pants.

Its slide had been dented by the killer's gun.

"Kirk . . ." she repeated.

"Other than banging my knee and knocking my head on the curb . . ." He showed her the damaged pistol.

She gasped in relief.

The slumped-over assassin now knelt with his forehead against the pavement like a Muslim in prayer, now rolling over to lie faceup in the parking lot.

Kirk grasped the front of his shirt. "You bastard, who sent you?"

The response gurgled up as foam from the man's jacket front. Connie Gail's bullet had struck him at the top of the sternum where chest meets neck. Even if he hadn't just died, he wouldn't have been able to utter a word through that broken throat.

Connie Gail shuddered and broke down herself, dropping her pistol to the sidewalk, buckling at the knees, moaning that she'd shot yet another man.

Kirk caught her before she could go down. He picked up her pistol and the man's .22 caliber with silencer, shoved her inside the room, and ran for the car.

He knew he had to get her to safety before she came completely apart. And he wasn't feeling so well glued together himself.

"Stand by?"

Pearson shrugged and repeated their instructions. "Stand by. Gerlach told us to wait for further instructions."

He'd expected the worst because they'd missed Kirk and they hadn't been able to get into Lee's house to search for a possible research journal. In fact, Pearson was still half expecting that he and Keeney would become quarry themselves, hunted down and dealt with because of their errors. By God, they'd even lost their damned car to that damned Kirk.

He'd expected to be recalled to Washington to catch hell. He'd never have gone. Catch hell was a euphemism. People recalled were never seen again. He'd observed that fact long ago.

But he didn't even get a reprimand. Gerlach himself had spoken to him to pass along the status of this project. Gerlach had seemed so calm. Pearson tried to fathom what the serenity could mean, coming from a man whose reputation was so vile.

Keeney interrupted his concentration.

"Well, what else? How come we weren't recalled? Why didn't we at least get an ass-chewing?"

"Seems we weren't the only ones to screw up. The people Barnaby sent to that motel in Speedway ran into a bit of trouble and got their own asses killed. About the only thing they did right was Barnaby did an electronic eavesdrop and reported that Kirk had a line on another one of those research logs and other stuff. We'da gotten into more trouble if we *had* killed Kirk. If anybody is gonna get a reaming, it's Barnaby. He come down here to run this little Hoosier project and instead it ended up running him. Hell, Gerlach said he never even got to the woman, let alone Kirk."

Pearson rolled down the car window and spat.

"Now what?" asked Keeney.

"You deaf? We stand by. Barnaby's supposed to be finding Kirk and the woman. If he doesn't, his ass is grass and Gerlach is going to be the lawnmower."

"When Barnaby finds them, we supposed to tail 'em?"

"Keeney, you got a mind like a steel trap."

Pearson shifted in his seat to relieve the pressure on his aching testes.

Keeney pressed him about a subject he'd sooner avoid. "You think we're being audited? Barnaby? You think this is all a trick? Think Barnaby is laying for us?"

Pearson stomped his foot, then groaned and clutched his crotch. The foot stomp had ricocheted back from the floorboard, up to his genitals.

"You know damn well our every move is being watched. And if Gerlach says so, Barnaby will kill us just as quick as he'll kill Kirk and that Gail woman."

The police had taken to hunting in threes for the fugitive, E. Gardner Jacobs. They would make no more mistakes, lose no more cops' lives. They'd find Jake and kill him trying to escape. There had never been any such instruction, but every grim-faced officer in the Iowa manhunt seemed to know that would be the outcome. Four dead cops added up to one objective fact: Vengeance must be exacted.

The pair of regular deputies and their reserve partner had already decided that would be the outcome of their approach to the ramshackle tractor shed behind the remains of a long-ago-burned farmhouse.

But for the moment, at least, they were confused. They had seen a figure from their cruiser, but it couldn't be Jacobs. This thing appeared too big, too awesome—too furry, like some kind of monster-ape, taller than a man, even slumped over, walking hunchbacked toward the shed. They had lost precious seconds as they argued about whether they would even report it. Finally the first deputy won out, calling for backup after reporting a guy in a fur coat. That was an okay way to call it in, wasn't it? he argued. The others agreed it would save them some embarrassment.

The regulars waved at each other with pistols and responded to each other's signal by moving farther apart as they neared the weathered gray door that dangled by one rusted hinge. The police reservist hung back uncertainly between them. They seemed to ignore him, and he resented that. He dropped to one knee, training his 12-gauge shotgun on the diagonal opening to the shed. He decided that their orders to cover them meant he should support their approach with fire from behind. It hadn't occurred to him that they meant he should watch to the rear. Maybe it hadn't even occurred to them.

He trembled as his gaze fell to the enormous footprints in the dust at his knee. The trail led up to the shed. Whatever had lumbered toward that outbuilding was not Jacobs, not a man at all, fur coat or no. He shuddered, although the chill was in the man, not in the darkening air. He sighed heavily and dried his grip, one hand at a time, on his denims so the well-oiled shotgun would stop slipping in his grasp. Concentrating, he placed the front bead on the doorway as the regulars moved in.

Concentrating, he did not hear the padded footfalls behind him.

Concentrating, he never heard the ragged breathing.

Only a whiff of gut-wrenching stench broke his concentration.

By then it was too late.

He spun and came up, only half on his own.

The 12-gauge exploded in his sweaty grip and flew out of his hands. He found himself lifted and torn apart in one movement, his abdomen spilling its shiny, coiled contents into the muggy air, onto the dusty earth to be coated in grass and gravel. His shriek died as the jaws of the beast closed on his neck and shook his body.

The two regular cops didn't know whether he'd died. And they didn't care.

They turned their pistols on him and the beast and fired without pause until hammers fell on expended cartridges. The pair saw their bullets smacking indiscriminately into the corpse and the furred apparition. Rosettes of blood broke out all over the reservist, and puffs of dust and gore peppered the beast.

The corpse fell in a heap.

But not the beast.

They fumbled with their quick reloads, shucking brass jackets, cursing, grabbing for six rounds that would insert at once—they'd done it dozens of times on the range. But never had their cardboard silhouettes looked like the monster before them. And never had the silhouettes attacked like this beast.

It went for the first deputy. He slapped his cylinder shut and began firing again, perhaps wondering why his partner was not supporting him.

The second deputy had dropped his quick load. He went for another and aimed as his partner began backpedaling, still firing.

The second deputy's first three rounds dropped the beast, but not before it had fallen on his buddy, not before the jaws closed on the screaming face, not before he heard facial bones crackling.

The beast lay heaving in its death throes; the first deputy lay squirming beneath, as if being raped.

The second deputy's pistol again snapped on empty cartridges, half a dozen times before he realized the .357 needed another reloading. He picked up his dropped reload and tried to jam the rounds into the cylinder. But he had not ejected the empties. He shook them out, not even bothering to curse.

Once he'd reloaded, he fired every bullet into the beast's carcass. There was no reaction but the smacking of slugs into flesh and the puffs of dust from the already soaking fur.

Still he felt naked, and ran to pick up the reservist's 12-gauge. He ejected the spent cartridge and walked unsteadily toward the pair in their love-death embrace, the quaking gun barrel leading the way.

The deputy didn't know whether to scream or cry or vomit. He did hear an approaching car but did not dare to turn away from this apparition that had taken life before him.

A pair of car doors slammed shut behind him.

His backup, he thought.

He glanced over his shoulder long enough to see two men in suits striding toward the scene. Feds, he guessed. But a glance was enough, and he snapped back to the riveting vision at his feet to find it still a reality.

"You got him," said a calm voice at his shoulder.

The deputy opened his mouth to answer or curse or cry or vomit. But his head imploded into jellied mush, and he never had the chance to express his anguish.

Guided by the beacon of a fire, several squad cars arrived an hour later. By morning there were two dozen cars, a useless ambulance, and a fire truck that did no better than to wet down and stir up the ashes of the shed. Days later, the authorities still had not sorted out the morass of broken remains for identification.

The search for Jake widened, finally granting him his most fervent wish, giving him the criminal celebrity status of the FBI's Ten Most Wanted List and the national news wires.

Kirk talked nearly all day.

He talked about the oddity in the national news. The only manhunt in the morning papers had been for an escaped convict named E. Gardner Jacobs. All the killings yesterday, the virtual elimination of the Fort Harrison command group, made the papers. But not a word about Gail and him. She must have been right about the FBI acting strangely. Maybe later in the day they'd hear about the search for the desperadoes named Kirk and Gail. And probably on the radio news.

But the radio news babbled about Jacobs, the cop-killer, and the panic that had seized the Midwest states of Iowa, Illinois, and Kansas. Reports from Fort Harrison became more vague rather than more detailed. The matter had been turned over to a Pentagon spokesman. Kirk smiled wryly at that. For all the efforts of the Defense Information School to teach openness, in practice, the first reaction to any disaster more unusual than a common plane crash was the military standard—stonewalling.

Nothing was said about the pair from Indiana. It astonished him that they were lucky enough to have avoided the attention of the press. It increased the odds dramatically that they'd get away with their escape.

Or else it meant that one hell of an undercover manhunt had been launched.

He talked because it kept him awake, because repeating what he'd read in the letter from PJ Payne might make it acceptable to his mind—maybe after the dozenth repetition. And he talked because he felt so much remorse for shooting Connie Gail—maybe talking to her would bring forgiveness.

But she barely paid attention. She remained distracted, either in pain from the stitches in her arm or drowsing from the pain killers.

They had boldly walked into a hospital emergency room. He told the admitting nurse their car had hit a lamppost on the street outside, that he would report it to the police as soon as his wife was treated. In fact, he did approach a policeman in the waiting area and talk to him —to tell him a drunk outside was brandishing a knife. Then he returned to tell the nurse the officer had left to investigate the crash. The doctor had disinfected and stitched the wound and wrapped her forearm from the elbow down to her wrist, anchoring the gauze around her thumb. He'd examined the blows on her face and glanced suspiciously at Kirk, looking for signs of an obvious wife abuser. They'd paid in cash and drove away before doctor, nurse, and cop could compare stories.

As morning dawned behind them, Kirk saw that the back of Gail's hand had swollen. Her fingers looked like wilted carrots stuck into a gray doughball. When she drowsed, she sometimes emitted a low moaning-sound as if re-dreaming the reality of the incident in the motel. She'd begun to perspire, though the air-conditioning had kept the car cool, and her hair became stringy and mussed from her tossing it from side to side.

Kirk knew Gail must be in her late thirties, but he'd always thought her beautiful enough, elegant—even regal —enough to pass for five years younger than her age. By noon she looked rough, every line showing around her mouth and eyes, every flake of skin at her hairline, every crease in her neck, every crack in her lips. She looked every minute of her age and then some.

He felt embarrassed for having to see her at her worst. He felt guilty, first for making her this way, then for not having the grace to ignore how bad she looked.

The car, a thoroughbred, a bundled, nervous-energy converter, leapt and shied at the touch of his foot or hand. It must have some kind of a police-special engine, Kirk thought. He didn't have time to check, though. At the all-night drugstore where they'd filled her prescriptions, he'd peeked in the trunk and seen rifles, shotguns, and suitcases built for carrying either sensitive electronic gear or explosives. A peek was enough. He shut the trunk lid hurriedly.

He would inspect the trunk's contents later. Meanwhile, he'd drive so the wheel wouldn't oversteer and the tires wouldn't squeal and the engine wouldn't accelerate to the eighties and attract the attention of the police. There'd be no way to explain some of those things to an Indiana, Illinois, or Missouri trooper, whose suspicions would be aroused, make that electrified, by a car registration that didn't match the driver's license of a driver with a bruised, wounded, delirious woman in the front.

Kirk doubted the car would be reported stolen. If he'd appreciated anything at all about The Corporation from PJ's letter and his own knowledge of intelligence organizations, it was that they feared questions, any kind of questions, but mostly official ones that could become public record. You never knew when an ambitious politician would try to make a career on something, when a reporter would try to repeat the miracle of Woodward and Bernstein's Watergate reporting.

By mid-afternoon, Kirk had fallen silent. Coffee helped not at all. It jangled his nerves and forced him to stop at every rest area. Gail alternated between sweating and shaking with chills. Finally a cup of watery soup and a cheap blanket from a truck stop settled her down. She lay huddled on the reclined passenger seat and slept.

With virtually no companionship except for the radio news broadcasts that had clearly run out of new leads on the cop-killer, Kirk began to nod off himself. Once he caught himself steering the car down the shoulder of the road.

This wouldn't do. He'd get them killed. Or arrested, first for suspicion of drunk driving, then for all the other suspicions that would come of the most cursory search of this car.

So he started talking again to keep awake.

"I'm a public affairs officer," he told the sleeping Connie Gail. "And I'm here to give you members of the press a briefing on the research log of a researcher, veterinarian, geneticist, and entrepreneur named Warren Howell, Mark Payne's brother-in-law.

"He was literally a beastmaker," Kirk told the huddled

figure. "He tried to develop subhuman slaves to do domestic chores and drudge labor for mankind.

"But Howell couldn't work out all the bugs. His creations kept turning violent and uncontrollable. What? You're asking if that made him more cautious? Hardly, ladies and gentlemen of the press, journalists extraordinaire. Howell was undaunted. And you may quote that very word, 'undaunted,' if you will. Howell kept trying for the perfect formula for subhumans to patent and sell as labor cheaper than illegal aliens without—in Howell's mind—the accompanying moral dilemmas."

Gail moaned. It sounded almost as if she were pleading for Kirk to shut up.

He didn't. He thanked the imaginary journalists for their attention and patience. Then he proceeded with his briefing.

"Howell broke new ground in genetic engineering. He combined the different species to make new animals. But . . . this is the spooky part—he came up with a ferocious beast that escaped and killed nearly everything in its path, eventually including Mark Payne's sister.

"My friend, Mark Payne, tracked down the beast and killed it and all its offspring. He also uncovered incriminating evidence on The Corporation, a government agency hidden so deeply between the Pentagon and the National Security Agency and the CIA, that it had taken on an existence of its own outside government—thanks to a turncoat within that organization.

"The only thing that had kept Payne alive in the last two years were copies of Howell's original research and the information from the rogue agent. Payne used them as insurance policies set to be mailed to certain members of the press and Congress and government and friends he could trust."

Kirk was silent for a long time, mulling over all that he knew, trying to get it to sink through his own barriers of disbelief. He wondered. How in the hell—having said all of this aloud now so his ears could consciously hear it— could he ever persuade anybody to believe it?

"So," Kirk summarized for his unconscious passenger, "now that you and I know that, we're going to be killed too.

"So why go to Texas?" he asked rhetorically of the lump under the cheap blanket. "That's where the logs and the other evidence against The Corporation are. If I can get my hands on just one of those things . . ."

He left the rest unspoken.

The lump didn't move; didn't acknowledge any of his monologue.

So he started in about his jungle crash. He told about Jud saving his life. It made him maudlin to talk about Jud.

"He saved my ass . . . dragged me all the way back to a hospital in Vietnam," he said.

Immediately he was sorry he'd brought it up. If he'd been drinking anything, it would have made him start bawling. If he kept it up, he'd be crying sober. He looked over at her. It would be embarrassing if she had heard—if she'd awakened and seen him like this.

But she was sleeping. That was good, Kirk thought. Maybe her pain was easing. That made him feel better. Relaxed. Sleepy too. Again. He shifted mental gears, ended the press briefing with a flurry of "no comments," and began singing along tonelessly with the radio.

Hours later, the sun had crept around to look into the windshield.

Kirk squinted into the silvering road, the strobing hood's reflection.

He found his eyes squinting completely shut against his will.

"I've got to stop," he announced. "Got to sleep."

"Where are we?" murmured Gail, surprising him.

"Hey, welcome back to the land of the living and sleepy. How do you feel? How's your arm?"

"Fine. Where are we?"

"Oklahoma, practically."

"Stop, then. You must be exhausted."

She sat up and twisted the rearview mirror around so she could see herself.

"My God," she said, and pulled away from the reflection. "Stop before I get picked up as a road hazard."

He readjusted the mirror so he could watch for a tail, as he had been watching all day.

"You look fine to me," he said. "Did you hear anything I said all day?"

She shook her head and raised an eyebrow and a corner of her mouth to smirk at him. "You've been talking all day?"

"Practically. No matter. Really, I'm just so glad to have you back, you look great." He meant it, despite her rough appearance.

She smiled ironically.

"Think about it," she said. "We've always been cool to each other. I've never passed up the chance to put the little major down on the job. We've been enemies for the last few days, spatting like a married couple. Early this morning we tried to shoot each other . . . you succeeded. All of a sudden we're a mutual admiration society."

"Amazing what a little shootout can do to cement a relationship," he said, returning her smirk.

She reached out her good hand and patted his thigh.

He reached down and clasped her hand.

"Truce?" he said.

"Truce. Now, you find a place to stop and sleep, a place where I can get a wheelbarrow full of makeup and get back to looking human—that's an order, Major Kirk."

She left the room while he was showering after he had lectured her about not using a check or credit card for anything she bought.

"And don't use a telephone," he'd said.

Her eyelids had flickered. Holding back anger, he thought.

"I won't," she'd said, and had smiled one of her new, warmer smiles. Even tinged in pain, even tired, the smiles were warmer than yesterday's.

But there had been that flicker. He wondered about it a second, but decided he owed her some credit for trying to keep it under control. Maybe she'd begun to like him. She came to him and pressed her cheek against his oily, whiskered face. She patted her purse, which now held the pistol she had used back at the motel in Speedway.

"I can take care of myself."

He nodded. She left.

He showered and shaved and tumbled into the firm bed with the cooling sheets. The damaged 9-millimeter he put within reach under his pillow, the .22 pistol he stashed between mattress and box springs. Mentally he rehearsed rolling off the bed, grabbing one gun or the other, and firing. Then he rehearsed it physically until on the third try he banged his elbow on the floor and decided three dry runs were enough. He tried to put some of the pieces of his puzzle together. But he fell asleep in minutes, sleeping the drugged sleep of the depressed, the dead sleep of the exhausted driver. He dreamed the troubled dreams of the combat veteran. These last days *had* been combat. The deaths of those children, the general, the beast, the Lees, McClean. The gore, the details, kept running by his mind's eye until he willed himself to be semi-awake, to remind himself these were dreams, to get a few minutes of untroubled sleep, to repeat the cycle.

Seiad Valley.

Adjacent to the Klamath River.

In Northern California.

Only a handful of residents in the Northwest could recite a single fact about Seiad Valley. The rest simply knew the valley as a place to drive through on the way to someplace else.

Pets had been disappearing for weeks. Families began to show some concern. The weekly community newsletter had run advice on how to combat the loss of cats and dogs to coyotes or bobcats or vandals or pet-nappers. It wasn't very good advice—because none of those things were responsible for the disappearing pets.

That became apparent when children began disappearing. Then some members of the search party didn't rally when and where they were supposed to . . . they didn't rally at all.

Authorities called off night searches altogether. They talked about requesting the National Guard from the governor. And they decided only day searches could be performed only by pairs of armed men.

That's why it was so odd that a full squad of men were moving soundlessly through the brush above the Klamath River at night. All the men were equipped with night-vision devices, infrared and starlight gatherers. They all carried rifles and pistols. A few carried tranquilizer guns.

The white beast heard the first pair coming. They made

noise; they talked and crashed through the underbrush. It could hear the branches swishing off their clothing. The beast adjusted its position, putting the tiny clearing between himself and the approaching men. It had done so before. It had lain in ambush like some lion at a bushland watering hole. Its prey had been drawn by the stench from the graveyard of bones and fur that covered most of the clearing. The prey, if an animal, would venture into the clearing and begin nosing around the rotting remains. If human, the prey would pause at the edge of the clearing and gag or simply stand stunned for a few seconds. In any case, the sight of the aboveground graveyard would hold the attention of any prey for a few seconds—more than long enough for the beast to lunge and larder its smelly lair with fresh bones and carrion.

But the prey surprised the beast this time by acting completely out of the ordinary.

Two men dressed in heavy clothing dashed to the center of the clearing. They stood back-to-back, talking excitedly. It was a minor variation on a theme the beast had played so many times before. With the barest of growls, it launched itself into the clearing, into the attack.

The first man to see it screamed and raised his gun. The second man was momentarily stunned by the ghostly sight, a white figure larger than a man that landed on all fours.

The first man fired his rifle, which let off a pop of air, sending a trank dart at the white figure. Its effect was to bring a yelp of surprise.

The second man began shouting into the open radio mike pinned to the front of his quilted canvas suit.

"Come on, come ON, COME ON! We got him."

The radio report was not entirely accurate. True, they did have time to throw their catch nets. And the second man also shot his dart at the lunging beast in white fur. The first man *did* bring up his pistol, the last-ditch weapon they were to use only if in imminent danger.

But they did not have the beast.

Rather, the beast had them.

The relief squad that had followed the noisy pair who'd drawn short straws, found a trio lying in the clearing.

Two nets of nylon mesh had been shredded. As had the heavy canvas suits and padding beneath. One man lay disembowelled. The other had been beheaded before the beast succumbed to the trank.

The tranquilizing drug acted in seconds—that was the claim of The Corporation scientists. But seconds amounted to too much time for the two men, whose canvas—supposedly claw-proof—clothes hadn't helped them a bit, except perhaps to comfort them on the trip up the trail to their deaths.

The third member of the trio was a figure nearly twice the size of a man. It lay breathing heavily in drugged sleep, its white fur spotted black and wet in the moonlight.

Two members of the squad ran puking from the clearing. It was not only the putrid scent. It was also the knowledge that the wet black would show bloodred when the lights came on.

The leader of the squad cursed them all for standing around dazed. He ordered them to rig the bodies for extraction . . . but the beast must be extracted first, he reminded them.

Keeney lay drowsing in the backseat. He leapt up at the sound of running outside the dark car. A breathless Pearson jumped into the driver's seat and brought the car to life instantaneously. Keeney kept shouting questions.

Pearson didn't answer until he'd hit the interstate and aimed the car west.

"Gerlach just told me Barnaby's found Kirk and the woman," he announced. "We got another chance."

"Where? Where are they?"

"Texas."

"Texas? Already? How the hell . . . ?"

"No, dummy. They're not in Texas . . . yet. They're on the way to Texas. We're gonna catch up to them. We'll be tailing by morning. Or else. We'll be redeeming ourselves, Keeney. Hot damn."

"Texas?" repeated Keeney.

"Hot damn," Pearson repeated.

Later—Kirk had no idea how much later—he heard the doorlock snap. In his unconsciousness, his hand closed on the semiautomatic, and he bunched for the roll from the bed.

"It's me," came her voice softly.

He relaxed.

Vaguely he heard the shower running, the sink tap, the toilet, a hair dryer whining in the distance, maybe even in the adjoining room. He smelled perfume, toothpaste, nail polish, antiseptic—these coming much stronger.

He thought she should hurry up to get some sleep. They needed to get going again, and he planned to travel about midnight or soon thereafter. He thought about making room for her on the bed. No, he should give it up and sleep on the floor. If only he could get his body to respond to his commands to be a gentleman.

Then it was quiet for a long time or else he slipped into a deeper unconsciousness. He knew she must be asleep in a chair.

Then the combat nightmares began again. He fought

back to semiconsciousness, hoping next time the dream would be of flying down Death Valley again. At the best of times he made the flight without even the aid of a helicopter. He just soared noiselessy, adjusting his flight path simply by changing the angle of pitch in his palms. At the worst of times he dreamt of the helicopter crash in the jungle.

But this dream was neither of those.

Instead, he felt a rush of cool air sliding between the sheets. Chilly, smooth skin pressed against his side. A pair of lips nibbled at his neck below his left ear. A woman's breath tinged with mouthwash and accompanied by perfume intoxicated him; aroused him.

It was better than flying.

She whispered his name.

He smiled.

She was asking for help.

He felt a tug on his shoulder, the rasp of gauze . . . This was no dream. This was Colonel Connie Gail in bed with him.

No, it couldn't be. This was just another of his fantasies, a realistic one at that.

"Dammit, Grayson, do you want me to leave you alone?"

"No," he grunted, suddenly realizing this was no dream. "For God's sake, no." His body found something to respond to.

"Then help me. My arm is sore."

He helped, turning over on his back. He had to open his eyes to believe his fantasy. It was her, beautifully transformed by her makeup, wonderfully naked.

She straddled him and lay on his chest, she soaking up his warmth, he extracting the coolness of her skin, the softness of her breasts. Her hair smelled so fresh, he inflated his lungs to the bursting point with the fragrance.

He felt so comfortable, they might have been made for each other. Certainly they should have done this before, he thought. With some women, it had taken him weeks to feel so at ease in bed. Maybe it was the pains they shared, he decided. Whatever, the only thing awkward was her right arm, which she rested carefully beneath the pillow. Neither of them were in the least bothered by the rigidity between them, neither seemed overcome by urgency.

Gradually, carefully, they made love. It was their unhurried concession to the wound, their shared exhaustion.

They reached climax separately, he first, she assisting his pleasure, then he helping her. There was no rush for either. It was as if they'd practiced mentally for just such a physical conclusion. Maybe, he decided, she had fantasies too. About him. Could it be?

But while he was calculating, he fell asleep. Much later, he felt her at his side, pressing her body into his.

He awakened enough to kiss her shoulder.

She rolled over to him again, and they made love again, this time desperately, as if each of them had suddenly realized the seriousness of their situation.

Afterward she searched his face.

"Truce?" she asked for the second time that day.

"So this is truce," he murmured. And he was asleep in seconds.

In the darkness of early morning, the motel operator awakened them on the first ring.

Automatically, they rolled out of bed and began dressing. Neither looked at the other's nakedness, although they had touched each other reassuringly during the night.

She seemed to have recovered completely from her fever. She chattered and sang as she showered. He shaved with a throwaway razor she'd bought, then doused himself in a cold-water rinse. Then he sat down to finish dressing.

She found him bent over his stocking feet. He wasn't moving.

"I thought we were in a hurry," she said.

He looked up into her eyes, his face suddenly gray and tired.

"What's wrong, Kirk?"

"I tore a hole in my sock."

She studied his face as if waiting for the punch line. He looked down. She followed his gaze to the sock, his large toe sticking through a hole.

She shook her head and laughed. "It won't kill you."

He swallowed hard and finished putting his shoes on. His manner left a pall over their earlier morning-after gaiety.

He stood up to gather their bags.

"Let's go," he ordered.

Obviously bewildered, she followed, thoughtfully chewing on her lower lip.

Keeney saw them leaving during his turn on watch. They stepped from the room to the car and pulled away a couple of minutes after two.

Keeney turned to Pearson, who was lying sprawled in the backseat, legs spread wide.

"They're on the move," he said, no louder than the snoring, fitful noises Pearson was making.

Pearson immediately sat up groaning. "Try the receiver," he ordered.

Keeney already had turned on the black box and placed it on the dash. Inside the box was an ADF loop antenna, an automatic direction-finder. Its readout was simply a glowing dot on a circular dial. The dial was divided into four equal quadrants, the center of the circle representing the receiver. The glowing dot, which brightened, then faded every ten seconds, represented the transmitter. Its position in the quadrants represented the relative bearing from the heading of the car. The closer to the edge of the circle, the farther away the signal. The edge of the circle could be calibrated by a turn of a selector to represent one, five, twenty-five, or fifty miles. Because the terrain was relatively open to transmitting a line-of-sight signal, Keeney had set the range to twenty-five miles.

Pearson rubbed his crotch gently and smiled at the dot, which kept winking at him.

"Let's get a cuppa java and hit the road."

The transmitter was mostly battery, a streamlined base with easily enough energy for three to four weeks, depending on the weather. It could be cemented or bolted onto a plane or boat. Or the magnetic plate would hold it to the body or chassis of a car.

Keeney had just put it atop the rear fender, clear of the trunk lid, and had extended the antenna to its full length of four feet. It looked like a CB radio antenna, something that would go with the electronic equipment in the trunk. It had taken all of five seconds to put it on.

Kirk watched the rearview mirror constantly, sullenly. He hadn't spoken since the occasion of discovering the hole in his sock.

"What is it?" she asked.

He broke eye contact with the rearview, looked at her without emotion, studiously, as if reading small print off her face. Then he turned to glare out front at the road unraveling beneath the soaring car.

"Kirk, what the hell's your problem?"

In answer he set the car on cruise control and crouched with his feet on the seat as she watched with wide, impatient eyes.

"Take the wheel," he ordered. "I'm going to climb into the backseat. You slide over and drive. Don't slow down."

She obeyed.

Once in the back seat, he lowered the window and leaned out. He pried the antenna off and took it inside.

"What's that?" she asked.

"ADF transmitter."

"What's ADF? How do you know all this?"

"Any pilot knows ADF. It's an automatic direction-finder. They're used in simple air navigation. The receiver shows bearing from . . . it points in the direction of a signal when you tune it in. This one is built to look like a two-way radio antenna, but it wasn't hooked up, so . . . As I said, I'm assuming . . . we have to assume somebody is following us. Did you notice it yesterday?"

She narrowed her eyes at him. He held the antenna over the seat and pointed out a dial in the base that could be used to select positions F1 to F5. Five transmitting frequencies, he told her. She wasn't listening.

"What do you mean, asking me if I noticed?" she asked into the rearview mirror. "How would I have noticed something like that? What are you getting at . . . love?" She raised her hands in a gesture of futility and flinched at the pain the movement brought her. The swelling had not gone down much in her right arm. She gingerly took the steering wheel again.

He put the antenna back outside, on the roof above the driver's window. Then he ordered her to slide over so he could resume driving again, glaring and staring again.

She broke the silence.

"My God. What kind of people are you dealing with? Kirk, how can you be sure . . . love?"

He smirked at her, a wiseass smirk that he made no obvious attempt to disguise.

They drove in silence for half an hour. Her sniffling broke the tension momentarily. But his reaction restored it fourfold.

"Stow it, Colonel."

Her expression was at first stunned, then wounded . . . then angry.

"Nice try, Colonel Connie, but tears don't move me all that much anymore. I guess I've seen them used too much. I've seen lots of things used. . . ."

"Used? USED? You bastard. What makes you so goddamned superior? What puts you above the rest of us mere mortals? I don't recall your objecting to being 'used,' as you put it, last night. What were you looking for, a virgin? Or are you just hoping to punish me today because your performance was a little rusty last night?"

"Ouch! When the tears run dry, you really know how to get vicious, don't you? Next thing you know, you'll be throwing it in my face that I shot you back . . . at the motel in Speedway." Kirk noticed that she was not a pretty crier—some women were, but she simply took on a shade of nastiness, a side of her he'd never seen. As if to confirm it, her tone grew sharply acidic as she snapped at him.

"Vicious? Me? What the hell *are* you talking about? And my tears weren't for you anyhow . . . well, maybe to pity you a little for the way you wrapped a towel around yourself like a damned newlywed this morning. But I wouldn't waste a lot of tears on you, Major. And pity yourself for shooting me, if you will . . . but don't try to wring sympathy out of me for it."

He retaliated instantly, jumping back at her, flinging his head toward her as if trying to sling his words into her face.

"What then, Colonel? What the hell have you got to cry about? You shed any tears over Jud?"

"Yes, you bastard." She'd begun screaming. "Yes, that's exactly why I've been crying, and you assume . . . you PREsume to think I'd cry over you."

"You're lying, bitch."

"No," she shrieked. "NOOOOooo-o-o-o, you bastard." She broke down into sobs. It took a while for her shoulders to stop shaking. She found a towel she'd stolen from the motel and wiped her face brusquely.

She looked at him.

He continued to stare to the front, his cheek and temple muscles knotted.

"It was the hole in the sock, wasn't it?" she finally said softly.

Somehow the knotted muscles tightened even further.

"The holes," he said. "Plural. Jud's and mine. I never thought of it till this morning. McClean wouldn't have walked out for cigarettes in his stocking feet. And the killers wouldn't have jumped him and gone through all the trouble to take his . . . his damned boots off."

"So," she said weakly.

"So it occurred to me that you lied."

She turned to him, tears welling in her eyes.

"Oh, Kirk . . ."

It was his turn to be silent. He knew he'd cracked her facade because these tears flowed without the nasty grimace he'd seen earlier. This time her appearance touched him. He was still confused about the lie. But he held his tongue, waiting for the explanation of what happened at the motel in Speedway.

"Kirk . . . I . . . I killed Jud McClean."

The car swerved completely out of its lane. He jerked it back. "What? What the fuck . . ."

Kirk started to pull over to the shoulder. He was struck by the thought that he'd need to stop the car to have both hands available to . . . to strangle this . . . woman.

"No, Kirk, I didn't actually kill him . . . not personally . . . not by pulling the trigger or using the knife . . . but I'm responsible just the same."

He bit his lip and gripped the steering wheel hard, as if choking a life from it, maybe her life in proxy. He put the car back into the proper traffic lane. All he could manage was a single word.

"Explain."

"I . . . told him I'd go out to get a snack for us. And while I was out, I used the phone to . . ."

"After I told you . . ."

"Listen, dammit. Just listen for a minute. Then you can call me names, hit me, throw me out of the car—nothing would be bad enough. I know you told us—me—not to use the phone or anything, but I have a friend, a mentor in the Pentagon. I called him to make sure we wouldn't be carried as AWOL. I talked to him to find out what was going on, to use his connections. He's a general, Kirk. I thought if you can't trust a general . . ."

Kirk snorted.

"I'm sorry. I didn't know. Until you told me those things about Payne yesterday, I wouldn't have believed it. Now I do believe it. I don't know how my contact in Washington could possibly be involved . . . I can't believe it. But he must at least have had his telephone bugged. I don't know how. But within an hour after I called . . . they came. I don't know how, but . . . Oh, Kirk, I'm sorry. I believe now."

"A little late, wouldn't you say, Colonel Connie?" The words were harsh but spoken gently. He realized nothing could come of thrashing her further. Not since she'd come clean.

"Yes. I deserve this, all of it and more. Go ahead. Please." She wept openly but silently. "I'm sorry. So sorry. I know what he meant to you. He saved your life in Laos, and I killed him—in Indiana, for God's sake, and with a telephone call. I wish . . . you hadn't redirected your bullet at the last minute. I wish they could have beat me to death or cut *my* throat. I wish . . ."

"You didn't use a phone again last night too, did you?"

"NO," she snapped. Then she started bawling again, her hands over her face. Her tears and slobber leaked down her wrists, dampening the gauze on her right.

Kirk felt a rush of contradictory emotions. She had been responsible for the death of his friend, a man who'd pulled him from the flaming wreckage of a Huey in some nameless part of the jungle. He knew what she was wishing about when she wished she'd died. Many times he wished he could have died himself so he wouldn't be facing the reality of now.

Yet . . . yet he wanted to reach out and touch her, to hug her. It dawned on him why she had come to him during the night, why she had been so careful and exquisitely slow, then so passionate, why she had been so contrite. At the worst, she was trying to soften him up, or at the least getting up her courage—screwing up her courage—to confess about Jud. He snorted at the bitter irony of his thoughts. He wondered if Jud would appreciate it.

He didn't know whether to reach out and pat her shaking shoulder or, in the name of Alva J. "Jud" McClean, to throw her ass out of the moving car.

Ahead, a flatbed eighteen-wheeler lugged low down the highway. Kirk sped up, his jaws clenching. He raced right at the rear of the trailer.

She uttered a tiny whimper as he whipped the wheel at the last instant and began passing the truck on the right shoulder of the highway.

Pearson had been driving in silence. They both watched the dot at the top of the dial, watched it glow and die, indicating a distance of about four to five miles ahead. Pearson slowed down periodically to fifty-five, then rolled ahead to a steady speed of seventy, highballing it toward Oklahoma City.

Every time the dot began easing toward the center of the dial, meaning they were closing on it, Keeney shook his head and muttered a curse. Pearson slowed until the dot drew up on the dial, then sped up.

The dot started sliding into the right upper quadrant of the dial soon after they crossed into Oklahoma.

Keeney tapped on the receiver.

"What the hell's going on?" Keeney finally said. "Something's wrong. He keeps slowing down and speeding up. . . ."

"Shit. Tulsa," Pearson shouted. He slammed his fist on the steering wheel and buried the accelerator.

"What?" said Keeney, immediately agitated that now something new had gone wrong, something he couldn't fathom. "I thought Gerlach said we were going to Texas. . . ."

"Shut up and tune that damn thing in to the mile range

ring. We *were* supposed to be going to Texas. But they turned north."

Keeney did so and the dot disappeared. In a couple of minutes, Pearson exited Interstate 40 to Oklahoma City, taking U.S. 64 toward Tulsa. The dot reappeared on the top of the ring as Pearson closed at 120 miles an hour.

"Careful we don't get picked up," Keeney cautioned.

Pearson glared at him.

Keeney said, "Why would Kirk switch to Tulsa? That's the opposite way to Texas. You think he saw us? You think . . ."

Pearson's glare hardened, his lips tightening into a wild Why-the-fuck-don't-you-at-least-shut-the-fuck-up-you-stupid-dickhead? expression.

Pearson let off the accelerator as a pair of 18-wheelers came into view grinding up a long, gentle grade.

"Maybe they're between the trucks," said Keeney hopefully.

Pearson gave him a sick, angry look, an expression that threatened murder.

Keeney moved away from the madman at the wheel.

Pearson sent the sedan dashing past the trucks. The receiver on the dash emitted a beep. They saw the dot drop below the center of the dial. Ahead the highway was empty for at least the mile to the top of the grade.

Pearson uttered a string of curses and braked, allowing the trucks to labor ahead. He savagely swung in behind the last trailer, a flatbed laden with bar steel. He swung onto the apron of the highway and began passing on the right.

"What the hell . . ." murmured Keeney, cringing as Pearson lowered his window and eased toward the whining wheels of the trailer.

Pearson reached out. When he jerked his hand back inside, he held the transmitter and antenna.

The receiver on the dash went wild, beeping and blinking.

Keeney looked as if he might bawl, Pearson as if he might kill. Finally, he did. He smashed the transmitter into the dial on the dash again and again until the machine went black and silent.

Edward Gates strode up to the front of Gerlach's desk and stood at attention. His knees started quivering immediately.

"Well, Edward, what bad news is in the shitbag this time?"

"Sir?"

"Your knees are playing jiminy fucking crickets," rasped Gerlach through a sneer. "When you have good news they play like a couple humping grasshoppers." He smiled broadly, showing the little yellow teeth he bared without shame whenever he wanted people to feel embarrassment. "Tonight it's crickets." He belched a laugh.

Gates flinched from the explosion of rancid air from behind the desk.

"Now, 'spose you tell me what the hell's going on in Texas, Mister."

With shaking hands, Gates lowered a sheaf of papers to a corner of Gerlach's desk.

"What's that?"

"Sir, those are two reports on the . . . beast hunt transactions we've been monitoring in Iowa and Northern California. Both transactions have been terminated at this point in time . . . terminated successfully. Let me preamble your perusal of the reports with a verbal condensation. . . ."

"Chrissakes, Gates, can you speak English?"

Gates's face went blank, his confusion momentarily replacing fear.

Gerlach shook his head hopelessly. "What happened in California, for crying out loud?"

"Our team captured the animal alive. The locals are unwitting of the nature of the pet disappearances and the humans as well. The team left a collection of crosses, knives, and symbols as a ruse to indicate a satanic connection. Our team lost two personnel. The animal was taken to the mountain. It was an odd specimen . . . an albino. The first reported in this latest series of outbreaks."

Gerlach grunted. "God, I love it when you give me the nitty-gritty details like this, Edward."

"Yessir. The second incident was brought to fruition with a similarly plausible cover, but it did not go as smoothly. This beast was pursued by civil law-enforcement officers in Iowa seeking a fugitive by the name of Jacobs. Unbeknownst to the three officers, they tracked down this animal instead. At this point in time, it appears the radio report transmitted did not reveal a beast's existence. But our team arriving on the scene was forced to dispose of the corpses, using a fire. No doubt pathologists will examine the remains and discover one of the carcasses was anything but human."

Gerlach chewed on the inside of his cheek. He looked up suddenly as his conclusion solidified. "No matter. No way will those yokels go public. We'll just have a sealed investigation for a hell of a long time. Not bad. Now what about the trek to Texas?"

"Pearson reports his regret at losing subjects Kirk and Gail."

"How the fuck they do that? They flunk tailing in the academy or something?"

Gates opened his mouth.

"Never mind, Edward. Rhetorical. I know why— they're too fucking dumb to follow Kirk. He's too smart. I ever tell you I knew the boy in Vietnam? Yeah, guess I did. We go back a ways. Even if he wasn't smart, those two shit-for-brains morons don't have enough brown matter to keep up. We're lucky we have Barnaby on this one. He's got another team traveling to Texas, right?" Gates nodded emphatically. "Thank my black stars Barnaby is down there keeping me up-to-date on this one." Gerlach waved his cigar. "Anyhow, it's not too hard to figure out where they're going in Texas . . . right?" He pointed the ash of his cigar at Gates.

"Fort Hood, sir?"

Gerlach nodded absently. "Probably around that area somewhere."

There was a long silence. Gerlach's color grew darker and darker. Gates's knees trembled harder.

"Dogshit," Gerlach finally said. "Dogshit for brains." He pursed his lips and shoved a short, fat cigar deep into his mouth. It came out wet and slow.

Gates respond to the visual image by shuddering.

"Bet you wonder what goes on in my dirty little mind, don't you, Edward, my man?"

Gates's jaw dropped perceptibly.

"Never mind," said Gerlach. His smirk said it was no accident he knew what his subordinates—his inferiors— were thinking.

"Edward, put on your thinking cap. You think we should call our little agents in from the cold?"

"No, sir."

"And why not?"

"Sir, I don't think they'd come. Unless we sent somebody to escort them back . . . maybe Barnaby."

"No, hell no. Barnaby can't be spared. Chrissakes, Gates, he's the only agent doing anything right. So. Do we deep-six them?"

"Sir? We need the manpower until we come up with the final package. We have Barnaby and the others . . . Pearson, Keeney, the new team . . . and . . . Texas is a big state."

"Where is the package, Edward . . . in your opinion?"

"Could be general delivery at a post office, sir. I first surmised Gatesville or Killeen. But our searches were fruitless. We can't burglarize every post office in Texas. Perhaps something will surface in the interrogation. Perhaps the Payne woman sent one or more to a friend or something."

"So, what do we do in the meantime?"

"Continue to attempt to reestablish contact with Kirk. Keep surveillance on Payne's friends. Should Kirk find the package first, dispense with him and the woman and the friends. Meantime, we keep trying to bring the Payne woman to consciousness enough to be able to use drugs and find out from her where she sent them."

Gerlach said, "Have our people in Montana try the woman on the drugs again. Hell with her health or the risk . . . just get it from her. We'll never get anything from Kirk, except by accident."

"Yessir."

He nodded at the door. Gates left.

He was thankful for Barnaby in the field. Actually, he was thankful he'd had the foresight to recruit and train Barnaby as his own eyes and ears. You had to have your own personal agent on the scene—or else you had to be there yourself, he thought. You just couldn't trust the regular line and staff, no matter how good they were. And Gerlach was feeling he couldn't even trust Gates any longer. He was glad he'd kept some of the best secrets from Gates. If he ever had to leave Washington and go to Texas or someplace else to wrap this matter up personally, he wouldn't want to leave an overinformed subordinate behind. For information was power. It had brought down his predecessor—actually *he* had brought down his predecessor with information, using the deputy's position. And that's precisely why he never filled the vacated deputy's job. Bad enough he had to have a secretary to share information with.

It was the chilliest of dreams.

PJ lay aching, throbbing, naked on her bed of foam rubber. She lay remembering, dreaming, fantasizing, hallucinating, and occasionally experiencing. But it all seemed to run together in a continuous stream of surreality that had no beginning, no ending, no intermissions, no borders or margins. So she could not tell one experience from the other. Reality was no more convincing than fevered fantasy. For all she knew, she was dead.

She remembered the icy water of Marion Lake. That had seemed real enough at the time, following as it did the heat and flash of the explosion, and before that the hot stings of bullets shot through her breasts and thighs.

She remembered wanting to die, to drown.

But the water temperature had not let her consciousness slip away, and the pack on her back would not let her sink. It kept pulling her up toward the surface of the lake. How ironic that the packaged research logs and evidence against The Corporation should be saving her life at the very instant somebody was trying to kill her for having them.

A grip of small rocks had held her down, tugging on her ankle, but finally one rock rolled loose and she had floated up into a cloud of pungent dust that hovered on the lake.

She'd gasped for air, heard the screaming and shooting, but could not see because she was enveloped in that cloud of explosives smoke and rock dust.

The cloud had floated toward the east. She rolled onto her back and let the pack support her. She kicked her legs to travel with the cloud, feeling the cold-hot ache of her wounds.

The yelling of the fighting men grew fainter.

She'd nearly fainted, but her awareness was sharpened by the sound of men running along the shore of the lake and by the coldness of the water. As the dust cloud thinned, she had seen them—three men running toward the fire and the fight. When they had passed, she kicked to the shore and crawled out onto the footpath. She lay there bleeding and shivering, wishing she could die. But the wish would not be answered. So she tried to stand and found she could. She had tried to walk and found she could.

There was nothing to do but try to do even more—in memory of the man she loved.

So she headed toward the hotel three miles below.

Somehow, she'd made it, found her room, addressed the two packages, written the letter to Grayson Kirk against the wishes of her husband.

Mark. He had been almost certainly killed. She should have stayed to die with him—would have, except that somebody had to try to mail those last two research logs to try to bring down the insidious Corporation. Safety of the type they had lived in the past two years was no good. They had seen it from the first. They should have sent their packages out then. Life as they had tried living it, even with the love they'd found with each other, just wasn't worth it. Trading that kind of life for the guarantee of not destroying The Corporation was not a good deal. Better to destroy it.

She hadn't gone near their own car. She actually walked down the gravel road to a cabin and found a set of keys in a pickup. She'd stolen it. Weakening, she'd weaved all over the road to drop the prepaid packages into a mailbox in the small community of Whitefish.

She was nearly to Kalispell when she'd gone unconscious at the wheel, the car seat drenched in her blood.

She'd felt the sudden stop, the rolling of the truck.

She'd known she was dead.

But then strong hands had pulled her from the wreckage.

From there, things were intermittent.

At first she was glad to be saved.

But she realized she was lying in a truck bed, not an ambulance. And the people tending to her were not friendly or gentle. She was a captive, not a patient.

She remembered a short helicopter ride.

Then she awakened in a cell, some kind of jail.

She was naked. Somebody had talked roughly to her, asking about the packages. Where had she mailed them? She fainted. She was awake again, delirious. They threatened drugs; they injected her naked, aching body. She simply fainted. They revived her. She fainted again. She remembered talking now and then. But to whom or about what, she could not discern.

She felt long periods of being alone with her wild dreams, dreams of screaming, wailing animals, dreams of beasts from her past. But when she awoke from her dreams, she found the nightmare of her reality even more frightening.

She refused food; couldn't have held it. She wanted to

die. But they force-fed her. She couldn't bring herself to choke on the food—her inborn will to live was too powerful, and she hated herself all the more for it.

Regrettably, she started feeling better.

They threatened her for information. She faked a faint. They twisted the hot flesh near one of her bullet wounds, and she came awake.

They injected her again, insistently asking questions.

But she'd known she could resist.

That's why it had surprised her so much to hear her own sleepy voice telling them she'd mailed the packages to Ken Poole and Sheriff Beard in Texas and a letter to Grayson Kirk care of Noble Lee at Fort Benjamin Harrison, Indiana.

And it surprised her to be left alone in a dreamworld where she felt neither pain nor fear nor depression nor heat nor cold. She floated about the cell floor naked, her feet not seeming to touch the concrete. And her cell had grown larger than a gymnasium. She floated into the walls and slept deep, dreamy sleeps on the cement. Yet she felt not a bit of pain or aching. She saw dirt and blood on her hands, knees, and arms; yet the blood—both dried and fresh—possessed the quality of wine—sweet, warm, cloying. Like wine, it soothed her pain.

And it surprised her to find herself clinging to the door of her cell, staring into the hallway, when they carried in an enormous white beast, itself dirty and bloody. But the beast's odor could not penetrate her dreamy state. Not even the shriek of the beast could offend her, in fact, could not even be heard among the heavenly voices singing in her head. The heavenly voices sang on as if they would never stop—not even when she fell from the door to sleep further in peace on the floor.

* * *

Six men had labored to carry the white beast into the mountaintop facility when it burst to life anew.

They had trussed the animal in chains and wrapped it in a cocoon of nylon nets. They had drugged it repeatedly for the flight from Klamath Falls, Oregon, giving it a new injection every time its pulse started to race, indicating a return to consciousness. Until finally a veterinarian ordered them to cease administering the massive tranks. Already enough had been used to euthanize a small herd of cattle, he said. They wanted the bloody thing alive, he commented incredulously.

So no more tranks were injected before the helicopter hop from the dark end of the taxiway at the Billings airport. Six men atop the mountain met the Bell Ranger, the pilot pressing his face to his window opening. They knew why, the instant the beast's acrid, rancid stench assaulted them as the doors of the helicopter opened. The passenger compartment bulged with the bulk of the beast. At first it looked as if a dirty carpet had been pulled up and stuffed into the compartment. But when they unfolded the beast, pouring the mass of stinking fur onto the helipad, anybody could see it was not a carpet. Anybody could smell it. And nobody would touch it as it began to quiver erratically. Although the only illumination in the blackness of night came from the blue bulbs that defined the square of the helipad, the men could see fleas hopping around their disturbed white home.

Somebody in command issued an order. Then the commander yelled the order at the frozen six-pack of men. Like pallbearers, they found a grip among the nylon strands and began to haul the gut-wrenching cargo into the building, even as the fleas began ricocheting off their arms and clothing, seeking relief from the cold mountain air.

Nobody had to tell the men to hurry. The jerks and starts of the beast, like those of some enormous, struggling fish, could be felt through the nylon and up the straining cords in the poles of their arms. Their steps mincing and fast, the crew strained to get this beast into its cage before it came to life. As they labored, each tried to turn his face in a direction so the air they gulped would not have passed over the horrid animal, would not kick them in the stomach. They gagged and cursed their way down the hall. The man in command urged them to shut up.

His command had no effect.

Because the beast suddenly screamed and went stiff, rattling his chains, jerking the net strands, throwing its pallbearers off balance, setting pandemonium loose in the hallway—shouting, cursing, earnest begging for help from God in heaven and the powers of hell.

Two men leaped away immediately.

A third man fell, his hand woven into the netting.

The three remaining men still holding the net couldn't have handled the beast in the bundle even if it hadn't been struggling. The trio staggered sideways, careening into the wall.

One of the trio dived over the netting to safety. He paused a moment to tear at the hand of the man who'd been caught. Once he'd freed the hand, these two joined the first pair in safety and turned to stare agog at the horror picture-show unreeling live a few feet away.

The beast's bulk pinned the last two pallbearers against the wall. The fifth man had managed to keep his feet, even though his back slammed against the wall.

The whitecap of fetid fur washed up against the legs, a stinking wave rolling up to the uniformed knees.

The commander of the group rummaged around in a kit bag handed off by the helicopter pilot. He found a syringe and tried to mate its needle into the soft cap of a half-pint bottle of tranquilizer. As he did, he shouted at the other four men to free the trapped pair.

All at once three of the four told their commander to perform a sex act upon himself. The fourth drew a pistol and offered to kill the beast.

A man's scream, long, drawn, pathetic, pleading, and cut off short, drew their attention back to the writhing men and beast against the wall.

When the beast hit the floor, he'd shed gravel, mud, twigs, flakes of offal, and a herd of ticks and fleas. As the monster rolled up against the wall, the flock of insects dispersed along the floor, looking for warm blood to suck.

The vermin did not have long to wait.

The man pinned against the wall bent over from the waist. But the mass of the beast against his legs threw him back. He couldn't move in any direction. He began to shout threats and promises to his companions. But they stood frozen, unable to answer his pleas as a huge white fist snaked out of the nylon mesh. Once free, the fist un-clenched, claws reaching the width of a dinner platter. When the fist reclenched, the man's upper thigh fit into the grasp. The ensuing shriek set up sympathetic tremors in the eardrums of every man in the hallway. The terror of the sound was diminished by the horror of the sight. The man tried to thrash about. But all he could do was bash first his own torso, then—as the claws and fingers disappeared into his flesh—his head against the cinder blocks of the wall. Five geysers of blood spurted from the finger holes, perfuming the enclosure with new smells.

The man in command cursed softly, then held up the tranquilizer syringe and ordered the four to help their comrade. The man who'd drawn his pistol aimed it at the scene. He merely intended to end the terror of his friend. The commander interpreted the move as an attempt to kill the beast—against orders from the highest higher-ups. So he drew his own pistol and spattered a smattering of human brains down the hallway. The man and his pistol clattered to the floor, where his body became temporary haven to some of the parasites there.

The commander waved his pistol to indicate his orders —he couldn't have been heard over the screams of man and beast—and the trio fully understood and flew into action.

They dashed across the hallway and began pulling on their comrade. In answer he shrieked. They released him. He begged them to continue pulling. So they did, heaving and tugging the screaming man in the grasp of the beast as if this were some company picnic tug-of-war. Meanwhile, the commander of the group blindly plunged his syringe into the mass of the beast.

The men won the tug.

And they lost.

With a lurch, they fell across the floor, never losing their grip. Finally, their man stopped screaming. He'd lost consciousness. And no wonder. The beast had not released its grip on the leg. But the huge thigh muscles had separated, both cut and torn from their anchors to bone. The femur, largest bone of their man's body, had been virtually stripped of flesh from hip to knee. A bloody broomstick poked out of the uniform pants where moments before there had been a muscular thigh.

The men gagged at the sight and backpedaled away, slip-sliding in their comrade's gore.

They let him lie, a ghastly wad of flesh bundled around his knee, which was still in the ghastly grasp of the beast.

The broken hose of the femoral artery flitted around in spurts like a small copy of a fire hose out of control, crazily painting the walls and floor. Growing weaker and weaker.

Gradually, the beast released its grip and went limp.

The commander stepped gingerly among the puddles in the hallway and kicked the beast in the back. No reaction. The commander waved his pistol—everybody had gone speechless. The stunned men tugged and pulled at the nets, rolling the mass of fur away from the wall.

These were tough men, tough and vile. They'd drawn blood on each other in training and their enemies in the practice of their trade. They'd endured torture. And they dished it out. Yet nothing had prepared them for what lay beneath the beast.

One man gagged.

A second man's stomach launched a projectile stream down the hallway.

The third sank to his knees.

Only the commander kept his senses about him. He simply refused to look.

The sixth pallbearer had fallen to the floor, stretched out beside the beast. He'd been the one to scream first, but his shriek had been cut short. The beast had rolled over his body and had pressed him into the angle between wall and floor.

For this man, the beast had used only its jaws.

It had lain face-to-face with the screaming human mouth.

It had cut off the scream with one huge bite from hairline to jawbone.

It had eaten through the mesh of nylon.

And it had eaten through half of the man's head.

It had lapped and vacuumed the contents off the half shell of the open skull.

The men who pulled the beast away found less than half a face and head, the skull cavity licked clean.

The beast had been tranquilized before it could swallow the human jawful of human teeth protruding from its muzzle.

When they dumped the mountain of fur into the enclosure, the thing was no longer white, but bathed in red.

The commander unlocked the chains. But he did not bother trying to remove the nets. He knew the beast would be able to free itself. Or the others would tear the newcomer free—whether they killed the albino was of no concern to him—he'd done his job.

The commander went into the hallway, not to examine the scene in detail, but to get a cleanup crew started.

Then he went off to be by himself when he vomited.

3

Central Texas in early fall is always late in getting the word to change seasons. Often September and October are indistinguishable from the dog days of August. Even many days of November are brutal vestiges of the sauna of summer. The grass has baked brown, gone brittle and dormant. Caliche clay dust coats the tough leaves of pin oak, live oak, pecans, and mesquite—just to ensure universal drabness. Only the juniper scrub, green in all the shades from jade to emerald to nearly black, seems to have any life. At that, it has virtually the life of a weed, for in Texas the juniper is an agricultural nuisance. The bushes, which are sold as ornamentals in many parts of the country, have to be fought back continually to keep them from taking over farm and pasture acreage.

Along I-35 south between Waco and Temple, Kirk drove, his body on autopilot, long since bored by the repetitive terrain. Gail slept fitfully, sometimes sitting in the front seat, other times sprawling in the back, always cradling her swollen arm. A shadow of her fever had returned to darken her spirit. When she slept, she did most of her talking, murmuring, groaning, occasionally uttering an intelligible word. Then she would awaken and demand to know what Kirk was staring at.

He would offer to stop for a doctor.

She would refuse.

Then they would be silent until she dozed off and re-started the one- to two-hour cycle.

In the last two hours, despite the efforts of the air conditioner, the late afternoon sun heated the front seat to an uncomfortable temperature. In the back she lay sweating heavily, her hair plastered to her forehead and down her cheek.

At about six she awoke, and he said, "We're almost to Temple. No arguments this time. I'm dropping you off at a hospital and continuing into Killeen on my own."

She smiled wanly, drying her face on one of the paper towels stockpiled from service station restrooms.

"Thank God," she said.

"You'll go, then?" He'd expected an argument.

"No. I'm thankful the fever has run its course. Feel."

She leaned forward and guided the back of his right hand to her forehead. It was cool and clammy. In the rearview, her coloring reflected gray, accented by dark crescents beneath her eyes. His anger hadn't completely cooled. Yet he felt relief that she'd recovered some. Maybe he could forgive her recklessness in using the phone that night. Perhaps it hadn't been the reason The Corporation people found the Speedway motel anyhow. In truth, he couldn't blame her entirely for being naive. Still, he thought, it had cost him the best friend he'd—

"Look," she said, extending the wounded arm toward the windshield. She flexed the fingers. The swelling had retreated. The gauze bandage on the forearm had loosened—now she wore it like a sweater sleeve. She sat back and began tending the arm, changing the dressing and applying disinfectant, studying the black pattern that stitched up her arm like fine boot laces.

He glanced at the stitches. A good sign. Earlier, the thread had been pulled out of sight into the wound.

She looked up from flexing her fingers, gingerly rippling the forearm muscles. And she smiled a wincing smile at him.

"No doctors," she said. "And no hospitals. This thing has turned the corner."

He offered her a painkiller.

She refused.

He gave her a grim smile. He knew it was useless to argue. So he didn't.

Soon they were entering the eastern city limits of Killeen, Texas, home of Fort Hood, largest military installation in the Free World, the sign bragged.

"How did you get . . . what made you finally retire from this . . . intelligence stuff?"

He flashed her an ironic smile. "Helicopter crash. I was a pilot for some significant intelligence operations in Southeast Asia. We gathered up some of the most important strategic elements of that war—they're things and places I can't tell you about. But those things were important enough to have given us a different conclusion, a different outcome of the war. We had winning within our grasp."

He sighed deeply with the recollection. "Our final project was called off at the last minute. Compromised, we were told later. But my crew didn't get the word. My helicopter was ambushed and brought down. Nobody but Jud McClean and I survived. And nobody came after us. He practically dragged me halfway across . . ."

Kirk couldn't finish. The memory of McClean then, sweating and hauling, evading, providing, for two weeks. The memory of McClean just awhile ago, lying on that bed, his throat slit, his stupid toe sticking through a stupid damned hole in his sock . . .

There had been the snatch team delivered alongside the

trail the week before. They had been given enough time to accomplish their kidnapping in North Vietnam. The general had moved down from the North along the trail with his entourage, moving with much more baggage than in the younger times when he'd moved against the French. But his move was to culminate in a parade. He was to have personally launched and directed the final assault against the South before the Americans could fully pull out. He was to have included them in the defeat. But the general had been betrayed. He was to be picked off, taken from his field command car before he could even get close enough to the South to be more alert. He was to be taken in broad daylight and spirited away to a night pickup area. Kirk was to have given General Vo Nguyen Giap an ignominious ride to the South as a wave of assassinations was to have taken place in the North.

As Giap had said, they could replace their soldiers like fish from the sea, all right. But let them try replacing the whole upper echelon of leadership. It might have meant ten years of peace. Well worth the gambit.

But no Giap.

Just betrayal.

There had been unmerciful examinations of the presidency by the press and Congress. And there had been the breakthrough at Paris at the peace table. Now the operation would have been an embarrassment when what was needed was a diplomatic coup—even if coup had to be spelled capitulation.

So Kirk had landed at an LZ of death, the entire snatch team mercilessly killed, a company of North Vietnamese soldiers waiting in ambush, a pounding of allied airstrikes on top of that. All followed by the Arc Light, B-52 bombers laying down their strings of 10,000-pound bombs.

They never even sent in Search and Rescue.

They never expected survivors. Why risk a SAR team?

An army and its opposing air force spent tons of munitions and effort pulverizing a spot on the ground where a single lightly armed UH-1N was to have landed and departed, flying below radar with its special navigation package, flying long distance with its auxiliary fuel tanks, escaping with its precious cargo of a North Vietnamese general, the defense minister of his revolutionary country. One lousy little helicopter and a crew of four. Total armament: two M-60 machine guns and four .38 caliber pistols. Overkill enough for a battalion. So why bother with SAR?

"Why are you shivering?" she asked.

He shivered once more and realized he was on the verge of reliving that nightmare that came to him so frequently. He was at the point of aiming the Huey down the stream of tracers, crashing into the gun carriage. He was near the feeling of welcoming death by fire, near feeling himself being dragged, broken and bleeding, from the cockpit. He was about to feel his body imploding again as the first of the bombs hit. He nearly felt the heat of the smoking earth and the burning fragments of schrapnel left in that first crater. He was about to be blown unconscious by the first rain of terror from the B-52s, then blown back to consciousness momentarily by the over-pressure of the second wave of strikes. The bombs could have been falling beside him. Or they could have been a half mile away. Or even just inside his head. For he could experience all of it again just by letting himself slip away.

He was sweating heavily, despite the air conditioner. And the chill, plus his being on the brink of his nightmare, was making him tremble.

She grasped his shoulder and gently shook him.

He thanked her.

"For what?"

"For waking me from my daydream."

"So," she said, "where are we going?"

"We're going to check out all the people who are supposed to have received the copies of the research journal."

"And what happens if we get one or both of the copies?"

"I notify a friend of mine. He was my friend before he came to be in a high place, the U.S. Senate. He'll know what to do with it—he'll know how to get action. And he'll clear the way for us to be brought in safely."

"I have friends in high places too. Generals. Lawyers. They could arrange for us to come in safely, to be protected."

"Maybe that's best," he said.

She brightened. "You'll do this my way?" she asked in disbelief.

"No." He smiled. "You use your connections to permit you to get in safely. Then you arrange protection for me. Or I use my own connections to get myself out of this mess . . ." She opened her mouth, but he held up a hand. ". . . but either way, I'm getting a copy of that journal first. There's more to this than just the need for safety. There's a group of people—a stand-alone outfit in government but outside the law, if PJ Payne is correct. Hell, they're operating like some government unto themselves with their own budgets, Swiss accounts, their own paramilitary units they just pull off the shelf, and . . . who knows what? I want to burn them."

"What are you? Some kind of redeemer? Who appointed you guardian of the Constitution?"

He found her narrowed eyes boring into him in the reflection of the rearview mirror. She was angry.

"Good questions," he said. "I'm not a redeemer. I used

to be party to operating outside the law myself. I thought I was right because my ends were righteous. I did a lot of things . . . I was proud of them at the time. Now . . . ?"

"Now it's none of your business . . . except maybe to report to the authorities. You're not responsible to correct these things, to risk your life for—"

His own darkening expression cut her off.

"This is not to save the country, not to rescue the Constitution. This is for Jud McClean."

"Jud, hell. For *you*, don't you mean?" she snapped. "Don't you mean your own revenge?"

He searched her face for an explanation of her reluctance.

She gave it to him.

"Kirk," she said softly, pleadingly, "what about us?"

His angry expression softened.

"What about us?" she repeated, her voice cracking.

She hugged him from behind, resting her injured arm across his chest.

"I love you, Kirk," she whispered.

He exited the interstate and stopped on a side street of Killeen. There he turned and knelt on the seat to return the hug gently.

After a time—he couldn't calculate how long—he pried her away and started driving. He'd relaxed thoroughly and had begun to reconsider some of his old ideas. He found the bus station.

"I'm going to call my contact in the Pentagon," he said. "By now he's gotten some kind of word on that group in Bertrand's basic-training photograph."

He returned looking pale within a minute.

"What's wrong?" she whispered.

"He's gone."

"Reassigned?"

He looked her in the eyes and gulped. "He died in a car crash. In broad daylight. Right in the middle of Alexandria."

They sat silently for a minute.

"Kirk," she said through set teeth. "Let me call *my* friend. He's in legal. He'll be able to do something."

He didn't argue with her this time. "But no more than a minute," he insisted.

When she came, she, too, looked drawn, even paler than the normal pain her arm had given her.

"What?" he said.

"Oh, Kirk . . ." Her determined expression convulsed into a mask of tears. "They pulled him out of the Potomac yesterday . . . drowned . . . foul play. . . . Oh, what are we going to do?"

"We've got to move fast," he said. He slid out of the car and leaned back into the window to speak.

"I'm going to look in this phone book for a Kenneth Poole or a Maggie Anzola or a Mr. and Mrs. Kenneth Poole. PJ sent the first copy to them. We have to hurry."

"Grayson," she whispered, "please be careful. I . . . don't know what I'd do if anything were to happen to you."

He leaned closer to her, and she leaned toward him. Their lips brushed. Each inhaled deeply, as if stealing the very breath from each other.

For a second Kirk wished they could disappear—to be alone forever with each other.

Then they kissed, greedily chewing on each other.

And for a while they did disappear to a private corner of the planet.

* * *

He was still dazed when they found the home of Major Kenneth Poole and his wife, the former Chief Warrant Officer Two Maggie Anzola, in Copperas Cove, the town just five miles west of Killeen. The home was a mobile one and a car was out front. He heaved a sigh and released the hand he'd been squeezing. She smiled back at him. Time for them to go to work.

But nobody answered Kirk's insistent knocks on the rattling aluminum door.

She had gone to the door with him because, they decided, a man and a woman were almost always less intimidating than a man alone. And with the wild line of questioning they planned to pursue, who knew how the Pooles might receive them?

"What now?" she asked.

He looked into her eyes. The blue in them had never dimmed, even in the worst of her pain and fever of the past two days. Now they were more alert than ever. Although her porcelain complexion showed the wear and tear as antique china shows its age—in tiny lines—she was ready for more. He was glad for her company. Her dogged spirit would make her an imposing adversary. He wondered how many military lawyers she'd worn down in military courts.

"Where would you go after work if you were a pilot?"

She flicked one corner of her mouth up in an ironic smile. "Church devotions?"

He'd heard of the officers club at West Fort Hood, because it was a pilots' club. Also, it was close to Copperas Cove, so Kirk decided to try there first. It was near Robert Gray Army Airfield and virtually alongside the route pilots had to use to drive home after work.

The sun had gone down, leaving a red sliver at the horizon. The flaming slit of color dulled to gray, then darkened to gunmetal-blue at the top of the sky. In the east the sky was black.

The club had begun to settle into its evening.

The pilots with nagging wives and husbands had already slugged down as many beers or tequilas as they could drink between quitting time and sundown. And then they had left before the bitching at home could get any worse.

The serious storytellers and drinkers had kept pace with the nagged. And now as drunk as the henpecked drivers careening toward their homes, they ordered food and more drinks, settling down for the long pull toward closing time. It was not a boisterous crowd as it would be tomorrow, a Friday.

Kirk and Connie Gail stopped inside, where the entry opened into darkness and the din of pilot chatter.

As his eyes adjusted, Kirk looked for a couple that might be the Pooles. There were no couples there. The men hung together in knots. The few women sat in a single cluster.

"I'll ask around," said Kirk.

Gail nodded and went to the cluster of women. He watched her go, again admiring her stamina. They had stopped for a few necessary minutes in the last thirty-six hours—to eat and use the facilities—and always in connection with refueling the car. Just half an hour ago they had made a foray into a discount clothing-store to buy a change of clean clothes for each of them. She wore a billowy, loose-knit sweater to hide her wounded arm. It was from a winter sale, but it looked incongruous in weather still in the eighties after sundown. She had spent ten minutes freshening up in a public bathroom, but a light dusting of makeup could not hide her enduring fatigue. They needed to sleep, he knew, but first they had to find the damned research journal.

Kirk carried the damaged pistol under his jacket and jammed down into the front of his pants. It seemed a bit loose there. He must have been losing weight these past days, he mused. Couldn't hurt. The silenced .22 he carried in his jacket pocket.

Kirk approached a solitary captain standing at the end of the bar staring down at an inverted leather dice cup, studying it as if trying to see the dots beneath the thick cowhide. Kirk stood at the captain's shoulder for a minute, ordered a draft, and took his first swig of the icy brew. The captain never moved, except for his slow, deep breathing, as if entranced.

Kirk cleared his throat. "There a guy named Poole in here?"

The captain never looked up from the cup.

"Battalion operations officer. I work for him," he said. "Poole," he shouted.

"Play, mother." The angry voice came from farther down the bar where three officers sat hunkered over beers.

"You shook three dice. No way do you got five threes."

"Then call, asshole."

Kirk studied the man called Poole. He sat slumped impossibly low over the beer, his flight suit bunched around his shoulders and neck. His black hair was slick with oil and dented from the band of his army cap and the support and padding of a flight helmet. His face was slick with body oil and pocked with scars left from the demolition of his complexion by acne. The eyes were angry—dark, small, and hard. It was a hell of a poker face, threatening and daring at the same time.

"You're bluffing," said the solitary captain. He had not yet even lifted his stare from the cup. He grasped the cup and jerked it away.

Kirk watched the oily, scarred face. There was no change in the expression. The eyes glittered a little, as if in a cruel laugh.

"Fuck," muttered the captain. He ordered another round of drinks for the bar, complaining to the studiously preoccupied bartender that there were five fives under that cup, that Poole had rolled three of them, that Poole had even given him an out.

The bartender took the captain's money without comment.

Kirk said, "Ken Poole?"

The dark eyes glittered at him. "Yeah?" said the voice. What the hell do *you* want, asshole? said the expression.

"I have a message for you from a mutual friend."

Neither the eyes nor the expression betrayed the slightest interest. Whether Poole had the package, Kirk would know by the reaction to the next words.

Kirk said, "It's from Mark Payne."

Poole's glistening face shone as it rounded off into a smile. "Hey, no shit. How's my boy Markey anyways?"

Bad news. Poole had not read the message that would have accompanied the research log. He had not received the package that revealed Mark Payne had been killed.

Kirk said, "He's just fine. He asked me to send you his best."

"From where?"

"Uh . . . where?"

"Yeah. Where is Markey these days?"

"Oh, uh . . . from California."

Kirk would have left it at that, would have disengaged

and left Poole to his game of liar's dice and liquor for the rest of his life.

But he saw Connie Gail move away from the knot of women to a separate table. She was followed closely by a taller, wiry woman with a masculine swagger. It must be Poole's wife, thought Kirk. He hoped Gail hadn't revealed too much. Better they move on to find Beard and try that source. Better they leave no tracks of themselves on the minds of the people in this bar.

Kirk moved across the room, wearing a look of what he hoped was caution. But Gail did not look up from her serious conversation with the woman until he pulled a chair back and sat down. His hand went below the table to adjust the barrel of the pistol pressuring his bladder. The two women stopped talking in their hushed whispers.

The blue eyes met his. "I didn't say anything, Kirk."

He bit his lip. To say you didn't say anything is to say everything, he thought.

"What's wrong with Mark Payne and PJ?" asked the woman, her question demanding more than asking. "We were friends together here—my husband was a company operations officer . . . we were pilots together until two years ago. Then Mark and PJ left suddenly, and we heard they were discharged."

Kirk looked into Gail's face.

She answered the question in his expression. "Uh, this is Maggie Poole. Mrs. Maggie Poole. All I asked her was whether she'd gotten her birth announcement from the Mark Payne family."

"And I said we might have missed it because somebody's been stealing mail out here and she just wanted to walk away. Now what the hell's going on?"

"Yeah," said a bitter voice at Kirk's shoulder. "What the

hell's going on?" Poole pulled out the fourth chair and
sat.

Maggie brightened and said, "Did he tell you Mark and
PJ had a baby up in Montana?" There was a measured
excitement in her voice.

Poole darkened and growled, "No. He said they were
in California."

There was a momentary awkward silence.

Poole broke the spell.

"Now. Suppose you two just come across with what
gives. What the fuck is going on here?"

If he had been alone, Kirk would have made up a quick
lie and disengaged himself, disappearing before they
could have collected themselves and compared notes. And
he would not even have been well remembered. Since he
was stuck here, the initial shock already subsided, re-
placed with suspicion, any attempt at quick extrication
might lead to a scene. The last thing he wanted was to be
remembered. There might even be a military police officer or Sid out here drinking. They couldn't afford a
scene.

He had to assume the people trailing him would have
long ago guessed their destination. It was possible they
were being followed already. And military authorities
and the FBI might already be searching for the two officers who vanished amid all the deaths at Fort Harrison.
Theirs was a tenuous situation.

So Kirk's only sign of distress was a brief glare at Colonel Connie Gail.

She glared back. "Well, excuse me."

Kirk sighed and started talking in a calm, measured
voice.

He told the Pooles only that he had received a distress-
ing letter from PJ suggesting that Payne was in some sort

of trouble. He told them a more detailed package was to have been sent to Texas.

"PJ thought I might be able to use the information in the package to . . . help Mark get free of his difficulty."

"You're sure it was to come to us? Through the mails?" asked Maggie. She traded knowing glances with her husband.

"That's right. And you didn't get it?"

Poole shifted in his chair. His eyes narrowed and looked even more bitter than his normal expression.

"We might have gotten it, but I drove in one day and caught somebody rifling our mailbox just behind the mail truck. He stole a package—like a Sears catalog, only bigger. I chased the somebitch all over the park . . . shit . . ."

He paused, remembering the disappointment of not being able to kick some ass.

". . . I lost him."

"It's just as well you did," said Kirk. He pushed his chair back. "I'm leaving. It . . . wouldn't be safe for you to be connected with me. If anybody asks—*any*body—that includes the FBI, just deny you ever met a man named Kirk. I mean it. It's for your own safety, not just mine. Thank your lucky rabbit's feet you didn't have a chance to open that package. Don't even mention Mark or PJ's name again. If I ever have anything to report on them, you'll hear from me by anonymous letter."

Maggie looked at him askance.

"I promise," he said.

"And you listen, fucker," said Poole under his breath. "You ever need help of any kind in getting Mark or PJ out of trouble, you let me know. I mean legal or *ill*egal help of any kind."

Kirk felt a hand under the table. He took it. Poole's

grasp crunched his. It was the fraternity handshake. It was the earnest grip of the brotherhood of drunk pilots, men and women who would do and say anything for each other as long as the liquor flowed. Kirk hoped Poole would remember to keep his mouth shut when the hangover wore off.

But Poole didn't release the grip on Kirk's hand.

Kirk stared into the angry pocked face.

"So. Where we headed now?"

Maggie said, "Yeah. Where we all headed now?"

"We?" asked Gail.

Kirk kept a straight face. Last thing he needed was a scene to be remembered by.

Maggie repeated the question.

Kirk dodged it again, his hand now growing numb. "Ken," he said, "what are you trying to prove?"

"Damn you, Kirk, you fucker, where we going?"

"Do we have to kick your ass, Kirk?" Maggie chimed in.

Kirk looked to Gail for support.

She'd grown serious, now understanding what was going on beneath the surface.

"Okay," Kirk said. "Do you know a Sheriff Jacob Beard?"

"Keeerist, I guess. Only he ain't a sheriff no more."

"That's where Gail and I are going." Emphasis on Gail and I.

"How you gonna find him without us?"

"Ask at the sheriff's office." The way Kirk said them, the words sounded more like a question than a declaration.

"Sure," spat Poole. "And I suppose you two wouldn't be nervous about walking into a lawman's office? Way you two've been acting, you'd get arrested on general principle."

Kirk sighed. "Okay. Lead us to the sheriff."

Poole smiled wickedly. "I tole you. He ain't a sheriff no more. He retired after spending the last part of his term trying to throw Mark Payne's ass in jail for murders he never done. He took over an old run-down roadside show. A zoo. Used to be Dodson's Zoo. He's got some kinda fuckin freak animal he charges people to see. It's up near North Fort Hood."

He released Kirk's hand.

Kirk rubbed the circulation back into his fingers and sighed. "I guess that's where we're going, then."

Kirk and Gail had left their stolen Corporation car hidden beneath dusty bushes alongside a trail used by armored units in training near the boundary of Fort Hood. They rode in the Poole's car.

Nearly an hour later, Poole waved a hand ahead at a security light on a pole.

"Don't slow down," said Kirk.

Poole drove by as Kirk surveyed the property as best he could. He saw a gravel parking lot with only a pickup occupying it. Behind a sagging cyclone fence, sagged a weathered trailer house without lights. Beyond that were some overgrown paths and rickety sheds. And the security light.

Less than a quarter mile past, Kirk directed Poole to take the left turn down a dirt road in a southerly direction. The dirt road dropped down into a now-dry streambed that ran back toward the east.

"Stop," ordered Kirk. Poole eased off the road onto a raised roadway grown over by weeds. The surface of the track was rhythmically rutted. Poole rattled fifty yards into the weeds.

"Used to be a railroad. Dismantled."

Kirk grunted his understanding and said, "I imagine this goes behind the zoo."

Not to be outdone in guttural communication, Poole grunted back and pointed at the faint halo of the security light barely visible beyond the crest of the hill.

Kirk ordered them all to stay with the car. He handed the 9-millimeter to Poole. "The slide is dented. You'd have to work it manually for every shot," he said. "So if you have to use it, make it count."

He adjusted the grip of the silenced .22 in his belt and started up the dry creek-bed. Gail followed.

"Are you deaf?"

"I'm going with you."

"Look. Gail, I'm just going to ask a couple questions, make a couple observations. All I want to know is whether he's received his package. As soon as he answers, I'll know. I don't need a whole crew for that." He flapped his arms out to his sides in supplication.

"And who's going to save your ass if you screw up?"

Poole snorted a sarcastic little laugh.

Maggie showed her approval with a husky chuckle.

Kirk decided against wasting precious time with an argument. If somebody *had* followed them . . . if somebody knew that Beard had received the insurance policy that research log represented, then no more time could be lost.

His walk was a brisk one, half in anger, half in haste. The going was easier along the hillside than in the creek bed, for cattle had grazed the grass low. In the feeble light from the heavens, the hillside looked white. Black sentinels of juniper scrub dotted the relatively lighted landscape.

It took only a brief recollection of his evasion training to keep him away from the occasional oaks and mesquite trees. Beneath those would be crackling twigs and acorn caps.

Only a half step into the low, mottled mounds of darkness taught him to avoid the cactus beds. Five minutes after swiping his sneaker against a needled prickly pear pad, his instep still stung. It was the foot that had been twisted by that beast in the helicopter. Just as the stiffness was about gone, he thought wryly. That beast . . . the crash . . . how long ago was that? Two–three days? It seemed months.

First the security light came into view.

Kirk worked his way from one juniper stand to another, staying in the shadows.

The pole came into view. Then the outbuildings, and Kirk saw the run-down, rusted cages. All seemed empty.

Except for one.

A dirty heap of matted carpet. Gray, stained, furry in the distance. That's what it looked like, except that it moved.

It crept across the floor of the only cage without weeds.

And outside the cage, draped across a chair, was an overweight troll of a man.

Kirk's pulse tripped, then ran a little faster than it should have from the exertion of their walk. He found himself hoping Beard hadn't been killed already. But he hesitated only a second. Either the man had been killed, or he had not. No point in wasting time waiting for him to either decompose or awaken from a nap.

As they came close, Kirk let loose a sigh of relief. He could see deep, heaving, slow breathing from the man's chest. He could also see the scattered broken piles of glass from liquor bottles, which explained the unconsciousness.

But something else snatched his attention away from the man. The gray, matted heap of fur took shape as an animal as they closed on it. It saw them approaching and crawled, snarling, to the wire of the cage to intercept them.

This beast defied descriptions even as Kirk tried to place it.

It had something in its appearance of wolf-man-ape with touches of reptile momentarily surfacing. It possessed the quality of an optical illusion, changing in the eyes of the viewer without moving.

Its body was that of a barrel-chested man with pitifully tiny waist and hips that couldn't support an upright, two-legged gait. Its rear legs were those of a canine, knees bending to the rear. The feet—long, flat, and broad like a snowshoe hare's, tipped with stout black claws and lizard skin—flippety-flopped nervously, raising dust devils on the floor of the cage. The front legs were arms, ape arms too long to be useful in a four-legged walk, with paws too unwieldy to be considered hands—more like exaggerated dog paws with a prominent vestigial thumb. Claws nearly three inches long, curved to needle points with a knife edge on the inner arc, armed the front paws. What the paws lacked in mobility and ability to grasp was more than compensated for in ability to slash, Kirk saw.

Its head had a particularly mesmerizing effect on Kirk. Its muzzle might once have been long and sharp, like a coyote's. Rows of enormous teeth had been implanted into upper and lower furry beak and the whole fanged collection had been stuck onto the face of a huge, furry pumpkin with chimp ears. Even at that, the freakish whimsy of nature hadn't been satisfied. The heavy musculature of the jaws and temples must have pulled back on the structure of the muzzle. Finally, the pressure must have been too great on the upper snout, collapsing it, pulling the top rows of teeth vertically up into a misshapen mast of teeth like the prow of a Viking galleon. The lower jaw bowed permanently downward, and the whole appearance of the face was that of some horrid cartoon character that had smashed head-on into a wall. The crushed muzzle cut off the nasal passages like collapsed mine shafts, so the beast had to breathe through its constantly open throat. Its serpentine tongue continually lapped the up-and-down smile, wetting lips that could never meet. The tongue wriggled like a snake trying desperately to escape the throat of the beast.

The jaws could only move a couple of inches to open.

The whole pitiful body was covered by a ratty coat of gray-black fur. Patches of oozing sores showed through in some places, black scars in others.

It lay in its own filth, unmindful of the clouds of flies around it, unconcerned with the maggots shed by its fur every time it moved . . . unbothered by the man who had tormented it for the two feverish years of its life.

Still, it might have been mistaken for a cartoon character, a kind of giant wingless bat preposterously drawn by a surreal hand. Except for the eyes.

Its eyes captured Kirk's, locking on and holding him in a stare. Hard black granite eyes flecked with quartz. Eyes full of emotion. Namely hatred. Evil, human hatred radiated from the eyes, inviting the viewer to come closer to be slashed, then sucked down that throat, bit by bit, crushed bone after slashed flesh.

"My God," said Gail, "what is that?"

Kirk knew. He'd read the excerpts copied from Warren

Howell's journal. This must be one more species of new monster created by the beastmaker.

Kirk tried to rouse the man. "Sheriff? Sheriff Jacob Beard?"

The man lay heavily half in, half out of a folding patio chair. His dirty T-shirt barely covered his beachball gut. One hand was stuck into the waistband of shiny, stained jeans, which were rolled up into four-inch cuffs. The other hand was clutching the neck of a tequila bottle.

He grunted, the sound coming up wetly all the way from the bottom of his lurching belly.

Kirk stepped around to the side of the man, keeping a safe distance from the wire and steel cage that housed the beast. He repeated his greeting.

"Sheriff Beard?"

"Nuhn-nuh. Not no more." His voice rasped through a dried, gravelly throat. Beard broke his own stare from the gaze of the beast.

"Well, I guess you've retired. They say you operate this . . . roadside zoo."

Kirk looked around at the empty rusting cages. Other than birds and a flitting lizard, the zoo was unoccupied.

"Well . . ." Beard looked up at Kirk. The black little beads of his pupils swam in pink settings.

The beast bunched tighter inside the cage as if it would spring against the bars. Beard's little eyes locked back onto the beast as if holding it at bay.

He shook his head, jowls flapping, cleared his throat, and spat.

Gail grimaced. Kirk turned his head away for a second.

Beard stiffened and rasped, "Well, what the fuck you want me to say? They was right. I'm retarred? Okay, I'm fuckin retarred. Hello? Okay, hello."

"No, sir . . ."

"You wanna look for nothin at this here freaka nature?"

"No. . . ."

"You owe me five dollars, for the two of you. And, you can't stay long. I should closed up a air ago . . ." He pulled a pocket watch and ogled it, trying to focus. ". . . couple airs ago."

Kirk smiled weakly at Gail. He dug down into a pocket, pulled out a crumpled bill, and stuck it into the dirty, stubby hand.

"Ninth wunner of the world, this freaka nature . . ."

"Sheriff."

"I ain't a sheriff no more, asshole."

"Mister Beard, we didn't come to . . ."

"Look, pal, you paid to get in here, and I'm gonna give you your five bucks' worth whether you like it or not."

Kirk glanced at Gail, and their eyes rolled up at the same moment.

Beard produced a can from a pail of water and popped the top of the beer and slugged half of it down.

"Well, folks . . ." He swigged from the tequila bottle, the caterpillar swirling in the bottom. The last of the beer chased the amber liquor down his throat and spilled over his greedy mouth. It ran down the whiskered neck that was lined with black grease in the wrinkles of the throat. ". . . You got yer pyramids in Egyp and the Gran Canyon. And you got Texas, which is a wonder by iseff, never mind the Big Bend Country, the armadilla, Lone Star Beer, and a bowl of Frank Tolbert's Big Red. . . ."

Kirk took a deep breath to speak.

Beard's volume went up, and the glaze over his eyes suddenly hardened to a flinty glare, a stare warning against interruption.

". . . And then there's this here freaky son of a she-wolf found crawling out of the belly—not out of the . . .

the proper birth canal, mind ya, but outta the belly of its
mother. Out near Smith Mountain, out . . ."

Beard's voice trailed off. His grizzled features softened
as his mind seemed to be re-searching the memories of the
day out near Smith Mountain. He seemed lost in the labyrinth of his own mind.

"I fount it myseff . . . I . . . well, it coulda been born
that way or it coulda killed that wolf . . . or . . ."

"Sheriff, I mean Beard . . ."

The pathetic bloodshot eyes crossed, then uncrossed
with a shake of the crew-cut head.

"Yer not innerested?"

Kirk shook his head.

He was looking at the cage, welded bars wrapped in
hog wire. Inside the cage was a second wire enclosure,
some kind of holding pen big enough for a large dog. One
hinged side of this pen had been propped up. Kirk supposed Beard put the beast inside the smaller pen whenever he cleaned up—if he ever did. At one end of the cage
stood a sheltered wooden enclosure, a giant rabbit hutch
with a low doorway.

Beard tipped up his beer can, then remembered why it
was so light and threw the empty away in disgust. It clattered unmusically against the cage. The beast inside
sneered even wider and hissed as it bunched for a leap.

Beard roared, "Then why the fuck you here botherin
me when I could be gettin some work done?" He waved
the tequila bottle at the shambles of the zoo. He burped.
"Or get some sleep or some shit. . . ."

Kirk decided to hit him all at once. In his state, he could
hardly hide a lie.

"Sheriff, you got a package in the mail . . . a large envelope with a research log. It came from . . ."

Beard sobered almost instantly.

"You. Yer the one, you, you . . . you cockbitin mother-fucker."

Beard struggled to arise from his patio chair.

Kirk looked at Gail. A hand covered her mouth, heightening the effect of her widened eyes.

Kirk widened his stance, putting his weight up on the balls of his feet, readying for combat.

"No, I didn't send it, but I'd be willing to buy it from you. It's got some very important research data in it. . . ."

Beard fell back into the chair and threw the half-full bottle.

Kirk flinched, although it was not flung at him.

The bottle shattered on the cage bars, and the beast lunged fullface into the bars. Its hiss rose to the shriek of a terrified child, then into a two-toned scream, as if two women were in panic, one a honking tenor, the other a trilling soprano.

Beard's gravelly voice roared above the beast.

"Warren Howell. It was his stuff in that book. Howell. What a asshole. Just like his brother-in-law. Just like that fuckin Payne."

Beard finally gained his feet unsteadily and cursed alternately at Kirk and the beast.

"This animal. I read that book. I know where this thing come from. Warren Howell created it. He brung the devil right up here to earth. This thing is the devil hisseff."

Kirk saw a pistol grip in the waistband of Beard's lowslung jeans—it hadn't been visible when he was slouching in the chair, his belly doubled over onto his lap. The fingertips of Kirk's right hand slid into his windbreaker pocket. A slit inside the pocket let him reach beneath the jacket to the silenced .22. It was a gun made for killing at short range with its small caliber and four-inch silencer.

Beard bent over awkwardly and picked up a handful of gravel and threw it into the monster's mouth, enraging it all the more, sending up a new chorus of shrieks and screams.

Beard's maniacal laugh and raspy cursing completed the insanity of the sight and sound.

His wild expression dissolved into a mask of hatred. He adjusted the pistol in his waistband and saw Kirk's hand inside his windbreaker.

For a moment, a wicked smile crossed his face. He wiped his full lips with the back of his hand and closed the wet fist around the grip of the revolver.

Kirk stood balanced on the balls of his feet, crouched, left arm wide, pushing Gail away. The right arm came partway out of his windbreaker.

"Shoot-out at the O.K. Corral, huh?" Beard growled.

"No, Sheriff. We're not here for trouble. I just want to pick up that package and maybe get your help with some people who killed my friend."

Beard dropped his hand. Then his body sagged into the patio chair, the belly effectively disarming him by folding over the pistol grips.

"Messy-kin standoff, kid."

Kirk's hand came out of the windbreaker.

"Payne?" said Beard. "Somebody killed Payne?"

Kirk nodded.

"A Payne-killer. Hah." Beard's laugh came as a sardonic burst that brought another shriek from the beast inside the wire.

Beard pulled another can from the pail of water, popped it, and pulled deeply at it like a sucking calf.

"I thought so, soon as I read in that package. Good," he said. "Now I can die in peace. Payne gone. . . ." His eyes seemed to glaze over as he looked toward some faraway place. Then he shook his head, returning to the coordinates of squalor on earth that belonged to him.

"Fuckin Payne. That sonofabitch killed my best deppity—or he was responsible. Don't matter. I found him with a knife stuck through his haid a couple years ago. Ever time I'd go out an investigate a fire or a accident or find a killin of any kind . . . there would be Payne. Chrissakes, I'm glad he's dead, make that fuckin esstatic. I only wish I coulda done it myseff."

Kirk grimaced.

"Who sent that package, anyways?"

"His wife."

"I member her. Little thing with the green eyes. I wunner why she sent it to me? She musta knew I hated him . . . hell, her too, for that matter. She musta knew I wouldn't spit on him if he needed a drink."

"Maybe she thought of you as a last resort," said Kirk.

Beard half coughed, half laughed, and spat. He put a finger to one nostril and blew his nose into the night. He switched nostrils and sent another glistening stream after the first.

Gail looked away. Kirk himself grimaced in disgust.

Beard now seemed completely sober. When he turned back to them, there was clearly a change of subject on his face.

"How much would you of gimme for that book?"

Kirk pursed his lips at Beard's choice of words. He tried to change the discussion back to the present tense. "How much do you want?"

"Ten grand."

It was Kirk's turn to laugh. But emptily.

"I'll give you a hundred dollars."

Beard joined him in the laugh. "Make it twenny grand." He and Kirk laughed until Beard began choking.

He finally coughed up and spat his problem and lit an
unfiltered cigarette, hunching over it to protect it from a
nonexistent breeze. Finally he looked up and smiled sardonically. "It ain't for sale. Not at any price. I burned
that package the day I got it. It was all lies anyways, and
if it was gonna help Payne, I din't want anybody to have
it. Shit, who you think believes them stories about monsters?"

Kirk glanced at the cage, where the beast was sucking
air wetly through the wires. The answer to Beard's question glared at them hatefully from that cage.

"Get outta here," Beard commanded. "Offen my fuckin
proppity. You got yer five bucks' worth."

Kirk and Gail began backing away.

"I shoulda kept that book, though. I bet I could get fitty
grand if I got you and your guvmint friends biddin on it."

Kirk turned and walked toward the parking lot—as if
they had parked a car there—one hand on Gail's elbow,
the other in his windbreaker pocket. He looked back once
in a while and Beard raised his beer can every time, as if
to toast him. When he did, his face broadened into a wide,
ugly, hateful sneer—his best imitation of a mock smile.

Once out of Beard's sight, Kirk urged Gail into a trot.

"What's the hurry?" she said.

"We're hurrying because he'll be coming out front soon
after he realizes we walked away instead of driving. I
wouldn't put it past him to start shooting blindly down
the road, would you?"

"No." She was silent for a second. "It's pretty evident
he still has it, don't you think?"

"No doubt. If he'd really burned it, he wouldn't have
been discussing a price."

"The man is crazy with hate. He gives me the creeps

. . . but what are we going to do? Search his trailer? Do we have a chance of finding that research log?"

Kirk shook his head.

"Kirk? I said, what chance do we have?"

"Sorry. I don't know. Try thinking like a drunken burned-out crazy redneck Texas sheriff. Where would you hide that log if you were nuts?"

She didn't speak for a while. Then she stiffened with the realization.

"My God, it's in the cage. Oh, Kirk, I'm scared. Everybody we've met in the last few days is either crazy or a killer."

"Odd, isn't it?"

"It's not funny. Do you think this Corporation is going to discover that Beard has the book?"

He nodded. It wasn't his distraction with Beard alone that kept him from speaking. He didn't want her to hear the inevitable anxiety in his voice. He was triply worried. First there was Beard and his insanity—he might even kill them if they went back to get that book, even to ask about it. Second, there was anxiety about The Corporation, which apparently killed as a matter of course. For The Corporation, murder must have been as easy as punching the time clock. And they must know—or would soon know—that Beard had that other log.

Finally there was that beast. Its purpose for existence was even more self-evident than The Corporation's. It could do nothing *but* kill. Kirk shivered. He knew he would have to get past this beast to get the research log.

This beast. That beast.

The beast at Fort Harrison—what was it, a hundred years ago?—was different from this wolflike thing in Texas. What did that mean? How many different varieties of these freak animals existed?

* * *

The Albino beast atop Judith Peak lay seething under the influence of the powerful tranquilizer. None of the drugs had been able to knock the thing into total unconsciousness. Even the heaviest dosages, those injected in the fight near the Klamath River, had not knocked out the animal. Although its muscles would not respond, it retained enough of its senses to be able to lie seething, hating, and hurting in the secret places of its head.

Now it lay where it had been dragged after killing the two men. It had seen the padlocks opened, the chains unwound partially. But then the men had abandoned that task.

The beast knew it could escape the netting and chains if left alone. Those feeble restraints did not concern it.

What concerned the beast were the scents like his own.

It was confused by the first such odors it had ever inhaled. It had reacted to the smells in the hallway—and that's why he'd stiffened, why these men had dropped him, why two men had died there. The beast had picked up the scent of other beasts. It had lashed out in confusion as the scents grew stronger. It had drawn blood; had feasted lightly on part of one man; had found new strength to resist.

But now it lay drugged again.

It lay helpless.

Confused.

Afraid.

Enraged.

It lay so it could not see into the cage.

The beast heard the sounds of the motor and the metal bars sliding on their rails.

It heard the soft padding on concrete, the clacking of teeth, the scritching of claws.

The scent grew hot and strong.

A shadow fell across the beast.

Had he been able, the beast would have lashed out in defense, would have attacked the presences in the cell.

That he could not enraged him all the more; frightened him in the extreme.

It felt a gentle touch.

One figure, then another, moved into his field of vision. Beasts like himself, he saw, only darker in color.

For a moment of curiosity, the albino forgot its fear.

Then the pair moved in on him. In his head, the albino tensed, recoiled, struck back. But the drugs held his body, keeping it limp.

The pair prodded him with curved spikes. He did not feel the rough touches, although a small spring of blood answered each of the pokes.

At the sight of fresh blood, the pair began to tear at the albino. He fought back, but only inside his head.

But no . . . they were not tearing at him. They were ripping the nets from him. They shredded the nylon and pulled it away, rolling his body over, touching, probing, sniffing.

When the albino rolled onto his back, he saw more beasts—three more who hung back.

Now free, the beast settled back inside his head. Now free, it would have its moment. It lay waiting, hating even his brethren.

For its inability to attack, hating even himself.

Gerlach chewed on the damp, acrid-smelling stub of a cigar. He parked it in the far corner of his downturned mouth and growled.

"Edward, pull up a chair."

Gates backed up to an overstuffed leather chair, but his

knees would only bend about thirty degrees, and he hovered, a question rising on his eyebrows.

"Sit, Edward. Tell me more about the news from Texas."

Gates let his knees bend to a full ninety degrees and sat.

"We have recovered Poole's mail and another copy of the research log. It was one the Payne woman mailed."

"For a total of?"

"With the one from the Pooles' mailbox, eleven. Five last year, six this year."

"Now, about number twelve?"

"Apparently Beard has it, sir. Two men are moving down from Albuquerque. And there's also Barnaby. And Pearson and Keeney—they're going after Beard and book number twelve. All the others are available for backup."

Gerlach smiled wickedly. "Send them in, Edward. Send in the clowns. I want to use them—all the clowns. I want this matter finished."

Gates nodded.

Gerlach cocked his head. His lip lifted. "Now, Edward. Get your ass out of that comfortable chair and get things moving."

Gates was at the door. Gerlach pressed the knee button in the well of his desk, releasing his secretary.

"Oh, and, Edward?"

"Sir?"

"Will you send me the certificates of destruction on every single one of those research logs when they've been shredded, burned, and the ashes have been made into wet mash?"

"Why . . . yessir."

"And any other copies we run into. I want this genetic warfare shit laid to rest once and for all. Ever since we've gotten into it, the most important damage it's done has been to this Corporation. Ever since we got away from the corporate charter . . . ever since my predecessor took this detour away from domestic intelligence into dirty tricks overseas and a kennel for monsters domestically, there's been trouble. If I do nothing else in my tenure here, I want to restore this organization to its rightful mission. Understand? Home intelligence only."

"Yessir."

"I wanna know when Beard is dead and his damned little beast is finished and when number twelve research journal is in our hands. Even if you have to wake me."

"Yessir."

Next to Poole's car on the dismantled railroad bed, Kirk told the others his plan.

"You're fucking crazy," said Poole.

Maggie said, "Can't we just call the cops or something?"

"No, Kirk," said Gail. "It's time we called a stop to all this madness. Your idiotic plan will just get us killed."

Kirk nodded slightly, then more positively.

"I'm glad you all feel this way. I recommend all three of you get into that car and get out of here. Then I can take care of this on my own—which is what I always wanted to do in the first place."

He looked at Gail and raised an eyebrow, inviting her to argue. She didn't. She just stood clutching her arms as if against a chill.

Poole muttered more obscenities.

"Screw this," said Maggie. "I'm too old to be falling for any Tom Sawyer gags. If he wants to be a hero, let him. Let him do it alone. Let's just get out of this mess."

Gail unfolded her arms. She put her hands on her hips and squared up to Kirk, face-to-face.

"Sorry, Maggie. Kirk, I can't leave you." She touched his shoulder lovingly, but her angry expression belied the gesture. "You stupid son of a bitch."

Poole looked helplessly at his wife, then angrily at Kirk. "Awright, you bastard, I'll help you, but there is no fuckin way on earth I'm going into that cage to dig around for some stupid book. I seen that monster before and I ain't fuckin going near it."

"Fine. You stand watch while I do the digging." He held up the .22. "I'll finish the bastard before I go in and start digging. And Beard will be passed out or asleep—or knocked out—until we're long gone with that log."

Gail shook her head for the dozenth time since Kirk had begun his explanation of his plan. "How can you be sure that book is in that cage someplace?"

"Where *else* would you put something both hateful and valuable?"

There was no answer to that.

Gail reluctantly gave up her pistol to Poole. Kirk left the partially disabled 9-millimeter pistol with the women and disappeared into the darkness, he and Poole becoming just two more juniper shrubs on the night landscape.

Except for a brief outburst of swearing by Poole at a cactus attack, they had crept quietly to the edge of the glow cast by the security lamp. Kirk dropped to his knees and sat back on his heels to watch and listen.

The astonished Poole swore under his breath.

Their plan had been to shoot out the security light so Beard couldn't open up with a rifle from the trailer. They would finish the beast in the cage with a shot to the head. Poole would stand watch as Kirk pried off the lock and searched the cage for the log.

It was not a particularly well-laid plan, but what they

saw was a complete surprise, something that would have disrupted even the best of plans.

The beast lay scrunched, locked inside the smaller wire pen inside the main cage.

And the main cage door was open.

From the hutch came the gravelly voice of Beard singing a drinking song and the sounds of digging—a shovel being thrust into dirt, dirt being thrown off the shovel blade.

Poole's small dark eyes met Kirk's as Beard's song reached down to seventy-eight bottles of beer on the wall.

Kirk whispered an answer to the question in the eyes.

"I don't know what to do now. We'll just wait and see. Maybe he'll just be bringing the book out to us."

Poole's oily face contorted into another question.

"I don't know why he's digging it up. Maybe he's trying to move it before we come back," said Kirk. "Hell, I don't know *what* he's up to. Maybe he found a buyer for the book. Maybe he's moving it to a safer place. Maybe he's leaving town . . . hell, I just don't know how to think like that guy."

The beast's tiny wire enclosure pressed in on it, preventing it from fully straightening on all fours. And it couldn't turn around. It hunched forward toward the singing in the hut, biting down on the wire mesh, then it backed off until its haunches pressed against the rear of the pen.

Twenty fallen bottles of beer later, the singing had not diminished. The beast had not wavered from its incessant pseudo-pacing. Kirk just kept staring into the cage, all his attention there waiting for Beard to give up a glimpse of himself.

Kirk felt Poole's elbow in his ribs.

"We gonna stay here all fuckin night?"

Kirk didn't give an answer. He had none. He turned his head toward Poole to say something anyhow. It was then he saw the movement.

It was the barest of reflections of the security light off glass. It came from beyond the trailer. A blacked-out car had coasted silently past the dilapidated zoo.

The next second he heard the muffled snap of gravel beneath a tire.

Poole heard it too, and hunkered down into the shadows. He looked at Kirk, and Kirk raised his eyebrows in question.

They didn't have long to wait for an answer.

Around one end of the trailer stalked a man dressed in dark clothes. He was carrying a pistol. From the other end of the trailer, his dark clothes full of burrs and thistles, came a second man, also armed, through the weeds.

As Kirk and Poole had been, they were clearly confused by what greeted them. They gestured at one another, at the trailer, and at the cage. Finally one ducked down beside a junked refrigerator and pointed his pistol at the cage, where the singing continued unabated. The other man cautiously opened the door of the trailer and went in. Only forty-four bottles of beer remained in the song.

Kirk took a deep breath. Poole mouthed a silent, multisyllabic oath.

They watched as a flashlight beam bounced around from one end of the trailer to the other, every once in a while coming to the door, where the man would look out.

At thirty-one bottles he'd finished his search. He came out and gestured some more with his sentinel. Then, treading carefully, they moved down the slope among the yard trash and auto parts toward the singing.

Kirk flexed his muscles and stretched closer to Poole.

He whispered into Poole's ear. "Get ready to move back down to the car. If I can't take them both out with a couple shots, you get down there and get the police out here as fast as possible. Tell them you want to report a murder. Mine."

Poole wiped a hand across his greasy face and nodded solemnly.

All at once, everybody within sight and hearing of it had fixed his attention on the beast's cage.

There were twenty-three bottles left when Keeney shuddered and stepped into the cage. Goddamned Pearson, he thought. What right did he have to order him inside first? For a moment he thought about just killing the beast outright and firing into the darkness at the singing. They could just continue digging in the hole Beard had begun and get that damned package that was so important, and this ridiculous affair would be nearly over. He and Pearson could courier the package back to Washington as directed and leave Kirk and the woman to Barnaby and the others.

He stepped to the middle of the cage and was only slightly relieved to feel Pearson right at his shoulder.

The hutch was dark. It was sending out an unbearable stench. How could Beard stand to work in there? Maybe he was good and drunk.

At twenty-one bottles he saw the beast sneering at him, drawing labored breaths through fluttering throat passages.

At twenty bottles he heard Pearson slam the gate to the cage. Momentarily, he wondered why, but he couldn't be diverting his attention from the darkness of that hole where Beard was armed with a shovel and who knew what else.

* * *

When the gate slammed shut, Pearson whirled. Instantly he saw what he had not noticed before. The gate was equipped with a self-locking latch. And he saw, even as he was throwing a shoulder into it, that the gate was deceptively strong, welded and anchored. He also saw a thin wire cable leading off into darkness. The cable was taut, he saw. And he saw that somebody had pulled the door shut behind them. He saw they were trapped.

He did not see a second cable go taut, releasing the beast as the side of the pen fell away.

At nineteen bottles the beast lunged at the back of Keeney, who was leaning into the darkness of the hut.

Pearson whirled, shouting a warning, leveling his pistol to shoot.

But the shot that was fired was not from his pistol. It was the blast of a shotgun fired from the darkness where the two taut wires pointed. Pearson's hand and pistol blew up into a bloody stump at the end of his black sleeve.

In his subconscious, Keeney of course heard all of that; the cage door, the shouted warning, the blast of the shotgun. But in his consciousness he missed all of it. For the only sensation that reached his brain for analysis was the overpowering sense of feeling eight claws stabbing him in the lower back and raking down through his buttocks and thighs.

His own scream emanated from his throat as he was on the way down. He felt and smelled and tasted the greasy offal on the floor of the hut. His voice was cut off in midscream by the toothed vise that clamped onto the back of his neck. Much as that hurt, he was thankful that it immediately severed all feeling from the neck down.

In his last instant he made peace with his god, asking forgiveness in words that never made it to his lips.

His final vision came in the dimmest of the security lamp's reflected glow.

He saw the tape recorder that had fooled them.

The tape recorder now counting down in Beard's triumphant voice.

To eighteen bottles of beer.

Poole had started backing down the hillside, deeper into the darkness and shadows—away from the horror picture they'd witnessed going on inside that cage. Kirk turned and caught up with him.

"Go on back," he muttered urgently into the oily ear. "Give me fifteen minutes, then get the hell out of here. Send the police—I mean it, just as we planned—tell them it was murder. If I can't get it, maybe they can find the research log and maybe they'll have enough sense to get it into the right hands."

"You gonna be all right, fucker?"

Kirk ignored the question he didn't want to tell the truth about.

"And make damned sure to take Gail with you," he said. "If you have to drag her by the hair. These people are probably backed up by somebody and they're going to want revenge for what Beard has done. They'll be killing everybody in sight."

Poole opened his mouth to speak, but Kirk was already on the way back up the hill.

There were eleven bottles of beer on the wall when Beard marched out of the brush, his shotgun pointing the way to the cage. He was singing along with the recorded voice.

Inside the cage, an astonished Pearson, pressing his left thumb deeply into what remained of his right wrist, suddenly understood the source of unchanged sounds of digging and singing coming from the darkness of the hut. Only now the sounds of crackling bones and sloppy eating mingled with the incessant bar song.

Beard stopped singing along. He was surprised too.

"Who the hell are you? I thought you was that friend of Payne's coming back . . . I din't expect you."

Pearson was dazed from the pain and from the symphony of horror emanating from the hut. He divided his attention between the hut and the half-drunk, half-crazed Beard.

Beard was now sweeping the double barrels of his shotgun back and forth from Pearson to the doorway of the hut.

"Is that Payne's friend in here . . . the guy who was out here earlier with that woman? Kirk?"

Briefly, Pearson's own eyes lit up, but they glazed over again with the hurt. He gave his captor no other sign of an answer.

But Beard, enraged and distracted as he was, already had his answer. As the seventh bottle of beer fell from the wall, he began a slow turn, pointing the shotgun along the line where the edge of darkness began.

He'd gone no more than a quarter turn, when Kirk's voice came from behind him, from Beard's own hiding place.

"Freeze," he shouted, using a command from the former policeman's own past. "Sheriff, I have a shotgun too. It's pointed at the back of your head."

Beard froze until there were only five more bottles. His face worked, his arms bunched.

Kirk stepped out of the shadows. He had no shotgun, but his arm and the pistol pointed at the tousled head.

"Don't do it, Sheriff. It's not worth dying . . ."

But Beard had already committed himself, perhaps thinking it was, after all, worth dying for.

On the fourth bottle, the shotgun barrels began inscribing an arc.

Kirk shouted again, loudly, violently, pleadingly.

But the crazed man kept swinging the gun.

Just as the eyes picked him up and hardened, just as the grip tightened on the shotgun, just as he was a degree or two in the arc short of being too late, Kirk made the pistol spit at Beard's head.

A wound that seemed no worse than a pimple scratched too hard appeared on Beard's forehead above the wild-haired left eyebrow. But it threw the head back, jerking the shotgun up so the shot from both barrels tore through the air high above Kirk's head.

Kirk shuddered, mesmerized by the sight and the idea of deliberately killing another man. For an instant he reflected that he had become as bad as any Corporation killer. Then he saw the one-handed man in the cage bend over his bloodied pistol. He shouted a warning. The wounded man straightened up.

Kirk reflected again that he had been forced to kill a man—a basically innocent man—in self-defense, yes. But a killing just the same. That shook him to the core of his gut, reducing his control over his body. He felt sick.

Yet he felt able to kill again. In fact, hard as he tried to resist the encroachment of the feeling—he *wanted* to kill again . . . if it would be this man, this Corporation rep who'd made a murderer of him and corpses of his friends.

He stared into the cage.

Pearson stared back at him, half in wonder, half in fear.

His eyes had filled with tears as he grimaced at his hurt. But he was nowhere near crying and he didn't make a sound.

Kirk wanted to kill the man in the cage. He was the representative of the organization, the so-called Corporation, that had driven him to murder, that had killed his friend Mark Payne, had thrown away all those lives at Fort Harrison as if they'd been eradicating insects, that had killed Jud McClean and the Lees—the whole family, including two innocent children.

On three bottles, he went through Beard's pockets and drew out a key and a fistful of shotshells. He reloaded the shotgun on two. On one, he stepped over beside the cage and aimed the shotgun.

The tape went silent.

There was no sound in the night but some daybirds protesting that their sleep had been disturbed by Beard's shooting. And there was the sound of ripping flesh. And Pearson's ragged breathing.

Kirk knelt down beside the cage door and fished out Pearson's bloodied pistol. He stuck it into his waistband.

Pearson just watched.

Kirk stuck the key into the door lock. But he did not turn the piece of brass.

"It's the right key," he said as the sound of a snapping bone came from the hutch. "With the proper behavior on your part, this key will let you out."

"I'm not going to beg you," said Pearson.

"Don't want you to," said Kirk. But he was lying. He wanted the bastard to beg for his life. His stomach had literally begun churning. He knew he might vomit and give himself away. He'd killed a man. He'd killed that beast at Fort Harrison. He kept killing things.

Pearson struggled for control of his breathing. "What then?"

"I need some information."

Pearson snorted through his pain. "Unless you have some pretty sophisticated drugs, you're not likely to get anything out of me . . . anybody with my kind of training for that matter. Might as well go on and finish me."

Kirk sniffed and turned his head to spit. He knew he'd have to match bravado with this guy. He knew the type. He'd almost been the type himself.

"I don't want to kill you," he said. "In fact, I won't. Whether you live or die is going to be up to you." A bone snapped with the loudness of a .22 pistol shot. "And that thing."

Pearson just stared through the dim natural light of the night as if he might discover some clue in Kirk's face.

Kirk took a deep breath, remembering Poole's savage poker face and trying to duplicate it. He spat nonchalantly onto the ground between them.

"Well, we both know that research log is probably just a few feet away . . . lying in there with your buddy and that . . . little pet of Beard's. I'm taking that log with me when I leave. So that means I'll have to kill the damned monster before I go in. But . . ." He left the word hanging. A new noise slurped from the entrance to the hut. From the darkness came a wet face, mouth wide with teeth, tongue snaking from the throat.

"As I was saying," said Kirk, "I'm killing that thing before the night is over. But I'm not laying a glove on it until you tell me what I want to know."

Pearson made no sound. But Kirk could see his throat working dryly up and down. Kirk welcomed that sign of fear.

"Never," said Pearson in a tone somewhat lacking in

conviction. "I mean I'll never tell. And I know something of your background . . . from when you worked for us . . . I know you never were involved directly in any of the assassinations. You're not a killer. You don't have it in the guts to kill."

Kirk glanced over at Beard's body. But he sensed the retort even before Pearson spoke it.

"That was self-defense. Doesn't count."

Right. Doesn't count. Ask Beard, Kirk thought. He continued to stare at Beard's corpse. He'd already done that. It didn't feel all *that* bad. He might be capable of worse. He didn't know. But this life—*all* the lives—*did* count, he knew.

He turned to glare at Pearson and heard himself saying, "I'm not going to be the one killing you, mister. That . . . *thing* is going to do it. . . ."

He groped through his mind for something to say that would seem threatening, something that would break down the tough guy. But all that came to mind was what the man with no hand had said about his not being ruthless enough to kill.

"You'd better start talking," he said, sounding a bit hollow even to himself.

"Maybe I don't know what you want," said Pearson, a little of the toughness gone.

For the beast had moved half its length from the hut.

Both men stared at it.

"I want to know where I can find . . . where your people are holding PJ Payne—her name used to be Larson."

Even as he spoke PJ's name, Kirk's mind was still on Pearson's introductory statement. "And what the hell do you mean?" he demanded. "What the hell is this idea that I used to work for you . . . for the same people as you?"

Even though the whole figure of the beast had moved into sight now, Pearson found a last laugh. "You never knew? In Vietnam, The Corporation moved into some other areas besides domestic work. In Vietnam we snatched people behind enemy lines, ran a few assassinations, rigged a few dirty tricks—you know, you helped with some of it."

Kirk whispered, "I never knew. I mean I never knew it was for a group like yours . . . outside the Pentagon."

"No need for you to know," said Pearson with an air of superiority.

"Where's PJ?" said Kirk, dismissing any preoccupation with his own past.

Pearson drew his knees up. The beast was within a yard. Its engorged belly was dragging on the floor of the cage. And because its appetite was sated, it no longer had the same sense of urgency with which it had dispatched Keeney.

"You won't do this, Kirk. You don't have the stomach for killing—not this way. In self-defense maybe. But this would be the same as murder."

"Murder? You mean like my friends Noble and Nancy Lee? And Jud McClean? You mean that kind of murder? And how about the children? You don't think that kind of killing could get me mad enough to murder?"

The beast stopped, its perpetually open muzzle a foot away from Pearson's ankles. It breathed wetly, spraying its rancid breath on the pair of men, one inside the cage, the other outside.

"Shoot it, Kirk," came the whisper from the cage.

"What's your name?"

"Pearson."

"Well. That's a nice start, Pearson. Now where might I find PJ?"

Kirk shifted, pointing the barrels of the shotgun at the beast.

Pearson took heart at the gesture. "Kill it, Kirk . . . now . . . please."

"PJ first."

"She's probably dead by now . . . ahhhh."

The beast had extended a tentative paw, the curved hooks fully extended, toward the shoe of Pearson.

"PJ."

"Fuck you."

The beast seemed to take offense at the epithet. It drew back its paw and flicked it out again. The claws hit the top of the shoe and penetrated. The leg was jerked straight.

Pearson let out a squawk.

"Kirk, please . . . oh, God . . . oh."

The claws sheathed themselves, and Pearson drew his foot away. But the paw flicked out again and raked the shoe back, tearing the laces.

Pearson again jerked his leg back, leaving the shoe in the grasp of the beast. His sock was wet with blood. The beast started biting into the empty shoe.

"Give me PJ's location, Pearson."

"Kill it, Kirk. Then I'll give you the place they're holding her."

"Right."

Kirk moved over behind Pearson, who had withdrawn as far into the corner of the cage as he could. He didn't want Pearson to see the weakness and sickness in his own face if this situation should worsen. For Pearson was right. He didn't have the stomach for cold-blooded murder. But he was prepared to rationalize this murder away if he didn't have the information that would get him to his friend's wife. The Corporation had driven him down to that level of depravity—he wanted to scream in rage for what it had done to him.

But instead of screaming, he muttered in a low, threatening voice, "I want to know where . . ."

Pearson's shriek cut him off.

The beast had flicked out a paw; had hooked the top of the shoeless foot; had jerked the leg straight.

And now it held the foot as a grizzly holds a salmon in two paws. In fact, the foot wriggled like a salmon. Then, as the bear bites the head off the fish, the beast turned its head to get a better purchase and crunched down on Pearson's toes, biting three of them off at once.

It was the sound that wrenched Kirk's gut, the snapping of bones, a noise as crisp as the crackling of potato chips.

Pearson was crying, begging, gasping for breath and succor.

He begged Kirk to kill the beast.

He cried for Kirk to put the gun to his own head and mercifully finish his own misery.

He pleaded for his own death.

Kirk raised the shotgun, pointing it over the shoulder at the mouthful of crunching teeth. The beast tossed its head and pulled the sock off Pearson's foot. It began to eat the bloodied cotton as well.

Kirk's finger tightened on the rear trigger, to the second barrel. Pearson had been right. He hadn't the stomach. Only God knew how he'd allowed this situation to go this far. The Corporation—could it be blamed for this extent of his depravity? Or would he have to take the blame for himself? Yet he hesitated. The rage. Only the rage stayed his trigger finger. Had he gone mad? He inventoried himself; felt his pulse beating in his head, neck, chest.

"*WHERE?*" he heard himself yelling.

"Montana," Pearson whined. "Now, get it over with. Kill it, please, please finish it, Kirk."

The beast opened its mouth impossibly wide and took two quick bites. All the foot below the ankle came off, strings of sinew connecting the mouth and leg.

Pearson screamed until his voice broke. Then he seemed to faint.

Kirk nearly vomited. He couldn't believe what came from his own throat, neither the sound nor the words.

"It's a big state, asshole. Exactly where is PJ, you son of a bitch? Tell me, or we'll stay here until he eats your leg off right up to your nuts."

Finally Pearson was persuaded by the threat of more pain to his genitals. He finally believed Kirk could be as cruel as any corporate agent. He began to cry, to moan, to shriek, to speak. Montana, he said. The mountains. *The* mountain. On top. A former radar tower.

The beast was readying for another bite.

"Where?" shouted Kirk. He doubted he could hold his stomach down much longer. "Where the fuck is this mountain?"

"Judith Peak. Near Lewistown. Central part of the state. Kill it, Kirk, you son of a bitch. Kill it or kill meeeee . . . God, please . . . please . . . pleeeese. . . ."

His pleas ended in a shriek.

The beast had taken off the ankle.

Pearson fainted.

Blood spurted from his leg and his wrist, splattering the beast.

Kirk wondered a second; hesitated while trying to guess whether Pearson would or could lie under such circumstances.

It didn't matter, he decided. He couldn't take any more

of the sounds. The beast began licking the spilled blood off the ground.

He poked the shotgun into the cage, literally into the beast's maw, and pulled off the rounds in both barrels.

The beast recoiled into a heap of matted fur.

The outpouring of blood was its only sound.

Kirk struggled to his feet and barely turned away from the carnage before his stomach involuntarily emptied itself. When the cramping stopped, he felt no better physically. Emotionally, he would always wonder about himself. How could he have done so savage a thing? He didn't know the answer. And he didn't want to dwell on it for fear the answer might actually be given to him.

Inside the hutch, he stepped over the remains of the other agent, felt around, and found a cheap lockbox nailed to the rafters. When he worked the latch, nothing happened. So he used Pearson's pistol to shoot off the lock. The bottom of the box fell away, and he found a heavy package wrapped in plastic bags. He didn't stop to inventory. He knew what it was.

He walked by Pearson.

The mortally wounded man had regained his consciousness. He groaned at the sound of footsteps.

"Don't leave me like this, Kirk." The words came as a weak whisper.

Kirk shrugged helplessly. "Do you want me to call an ambulance?"

Pearson choked on a thin laugh.

"Use the shotgun. Give me peace."

Kirk looked at the empty weapon, its barrels still poking through the wire as he had left it.

"You were right, Pearson. I haven't the guts for it."

"Bring it to me, then, while I still have the strength."

Kirk reluctantly carried the gun around, broke it open, and removed the empty shells.

He laid the gun beside Pearson's left hand, his good one.

"Not that way, stupid."

Kirk looked up, offended.

"Point the muzzle up this way. And take off my shoe . . . my good shoe." He sobbed. "My *only* shoe."

Kirk's sick expression turned into a question.

"So I can work the trigger with my toe."

Kirk did as he was asked. Then he fished in his pocket and brought out the last shotshell.

"I only have one left."

Pearson gave him a sarcastic sneer.

Kirk put the shell in. He was careful enough not to cock the hammers so Pearson could turn the gun on him for a last-second bit of revenge. He could fumble with the hammers for himself after Kirk was safely out of danger.

"That's good," Pearson observed. "You might make it as an agent after all. You have to be careful. And you have to be ruthless, Kirk. You'd better work a little on your ruthlessness. You could get your ass killed by being so hesitant to kill. You have to learn not to hesitate. You have to kill first. You . . ."

But Kirk was gone. He'd had enough of The Corporation line and lecture. He had barely started down the slope when he heard the blast of the shotgun.

The sound spurred his imagination enough to see Pearson's head blown apart as the beast's had been. It was vivid enough to make him vomit again, and it took several minutes for him to get over the dry heaves.

Kirk's head pounded as he worked his way downhill. He felt as if he'd just awakened with a champagne hangover.

He didn't feel at all like being careful. Poole would have long since followed his instructions to leave, to get away and call the police. After so long a delay, they wouldn't have expected him to return at all. In fact, Kirk was himself surprised to be walking downslope among the junipers with that infernal package under his arm. And alive. He thought he might find a soft, sandy place in the dry creek-bed and curl up for a few hours sleep. If only there wasn't so much to worry about.

His mind jumped ahead, and he began to wonder how in hell he was going to make his way to Montana. How was he going to find a mountain called Judith Peak? And what was he going to do about it if he ever did get that far in this journey?

Before he could answer his own questions, a flash of lights from below brought him up short.

He dropped into a crouch.

Pearson had told him about the need to be careful in virtually his last words. And here he had let down his guard completely. He was strolling across the hillside like a Boy Scout exploring for arrowheads. He needn't worry about Montana, he told himself. If he continued to act like an idiot, he'd never make it out of this county, let alone go searching for a place on the northern edge of the country or wherever this Judith Peak was.

The lights flashed again. Then several more times hurriedly. A signal? Kirk thought of Gail. She might be in trouble. The thought worried him. But that he cared about her was a sign—however tenuous—of his concern for one small fraction of a percentage point of humanity. As long as there was that, he could rationalize that he wasn't *all* bad. Maybe he even loved her.

As the lights continued to flash, he tried to get in synch with the dark periods. Each time, he sprinted from one juniper bush to another until he found the creek bed. Finally he was in it, gasping for breath, but safer now that he'd stumbled down off the exposed hillside.

He raised his head to recon a route to the car. A direct line was no good, it was straight into the headlights. If they should come on for any length of time, he'd be spotlighted like a deer in a poacher's beam.

He decided he would go over the abandoned railbed and approach from the opposite side until he could see what was going on at Poole's car.

He eased out of the creek bed and started breaking a wide arcing path through the night. As he tried sneaking over the railbed, the weeds made a racket against the plastic wrapping, and he decided to stuff the package— about the size of a ream of typing paper—under his shirt. He knelt to do so, keeping low in the weeds so the flash of those lights fifty yards away would not catch him. When finally he'd packed the journal and papers into his shirt and buttoned it tightly, he started crawling on all fours.

The lights would flash on—for longer intervals now.

And then they would shut off.

When they were off he crawled.

When they were on he stopped.

He was almost across the railbed when they came on again.

And he saw an all too familiar sight of these last few days.

He saw another slashed throat.

This time on the body of Maggie Poole.

He cursed under his breath. He was at once shaken and angry about this killing and worried about Gail. He slid down the other side of the embankment, fearful that he would stumble over her corpse as well. He found himself trembling, and his stomach was lurching again in a kind of anxiety sickness.

But he did not find another body, and his stomach settled down to a quivering tenseness. He cut down his arc toward the car, deciding that carefulness was no longer as important as revenge. He wanted to make somebody pay for that death. And as far as he knew, for the deaths of Gail and Ken Poole as well. His breath began to come faster as his rage worked up, his anger becoming focused on that car and those lights. Was this caring? he asked himself. Was this love? Or had the latent killer in him finally come out for good?

Finally he could see. He was abreast of the passenger door just twenty yards away. Poole was the one flashing the lights. He was standing on the driver's side, reaching inside, flashing the lights, hissing into the darkness.

Kirk's heart fell back a stroke. He had wanted the flasher to be Gail. He'd rather have seen Poole dead and Gail alive at the car. So. This selfishness was caring—this was love. It didn't seem worth a whole hell of a lot.

He stood up and strode directly to the car, his pistol at the ready in case Poole was being forced to flash the lights at gunpoint.

But he was not, and when Kirk spoke his name, Poole leaped a foot away from the car.

"You scared the shit out of me, fucker."

"What the hell are you doing, Ken? You could get yourself killed." Like Maggie, he thought.

"Maggie. She's gone. Gail too. When I got back here, they were both gone. I walked around. I called under my breath. I heard the shooting and started flicking the lights so they'd know to come in . . . you know, in case they was out there hiding in the dark."

Kirk shuddered, knowing the decision he must make, feeling the sickness in his stomach for the lost Gail.

"Poole, we have to go." So much for caring.

"Fuck you, Jack."

"Ken, it won't do us any good to stay here."

"I ain't leaving . . . why do you have that fuckin sick look? What ain't you tellin me, asshole? Where's Maggie?"

"Ken, there may be agents all around here by now . . . your lights have probably slowed them down for a second, but they'll be here. They want this. . . ." He patted his chest, where the package was outlined.

Kirk walked around the car to the driver's side.

"Let's go, Ken. I'll drive."

Poole went into a wrestler's crouch, low and balanced.

"The fuck you say. I'm gonna bend your fuckin ass if you try to move this car. I'm only goin when I find my wife and not until."

Kirk threw his hands out wide and moved to clap his hands on Poole's shoulders.

"Ken," he murmured, "Maggie . . . and Gail are . . ."

The word "dead" was unheard, flattened by a pistol shot.

Kirk was sprayed by Poole's blood and struck in the chest at the same time by Poole's punch.

Poole, still in his crouch, fell forward.

Kirk caught him and threw him into the front seat. In an instant he was behind the wheel and backing away.

A second slug hit the windshield.

Kirk floored the accelerator and tried to keep the bounding, bouncing car under control.

He hit the dirt road and threw the car into the forward gears. His chest ached from the rap he had taken in the sternum.

He checked Poole. It didn't look good. Sounded worse.

Poole gurgled in his blood.

Kirk saw him trying to sit up, clutching his face, trying to talk.

His wife's name kept trying to force its way through his blood. But the sound of the name and his gagging kept getting in the way.

And all Kirk could think of was the woman he loved—yes, he must finally face the fact he loved her—now that he loved her and could admit to it, she was dead too. She'd told him she loved him. He hadn't returned the words; hadn't been certain enough to lie. And now he'd never have the chance. Dead. Lying in the weeds somewhere. Like Maggie. Her throat cut and smiling up at the starry sky like those throats from out of the past. There were those throats from the jungle landing zone.

Now that he finally cared about somebody to the extent he could say the word love in the same breath as her name she was . . .

Ambushed.

Dead.

"Magg—ssss," hissed Poole.

Gail, whispered Kirk.

"A total fucking disaster."

Gerlach was beginning to repeat himself. He had rehashed the whole night's events time and again to his secretary.

Then, as if to confirm the inefficacy of his tantrum, Gerlach began to repeat his considerable repertoire of obscenities, not even bothering to order them differently for variety.

Gerlach stopped in front of a window. Outside, the first streaks of gray had begun to erase the blackness of night.

"It'll be light out west in a couple hours," he growled. "Edward, have we got anybody cleaning up that bloody mess? Disposing of the bodies and such?"

"Two men, sir."

"We have to assume the log is in Kirk's hands, don't we?"

"Yessir."

"Do we know for sure Kirk got away in a helicopter, son?"

"Yessir. And we know the chopper had long-range fuel tanks."

"Damn," Gerlach whispered. "I shoulda brought Kirk into The Corporation with me. I never thought that boy was stuffed with those kinds of balls. I could be grooming him in the very job you have. I could be preparing him to take . . ."

A sudden look of wariness crossed Gerlach's craggy face, made even more granitelike by the lack of sleep and excess of cigars and coffee.

"Edward, my boy, I want you to take care of a couple things for me."

"Yessir."

"First, get ahold of a certain Colonel Winton Handley in the Montana Air Guard—they're parked at the airport in Great Falls. Me and Whip go way back. Fighter jock."

"Yes."

"Do that in the next ten minutes or so, and don't take no shit off the duty officer—wake him up if you have to. Tell Whip I'm coming to meet him . . . probably blow his cover for good . . . but I gotta use him. Then I want you to fix it with one of our people down there at Fort Hood. I don't want that helicopter reported stolen or missing. Fix it up on a long-term flight plan or something. I don't want it found until it's a heap of molten metal and ashes."

"Anything else, sir?"

"Yeah. Get me some kinda travel connections to Montana . . . Billings, or something—I think planes go there."

"Yessir . . . and, sir, what about Barnaby? You want him to come back up here for a debrief?"

"Naw. I'll send a personal message. I'll have Barnaby meet me on toppa Judith Peak."

"Yes, sir."

"Judith Peak," muttered Gerlach—as much to himself as to Gates. He shook his heavy head. That Kirk could have come up with that research journal was next to miraculous. It alone was enough to damage The Corporation—at least enough to have it disappear from the face of the earth in its present form. At the very least, it would have to be reorganized and renamed if that book got out. True, one book coming from an officer with an apparently mediocre military career and no important connections wouldn't do the same damage as all twelve hitting in all the places Payne had set up. But it would be enough to cause panic from certain officials who never liked the idea of an extralegal corporation anyhow. Kirk couldn't kill with that research log . . . but he could inflict a wound.

But, thought Gerlach, if he somehow had found out about the Judith Peak complex . . . if he got to it, got inside, got the Larson woman out, found out what was there . . . he could inflict a killing blow to The Corporation.

Chances were good Kirk and Poole had stolen that helicopter and taken off for Mexico to hide out and recuperate. Odds were, they'd be reported AWOL and that would be the end of troubles. Maybe later . . . with international cooperation, even with connections into the world network of drugs and guns, he could send an assassin after them. . . .

But if by some incredible happenstance Kirk ever got hold of the name Judith Peak . . .

Gerlach couldn't take a chance. He'd have to send the best agent in The Corporation to the top of that mountain. He'd have to go himself.

He'd left it to others to dispense with one First Lieutenant Grayson Kirk and his crew before—in a remote, nameless Laotian landing zone, a space barely large enough to accommodate the silenced Huey blades. Kirk was a nobody then too. He was just a pilot, just a tiny particle of an important task force on a consequential mission—consequential if it succeeded, nonexistent if it failed—that had gone awry. The whole crew was to have been erased and the whole project forgotten. But Kirk had survived. It couldn't be left to chance that he would survive again. One flaky army major couldn't fuck up the whole domestic intelligence operation.

"It's a fucking national security disaster," he murmured.

"Sir?" said Gates.

Gerlach sighed heavily, tiredly.

"The way people been fucking this project up, I imagine if Kirk gets past old Whip, I'll have to settle with him myself.

"On toppa Judith Peak."

4

By the time daylight showed itself at Kirk's right shoulder, the Red River had slid past a hundred feet below. So, depending on their east-west drift, he had flown into Oklahoma on a line toward Montana.

He adjusted the headphones that kept trying to pinch through his skull. It seemed pointless to be monitoring radios, since he had no intention of answering any calls, and they would be landing only at uncontrolled airfields for fuel. Still, he had decided it might be useful to listen to the guard frequencies, the universal aviation emergency channels. Just in case somebody tried to contact them with threats or promises.

If he hadn't been so exhausted, he'd have flown on the very deck, his skids virtually—sometimes literally—brushing the treetops, or in this case, the tops of grasses and prairie shrubs. That had become the safest way to fly in Southeast Asia—at least those parts of SEA outside of South Vietnam. Anywhere near the skein of trails in Laos or the various strongholds in Cambodia, there were at least 12.7 millimeter guns and up. And the farther north you flew, the more likely it was to find surface-to-air missiles. Though nobody out of the conventional mainstream was told or would believe it, the NVA were using shoulder-fired SAMs every bit as sophisticated and deadly as the American Redeye missile. So, to avoid radar detection and lock-on from the SAMs and tracking by the shoulder-fired missiles, it was on the deck. Down there, the sound of an approaching helicopter deceived the ground observer. It seemed to come from every direction. So the enemy had only one incautious recourse, to point their small-arms weapons into the sky and shoot randomly until the black shadow buzzed their heads.

Kirk shook his head. He was getting punchy. This was not Vietnam or any other Asian country. He would not be under attack from the ground. It would have been best to fly even lower to avoid FAA radar. But too low would only endanger him and Poole. Too low would mean risking flying into the virtually invisible wires on utility poles and high-tension towers.

So he had to stay at a hundred feet or higher—low enough to read the biggest road signs and the water towers of towns. Water towers. He smiled tiredly to himself. The greatest aid to visual navigation ever devised for use by army pilots was none other than the ubiquitous water tower: Shelby—Home of the Fighting Coyotes—Go Coyotes.

Kirk shook his head again and tried to look at the map vibrating on the radio console. It was a bound road atlas of the United States. Poole had taken it from his car at the last minute and had thrown it into his flight bag. Kirk smiled and looked back into the cargo area, where Poole lay sprawled, still clutching a towel to his face.

He smiled because Poole was proving to be a valuable ally. He'd not been injured all that seriously. At least his wound wasn't life-threatening. Painful, yes. The slug had passed through his right cheek ahead of the jawbone. It had taken the caps off two molars, sliced a groove diagonally in the tongue from right rear to left front, nicked the left upper canine, and torn a piece from the upper lip.

But most of the slug had exited Poole's open, cursing mouth. Flying fragments of teeth had put a dozen jagged cuts inside the lips.

Poole had finally stopped trying to talk, stopped insisting on saying Maggie's name.

Kirk wouldn't—couldn't—tell him about the slashed throat he'd seen in the weeds. Poole seemed to sense the word dead had been spoken, but he didn't ask again. He had almost cried, but didn't. He'd filled up with rage at what had been happening to him and his wife since running into Kirk. He readily adopted Kirk's sense of vengeance as his own and seemed ready to kill. To Kirk it seemed all he would have to do was point at somebody and give the order to kill. And Poole would do it.

So it was nothing to him when Kirk had asked first if he had access to helicopter keys—then if he'd help steal one.

Poole, his eyes glittering with emotion, had grunted twice. It was as if his greatest disability in this experience was the inability to swear through his wounded mouth.

"How about one with auxiliary fuel tanks?" Kirk had asked hopefully.

Poole had grunted his assent. He wrote a quick note: "The battalion commander's bird has internal aux tanks."

Kirk wondered aloud how they might get into the headquarters to get the keys.

Poole had launched into a tirade, cursing unintelligibly through the hanky stuffed in his mouth. He pulled a ring of keys from the leg of his flight suit. Then he wrote another note: "I'm the ops officer, fucker."

The last word was underlined heavily four times.

Kirk looked into the defiant eyes.

They were sad eyes as well.

Poole was on the verge of tears for what he knew must

have happened to his wife, for not having the courage to hear the answer to the unasked question.

Kirk thought, this was not bravado. This was bravery. This was caring—loving, really.

Now, as he flew, putting the last glint of the sun off the Red River behind him, he felt a welling of tears in his own eyes. And he knew it was for Gail.

Then he felt a hand on his shoulder.

Poole thrust a note into his shirt pocket and climbed over the console into the copilot's seat and put on another headset—a helmet could not be pulled over the wound.

The note read: "I'll fly. You rest. Heading???"

Kirk pointed at the radio compass.

"Three-three-oh," he shouted over the noise of the helicopter.

He climbed into the rear.

There lay the package wrapped in plastic film and tape.

He tore it open to start reading. But the fatigue overcame him before he'd gotten through the first page. And he couldn't get Connie Gail out of his head. So he fell into a troubled sleep on the vibrating massager of the cargo floor, his last waking thought a memory of that long, transporting hug he'd shared with Gail in the car outside Killeen.

Uncharacteristically, Gerlach was laughing. And not lightly. He practically gagged into the phone, trying to catch his breath.

From the receiver came answering laughter.

Finally, after a long period of ragged breathing from both ends of the conversation, Gerlach spoke.

"It's not that funny," he said. "Kirk got away."

The tone from the other end was a reassuring one.

"You're right," Gerlach said. "He's bound to find his

way to the toppa that mountain. We'll wait for him there. But he won't bring that log with him. We'll have to get it after we take him. . . . This means we'll have to take him alive . . . damn."

Suddenly, both voices were serious.

"Barnaby," Gerlach said, "are you sure you shot Poole?"

The offended voice affirmed it.

"And Poole's wife?"

The tone raised a point of order.

"Okay, cut her, then. And Lieutenant Colonel Connie Gail? You had to finish her off too?"

Barnaby affirmed it with a shrill laugh.

"Cut her or shoot her?" asked Gerlach with a giggle.

Another laugh answered him.

And Gerlach choked on his own laughter again.

To PJ, day and night had no meaning. For the light recessed into the ceiling burned continually, casting it's own naked yellow glow onto her naked, scarred body.

She'd stopped floating in what she now knew was chemically induced ecstasy. In its place came the dreary depression of a chemical hangover.

She had tried to stand on her bed to pull on the light grating. She thought she might stick a wetted finger into the light socket and finish herself that way—or maybe some glass from the light bulb would stand up to the soft flesh on her neck.

Against her will, her strength had come back. Her wounds had started healing, even itching at the edges. And she felt strong enough to explore her tiny cell. Her bed was a piece of plywood bolted to a wood frame, her mattress an uncovered piece of foam rubber. She had no blanket or sheet that might be torn and woven into a rope for hanging. There was no mirror over the sink basin. Nothing from the plumbing could be used as a weapon of death or self-destruction.

It was beginning to bother her that she was so preoccupied with suicide. It bothered her so much so that she realized she had practically climbed out of the depths necessary for a suicidal depression. If somebody had marched in with a tray of knives, guns, and pills, she'd probably not have the passion to kill herself anyhow.

So she was a failure again.

She'd failed Mark.

Again.

She hadn't been strong enough to keep him out of the mountains he loved. Otherwise they might not have been trapped like mice in a giant outdoor cage.

She hadn't had the decency to die in the lake when she went under. And she hadn't had the courage to sacrifice herself when she knew he must be dead.

If Poole and Beard had done anything with the packages they received, there might have been some action by now, some change in the routine at her prison.

Ditto with her letter to Grayson Kirk, care of Noble Lee.

Finally, she'd heard herself talking under the influence of those drugs. She'd told the names of the people she'd sent the logs to. That made her more than a failure. For failure indicated merely an inability to succeed. Her failure more likely meant an active wave of destruction. By sending those logs and letters to those people—people like Lee and Kirk, whom she didn't even know—she probably had condemned them to die.

More than a failure, she was a nuisance killer, a kind of mail-order Typhoid Mary.

She lay on her foam pad and began to cry.

This was better.

Maybe she could get low enough to make another run at suicide.

Between sobs, she heard the metal sliding in its channels. The access door was being opened. She was being watched through a one-way glass. She lay with her back toward the door, feeling ashamed. She folded up into a fetal position. At first, the stale animal odor reached her. But then a warm, salty scent overpowered that one. Food.

Why were they feeding her anyhow? She had yielded up everything she had of material value. She'd given up her husband and all copies of information that could have been damaging to them. And she'd lost her clothes, her strength, her will to live—at least temporarily—certainly she'd lost any reason to want to live.

Why didn't they just let her die?

After they'd used their drugs to get the information they wanted—and even though she wanted to lie, she could not, literally did not, have the power to, but simply told the naked truth to every question—why in hell didn't they just give her an overdose of something and let it peacefully be over? Or why couldn't they have given her the means to do it to herself? She would have earlier.

She decided she wouldn't eat today either. She could fast. Starve herself. But the scent of food stimulated contradictory commands from her body. So she sat up and looked at the tray, thinking perhaps that she could start her hunger strike tomorrow.

But what she saw made her want to eat.

It was kindness and it was cruelty.

Although such a tiny gesture, it was a dramatic shift in her expectations, it overcame her emotionally.

She clamped down on her facial muscles to avoid giving away her relief, her delight, her first joy in days and days.

Something *had* changed after all.

Try as she might, she could not keep back the tears. They flowed involuntarily.

And she wanted to thank somebody—some unseen somebody who had given her back this the slightest shred of her former existence. They had given her back her underpants, her sweatshirt—with the bullet holes darned crudely—and they had given back her jeans and tennis shoes.

She took the clothes before the food.

She hugged them to her body, ignoring the hurt where she rubbed her wounds.

There was no bra—that too easily might have been used as a noose. And the sleeves had been cut off the shirt, perhaps for the same reason. But her jeans were intact. And once she put the clothes on, her sense of decency was restored as well.

She lay on her bed and cried with relief and joy and disappointment, a jumble of emotions.

Something had changed. However remote, there was hope some action might be taken to save her. She realized she wanted to live, and probably did so even when she was so preoccupied with dying. And now that she was sure she wanted to live, it made her life all the more vulnerable. It once again gave them something to take away.

When she had composed herself, she drank her soup greedily and wiped the last trace of flavor from the bowl with a piece of bread.

When it was all gone, even the crumbs on the tray, she realized she wanted more, needed more. She needed her strength. She needed to build up her drained reserves of hatred.

Whoever these people were, they were deserving of her loathing. She wanted to oblige in person if she were ever given the chance. She wanted to live now. To see. To hate. Perhaps even to kill.

She lay back on the foam to sleep, to regain some of her lost strength. Her wounds were itching painfully. She took that as a sign she was on the mend. She hated her body for that resilience. Why wouldn't it just die, dammit?

It had been nearly twelve hours since their takeoff from Gray Field.

Twelve hours since the guard had approached Poole, who had a towel wrapped around the lower part of his face and a hanky stuffed in his mouth to stanch the insistent bleeding.

Twelve hours since Poole, looking like some poor imitation of a Lawrence of Arabia, had turned his charm on the guard, shouting indistinguishable but unmistakable obscenities. The guard had backed off; had unshouldered his shotgun.

Kirk had stepped up behind him, murmuring softly twelve hours ago, placing the cold steel of Pearson's pistol against the kid's neck, just below the corner of the jaw, the sweet, sensitive spot where humans want to be nuzzled by human lips, not by the muzzles of guns.

So the kid had cautiously handed over the shotgun and allowed his own crinkled hanky to be stuffed into his mouth, allowed his mouth to be taped shut with the green tape, so-called hundred-mile-an-hour tape, its stubborn black adhesive able to repair many a helicopter ill and even withstand the airstream at a bird's top airspeed.

Just twelve hours ago, when Kirk left the guard hugging a telephone pole behind a hangar, his wrists taped together with the same green-and-black tape.

Still there had been not a single problem, except for a minor but persistent hydraulic leak.

Around mid-morning he'd been awakened by the chopping of a Huey in descent. By the time he'd gotten his bearings, Poole had them on the ground at some airfield.

During cool-down time, Kirk read the note that said they had just landed at some forlorn place in Kansas. He walked across the tarmac with a government credit card in his hand and the lump of a pistol in his belt. Surely they would be a hot item by now—even in Kansas.

Poole kept the Huey at flight idle, in case they needed a quick getaway. They had about an hour of fuel left. Enough to get them some time to land elsewhere and escape on foot. Escape to where, he did not know.

But there had been no problem there either. So they shut down to refuel.

The Huey took the full 300 gallons in the internal aux tanks and 119 more in the normal tanks.

Kirk performed a walkaround inspection of the Huey, peering into access panels, checking fluids, searching for leaks. He found a puddle of watery pink hydraulic fluid on the engine deck. Nothing serious, but he made a mental note to keep an eye on the hydraulics. He told Poole they'd have to make more frequent stops between refueling—to check on the helicopter's condition. More so than with any other machinery, the life of rotorcraft is a continuous cycle of major and minor malfunctions, corrected by constant repair cycles. Once the preventive maintenance functions cease, the malfunctions mount rapidly. Kirk ordered hydraulic fluid from the fuel truck attendant. He didn't know the capacity of the system, but the refill took two quarts. Kirk directed the attendant to toss a case of quarts into the cabin in case they needed it later.

After takeoff, Kirk wondered aloud about the hydraulic leak.

Poole listened briefly to Kirk's rambling on about their need for more frequent maintenance stops. Then he waved a hand in Kirk's face to silence him. Poole insisted in sign language that he would be flying again on the next leg of the trip. He said in an angrily scrawled message that he felt a fever coming on. By mid-afternoon he'd be too sick to fly. So he'd better do it now.

And by mid-afternoon he'd been proven right.

They had flown across the desolation of western Kansas and eastern Colorado, matched only by the humdrum of Wyoming's vistas. In the distance was always the black-and-blue line of the mountains, but below was blowing dust and sage-dotted brown scenery, slashed occasionally by sun-bleached gray highways.

But Kirk had missed most of that. He'd been reading. He'd been cover to cover through the research logs and the typed and handwritten marginal explanations of Mark and PJ Payne.

And now he understood everything.

At least he understood how damaging the material could be, not so much the monstrous scribblings of the researcher, Warren Howell, but those of the agent who had turned on The Corporation, the revelations of domestic surveillance, the breaking of laws at every turn from inside the CIA or Pentagon or both, probably with at least the knowledge and tacit consent of somebody in the administration—several administrations, for that matter. Every one since Eisenhower's, in fact.

Kirk understood that Beard's beast may have been the last remnant of a genetic accident created by Payne's brother-in-law. Possibly the beast he'd seen at Fort Harrison had been another one. Or it had something to do with the Michigan group, which he'd divined was the group of basic trainees bound for OCS. It was Payne's group and it was Bertrand's. It was the group with the foil stars. They had been exposed to drug experiments, which had made them first become ill, then, over the years, made them vanish. How these things were related, he didn't know. Maybe later he could find out.

Maybe atop this place called Judith Peak.

They had refueled again in central Wyoming, although Kirk had calculated they could make it all the way to Montana and have a small reserve. But he wanted a large reserve. He wanted more than just to get there. He wanted to get up to Judith Peak and get back down and out of the state—far out. And he'd needed to check that hydraulic leak again. This time the refill required nearly three quarts. Kirk began to worry about what a sudden demand on those hydraulics might do. Would it blow a line or a seal? Would they have to call off everything because of a lousy hydraulics failure? He refused to think about it.

At the Wyoming fuel stop, Kirk also found an airfield hand who agreed to mail the package for the change in a $20 bill and another one to boot. It was too valuable to be carrying around like some dime novel. He brought sandwiches, coffee, and soup from a machine, though the best Poole could do was let some water and blow-cooled broth flow down his throat.

Kirk looked into his eyes.

They were reddened by a network of veins. And they were wild. Poole was nearly done.

Kirk offered to leave him to seek medical care.

Poole's eyes said his obscenities for him.

Kirk thought about diverting and dropping off his co-pilot, who had given him this chance by giving him the helicopter, a few hours of revitalizing sleep, and the opportunity to read the research log and gain some understanding of the shadow government that was causing this insanity.

But he could not divert.

As it was, he was getting more nervous.

His road atlas told him they were less than two hours from the Montana state line. He had made two fuel stops. All anybody had to do was take a map of the United States and draw a line between Killeen, Texas, and either fuel stop—not even both were needed. And they would know Kirk's destination.

Clearly, they could know he was coming if they wanted to. Up till now he had been so predictable. He *had* to assume they knew.

And he had to think.

Thinking like Beard had led him to the research log hidden in the lair of that beast.

Now he had to extrapolate from what he'd learned from that package he'd mailed to himself, general delivery, in Billings. He had to begin thinking like macrocriminals, those human animals that had been behind the freak animals. Those men who placed themselves above the government by creating agencies not subject to ordinary constitutional scrutiny.

He looked over the wing of the Huey's armored seat. Poole lay in back tossing feverishly. He was through as a helpful ally in this excursion. The least he could do was drop him off where he could get some aid.

But no. That would never do. He mustn't think like a humanitarian. He must think like a shrewd, ruthless killer. Pearson had told him to be careful. To be ruthless.

Suddenly he jerked the cyclic of the helicopter to the left. A cold chill had swept his body—and not merely because of the careless movement's effects on the leaky hydraulics system, although he wished he hadn't been so reckless. What really shook him was the realization that had dawned on him in the last instant.

This was no accident that he hadn't been impeded on his flight to Judith Peak.

They were letting him come. They were expecting a helicopter on a beeline from Texas to Montana.

They were expecting that the pilot of the helicopter would be stupid enough to fly straight to the designated mountain, maybe even try to land on top.

And they were right. The stupid little pilot had flown his stupid little helicopter like a stupid little bee—straight and predictably.

And when this little bee got to a remote enough spot on the planet, say a couple hundred feet above north-central Wyoming, they would swat him from the sky with their little bee-swatter.

Kirk flew straight westward. From checking the atlas, he knew he was north of I-90. He'd been following the Powder River, funneling himself between two north-south ridges. Soon he would have exposed himself to the wide-open spaces of southern Montana.

If only he had come to his senses in time.

He began to think he had it made when he had flown far enough west of Sheridan to cross Granite Pass at nearly 9,000 feet. He was off the direct route now. He'd done something unpredictable. Not much. But at least he'd put a bend in the beeline.

Half an hour later he crossed into Montana.

He was now flying among the trees, the skids and fuselage sliding between the sharp points of pines, and firs.

There would be little chance of his being shot down now. Nobody could get enough of a bead with a normal gun or even a shoulder-fired heat-seeker like the Redeye or Stinger.

He mused about the geographical fact that the Custer Battlefield National Monument was less than an hour's flight from here. He wondered if he'd make it as far as Custer had.

And from now on, his route would be unpredictable, circuitous. They might know his destination. But they'd never figure his arrival time or his route. Maybe that uncertainty would give him an edge Custer never had. And maybe the hydraulics would hold out long enough.

He flew through the Bighorn Canyon National Recreational Area, skirting the edge of Yellowtail Reservoir, until he found a meadow, a natural one, not connected to the rest of the world by logging roads.

He landed on the western edge of the clearing, where the lengthening shadows of evening would find him first.

He shut the Huey down and vowed to get some rest for what lay ahead and to let some time pass, to put them a little off a predictable timetable.

Poole took a little water.

Kirk made a watery aspirin paste from tablets in the first-aid kit and forced him to choke that down too.

Then he climbed up on the roof of the Huey to conduct a thorough inspection. Actually, he didn't want to do that. He didn't want to find anything wrong that he couldn't repair with his almost total vacuum of maintenance knowledge. The main rotor head was coated with grease and oil, though nothing looked excessive. If the crew chief of this bird knew how little attention had been paid to his helicopter over this grueling flight, he might have cried, Kirk thought. Or he'd have killed a couple of pilots.

The rest of the preflight revealed no new problems.

Except that two more quarts of hydraulic fluid had been lost in the relatively short flight from Wyoming. Kirk filled the reservoir and sighed. Then he overfilled it. He'd decided to stretch this flight every possible second. He'd reasoned it might be the helicopter's last.

Oddly enough, he suddenly felt the stabbing of hunger pains. He rummaged through the remnants of candy wrappers from the Wyoming stop and found what he knew was there . . . nothing. Probably just as well, he thought. After all, Poole wouldn't be able to eat. He looked over the prone, deep-breathing body of his co-thief, copilot. Poole wouldn't expect him to starve, would he? Of course not.

Almost desperately, he started ransacking the Huey. Surely the crew chief would have a stash of some kind. And sure enough, he did. Underneath a pair of phosphorus signal flares, Kirk found a half-pint of Wild Turkey and a drawstring bag full of bubble gum. The gum chunks resisted chewing like golf balls, but he kept after it until he softened them and sucked the sugar from them. The whiskey burned but mixed pleasantly with the syrup he'd extracted from the gum.

The scents were too much for Poole to sleep through. He sat up and directed his scowl at Kirk, who proffered the bag of gum. Poole responded with a flip of his middle finger. He took the bottle in one hand and covered the hole in his face with the other. He kissed the bottle deeply, and half the amber fluid disappeared. Poole grimaced and lay back. Immediately, he was asleep or unconscious again.

When he'd drained the last of the burning whiskey and his jaws could no longer take the rocky gum chunks, Kirk climbed back up to the helicopter's roof. He lay down and thought about praying . . . drinking . . . killing.

Luckily the breeze had stilled, for the air was chilly. At this altitude and this time of year, air seemed thinner, less able to sustain mists or dusts or any occlusions to the visions the mountains spawned. The peaks wore their first dustings of snow, and high winds up there formed white plumes of blowing crystals against a sky so blue, it defied reality.

The mountains and weather of Montana defied Kirk's credulity as well. The grasses in this meadow were lush, thigh-high, and the trees sprouted upward, sentinels forming a wall against the outside world's scrutiny. The helicopter, and indeed men, did not belong in this pristine setting. Especially out of place were men in possession of such knowledge and missions as Kirk had.

The wind hushed through the brushes of pine and fir. The sound, indistinguishable from that of a distant waterfall, became both chilling and mysterious. Light shone so pure, it exposed every blemish on man and earth. It was a white light, not at all filtered through the blue of sky. And Kirk could see every fault in the earth exposed to the sun by mountains that had somehow been uplifted by mighty forces below the surface. Climbing up the lower slopes of the mountains were fields of brilliant yellow. Aspens. Although Kirk could detect no breezes, the leaves fluttered, flickering their brilliant colors like millions of postage-stamp flash cards.

Kirk realized he did not have to pray. This vision of the earth was itself a prayer, and he felt a part of it.

The pure sun spilled its narcotic, warming effect on his face and clothing, making him drowsy. And he fell asleep.

To dream.

Of flying.

Down Death Valley.

Again.

* * *

The chill brought him awake. Indeed, he shuddered because the sun was no longer soaking him with its tranquilizing rays. The shushing conifers had now begun to filter the light as well as the air, and dappled shadows lay across his belly.

The helicopter rocked now and then when Poole shifted his weight in the cabin or if a breeze caught the untied rotor and made it teeter-totter against the rotor hub-stops.

He opened his eyes.

If anything, the sky's blue had deepened. The only signs of civilization—if that's what he was part of—were the rotor assembly above him and the contrails streaking across the otherwise perfect blue.

He had slept. He had dreamt. He had awakened.

Things were as he had left them.

His dreams were not nightmares. Reality was the nightmare.

Nothing had changed. He would be forced to some kind of action. He still had no idea for a workable plan.

He did have a few more regrets.

First, about that package left in the hands of a Wyoming fuel-truck driver. Kirk wished he had kept the log. Second, he wished he had pointed the helicopter toward California or Mexico—anyplace but the remote regions of the country. And he wished he could be ruthless enough to run away and leave PJ to her fate on Judith Peak. For chrissake, she might not even be there. All he had to go on was the word of a white-collar criminal perfectly capable of using his last breaths to lie.

Was all this worth it?

Should he care?

He thought about the Lees and Jud McClean.

He thought about Gail and concluded he probably did love her.

He owed them something.

At least he should care that much.

And Poole. What about his Maggie, by now decomposing like some road-killed varmint in the Texas sun? He owed him a shot at revenge.

He shuddered yet again. The chill of the mountain air would not let him lie with his idle thoughts any longer.

He climbed down stiffly.

Poole slid open a cabin door and slid out into the last of the sun.

Kirk glanced at him and would have averted his eyes, but he forced himself to be kind. Poole looked awful. His face was swollen fatter than if he had a double-sized chaw of tobacco on one side. Inside, the mouth could not have been much better, because his tongue seemed to be pushing out between his lips, so much was it puffed up. Watery fluids had streaked down his chin as he slept. And the streaks had dried yellow.

Poole urinated; turned to Kirk; saw his sympathetic gaze.

What he muttered was a muffled obscenity, part of which leaked out in a puff of air from the hole in the side of his face. He tried to guzzle some water, and part of that ran out the side of his face too. He held a finger over the hole in his cheek and drank again. When he was done, he had the semblance of a smartass smile for Kirk. And Kirk recognized the very smile he'd been seeing in the mirror all these years since his own crash.

They completed a preflight, Kirk studious, Poole distracted by his pain. But at least the delirium of fever seemed to have passed for the moment.

Before they climbed into the cockpit, Kirk said, "You

want me to drop you off at some civilized place so you can see a doctor?"

The answer was a shake of the head.

Poole started to step up on the toe of the skid.

Kirk touched his shoulder. "Ken. This is serious shit. We might be killed before we can get even with the bastards."

Poole pulled a pencil from the sleeve pocket and scribbled a note on a page of his small spiral pad.

Kirk waited until he saw the question mark swirled onto the end of the sentence.

Three words.

Is Maggie dead?

"I'm sorry, Ken. Yes. I saw her."

Poole sniffed and climbed into the cockpit.

Kirk looked to the sky for forgiveness. He asked to be absolved from guilt for getting all these people killed.

Poole mechanically went through the checklist sequence, depressed the starter trigger, and the turbine began to tick, then whine.

The blades began to catch as the whine grew to the roar of a fiery blast furnace.

Kirk studied the atlas. Flying direct, they might arrive in the area of his destination in an hour. He had found the Judith River and a town called Judith Gap. He was guessing there'd be a mountain in the vicinity of those two. A mountain called Judith Peak.

"After this I saw in the night visions, and behold, a fourth beast, dreadful and terrible, and strong exceedingly; and it had great iron teeth; it devoured and broke in pieces, and stamped the residue with the feet of it: and it was diverse from all the beasts that were before it."

—The Book of Daniel, 7:7

BOOK III

INTO THE DEN OF BEASTS

1

The albino beast had asserted itself the only way it knew how. Violently.

Once the drugs wore off, it struggled to sit up. For a while it couldn't balance well enough to do that. So it clawed its way across the floor and pulled itself up on the bars of the inner-cell door. It huddled there, regaining its senses.

The bolder pair of beasts approached and prodded the albino again, as if testing the newcomer. The albino clutched the bars and tugged at the shreds of netting that still entwined parts of his limbs. The pair became bolder yet and began slashing at the netting carelessly, catching and pulling off tufts of bleeding white hide as well.

In half an hour the brown beasts tired of toying with the odd white one. They turned toward the darker recesses of the cell, the little caves of dimness where two other pairs of beast eyes watched.

The albino struck the instant their backs turned. He lunged, clubbing one beast at the back of the head, sending it sprawling, whimpering, wailing on the concrete. But the other, the biggest of the pair, the albino seized by the head. His jaws closed on the back of the neck as his claws tore into the thick fur beneath the muzzle.

The brown beast barely struggled.

Its vertebrae crackled, and the animal went limp.

The albino ripped away the front of the neck.

Suddenly the walls and floor turned crimson.

The albino dropped its kill and shrieked in triumph. The other beasts cringed deeper into their caves of darkness.

And the albino began to feast on the carcass of his victim, growling a warning even as he gobbled his cell mate.

The sound of a sliding door at the rear of the cell broke the spell of wet eating-noises. The three darker beasts sidled toward an opening in the wall. Down a chute slid the carcass of a dead steer. The trio tore at their own meal immediately, but nervously, their six eyes flashing intermittently out of the darkness toward the albino.

When the albino had eaten its fill from the viscera of its enemy, he growled a warning at the others and took over the steer. They gave way, instantly surrendering dominance to the more powerful, more aggressive of their number, each one fearful it might become the next meal.

Kirk had decided on a long way around to his destination. He decided to at least double the flight time to two hours or even three, flying east from the Bighorn Canyon, crossing the Custer Battlefield low level, moving across to the Rosebud Creek, heading north to bypass Judith Peak and then to circle toward the west and fly in from that direction. He didn't suppose there were many ways to sneak up on a mountaintop, but then again, what was the point of taking that beeline? As soon as he was airborne, he wished they'd departed earlier. It would darken early at this latitude and especially in the mountains. It would be night when they arrived in the area around Lewistown.

Poole was at the controls as Kirk began drawing his pencil line on the atlas page of Montana. The Huey approached the Custer Battlefield, following its own shadow cast ahead of them by the setting sun. Kirk marveled at how insignificant a spot the battlefield seemed topographically, for all its effect in history and legend. A low, brown ridge ran alongside a river barely larger than a creek—that's all.

The fading sunlight caught the white markers on the slopes, the spots where soldiers had fallen and were once buried, then exhumed. The markers were strung out, leading toward a darker area below the crest of the ridge, the spot where the monument had been placed, the spot where Custer had made his terminal mark.

Poole's flight path would pass directly over the monument and burial site two miles away.

Kirk didn't want to overfly the park buildings near there, didn't want an outraged park ranger reporting a rogue helicopter in violation of the sanctity of a national monument to FAA officials. Not now. Even if The Corporation knew Kirk's intentions, he didn't want his timetable confirmed.

So he gently took the controls and, mindful of the hydraulics, changed course toward a spot farther south on the ridge where the hills dropped away to a creek.

As the Huey's shadow dodged right, the grassland to the left front erupted in a massive explosion, just missing the shadow.

The startled Kirk, now totally mindless of the hydraulics, jerked the cyclic right again. Again the earth to the east blew up again, this time in hundreds of smaller explosions.

He swung back toward the left. Would it happen again?
Yes.
Again.
The shadow dodged yet another set of explosions.

Poole was trying to look behind. Even as he jerked his face left, the wound in his swollen cheek began bleeding again.

Kirk didn't need to look. Incredible as it seemed, the eruptions could only have come from one thing.

He saw the swooping shadow, the silhouette, the glint off the canopy, the blackness of the camouflaged fighter as it swept by less than five hundred feet above, leaving them in a buffeting, roaring vortex of noise.

"Holy shit," marveled Kirk. "They've launched the goddamned air force?" The Corporation had *this* much naked power?

Poole, who would have been swearing even worse if his face had permitted, gave him a half frightened, half sarcastic look that said: What does it look like, dummy?

Something in the distant reaches of his training came back to him. "Ken," he ordered, "punch the clock."

Whip Handley hacked his own clock as he shot by the spot where the darting helicopter should have been splattered on the ground. Instead it had flown beneath his field of view seconds ago. The grizzled Guard colonel pulled harder to get into a climbing arc to reacquire.

He made a mental note of the dust he raised with his ordnance. The helicopter would be flying at 120 knots. In the minute or two before his next run, it would move two to four miles from the spot.

He cursed himself for not believing Gerlach. He should have taken this damned army pilot more seriously. Till now it had been too damned easy. He bumped his alert pilots and took the armed F-4E Phantom alone from the hot spot. Easy enough, although he'd probably be catching hell when the old man found out. And he'd acquired the helicopter easily enough too. Flying low level down the Bighorn Valley, his air-to-air radar picked up the Huey as it crossed the ridge toward the Little Bighorn. From then it'd only taken a minute to line up his run of three miles with only a slight descent.

He checked his airspeed. Four hundred twenty-five knots. Climbing through 4,000 feet indicated, about 3,000 above the terrain here.

Should have used the Gatling gun first, Handley told himself. Dammit, should have used the gun—even the AIM-9's, the heat-seekers, would have done it. But no, he'd wanted to use radar. Real air-to-air demanded the whole electronics works.

He'd acquired the Huey from behind. Radar lock-on was solid at four miles. At three and a half, it became intermittent. Ground clutter, radar returns from the irregular features of the earth around here. A backseat could have screened that out, but he'd decided against eyewitnesses . . . actually Gerlach had demanded he fly solo for this job.

Lock-on came again at two miles. He'd fired the Sparrow instinctively, waiting till the last moment to see if he'd need to throw the throttle arm-switch to "GUNS." He lost lock-on almost at the instant the AIM-7 Sparrow missile launched. It went ballistic immediately—even at that, it might have come awfully close had the pilot not jinked right.

Gerlach hadn't been bullshitting. The army guy was pretty good. He jinked twice more to evade the gun's firing pattern. Then Handley's Phantom had closed to less than 1,000 feet, too close for firing any kind of ordnance effectively.

Did that guy have eyes in the back of his head? Or did he have a radar receiver of his own? No, Gerlach had told him that only a few Hueys had such electronic arrays as

Radar Air Warning. It had to have been pure, damned luck.

Shit, not time enough for that kind of concern, he told himself as he calculated another problem.

The F-4 carried a basic load of fifteen hundred rounds of twenty mike-mike HE for the Gatling gun. Six hundred rounds a second, rate of fire. Three seconds total available, and he'd used half or more. The Sparrows would be useless. He'd use the remainder of high-explosive ammo on this pass. Then it'd be gone, but so would the Huey. The bastard couldn't have had extra eyes, right?

Right, he told himself.

He swept upside down at 6,000 feet indicated, picking up the landmark of the Custer Museum and the national cemetery, then the dust. He checked the clock. One minute elapsed. He wanted to be quick about this. The sun was getting low. Not much useful time left on station. He rolled back, sweeping his eyes across the brown earth for the twin black dots of the Huey and its shadow.

Kirk guessed he'd have little time before the jet returned. As his clock's sweep-second hand scratched by at the minute mark, he started getting antsy. How long was it before a fast-mover could reacquire again? He searched his brain for a little recall of the anti-MiG training he'd gotten before flying over the borders of South Vietnam. The most memorable maneuver he could remember was the one Jud McClean had given him after he heard about Kirk's plan of action for the crew to take in case of attack by fast-movers. Jud had said, "Forget that shit. In case of MiGs, best thing for you to do is drop the collective, shove the cyclic out the front of the cockpit, bend over, put your head between your legs, and kiss your ass good-bye."

Kiss your ass good-bye.

The harder he searched for a practical response to this fighter, the more insistent became Jud's advice. He couldn't think of anything else.

Kiss your ass good-bye.

The best he could do was break into a harsh laugh.

Poole, daubing a sleeve at his cheek, looked wildly at his flying mate. But Poole could understand idiocy. He smiled, loosing a fresh rivulet of blood. A little cry of maniacal laughter ushered from his throat into the intercom, and air bubbled out of his cheek wound.

Kirk looked away, suddenly made serious by the sight of his friend. Terrain mask. Go for the shadows. The words were coming back. Jink. Never do the predictable.

All the time, of course, Kirk had been shoving the cyclic over, tipping the rotor plane as deeply as it would go so the blades would bite into the air more greedily and pull the craft along faster, predictably running for the cover of the river and the bluff.

At about 128 knots, Kirk found VNE, the top speed possible with this helicopter. The nose kept trying to pitch up, to warn him he could get no more from this craft. He backed off to 125, which was still more than most UH-1Hs had ever given him. This was a thorough-bred.

The Huey closed on the trees along the Little Bighorn River, and Kirk became even more nervous. Minute and a half.

The Huey crossed a railroad and highway, and still there were no more explosions. Maybe he'd make it.

Mentally, he had this picture of fighters on gun runs in Vietnam. By now, the jook behind him had long since reached the top of his orbit. By now he'd be rolling in with a long, deliberate, deadly accurate run.

Or he might have made a hurried, tight arc, ready to roll in and make short work of what he should have accomplished on the first pass.

Mask.

Jink.

Do something unpredictable.

Or kiss your ass good-bye.

Kirk guessed short run. If he was wrong, no harm. If he was right and didn't act in a hurry, he and Poole would be two more soldiers dead at the Little Bighorn.

He did something unpredictable.

He jinked.

He tossed the cyclic right and back to the stops.

The helicopter bucked, snapping in the air like a trout darting from the water.

He no longer was able to see the earth beneath his feet as the Huey swooped up and arced over on its side.

He dropped an eye to the rotor tachometer and saw the rpm building dangerously because the sudden maneuver forced the blades to speed up. He pulled power in with the collective in his left hand, and the rotor speed bled off to the caution area on the tach as the blades screwed into the air.

His eyes swept the skies, looking for the deadly fast-mover.

Handley had gone through his pre-attack checklist in seconds. Everything was set up as he began the final three-mile run. Airspeed, four-fifty. Dive angle, fifteen degrees. Switches armed. The pipper would fully cover the helicopter at a half mile. He throttled back to stabilize his aircraft. He wanted the option of two bursts if the first cannon fire missed.

The helicopter ran straightaway before him. Gerlach had been wrong after all. This guy was a dummy.

Handley's finger received a signal to fire from the colonel's brain. It obeyed.

"Fuck NO," the colonel shouted, trying to reverse the brain's command as the Huey suddenly bucked out of the pipper.

But the finger expended nearly all the twenty millimeter from the Gatling gun before it could release.

Handley's temper flared up and he aimed his craft for the Huey.

Everything was going wrong with this damned mission. The lousy army guy was beating the hell out of the shit-hot fighter jock. He'd already blasted the hell out of the peaceful countryside, attracting attention from somebody. He'd never get away with this one now. It wouldn't merely be written off or excused or forgotten. And a court-martial would be unacceptable. He'd blown his deep cover as a mere air force officer. He'd have to disappear into some other job in The Corporation . . . if he was lucky. Thank his stars Gerlach was his big buddy, he told himself.

The Huey slid out of sight beneath his instrument panel.

Handley half wished they'd collide.

It'd save a hell of a lot of explanations.

Kirk couldn't see the explosions of the gunfire, but he heard and felt them. He felt self-satisfied for a moment because he knew that the jet jock could only have made a short run because he'd had so little time to line up. And the moving target to the Huey would be nearly impossible to hit.

Of course, if the jock had used his heat-seeking missiles in the first place, the war would have been over while he and Poole were gawking long distance at the battlefield, Kirk knew.

As he came around, he expected to see the fighter going by.

But it hadn't been going fast enough for that.

It was practically head-on.

Kirk slammed the cyclic to the left and dumped his power just as the nose of the jet began to sparkle orange.

He saw the smoke trailing from the F-4's nose for a fraction of a second.

He expected the Huey to disintegrate.

But the jet jock hadn't been able to intercept the turning arc of the Huey, the right, climbing turn of a few seconds ago. Now Kirk had shoved left and bottomed the collective pitch. The Huey fell away like a flat rock being spun from a kid's fingers.

The jet passed over the Huey and very close. As it went by, Kirk recognized the horizontal stabilizers angling down characteristically. For the first time, he could positively identify it as an F-4 Phantom. He remembered they had been turned over to the Air National Guard—and he knew he must be up against one hell of a pilot with lots of combat experience.

But there was no time for a feeling of camaraderie, one combat veteran to another. The F-4 had powered up and kicked in its burners, twin torch flames shooting back at him explosively. He pulled collective and climbed, turning perpendicular to the Phantom's flight path. The Phantom had planted an invisible weapon in the turbulence it left behind. The disturbed air could swamp the

Huey like a dinghy in heavy seas. He had to clear of that invisible, boiling wake spiraling off both wingtips, growing into horizontal tornadoes.

In seconds he was beneath the danger on the deck, flying barely above the pasture grasses. He had to jerk the nose up each time he neared a barbed-wire fence line so the Huey could leap over each fence like a steeplechase mount.

Finally, when he was sure he was clear of the jet's wake turbulence, he pulled his mount to a halt.

Literally.

He jerked the cyclic back, raising the nose abruptly. Simultaneously, he dropped the collective so the Huey would not swoop up into the sky and he stepped down with right pedal to keep the nose straight as the torque between the transmission and the rotor head diminished.

He nursed enough power in to prevent an overspeed and wondered how many were left in the system before the rotor head disintegrated from the centrifugal forces he'd given it in just the last minutes.

The hydraulics. A vision of the engine deck painted in thin pink oil recurred, a reality he'd seen repeatedly in his preflight inspections. He erased the thought from his mind. No time for that. Right now the hydraulics weren't the immediate danger.

He worked the pedals, sweeping the nose right and left, looking to the west, following a streamer of black exhaust to the climbing tail of the F-4. The jock had started another long, arcing turn back. This was going to be his final deliberate run. No more hurry-up jobs. This time he intended to do the job right, to bury the helicopter pilot at the end of a flaming plume of black smoke. He'd be coming out of the west. Out of the half-set sun.

He looked over at Poole. Poole looked back, the fire

having returned to his eyes. Poole gave him a puffy grin and jerked off an imaginary penis in his right hand, the universal sign of delight for pilots everywhere.

Kirk looked for a tree line, looked for a place to hover, to hide the Huey in. Columns of dust rose up around the helicopter. The dust turned pink in the setting sun. It would give him away. Scratch that idea. A quarter mile away, the Phantom's exhaust trail had begun to touch down, lifting pink whirlwinds of dust and dry grass into the air as well.

Kirk knew he needed a brilliant idea in a hurry. Most likely, he'd be facing heat-seeking missiles on this run. Most likely, more than one. He needed a brainstorm.

"Take the controls," Kirk shouted into the intercom.

Handley could see the sun. All of it at his altitude—he checked . . . seven thousand indicated. But the elongated shadows on earth told him it had nearly set. In a while, the earth would be blacked out and there'd be no more chance of attacking the Huey. He'd expended the last of the 20 millimeter. No matter, this was it. This would be a longer, steeper run. He'd find the hot engine of the Huey and slave the missile's IR-seeking head to it. His missiles would find the target. End of mission.

No place to hide. No smoke or dust or shadow could defeat the infrared-seeking AIM-9 missile.

He lined up a twenty-degree attack angle.

Below, the dust rose out of the shadows beneath the bluff. He aimed the Phantom. His IR slaving system began sweeping.

He began his checklist.

Arming switches on—heat-seekers selected.

Arm lights on.

Master lights . . . check!

Step-ladder lights . . . check! Shoot lights . . . flashing!

The slaving system identified the Huey, sending an
electronic message to the pair of missiles hung below.
When one launched, it'd be on its own seeking system,
but the slaver would have identified a starting point.
Down the flight path, changing data would be relayed to
the missile's fins. Course changes would be automatic.
Persistent. Deadly.

At a mile his finger tightened on the trigger.

Handley felt the thump beneath the Phantom as the
missile was blown down.

He heard a whoosh as the rocket motor ignited.

A swirling trail of white smoke.

Tracking, tracking.

He hauled the nose up and cranked the Phantom over
so he could see out and pick up the effect of the missile on
the Huey as soon as possible.

Poole gave Kirk a wild, wide-eyed stare of incredulity
when he saw what the man had in his hands after rooting
around in the cabin and climbing back into the pilot seat.

Poole's lips formed an F-word.

"Flares," Kirk said into the intercom. "Signal flares."

That wasn't the word Poole kept forming, kept mouth-
ing at Kirk.

Kirk grinned, propped the flares between his thighs,
and took the controls. He shoved left pedal to spin the
craft around the mast. He looked to the ridge line. He
might make it. Or he might not. But he had to get there
before the jet could finish its run. At least with the ridge
behind the Huey, Kirk knew the jock would have to adjust his attack angle and pull out a little higher.

No point in making it too easy.

Kirk started a tacking run to the southeast. He crossed the highway and noticed several cars and pickups had stopped to watch the aerial demonstration. They probably thought it was a hell of a show. He wondered how they were going to feel if the jet jock let off a few bursts of gunfire a half mile short. Or if a missile went ballistic on their stupid asses.

There was the bluff. At the base of that was the river, slowly winding along. West of that was a tree line, then pasture. Then, west of that was the Phantom, now invisible, but no doubt arcing out of its turn somewhere and beginning to roll in.

Kirk hovered over a hayfield and searched the sky for the jet.

Nothing.

The jock had obviously put his Phantom's shadow on the helicopter because Kirk couldn't even see the F-4 for the fireball of the sun. All he could see was the trail of black exhaust leading into the top of the fireball as if the sun itself were on this attack run.

He began pulling collective, increasing the pitch angle of the rotors so they began to screw into the air, pulling it down, washing it outward, creating a dust storm fanned by the giant blower of the rotor. Then Kirk jerked the Huey into the air, turning the jet a profile, knowing the heat of the exhaust could give a missile a lock-on. He wondered for an instant if this guy flying could possibly have been the same guy who'd given him his Vietnam briefing. If so, this could mean the end of the dogfight, such as it was, the Doberman versus the Chihuahua. The Chihuahua was now offering its ass to the Doberman.

How long to wait? How many missiles? More twenty mike-mike?

He didn't know.

It felt like too long.

"Take it," he ordered Poole. He shoved his window down and held the flare out toward the sun, the cap with the firing pin against the door.

The rotor plane flickered through the fireball of the sun. Kirk reached inside and shoved the collective to the side, lifting the rotor disc, putting the Huey into a side-wise hover. With the other hand, he bashed the flare's base against his door and shot a fiery red cluster at the sun.

Then he grabbed the controls and took off perpendicular to the attack path. He flew directly over the river, the line of cottonwoods between him and the jet. And beyond the trees, a grass fire had already sprung up as the phosphorus bundles burned up red and hot. Then he could see the Phantom, then a white whip of smoke. He squinted, trying to pick up the rocket. Could not.

Kirk bottomed the collective.

The Huey fell below the tree line.

An explosion struck the ground in front of the trees. Now the jock would be pissed. He'd be cutting loose with his guns, which the cottonwoods could hardly hold back. So Kirk headed upstream, retracing his route to where he had started his maneuver. Unless the jet jock outguessed him, he'd be firing into the trees on a line where the Huey would be if it had not stopped.

Kirk yanked the Huey around and saw the fighter break off in a steep climbing turn south, then back toward the west.

The sun was now being completely swallowed by the hills in the west. Even if he made a hasty run, there might not be enough light for one more attempt. If he tried for a longer shot, Kirk could hide forever in the shadows.

He saw his grass fire had grown to a regular range

blaze, further reducing visibility. This little fight was about over. And the Chihuahua was about to win, about to kick the Doberman's ass.

Kirk searched the western sky for the Phantom but he could not find it.

It was not there—even in the sun it would have been visible by its exhaust tracks.

Kirk wouldn't allow himself to think for a second that the pilot had given up and gone home. Not while there was light enough for one more run—even if his guns were empty, he'd have tried to catch the Huey in the turbulence of a near pass.

He smashed his right pedal and flipped the Huey 180 degrees to check back to the north.

Nothing.

He spun again, checking the western sky for a black dot against the glowing red, continuing the dizzy spin to the south.

Nothing.

He looked at Poole.

Poole felt the urgency. He'd lost the Phantom too. Then Poole pointed east.

But that was impossible. The ridge was in the way of a run from the east. And the sun's sliver on the horizon— no pilot would . . .

Chrissakes, Kirk told himself—it would be fatal not to expect the unexpected.

Kirk yanked the Huey to the left, to the east.

Already, he felt he'd occupied his spot above the river for too long. No matter which direction the F-4 came from, he couldn't afford to be stuck at a twelve-foot hover over the goddamned river.

He started up a coulee that cut between the bluffs. In

spring there would have been a creek until the end of the snow meltoff.

He saw nothing to the east.

He felt a chill.

If that jet jock was indeed coming from the west, he was now trapped in the coulee—the same damned coulee where Custer had been routed more than a hundred years ago—unable to make his run above the river again.

Suddenly Poole was slapping his left forearm.

He looked.

Poole was pointing up through the greenhouse glass above his head.

He tossed his head up, bringing the nose of the Huey up as well.

And there was the exhaust trail. Black and seemingly vertical, although that could hardly have been possible.

"Take it," Kirk screamed. He dropped the controls almost before Poole had taken them. He fumbled with the other flare. He got it out the window and banged it on the side of the door. It would not fire. He banged it harder. The cap, the firing device slid off the butt end of the flare. Kirk grabbed for it. But it was gone.

The Huey started drifting crazily up the coulee toward the bluff.

Kirk tried to wrench the controls back from Poole.

Poole wouldn't let go.

They were fighting for the cyclic.

No.

They were *not* fighting the cyclic, after all. The cyclic was fighting them with a powerful, vibrating feedback in the control.

The hydraulics had given out.

They fought at cross-purposes, one trying to go left, the other pulling right, the cyclic going with whoever was strongest at any one moment. They flew into the shadow of the bluff. Next they would fly into the bluff itself.

Kirk screamed a torrent of obscenities to encourage Poole to let go of the cyclic . . . to shut off the hydraulics switch . . . to pull the circuit breaker.

For if the power were now restored by some fluke— even for a second—the tugging, pulling, pushing, would jerk the helicopter over into an impossible attitude at once.

Handley had seen the red-star cluster explode; had watched the missile jink, preferring the hotter target; grimaced and cursed as it flew harmlessly into the earth. He climbed out toward the west, then had slipped them high and east. Now he was rolling from the east down the coulee. He took a thirty-degree attack angle to reduce the effect of the sun in his face.

High. Maybe too high.

He didn't care much anymore.

He'd become a raving madman in the half minute since the missile had been decoyed away. But now he'd grown deadly calm. He vowed to finish the helicopter—one way or . . .

Kirk had only two choices. One was to pull the Huey's guts out, asking it to climb up the coulee to the east. The other was to die on the Custer battlefield.

Kirk pulled pitch. The collective fought back.

He screamed at Poole to help.

Together they made the Huey respond with everything it had, though the engine rpm began to bleed off because they'd demanded too much too quickly. Against every instinct, he held the power. And took the cyclic in both hands.

The Huey was raising an enormous dust cloud in the clay of the coulee.

Great.

Just in case a vertical shot of the rotor plane was not enough, the white cloud could mark the spot as well, thought Kirk.

But the rpm stopped bleeding off, and the Huey kept flying.

It did occur to him that the jet jock might be having a tough time as well, though.

Colonel Whip Handley squinted into the brilliance coming through the canopy. The ground *was* dark and indistinct, lying as it did in the long, westerly shadows. There was only that dust cloud. And the sun. His eyes kept sweeping, looking for the helicopter.

He went through the firing sequence and launched the final heat-seeking missile. The missile found a hot spot but it had failed to acquire the Huey. It took off toward the fireball of the sun instead.

Handley roared as he saw the missile homing on the sun. The roar came out a vicious oath.

The erratic Huey began flying directly under the belly of the Phantom, flying toward his tail.

Handley read his instruments; saw his safety envelope shrinking.

He had only a handful of seconds to decide.

It took only one.

He shoved the stick forward, steepening his angle, aiming his jet at that damned helicopter.

Kirk kept waiting for this world to blow up.

It should have been over by now.

He could no longer keep track of the Phantom. He kept fighting his helicopter. He reversed direction.

Where? No . . . when would it be over?

Had he won? Had the jock pulled out and left?

But no. He wouldn't allow himself the peace of mind to think he was safe. This was by no means over. They would be out on the open prairie and vulnerable to another attack.

He shouted a frustrated curse at himself.

Handley aimed to intercept the helicopter's flight path.

When it reversed direction, he only had time for another frantic, throat-rending curse.

An explosion behind them shook the Huey.

Another set of rockets?

Another fighter?

A bomb?

He reached the ridge top and turned, ready to dash back down toward the relative safety of the Little Bighorn River bottom.

He heard the unnatural squeal from Poole's throat before he saw.

It was a black, billowing tower of smoke punctuated by ominous orange flames. The grasslands of the Little Bighorn Battlefield would be burning for a long time.

At least until the fuel and metals of the F-4 Phantom had burned themselves out.

Poole was clapping his hands, his body language uttering the obscenities his mouth was too puffy and tender to shout.

He masturbated an enormous imaginary penis.

And the rush of his exuberance caught up Kirk as well. He shouted a stream of invective at the fire, cursing for

himself and on behalf of the orgiastic pantomime who
was his copilot.

Kirk's excitement lasted only a short half-life.

He'd gained almost nothing in defeating the jet jock—
or rather, letting the jock defeat himself. Perhaps a little
time.

Time for what.

Every passing minute just meant more aches in his
hands, arms, and shoulders.

The Huey seemed to fly better at cruise airspeed than
at a hover. Maybe the airstreaming effect helped. Still,
every control input required an exertion of force. Always,
the movement of the cyclic or collective resisted, then
gave in, taking an overcorrection, which required that another exertion be overpowered by the pilot. The resultant
cumulative effect was a drunken, weaving flight pattern
of irregular altitude and flight path.

Kirk debated about stopping to add more hydraulic oil.
But hydraulics-off landings required too much finesse, a
running approach, a hard surface preferred. At least by
the book. They'd probably have to try hovering down,
one man on the collective, the other on the cyclic. Kirk
didn't want to be doing more of those than necessary.

He could handle the moderate feedback through the
controls, now that they weren't trying to hover around
evading a Phantom in the attack. But every half hour or
so his arms began cramping, then his back. He and Poole
traded the cyclic every time the pains grew too severe.
The intervals of piloting grew shorter and shorter as the
aches grew into meaner and meaner cramps in the men's
shoulders.

And there was still that mountain, still the question of
how to sneak up on it. No, that was no question at all. If
the Phantom pilot had found him, he'd been reported to

somebody. There was no sneaking up that hill, wherever it was. He'd be better off skipping that prospect altogether. He should slip into Canada and hide out. Or he should ditch the helicopter and thumb his way to Billings to await the research log. Then he could find the authorities. Or . . . hell, he didn't know what.

Even as he was thinking of quitting . . . again, he was still flying toward the general area of a mountain he'd never recognize, even if he flew right into the side of it. The mountain beckoned with its invisible, powerful force —the possibility of vengeance. And like a moth toward a flame, the Huey kept homing.

The moon was low in the sky and about three quarters toward being full.

They had flown their wide arc. Now they must certainly be west of the peak. But there were mountains and buttes of varying sizes in every direction. They would fly down any number of valleys between ranges large and small, peaks, some tree-shrouded and some snow-capped.

They were in such a valley now, slopes left and right. To the south was a black, dark range of mountains. That could be it. There was no way of knowing without a topo map.

Unless . . .

Kirk had been lost before.

He knew what to do. All it took was enough guts. All he had to do was land and ask for directions.

He found a collection of buildings—a medium-size ranch, by the lights and number of outbuildings. He picked a landing spot nearby, beyond a grove of trees.

He set the Huey's approach to be long and shallow. He directed Poole to help him with the collective. On his signal, he instructed, Poole would have the collective alone and Kirk would use both hands to wrestle the cyclic.

Now at ten feet off the ground, Kirk gave the command.

Poole heaved his weight over and pushed the collective down with both hands. Kirk tried to finesse the cyclic to keep the skids level, to hit the ground—he had no doubt that they'd be hitting rather than touching—to keep the aircraft straight with his feet on the pedals.

The Huey bounced and skidded.

It took off again and flew three feet off the ground.

Kirk pulled back too hard, then corrected. The tail stinger hit and whipped the tail back upward, exaggerating Kirk's forward overcorrection.

Poole grunted heavily and kept pushing down.

The Huey dropped again.

Kirk had barely leveled when the skids hit again.

He leaned left and added his weight to the collective.

Their combined force unloaded power.

The Huey stuck to the ground and rocked.

They pushed the collective down to its stop and sighed together. "Goddamned controlled crash," said Kirk. They laughed, Poole spraying fresh blood from the hole in his face.

They began the cool-down and shutdown of the Huey together. While the main rotor blade was still whisking through the air and the engine metal ticking as it began to cool, Kirk set off toward the house on foot, the motion of walking so unfamiliar after so much time in the air. He waved his arms and shoulders to work out the tightness. His body chilled quickly, the sweat of his exertions seeming to freeze in the Montana air.

What he hadn't seen from the approach was the rushing waters of a creek blocking his path to the house. He started upstream to find a crossing. He found a small natural park that had been improved upon by a rancher. It was fenced, and a pond had been scooped out for swimming. Short-cropped grass ran up to the edge of the pond and on the north edge was even a small boardwalk.

When Kirk began walking around the pond, he realized it was not a pond at all but a huge natural spring. The creek had its beginning here. He lay flat and scooped a handful of water. It was tepid and not at all the frigid drink he was expecting.

Kirk immersed his head fully into the pond and washed his face.

It seemed to wash away a week's tension to feel that pure, tepid water in his face.

So he took off his shirt and splashed water on his chest.

But that only cleansed him more and left him wanting more of the cleaning, and the chill of the air on his wet skin demanded he splash on more of the warm water.

In a minute, all his clothes were lying in a heap on the boardwalk, the pistol hidden beneath the pile.

And Kirk jumped naked into the spring. It was a squandering of precious time to be indulging in such an ablution, he knew. Even before he hit the water, he was cursing himself.

But what time did they have left anyhow? he asked as the water enveloped him. Would there even be another sunrise for him?

The bottom was gravel. He pushed off to the surface, feeling the sensual warmth, deciding he could spare a few seconds of his life before trying the certain suicide of Judith Peak.

Bubbles and the current rising through the gravel climbed up his legs. He stretched out and swam, easing the aches in his body and mind.

The Huey had finally rested quietly. The night air was heavy with silence and chilly on his head. So he kept ducking himself in the warmth of the water. Elsewhere tonight, the state of Montana would probably endure a freeze. But in this tickly, rising current, there would be warmth and comfort.

He decided.

Hell with Judith Peak.

He was no hero. He should report his whole story to the police or FBI or somebody. Plenty of witnesses had seen the air-to-air assault of that Phantom against the Huey. He could probably make a report to the Air Guard or the National Transportation Safety Board. It was the kind of thing impossible to hide. It was enough of the truth to confirm the other incredible things he could tell. Ditto the things he could show in that research log.

First he'd check with Poole. He owed him that much. Their luck was bound to run out soon anyhow. No sense in risking their lives anymore.

He asked himself: Was he being persuasive? Could he get Poole to believe him? Did he believe himself?

There was no time to answer.

He reached up to the bank on the far side from the boardwalk and was about to push off and swim back to his clothes when he was startled by a blubbering snort. He felt a mist.

" 'Lo," said a man's voice.

Kirk's racing heart threatened to burst from his chest.

"We saw you land," said a woman. "You having any kind of trouble?"

He saw a pair of people belonging to the voices sitting ten feet above him on horseback. The horses snorted at him again, spraying him. Unconsciously, he scrubbed his face with the warm water.

"Uh, no problem. I . . . we're lost. I, uh, stopped to ask directions. I was going to knock at that house down there. . . ." He pointed.

"Well, that's our house," said the man. "Nobody's home —'cept Kalea, our baby girl." He laughed.

Kirk returned the laugh. He wondered if they could see down into the water. He looked down and couldn't see his own nakedness. Standing in the gravel and bubbles, the water was nipple-deep. His shoulders shook in the cold of the air. He ducked down again.

"Well," said the man, "whatcha looking for?"

Kirk shrugged.

"You said you were lost," said the woman. "Where were you going?"

"Oh," said Kirk. "Yeah. I'm looking for Judith Peak. Do you two know where it is?"

They both turned in their saddles at once, the leather squeaking in protest, and pointed east.

"There it sits," he said. "About twelve miles as the crow . . . chopper flies. Govermint's got the road closed." He nodded toward the dark spot on the landscape that was the helicopter. "I guess you don't care about that, though."

Kirk said, "No. Uh, you have any idea what's up there?"

"Sure. It's an old radar station. I think the Federal Aviation Administration used to use it. Or else the air force used it. But it's been shut down for years. And a landslide took out the road a mile or so below the summit. All kinds of rumors why."

"Oh?"

"They say they closed it because of a chemical spill that contaminated the area. Some say it was radioactive stuff from inside the instruments. One engineer told us in a bar one night the top of the mountain had slid a yard in the last year and any day the whole damn thing was going to drop into the valley. Anyways, it's blocked off and fenced and even guarded . . . men *and* dogs. They cut a ditch below the landslide and leveled off a spot for helicopters to land . . . they're the only way up top now. Hell, it's tighter up there than at some of them Minuteman Missile sites across the highline. I say it might be one of them command centers inside the mountain in case of a nuke war. It might even be the headquarters for the whole damned missile force."

Kirk said, "You seem to know a lot about strategic missiles."

"Hell," said the man, snorting like one of his horses. "I just work for the railroad. All I want to do is raise my horses. Wisht I had a few head of cattle to go along withem. Wisht Montana had never been made a state. I'd feel a hell of a lot better if it was still just one of the territories."

Still feeling naked, Kirk had nothing to say. He was overwhelmed by sadness. He, too, wished he cared about land and horses and cattle and even people.

"You sure you don't need anything?" asked the woman, interrupting his self-pity. She tossed her long, straight hair.

The water had relaxed his body. His stomach had come alive too. It told him to ask. "Ma'am," he said, "my co-pilot and I are so hungry, we could drop. Have you got anything we might eat? Some soup? We could pay."

She laughed at him derisively. "Pay? You are lost. In this part of the country, that's an insult. Come on down to the house and I'll throw something together for you."

But Kirk didn't think Poole's appearance would bear any civilized scrutiny. "No, ma'am, we . . . we have to hurry. If I could just run down and pick up something quick to drink and maybe a snack to split, that'd be enough."

It was the man's turn to laugh. "You just get your naked tail out of the water and I'll bring you back something."

They wheeled their horses and galloped off into the darkness, leaving Kirk to wonder if they'd be back or send the police.

Kirk returned to the Huey. Poole stood beside the open engine compartment, scowling and shaking his head. Hydraulic fluid painted the deck and the skin of the craft. Poole had poured in five quarts of oil to refill the system. The craft had taken it all, but nothing showed in the window of the sight gauge. Beneath the fuselage, an oily puddle was soaking into the Montana soil. Together the men cursed under their breaths.

The horseman did as he promised. He shared a few bites in the darkness with them, and sipped at his coffee noisily. He remarked at how untalkative Kirk's copilot was and that he didn't eat a bite, just sipped at some soup. Poole grunted. Kirk explained the copilot was sleepy. Meanwhile, he stuffed himself with thick cheese sandwiches and a beer and hot coffee.

The beer gave Kirk a second's pause. Regulations forbade flying within twenty-four hours of drinking. He thought about the rule, smiled to himself, and slugged the beer down in one long pull, spilling part of it defiantly down the sides of his mouth, down his neck, and into his clothing. If he lived to be court-martialed, it'd make an interesting charge alongside murder and helicopter theft, AWOL, and the rest.

He was clean, relaxed, full-bellied, and sleepy when the

horseman finally mounted up and left them to their dilemma.

Kirk sucked air through his teeth squeakily.

"Let's forget the mountain, Ken. We don't have a prayer."

Poole looked at him angrily. Even in the dimness of the partial moon, Kirk could see fury seething in those eyes. Kirk tried to explain about the package and security and the FBI and the Phantom incident witnessed by so many.

While he was saying it aloud it sounded so thin in comparison to when he was rationalizing it to himself.

But when he was done, Poole shrugged.

Kirk thought he'd given in.

Poole scribbled a note and handed it over.

Kirk read it.

Two words.

Fuck you.

Poole snatched the paper back and scribbled an afterthought.

Asshole.

Kirk argued for a while. In writing, Poole offered to let him stay and eat cheese sandwiches. He'd lost his wife and he planned to get even if he had to fly the fucking helicopter into the top of the mountain, hydraulics be damned.

It was a long message for Poole to write. Halfway through the last word, the lead snapped off his pencil. Kirk got the gist anyhow.

He tried to devise a plan. Nothing seemed sensible, not even moderately sensible. But Poole would not agree to leaving.

Finally, Kirk felt he'd been reduced to the level of Poole's own madness.

"I ought to fly right up the damned mountain. By the

time we get to the damned top, if something hasn't damned well occurred to us, I'll crash-land the damned helicopter and kill both our damned asses. How would you like that?"

Poole smiled painfully. He loved the idea.

"You're suicidal, pal. I'm not."

So he suggested a more sensible plan. Poole would drop him off not far from the top, and Kirk would pull a recon on foot. Poole would return in an hour and pick him up. They would develop something of a plan from there.

Poole agreed reluctantly with a hesitant nod.

"You're right," Kirk said. "It *is* a stupid idea."

But before Kirk could elaborate, equivocate, or evade further, Poole hit the battery, fuel, and governor switches. He set the throttle and pulled the starter trigger. From habit, Kirk switched on the radios and clamped the headset over his aching ears. His mind was elsewhere. He was thinking of how long ago it was that he was making love with Gail. He wondered if they would be meeting again after his death. His imminent death.

Then he looked over at Poole. He wondered how hard he'd have to tap him on the head to just knock him out. He could tie him up with some of that tape and drop him off at a hospital's doorstep. Then he could pick up that research log and attempt something rational.

But rational was not to be.

A voice from the past came across the headset as he pinched it to his aching head.

"Kirk," said the husky voice. "Kirk, I'm calling you on Guard frequency. Come up Gray tower freq so we can talk."

Kirk froze. And not because he didn't know the tower frequencies for Gray Army Airfield a couple of thousand miles away.

Poole knew them and dialed the FM, UHF, and VHF radios to the proper numbers.

Kirk hadn't moved. Physically, he was sitting inside a helicopter in Montana. Mentally, the voice giving instructions in the night, the coarse, arrogant voice coming through his earphones, a voice from his past, transported him to a remote elsewhere, a staging area in the northwesternmost corner of South Vietnam. The voice then had given him frequency instructions, just as it had given him instructions now. And he was to have changed channels, just as Poole had done. And he was to be given a coded message citing a set of coordinates for a pickup of a V.I.P., Very Important Prick, in the pilot's lexicon. It was to be a snatch of the Defense Minister from Hanoi. A BIG prick.

Poole slapped him on the arm, bringing him back to Montana. He waved a palm at the radio console to indicate he had a choice of sets.

Kirk shook off the feeling he'd felt all those years ago.

He tried to make his wavering voice contact his caller via VHF.

No luck.

Poole slapped him again when he hesitated so long before trying another call.

He switched his selector from 3 to 2, to attempt UHF contact.

"This is Kirk," is all he said. He didn't have breath enough for more.

"Kirk," came the reply, rich, rough, heavy. The voice broadcast an element of satisfaction—*arrogant* satisfaction.

Kirk's breath came faster.

He felt a grip on his shoulder.

Poole gestured wildly at him, combining obscene finger

language with the shrugging of shoulders and the raising of eyebrows to indicate in signing: What the fuck is wrong?

Kirk didn't have an answer to that question. Something in the voice swamped him with memories and emotions. He remembered fears from long ago.

The gravelly voice challenged him. "Is this *the* Kirk? The fearless first lieutenant pilot of army helicopters flying into forbidden territories and forbidden cities?" Sarcasm tinged the tone, gloating, born of having knowledge not shared.

It raised the skin at Kirk's neck. He prickled all over with the new heat generated by that tone and those words. And he knew.

This bastard he'd come to know by voice only. That radio contact from the past for nearly a dozen missions now spoke to him again. Always the same arrogant voice. Always the same challenging tone, daring Kirk to fail. Never saying but always suggesting he'd hang the lieutenant's ass.

Kirk had always guessed his contact was CIA. The military lilt to his speech divulged a background in uniform, but this kind of work was left to people outside the Pentagon. That was what he thought. And now he was meeting the voice again.

The voice that had sent him to die.

That voice must have known the mission had been betrayed somehow. He must have had some fail-safe code or signal that could have brought Kirk back from destruction. But he had not called. He had let Kirk and his crew go in, landing to certain death.

And then, to eliminate any trace of the operation, he had sent in the air force on top of the enemy troops and friendly corpses. What was the big deal about a few more missing in action?

But thanks to Jud McClean, the operation had not been swept away by the explosions of tons of ordnance.

Jud had carried and dragged and cajoled him across miles of enemy territory, finally bringing Kirk's wounded and broken body to a South Vietnamese base camp. The Viets then delivered them to the Marines. And the Stars and Stripes reporters who splashed their miraculous escape and evasion across the paper had ensured they would not permanently be exiled back to MIA status.

"Kirk, we need to talk."

"Tell it to the judge, the cops, the Congress . . . asshole."

Poole clapped him on the shoulder. He bounced in his seat. This was more his style.

"You have something I want. You have the package you took from Beard's. I have Payne's wife. We can trade."

Kirk laughed loudly inside the cockpit, though he did not key his mike to let his derision go out over the air. This voice did not care about that package. The voice had felt confident enough to send a fighter jock out to destroy him without knowing or caring whether the research log had been aboard the helo or mailed or buried or anything. This voice no longer cared about that log. The funny part was its believing that Kirk would be stupid enough to believe a trade was possible. The voice still thought of him as a devoted, naive, idealistic lieutenant.

Fine. If that's what they wanted to believe.

"I don't have it with me. I can't make the trade tonight."

"Yes," said the voice. "You *can* make a trade. We'll give you the woman. You tell us how to get the book. You fly away . . . leave the helicopter where we can get it back to the army. You go back to a normal life. We'll trust you."

Sure. As if an organization like this would even trust its own people. Kirk decided to test him.

"No. I'm going to make copies and mail them around. I'm going to send them to the papers. I'm going to bring you bastards down."

"Suppose we talk about this, Kirk. Do you reckon I could mention a proper dollar amount that would sweeten the trade?"

Absolutely the wrong approach, Kirk thought. So weak an effort. The owner of this voice must have known he wouldn't respond to a bribe. The feeble tone confirmed that. Then why offer one?

Suddenly Kirk felt vulnerable. The voice had begun to sound like one of those television detectives who want to keep the kidnappers on the line until the trace can go through.

He and Poole had sat in the same spot for more than an hour. Somebody might be sneaking up. No, somebody *would* be sneaking up. He'd not been careful. He'd not been thinking *ruthless*.

He looked over at Poole and nodded urgently. Together they picked the Huey up. Kirk aimed south, toward higher terrain a mile away to continue this conversation.

The helicopter barely broke ground before the cockpit was bathed in the brilliant white light of spots—at least two. Kirk broke his take-off path sharply right, barely stopping the lost hydraulics' overreaction before the Huey lost its climb. The rotor wash caught the dust of the road and threw up a cloud.

His heart pounded. He knew what followed the lights.

He couldn't hear the shots but he felt at least two bullets strike the Huey. They were like yardsticks being slapped against the skin. He tacked left and right and the spotlights could not catch the helicopter again.

He pointed at the gauges, but Poole had already begun scanning, looking for temperatures rising, pressures dropping, caution lights illuminating.

Kirk felt a new vibration, a one-to-one bounce or a slight lateral, an irregularity that came with every revolution of the main rotor blades. It probably meant a strike in one of the blades. It was not likely to be serious, perhaps a slug lodged in the blade, setting up a slightly imbalanced condition. The other strike might be more dangerous if it nicked one of the fuel or oil lines. It couldn't have been the worst hit. It couldn't have been a shot to the tail-rotor drive or blades. That effect would have been instantaneous.

Then he saw a new light on the panel.

The red light every pilot fears.

His heart stopped.

FIRE, the red light on the dash screamed.

Either the engine compartment was actually burning or the warning system had been damaged.

There was only one thing to do.

Kirk found an open spot in a pasture. He scattered several dozen cattle as he and Poole hovered in the dark, resisting the urge to use a landing light, fighting the controls as they looked for a spot without rocks or snags in the faint light from the skies.

Finally they planted the tap-dancing Huey skids in the dirt. Kirk jumped out. He dashed to one side of the Huey and batted at the spring-loaded inspection door in the cowling. No flames. He ducked under the tail boom and repeated the maneuver. Nothing. He decided to keep his composure. He would not yell and scream and curse, although the rage inside him threatened to exhibit itself in exactly that form. He would remain in control. Of himself. Of this situation. Control. And he'd remain careful and *ruthless*.

He went to the skid beside Poole and pulled on his copilot's boom mike. He reached inside and keyed the intercom switch and talked to Poole through his own mike to tell him there was no fire.

"Pull the circuit breaker," he ordered.

Poole patted the sides of his headset and pointed at Kirk.

The voice wanted to talk to him.

Kirk went around and, standing on the skid, put on his own headset.

"Yeah," he uttered.

Pause.

After a moment's hesitation, the voice spoke. It sounded a little more tense. It must have heard from its force on the valley floor by now. By now the owner of the voice knew about the failure of the ambush. Like Kirk, he seemed to be struggling to maintain his composure.

"Kirk, are you still there?"

"What kind of money?" he heard himself saying.

"Does something in the high six figures interest you?" The voice wasn't buying Kirk's greed any more than Kirk had been persuaded by any offer of anything.

"Not enough."

"Seven figures."

"And PJ."

"Of course."

"And some form of insurance. A written promise."

"That goes without saying."

Kirk laughed harshly, again only inside the cockpit. Two desperate liars both lying to each other.

Kirk's skin still felt prickly from the hatred he was feeling. Hatred of this voice—make that the owner of the voice. The ruthless bastard that had tried so often to kill him.

"I want to meet you," said Kirk. "Alone."

"Why . . . yes . . . to make the deal."

"You'll bring PJ Payne?"

"Yes. And the money."

The money didn't matter to Kirk. He just wanted PJ to be safe. And he wanted a few seconds alone with the man who belonged to the voice. It would take only seconds to repay the debts he owed those men in the LZ, Jud, Gail, the Lees, the others. All his ambivalence about going to the top of Judith Peak had begun to dissolve the second he heard that voice. By now his indecision was all gone. Nothing could keep him from going up there.

"Prove she's all right. Put her on the radio. Let me talk to her right now."

The speaker laughed confidentially.

"I'll do better than that," said the voice, as if its owner could toss out any number of enticements.

For a second, Kirk wondered if he'd made himself sound too easy to persuade to come up. Had he given in too easily to be believed? Besides, he didn't know PJ. How could he be certain . . . well, Poole would know her voice.

Then a woman's voice came over the radio.

But it could not have been PJ. Because he *did* recognize it. A sudden chill gripped him and shook all his inspirational hatred to its foundations.

"Grayson. Grayson Kirk, please do what they say. I love you, Grayson. Please, I need you, darling. They're going to kill me."

The groan that escaped his lips came as if from a kick in

the stomach. He came very close to losing the control that he'd been struggling for.

He looked over to Poole to see whether his own ears had somehow tricked him with the voice from the dead.

Poole's fat face looked just as stunned as his own must be.

They both had heard the plea correctly.

In the voice of Lieutenant Colonel Connie Gail.

After the initial shock of hearing Gail's voice, the decision to go up the mountain was simple for Kirk. Hearing her only stoked his hatred of the man who'd sent him to die before. He doubted he could get safely in and out. All he wanted to do was get in. All he wanted was one shot at the owner of that coarse voice. If he could just get even with him for the past and for the sake of Gail and the others. That would be enough.

But how?

It was time to move. He needed time to think about how to get to that voice without being blown away. But he'd have to gain that time in the air.

The voice called his name.

He ignored it.

He began to climb in.

Poole touched his arm. He pointed at the extinguished fire light and motioned for Kirk to check the engine again —just to be sure.

Kirk stepped down into the night and stretched. The days of fatigue were doing awful things to his body. Next would come the cramps in the buttocks and thighs, sending him into gyrations in the seat. But that was nothing compared to the problem of the lost hydraulics. How would they land without hydraulics up on that peak? That was the main problem.

He hardly had time to worry.

He was standing on tiptoe beside the fuselage, peeking inside the cowling. The roaring of the turbine was angry and deafening. He didn't pay much attention to the slight change in the pitch of the noise. But he did feel the downwash of the rotor suddenly. He ducked down and prepared to scoot under the tail boom to check the other side.

But the damned Huey had begun to lift.

He straightened and cursed, though nobody on earth could hear his shouted obscenity. Then he hit the ground as the Huey peeled its skids off the pasture's grass and dust and cow splats.

The tail boom came around as the Huey fishtailed violently in its take-off. And then the dust ground into his eyes, and he flattened, resting his forehead, cursing into the curly buffalo grass.

Poole had finally snapped. He'd taken off to do something crazy. Maybe to fly up there and pull a Kamikaze strike on the radar site. But no, he wouldn't do that with Gail and PJ inside, would he? Was Poole *that* crazy? He'd been in pain for days. He'd not eaten and had drunk only a little. And two days with no booze but that one swallow? Maybe he was crazy enough to do it.

But would he?

No.

Never.

The breeze from the blades died. The angry buzz of the Huey had begun to fade.

"Poole, you bastard," he muttered into the night. "Why?"

And how? he asked himself. How would the stupid bastard land that Huey up there alone without hydraulics. When two men would have a hell of a time.

Then he heard the answer to his why-question.

It was the whine of another set of blades at flat pitch. A smaller set of blades. It was the buzzing sound of an OH-58 Kiowa.

Poole must have seen it first and he must have taken off to avoid getting caught. But why? They could have lost the Kiowa in the dark.

Then Kirk saw what Poole might have seen.

The crouching man was pointing a long, thin tube with a bubble on the end. He was pointing it at the orange-ish, blue-ish oval of fire that was the exhaust of the Huey.

Kirk almost shouted, though he knew that would have been pointless.

He gained his feet and began running, fishing in his belt for the pistols.

It was a hundred yards.

He'd never make it.

He stopped and aimed the silenced .22.

The crouching figure was bathed in a flash and a string of sparks whooshed into the night. The sound and sparks began tracking the rattle of the Huey.

Kirk again wanted to yell.

But he didn't.

He didn't even bother watching the missile fly toward its target.

His attention was on the crouching man dressed in a camouflaged army field jacket. The man continued tracking the heated oval of the exhaust, somewhere between 400 to 610 degrees Celsius of heat attracting the infrared seeker in the nose of the missile. In the neighborhood of about 1,000 degrees Fahrenheit.

The Huey exploded—or the missile exploded, and the Huey fell in a heap of orange flame.

Kirk saw the firer stand up and brush off his knee. He was close enough to see a satisfied grin on the face.

The man never heard the footsteps across the pasture. Why would he expect them? And how could he, what with the whine of the Kiowa at flight idle? A word occurred to Kirk.

Ruthless.

Kirk put the silenced .22 behind the ear where the skin was wrinkled from the grin. The gun spat and the grin was wiped away, the smugness converted to . . . what? Pain? Surprise? Anger?

Kirk knew Poole would have appreciated seeing that lousy grin erased. He smiled sickly for Poole's benefit and at the corpse at his feet. He stepped up to the left door of the Kiowa and looked across to the pilot. He was talking calmly, smiling, apparently making his report of the shoot-down. Kirk waited until the lips had stopped moving and the pilot looked over for his companion.

Kirk jerked open the copilot's door and with his free hand held down on the collective so there'd be no accidental take-off.

He saw the finger tighten on the radio button on the cyclic. But the .22 slug cut off the astonished utterance before it had time to escape the mouth.

There was nobody else in the craft.

He walked around the nose of the craft and strapped the dead pilot in, locking the shoulder harness so the man, drooling blood from a hole beside his nose, would not fall over on the controls. Kirk pulled the man's visor down over the eyes, eyes still open and astonished.

He released the seat belt and put the gloved hands neatly under, then snapped it again so they would not flop around, perhaps wedging against the collective as he flew. He found a survival knife strapped to the man's boot and took it for his own. Then he went back to the dead missile firer and stripped him of his field jacket. It pleased him to find no blood had ruined the jacket.

He was becoming quite the efficient killer, he thought to himself. He should have been part of this Corporation instead of its enemy. Well, apparently, he had been part of it once—unknowingly. But they had tried to dismiss him. They had tried to fire him and leave him without compensation in a jungle spot in Laos.

And he now had his ride to the top of Judith Peak at last. Maybe he couldn't save Gail or PJ. But there was always hope for payback time for what they had done to him and all the others—people he might have loved if he'd known what love was. "Goddammit," he muttered to himself. Poole lay burning in that fire just a couple hundred steps away. All he could think of now was revenge. The hell with anything else.

2

Much too simple.

Kirk landed between the corners of the square marked by the dim blue lights. The flight had been too simple, without challenge. He had simply taken off in the Kiowa, simply confirming the wind direction by the blowing, smoking, flaming inferno fueled by Poole's body and the Huey's fuel.

It was a west wind.

He'd avoided flying through the smoke plume which the wind had carried. Already sickened by the death of his friend, he knew the oily smell of his ashes would launch his recent meal straight up and into his lap.

So he climbed to 10,000 feet into the wind. Then he started crosswind, heading south. It was so simple to find. There out the left door to the east sat a fat, hulking mountaintop bathed in the light of security lamps. He headed downwind for ten minutes and began a long, shallow turning descent back into the wind until he picked up the blue markers a hundred feet below and adjusted his glide to the ground.

Simple.

No challenge by lights or over the radio.

No codes.

No welcoming committee.

Nothing.

Nice flight.

In a helicopter with hydraulics, a real breeze.

It gave him time to think.

About the simplicity of it all.

But it wasn't this mechanical simplicity that bothered him. He didn't suspect a trap of any kind. For the bane of an organization like this Corporation was its belief in its righteousness and its invincibility. Kirk had probably put their corporate presumptuousness to the test, particularly with the Phantom—he hadn't merely escaped its overwhelming advantage . . . he'd brought it down.

But now the Huey was burning down on the rolling flats. Kirk's body was expected to be in it—he had no doubt that was the report of the pilot he'd killed, the man sitting beside him. Just like Poole. Dead. He shook off the idea of grief.

His revenge would be systematic and mechanical . . . not emotional. For now, he needed to keep his wits about him.

He figured he could assume they had no idea he had commandeered their own aircraft.

He shuddered, unable to fight off his emotions. Not the grief, necessarily.

No, that wasn't simple grief that nagged at him, eating away like acids against his naked sense of morality and values.

It was the simplicity of the killings—the murders, really.

Had he felt a bit of smugness himself when he'd popped the brains of the Redeye firer, wiping the smile away, replacing it with a death mask?

And the pilot. Might he have wounded instead of killed? Couldn't he have jerked out the mike cord instead of pulling the chain on his life? Flushing him out of existence?

Killing was more certain. And certainly it was simpler. But didn't that make him as bad as one of them?

He'd killed in the army, yes. But that had been in battle. And he'd only shot Beard in self-defense, while he was yet an inch or so away from being killed himself.

Ah, but then he'd let Pearson be partially devoured—just to get some information. And he'd left Gail behind in the brush at Beard's, though he couldn't be sure she'd died, because . . . because the mission had suddenly become more important than her life. And now she'd been captured by . . . *them*. Try rationalizing that away.

And wasn't that exactly the same kind of reasoning you'd expect to hear from The Corporation if it was ever brought under scrutiny? The mission? Orders? It was an old argument. It dated at least back to Vietnam and Calley, My Lai. Before that, it was heard as a defense at Nuremberg, for God's sake.

About all he had time for was to decide Pearson was wrong in his advice on how to survive. Careful, yes. But ruthless was not for him. He'd never make it in this business. Killing made him ill.

Yet he began the deliberate shutdown of the Kiowa. He'd kill some more if he had to, and he'd kill for Gail, a woman who loved him, a woman he loved. Just thinking of her in the hands of these people made him want to kill —now there was a new one—he'd kill for love. And he'd even kill for PJ, a woman he'd never met.

God, how low was his threshold?

He cut the fuel and reset the Kiowa for a quick restart. All that would be needed was battery, fuel, and starter trigger. The positions of the switches were unfamiliar to him after he'd spent so much time in the Huey. He rehearsed the starting sequence. Paused. Took a deep breath. Stepped out into the thin Arctic air atop Judith Peak.

The field jacket barely cut the wind.

His eyes started watering instantly. He strode across oversized chunks of gravel toward a gate in an interior fence. He looked around and saw a double stand of security wire enclosing the scraped and graveled area where the buildings squatted low, probably partly underground to anchor them from the winter winds that must sweep by at this altitude. The gravel chunks must be so large to keep them from being blown away by gales, he thought.

Between the outer fences were dogs.

More dogs ran among the cinder-block buildings. Only a path protected by a tunnel of wire from the helipad to the first building kept the dogs away. Two of them, shrieking and yapping, bit into the chain links. Kirk wondered if they greeted all people that way or if he was getting the treatment of a stranger.

A figure stepped from the entryway at the end of the tunnel and shouted at the dogs to be quiet.

"Heard you got a shoot-down," the figure said to Kirk.

Kirk wiped his eyes and nose with the sleeve of the jacket, trying to hide his face as well. "Yeah. Where's the boss?"

"Gerlach? He's over . . . hey, who the . . ."

His last word was the Anglo-Saxon curse word of choice. It stuck in his throat. Even as the blade of the pilot's survival knife drove up under his sternum and stuck in his heart.

Kirk gulped down another murder. He had no time for remorse now. It didn't matter whether this was killing in self-defense or simply offensive military maneuvers.

He'd obviously found a guard shack. Security. Dog

handlers. Probably kitchen help, pilots, and other support staff stayed there too.

There was probably another entrance for V.I.P.s, people like this Gerlach, the "boss" that the dead man had identified by name. Better to try here than to attempt a bluff through an entrance reserved for the brass. There the security would rarely be lax. Here he might have a chance.

Yes, pilots and gunners would be billeted with security people. He should enter here.

He did.

He opened the door and stepped down. He found himself in an alcove. It was an airlock of sorts, built to keep the interior heat where it belonged when people exited in numbers—people such as guards relieving each other in shifts. Overshoes and snow gear lined the right wall. To the left was one door. Ahead was another. From the door ahead, he heard the canned laughter from a television.

Off-duty guards. He shoved the blooded survival-knife blade into a wood seam. It would keep the door from opening right away in case of an alarm. It might buy him a few seconds.

Then he took the left door.

It led into a dim hallway, naked bulbs burning above, recessed into the concrete ceiling, grates over the yellow, glowing globes.

This interior looked familiar. To the right of the fifty-foot hallway were doors. Steel doors with dark glass panels. At the end was a set of bars and a larger steel door.

He studied the door he was holding. It was another steel door with a heavy self-locking latch.

He remembered.

Fort Harrison.

Several low cinder-block buildings like this had been

left over from World War II. They served as secure storage areas, and one had been converted into a classroom and darkrooms for photojournalism training in the Defense Information School. But they had not originally been intended as darkrooms. They had been built as cells to house German prisoners of war, those with strategic importance, especially if they needed to be shielded from the postwar trials.

He now stood in a similar cellblock.

It was a smelly place, too. It made his nervous stomach jump.

Awkwardly, he fished in his wallet and took out a credit card. He held it between the tongue of the latch and the iron doorjamb as it went closed. He could escape this way now if need be. Now he knew why they had always warned him never to leave home without that card.

Quickly and silently he walked down the hall, checking the dark glass in each door. The glass was a one-way mirror. He opened one door and saw a compartment. For feeding, he guessed. He opened the interior door.

An empty cell.

The second door's compartment was open. And this cell was empty too.

Likewise the third.

He noticed that the closer to the end of the hallway, the stronger became an animallike stench, a hatefully familiar smell.

He tried the door latch, heavy steel handles and deadbolt locks. But the empty cell was open.

The fourth was the last cell in this hallway. He saw the passage went right, deeper into the interior of the building. This seemed not to be going so well.

But when he looked in, he saw a woman—no, his unbelieving eyes found a pair of women in the cell. Would it really be so easy? The women were Connie Gail and PJ Payne—well, he'd never seen PJ, but it *must* be her.

He drew a breath to greet them, then decided against it. He couldn't afford to have them shrieking or asking questions—the cell might be bugged. He'd need to free them, and they'd need to run.

He heard footsteps.

They came from the hallway to the right.

They were careless, clopping heels. He guessed a guard on patrol of the occupied cells. God only knew how many more prisoners this bastard organization had taken from among the citizens of America. He was glad he'd not spoken to the women. They might not be able to disguise their excitement to the prying eyes of a guard.

Kirk stepped into the third cell and pulled the door carefully shut. He kept the latch turned so the workings would not snap.

The footsteps squeaked a bit of grit between the soles and the concrete floor as they turned the corner.

Kirk bunched.

If that guard's face appeared in this doorway, it was going to be flattened.

He heard the jingle of keys.

The lock at Gail's cell was going to be opened.

The other cell door was all of six feet away. He'd have to swing this one out and go around. But he did have the element of surprise.

He waited until the key scratched at the lock. He heard it slide in and turn.

Kirk burst out.

The guard's jaw fell. Before he could utter a sound, Kirk smashed him on the forehead with a fist hardened by the pistol grips of the .22. The guard dropped to his knees suddenly, like a saved soul dropping at the feet of a charismatic preacher. Kirk threw a knee into the point of the slack jaw and the man smashed the back of his head on the concrete floor.

Kirk turned to the key ring still stuck in the door. The man might die of brain damage, but compared to his earlier murders, that would be wholly accidental. It gave him a second's pause—the ease with which he rationalized.

But this was no time for self-analysis.

He jerked the door handle and came face-to-face with the astonished, astonishingly beautiful face of Colonel Connie Gail, more rested, better colored than when he'd stranded her in Texas. She blushed, her eyes blinking rapidly.

He smashed his lip against her open mouth, cutting his upper lip on her teeth.

She stepped back in disbelief. "They said you were dead," she whispered.

He smiled and cocked his head to show he was alive and still capable of that wiseass grin.

"And I was sure of the same thing about you . . . but, come on, Gail, drag this bastard in here."

He stepped in and touched the shoulder of the other woman.

"PJ?" he said.

She nodded. Both her hands were holding her face as if holding her jaw against becoming unhinged.

"Grayson Kirk," he said. "A friend of Mark's. Come on, you two, we got to get the hell out of here."

He was becoming giddy. He was going to make it.

It was so simple.

He was going to march right into the stronghold atop Judith Peak, grab the two women, and fly away in The Corporation's own helicopter. He was going to fly to Billings and get that log and destroy this organization. He wasn't going to be a loser, a killer, a spy, or anything. He was going to become decent again. He was going to love somebody and he wanted to be loved. He was going to get a second chance.

"Grayson," whined PJ desperately, fear now filling her eyes along with a rush of tears.

"Not now, PJ. Outside. I have a helicopter."

"Grayson . . . she . . . she is one of *THEM.*"

It was the turn of his mouth to fall. Maybe if he were more suspicious, ruthless, careful. Maybe he would have ducked. Or earlier, he might have wondered why Gail looked and smelled so fresh compared to the drawn, haggard PJ.

But his own jaw fell.

And he turned halfway toward the door of the cell . . .

. . . just as the side of his head seemed to cave in.

He felt PJ's hands trying to hold him up. Uselessly trying to hold him, for he was much too heavy and too limp. He hit the floor and bounced.

He felt hands feeling him, frisking him.

He felt the .22 pulled from his belt.

He felt a kick in the ribs, a sharp, pointed kick, as if from a woman's shoe. And he felt the sting of a woman's curse insulting his very masculinity.

And then he was unconscious.

When Kirk awoke, he wished he hadn't.

His head must literally have been cracked by the blow Gail had given him and by his head bouncing on the concrete. It gave him a second moment of pause, a fragment of sympathy for the guard he'd nailed on the forehead, chin, and back of the head, in that order.

But even worse was the stench that invaded his head.

He opened his eyes. PJ was in this new cell with him. It was an open cell, with bars all around. They were under bright lights.

PJ was cringing away from him.

He was sick, on the brink of vomiting. The headache, the smell, and the sunken feeling of having thought he might be in love—might have been loved. And she had been one of them. Relaying information and his intentions. She had been involved in the killings, the betrayals. No wonder he hadn't been able to shake the agents following them. And that night in bed . . . God, what an actor she was.

PJ was softly crying.

"I'm sorry," she sobbed.

"It's not your fault," he said. "I'm the sorry one, kid. I might have done better." He choked down the bitter reality. "But how could I have known?"

"It's my fault," said PJ matter-of-factly. "I could have jumped her or something when you came in. But I was expecting a guard. And she had just finished telling me . . . laughing about it . . . that you'd been killed in a crash. Before you introduced yourself, I wondered if maybe you were one of them too. Then . . ."

"PJ."

She sniffed and wiped away tears. "What?"

"It doesn't matter now," he said. And he knew it certainly didn't.

She snorted, a hysterical half laugh of ironic helplessness.

He joined her in the laugh, though it hurt his head. "God," he said. "And I thought I even loved . . ."

He looked around. The wall she was cringing against had a door just beyond the bars. The cell was a kind of cage within a larger room.

He fought to keep his stomach down and said, "What is that awful smell?" But he already knew the answer. He remembered it. He'd smelled this stench the day the blue-eyed monster killed Major General Harry X. Ford.

She shuddered and pointed over his shoulder.

He turned and saw nothing. The room was dark around the edges with deep, dark caves built into the walls.

But then he saw movement. One of the areas of darkness in one of the caves shifted.

It was an animal.

No, it was a man.

No.

"My God," he whispered.

It was both.

He asked God again for help. "What in God's name . . ."

A growl of a voice responded. "Not in God's name. A man's name. It's in the name of Mark Payne's brother-in-law. A certain Mister Warren Howell, once of Texas A & M University, College Station, Texas—he . . . was a maker of beasts."

PJ whimpered.

The voice came from an open hatch in the doorway, a window without glass.

It was the same voice he'd heard over the radio.

Kirk's head cleared as if cleansed by fire. It *was* fire at that. It was the fire of hatred stoked by the sound of that voice.

But the owner of that voice did not step up to the window in the door. Instead, there came another face.

The face was familiar, the expression was not.

Clearly, Gail had harbored her own measure of hatred for him and had suppressed it well in the days they had known each other—in every way. For her sneer was so derisive, it instantly wiped out any romantic notions he might have suspected in her.

"Fancy meeting you here," she said through the sneer. "The things I had to do to try to bring you under control. Then, as soon as I stop trying, you show up."

He didn't say a word. He was thinking how the cruelty that showed on her face must have manifested itself so often in murder in the last few days.

Suddenly things began to fall into place. She probably had killed Keating, the chief of staff. She had been an agent on site at Fort Harrison for a month, arriving about the time Bertrand, a member of the Michigan group, had disappeared. He wondered what she might have had to do with that. She had been a direct information pipeline from the post headquarters to The Corporation's headquarters. Kirk wondered how many other military organizations had been infiltrated in that way.

"Gail," he said. "If that's your name."

"Oh, it is. Gail Barnaby. I work directly—and exclusively—for Mister Gerlach here. Even within my organization, nobody knew I was a woman . . . I finished using the Connie Gail name that night at Beard's—the night Connie Gail died with Maggie Poole."

"Not *died*," he corrected with a sneer. "Killed. You cut Maggie's throat."

PJ inhaled sharply.

Gail Barnaby lifted the corner of her upper lip into her own sneer.

Kirk clenched his eyes shut for having revealed it so cruelly to PJ. When he opened his eyes, he spoke in a low, angry voice.

"Why didn't you just finish me instead of pulling me out of Fall Creek?"

"We found the blood trail beside a lake here in Montana. Then we found her. She . . . we couldn't risk the possibility that she might have sent something about us to you through the mail. Turns out she did. We wanted you to get it. Then we wanted to take it away."

Kirk remembered the night outside the bar. She had rolled away from McClean's oncoming headlights like an athlete—or a trained agent. He should have known enough to suspect her then. It might have made a difference.

"You did kill Jud after all," he said matter-of-factly. He remembered: She'd been struck on the right cheekbone. Jud was a lefty. His tone belied the surge of hatred that shot through his chest at the realization.

"Well . . . yes, quite literally. And Martin Grier. Now that was a close call. I'd just left him dead at the hospital and got a call from the FBI. I couldn't take a chance they suspected me."

"Jud," Kirk repeated.

"He caught me making a phone report. He was the one who slugged me and cut one of my best men. I had to finish McClean. . . ."

"Finish? You cut his throat *and* shot him?"

She smirked. "He pissed me off. And I would have shot you if you hadn't done this. . . ." She held up her lightly bandaged forearm. "And I would have cut your throat too. 'Course . . . at the time I still didn't know about the letter from the bitch." She flicked an evil glare at PJ.

So cold. Her eyes were so bitter and cold. He knew she would have cut him.

He remembered how he had purposely jerked the shot off its aim at the last instant. He regretted that.

He remembered.

"The hole in the sock . . ."

She laughed. "You had me, Kirk. But then I sprinkled a few tears on you. No problem." She gave him a condescending glare. "You were starting to become too analytical. I thought I'd raise your emotions a bit, you know, evoke a little pity. I thought it might make you trust me . . . that and a little tactical use of sexuality is usually enough to bring most men to their knees. So to speak."

It had certainly been enough for him, Kirk reflected bitterly. The sex. He wondered. Was that faked too? Hell, what did it matter to his damned stupid male ego now?

She apparently read the question on his face.

"I'm a pretty good actress in bed too," she added sarcastically.

Kirk couldn't suppress a pitiful laugh. "You are one cold bitch."

When he spoke again, it was half to himself as the realizations dawned with the names. "And Maggie. And Poole. And . . ."

"And Duda. And Ferrin. And the little girl . . . what was her name? Grace?"

"Mazey," Kirk whispered. He choked back the rising bitterness in his throat.

"And I would have had you again that night at Beard's if I hadn't let you leave the pistol with the jammed slide. I had to screw around with it . . . but . . ." She flashed her perfect teeth. "Here you are."

So cold. So utterly devoid of emotion. He wondered where she had learned that.

"You monsters," said PJ.

"If you only knew," said Gail Barnaby. "If you only knew the half of it."

Kirk kept putting details from the past together. And plenty of them had been laid out . . . enough to have exposed her . . . if he hadn't been so damned rusty . . .

no, that wasn't it. He'd left his stupid brain in his shorts, that's what. He could have figured her out. It was all there to see.

Laos. She had known he had crashed in Laos, although he'd never actually told her the classified tidbit of the name of the country. And the burning helicopter. It hadn't been burning when he left. She'd killed the pair of military lawmen and set the fire. With help? he wondered. No, she would have done it alone. She was ruthless and efficient enough.

And Texas. Back at the officers' club, she'd told Maggie the Paynes were in Montana. Only later had Pearson revealed that. He might have suspected then . . . if he hadn't been so much in love with the idea of her loving him.

He looked beseechingly into her eyes, looking for the slightest hint of compassion, the faintest contradiction of the evil she had spawned.

All he saw was acrid spite, the blue smoke of hatred in her eyes.

"You . . . did in your own man? The one in the Speedway parking lot?"

She shrugged. "An incompetent. He nearly killed you —would have if I hadn't nailed him, if you hadn't been lucky enough to be wearing the 9-millimeter jockstrap."

So that was ruthless, thought Kirk. She had almost killed him from the tub a few minutes earlier, nearly made the same mistake she'd killed another man for. So . . .

"I could have had you anytime, Kirk. Even in bed. Did you know you had sex with the loaded pistol pointing at your temple? I even thought about taking you out then . . . just to see how it would feel to live out a snuff-sex scene. Does it turn you on to know that?"

His stomach lurched.

She laughed and stepped aside. The open space in the door was filled by an immense gray face.

"Kirk," said the voice he'd heard so many times on the radio—in South Vietnam and Cambodia and Laos and North Vietnam. And tonight, in Montana. "Too bad I didn't bring you into The Corporation with me. You've got it all, boy. You've got the brains and you've got the balls. How the fuck did you ever beat Whip?"

Kirk's puzzled face asked the question.

"Whip Handley, the fighter pilot."

Kirk never answered. He just studied the gray face as if he might need to know it if he met it again. Or as if he was trying to decide whether this face could explain the treachery the owner of the voice had wrought. He hated the face as easily as he had come to hate the voice.

Kirk waved his hands at the dark edges of the larger rooms where the caves seemed to be built into the walls, where the beasts lived.

"What are these . . . things?"

Gerlach sighed heavily. "Long, long story, my boy. Fact is, until just this week we didn't know what they were . . . or where they came from."

"You're going to kill us?" asked Kirk, though it sounded more a statement of fact.

"Smart as you are, I should think you wouldn't have to ask."

"What about the package? I mailed it to myself. The return address, after thirty days, is to a friend of mine in the Senate."

Gerlach held up a bundle. The paper had been torn off, but Kirk recognized it. His heart sank.

"You mean this? We tracked it down about an hour after you left it off at the flight service station in Wyoming.

It didn't even cost us very much to buy it from the fuel handler."

Gerlach's smile was savage, gray, and dirty, exposing yellow teeth.

Kirk looked at PJ.

To PJ, this was the worst news of all. She had resigned herself to death a hundred times since being captured. She had wished it. Life was worthless without Mark. But she had always held out a faint hope that the research logs might be used to bring down The Corporation, which had caused all the harm. Now she knew even that hope was gone. Now all she had to look forward to was death. And death would not be the victory it once seemed.

Gerlach held up a wrist and inspected his watch.

"Well, we'd love to chat, but we gotta be getting out of here. In about a minute the bars of your little cage will be sliding aside, and you will be introduced to your . . . cell mates in the larger cage. About ten minutes after that, the top of this mountain is going to blow you and them to hell." He showed them a remote control. "The place is wired," he said. "The jet crash . . . the chopper down . . . the Feds are going to be snooping all over the place when it turns out both were stolen. This . . . operation can't be compromised."

"Wait." Kirk was desperate. "Why Mark? Why the Michigan group?"

"No time. . . ." Gerlach hesitated and smirked viciously at PJ.

"The blackouts," PJ murmured. "Mark had blackouts. In the end, he was getting sicker and sicker. He would have died from those drug experiments if . . ."

Gerlach's face shrugged. He laughed a vicious laugh.

"You'll never know the whole story," he said. "Lady, you don't want to know. Now. Enough of the parlor mystery shit," he growled. "We got a flight to catch."

The receding sound of footsteps left them alone with the smell and the threatening forms lurking in the shadows at the edges of the room.

PJ was weeping softly. It was not so much crying as the simple emotion-draining flow of tears. She was not angry or frightened. She was just defeated. She hugged herself and sat against the wall, staring ahead, waiting.

Kirk laughed suddenly, harshly. It was a humorless, bitter laugh.

PJ looked up at him as he paced from the door to the outside to the bars.

"Are you crazy?" she asked.

"No." He smiled wildly at her. "But I just had one hell of a crazy thought."

She cocked her head and waited for a revelation of his insanity.

"Stand up," he ordered. "Are you still hurt too badly to move, to run, to put up a fight . . . to fly?"

"What? Kirk . . ."

"Call me Grayson. *SHE* . . . used to call me Kirk."

"Grayson . . ."

"Quickly. We may not have much time. Get on your feet and loosen up. Well, we may have all the time in the world—the rest of our lives—but there is *one* chance."

"Come *on*, Grayson." She sounded out of hope. But she did stand up and limp around the cage.

"Listen, PJ. This is the only chance in the world for us. They may have a pilot in the barracks or they may not. If they do, we're dead. But I'm the guy who flew that Kiowa up here. And you may be the only other live pilot on Judith Peak—the other guy is hopelessly dead. We'll know in a minute or two. If they don't come, we can't do anything about it. But if they do, we'd better be ready to be very much damn smarter than they are."

Kirk stood at the door listening. A minute had elapsed. No footsteps in the hall outside. He couldn't hear a helicopter outside, but then he couldn't hear the whistling of the driving wind out there either. He turned and shrugged to PJ. He'd been wrong. Not the first time. But quite possibly the last.

His shrug said it all.

But before PJ could answer either with words or body language, they heard the whine of an electric motor.

Kirk looked up at the ceiling.

He saw the metal linkage snap taut, heard the clanking.

The whole front wall of the cage began to move, sliding to the side on overhead tracks, exposing them to the rest of the room, to the figures there in the darkness.

For the longest time after the door stopped sliding and the motor's hum died, there was no sound at all except their nervous, halting breathing.

Then came the padding and shuffling of feet, the scratching of claws on concrete.

PJ and Kirk stepped together, pressing side to side, slipping an arm around each other's waist.

Three beasts padded into the glow of the light, one an awesome albino, heavier and more savage-looking than the other two. There was no fight left in Kirk or PJ. There was awe, fright, perhaps resignation. But no fight. It was going to be over.

Kirk stared in wonder.

He saw the long fur, the smashed foreheads, elongated muzzles. He recognized these as members of the same species that had killed Major General Harry X. Ford at

Fort Benjamin Harrison. It had taken a whole clip of .45 rounds to finish that one. What chance did they have with bare hands against three?

So. These were the legendary Bigfoot monsters. He'd heard of them, seen paintings that looked like poor fakes of monsters. But here they were, the Sasquatch in the flesh and fur.

Why in hell's name had The Corporation gone to the trouble of searching the northern woods and southern bayous to round up such things?

He arrived at no answer to his question.

There wasn't time.

For the curious stares in the animal faces turned to glares. Then the volume in the room was turned up as first one, then the others, began to growl. The albino brandished a paw tipped with dagger claws. The rest followed suit. The albino then exhibited his teeth. So did the others, their breaths hissing a foul stench across the ten feet that separated humans from beasts.

Kirk and PJ had stood their ground, as if each had chosen a spot on earth to die. But the smell of the collective breath set them back a step. They kept sidling back until their backs pressed against the door.

They hugged each other now.

"Any last words?" said Kirk.

"Huh?" She broke her gaze from the apparition to see if his face showed that his mind had snapped.

He looked into her eyes. "I'm hung up on last words. I had two chances at them before and I said . . . I said curse words . . . I said the F-word."

She giggled, not humorously but hysterically.

"I want to say some new last words," he said.

"You're certifiable."

"That's not good," he said. "Try again. My last words are I love you."

"You can't."

"I know. But I want to say something nice for a change." He hugged her. "I love you, PJ."

"You're nuts," she whimpered. She clutched him tighter. "I love you too," she sobbed, and she began crying silently.

They held each other and prepared to die incongruously, impossibly in love with the idea of being in love.

The monsters now stood on the tracks at the spot where the wall of bars had slid away. They hesitated. Then the first one stepped across the threshold. The others followed.

The next sound, when it came, was a hiss.

Kirk and PJ looked left.

There was a fourth beast, whose fur was dark, patchy, and bloody. They had not seen it before; wouldn't have seen it if it had not staggered out of the near shadows and lurched toward the trio of beasts.

They backed away from the inner cell.

The fourth beast brandished claws and hissed again. The others took another step toward the darkness.

Kirk looked at PJ.

The injured beast moved into the inner cage with them and turned.

Kirk studied its back.

It had a huge seeping scab on the back of its neck. The wound drew the neck muscles tight on one side and pulled the right shoulder up higher than the left.

And its ear had been damaged—a crescent had been cut into one ragged edge.

The beast turned.

Its chest had been operated on. Clearly, the fur had

been shaved down to bristles and the staples holding the breast together still were embedded in the chest.

The eyes.

The pained, bloodshot eyes were gray.

PJ moaned, then began sobbing anew.

Those eyes, those pitiful eyes.

Kirk stood watching, frozen. He didn't know what would come next. Whatever it was, he would not be the one to initiate it.

PJ whimpered in horror, "Mark."

Startled, Kirk said, "What?"

She had no time to respond.

At the edge of the darkness, the three beasts started growling, edging back toward the inner cage.

The wounded beast crouched and hissed back.

But they were no longer to be cowed. They advanced on the open cage.

Suddenly, the fourth beast attacked the others, lunging haphazardly, slashing ineffectually.

The din rose to ear-shattering levels with the growling and shrieking of the animals.

Hardly a battle.

The wounded beast was wounded yet again, bitten and slashed until it dropped. The others stood back a second from the bloody mess they had made.

PJ stepped toward it.

Kirk grabbed her arm and tugged her back.

But the wounded beast was not finished. It struggled to its feet and dragged itself between the humans and the other beasts.

The others brandished teeth and claws and moved in for the kill.

The wounded beast crouched for a last lunge.

Then, in the distance, that electric motor started up.

The linkage clanked taut again and the cell door began to slide shut on its track.

"They're coming back for a pilot," whispered Kirk.

PJ clung harder to him. She was trembling, anguished.

Two of the beasts realized what was happening—they backed away. The aggressive albino attacked. While the others stared in awe at the sliding wall of bars, it leapt to the shrinking opening.

The wounded beast lunged for the same spot from the opposite direction.

They met in a clash of roars. The collision's force threw the weaker animal back into the enclosure, and the albino attacker roared triumphantly, sticking its head out and bellowing.

Until the bars of the gate closed on its neck and kept closing. The shriek died into a whistle, then a hiss, then a gurgle. The neck snapped.

The remaining two beasts attacked the dead carcass triumphantly, ripping it into shreds of flesh and dirty white hide.

PJ buried her head into Kirk's chest.

Kirk watched the wounded beast lying against the closed cell door at their feet. There was barely a movement in the chest. A pool of blood leaked from the spot where the staples had been torn loose, and the pool began to spread across the tile like a tiny scarlet tide. It had saved their lives. Now it lay dying.

"Mark," PJ whispered.

"PJ," Kirk barked. "What the hell. . . ."

The square access port in the door opened, and Gerlach's swollen, angry face appeared. Savage, expectant eyes surveyed the damage and brightened when they saw the pair of pilots still standing unbloodied.

"Larson," he snarled. "Come out here."

She looked at Kirk. "No," she said weakly.

"With a little conviction," whispered Kirk.

"No," she repeated, but hardly louder.

He saw she had been stunned by all the gore in this cell. He hoped she could tough this out.

"You. Kirk, get your ass out of that cage."

"No. We'll both go, but neither of us will go alone."

"I'll kill the woman if you don't come, Kirk, you asshole."

Kirk looked at her and shook his head. Don't go to pieces on me now, PJ, he pleaded with his eyes.

Gerlach tried her again. "Larson. . . ."

She stared at the beast and reached out to pat it, then anger snapped the sadness from her face as she whirled on Gerlach.

"My name is Payne, you bastard. Mark Payne was my husband. You may threaten to kill Kirk—and you may actually do it. But I'll never fly you alone—unless it's into the side of this godforsaken mountain. It's both of us or neither of us."

Kirk hugged her hard.

She winced, her wounds still hurting.

The port slammed shut.

Kirk looked at PJ and smiled.

"We've got them," he murmured.

There was cursing and arguing outside.

"How can you be sure?"

He smiled as the access port opened and Gerlach's angry, dirty face showed. He cursed them through the opening. Then the door lock snapped and the latch opened.

When the door swung open, Kirk saw two pistols. Ger-

lach waved the barrel of his short-barrel .357 magnum
impatiently.

"Get moving," he commanded. "Get out of that cage
before that . . . thing . . ."

PJ responded by leaning toward the opening. But Kirk
held her back.

"Give us one of your guns."

Gerlach and Gail Barnaby laughed at once.

"I'm not kidding. The only thing we have going for us
is a standoff. Once we land at the base of this mountain,
or whatever, we'll lose that. Give us a pistol so we can
maintain the status quo. You can keep your gun."

"Fuck you."

Kirk shrugged. He reached out and tugged on the steel
door to shut them out again.

But before it could close, Gerlach slammed a shoulder
into it and motioned for Barnaby to give up her 9-milli-
meter to them. Reluctantly, she did.

Kirk stuffed the pistol into his belt, offering no threats.
For the moment, he knew he was completely in command
of The Corporation and would remain so until they got
off this mountain. Time enough to worry about that part
later.

He and PJ stepped into the hallway.

Gerlach shut the door and brandished his pistol in one
hand, the remote firing device in the other—the last bit of
power at his command.

"Let's get the fuck out of here," he ordered.

PJ turned. Barnaby turned. Kirk started to turn.

But for Gerlach there was no getting out.

He never saw it coming, never sensed the hairy arm
coming through the access window in the door until the
paw closed on his throat.

Kirk saw it, but his own throat froze on the warning he

might have shouted. Even if he had shouted, it would have been too late.

The hairy arm was already drenched in its own blood, but the daggers at the tips of the fingers punctured the throat of The Corporation's chairman and sprinkled the hallway with blood.

First the .357 bounced on the floor, then the detonator.

Kirk winced, as if expecting an explosion.

Gail leapt for the gun.

Kirk's reaction came absolutely without reservation or chauvinism. He caught her in the face with a roundhouse right hook. The blow knocked her on her butt. She sat there with a surprised, hurt expression on her reddening face. She'd always been able to gain a second's advantage because of her womanhood. But not this time. This time, she'd hardened Kirk with her vengeful speeches. He'd not spare her an instant's hesitation again. He'd slugged her with the full intention of hurting her, of smashing that mean porcelain face. Keeping his eyes on her, he picked up the detonator.

Gerlach's expression was one of surprise, then agony. His body was slammed back against the door by the enormous strength in that arm. A second paw came out and closed on the face. Gerlach's pocked and scarred complexion was suddenly even more damaged. The first paw shifted from neck to a higher grip and pulled, tearing the very face off the writhing, struggling body of Rodney Gerlach.

The beast's arms disappeared into the access port.

Gerlach's head followed, lifting his feet from the floor.

There was a horrible wrenching and the body jerked stiff, nearly horizontal. In the distance, bones snapped.

Gerlach went limp. Then he fell into the hallway.

That is, all of him but his head fell into the hallway.

He lay there, his legs twitching, his blood gushing.

The gray eyes appeared with the face of the beast in the access port of the doorway. Then the eyes glazed over and the face fell away.

PJ sobbed. "Finally," she whispered. "Finally Mark has his revenge."

The stunned Kirk suddenly realized he'd been avenged too.

Again Barnaby went for the pistol on the floor.

Kirk stepped up and kicked her hand away. He pointed the pistol at her face.

"You're a determined one, Connie. I guess now we have better than a standoff," he said.

She sniffed a trickle of blood back up her nose, then exhaled. But she was anything but defeated. "It's not Connie. I told you I finished her off that night in Texas. Gerlach and I laughed about it. You fell for a fake, Kirk. My name is Gail, Gail Barnaby. And you are a eunuch. You don't have the balls to use that gun, Kirk."

Ruthless. That was one of the essentials Pearson had told him about. If he didn't have that, it could get him killed.

Kirk imagined the bullet smashing the pretty, cocky face, knocking the smug look away. He saw a rationalization for his violence in his mental image of Jud's and Maggie's slit throats. All the deaths in these last long days, weeks—hell, years. She was a part of them. He could achieve revenge on behalf of all who deserved it with a pull of the trigger. He could finish her and earn his own revengeful satisfaction for the bedroom betrayal of him. For the actual betrayal. For leaving him to die in the maws of those beasts in that room.

Or he could just leave her here and blow the mountain away.

If he were ruthless enough.

But she was right.

He wasn't ruthless enough.

So he let his arm fall.

PJ touched him on the shoulder.

"Thank God."

"For what," he said absently.

"You still have your soul."

He knew she was right. Perhaps he *had* recovered his soul.

"We'd better go," she said.

"Where's that research log, Gail?" he asked.

"It's already in the helicopter," she snarled.

Kirk started down the hallway. PJ was beside him, step for step. Gail Barnaby stood rooted to the spot, a disappointed look on her face.

PJ whispered, "I think she would rather you killed her."

"Come on, Gail. I want you alive to explain a few things to my senator friend."

Barnaby sighed and followed.

They were in the helicopter, the engine whining in the start, Kirk sitting in the pilot's seat, the dead pilot lying fetal on the ground, the research log and remote control detonator resting on the copilot's seat.

Kirk snapped the throttle, and the Kiowa's internal fire roared to life. In seconds the blades would be up to speed and they could take off.

He glanced over his shoulder into the passenger compartment. PJ was pointing the pistol at Barnaby, who seemed sullen and angry, more the aggressor than the woman holding the gun.

Kirk hoped there would not be trouble. He doubted if

PJ could kill somebody in cold blood any more ruthlessly than he had been able to.

A cluster of guards had run from their quarters into the frigid night.

The blades had the rpm, and Kirk started pulling pitch.

The helicopter lifted off.

Kirk pulled more power and tipped the nose.

Suddenly the helicopter was being rocked.

He glanced over his shoulder and saw the women wrestling. The word occurred to him again. Ruthless. Now PJ was in danger again. If only . . . no—he wasn't about to start that again too.

Meanwhile, Gail was lying atop PJ, punching her. Kirk reached back and swung awkwardly with a fist. But he missed and smashed his knuckles against the door.

The Kiowa careened into the night sky, barely under control.

Kirk settled it down. He put it into a climb toward the east, downwind, the quickest way away.

In the back, they were now fighting over the pistol, all four hands clutching and scratching for it.

Kirk saw dark blood patches on PJ's chest where her wounds must have reopened.

Finally, with an extra effort, PJ wrested the gun away. She did not fire it, though. She opened the door to the passenger compartment and tossed it out into the night air.

Kirk took another swing at Barnaby and missed again.

Again the helicopter lurched wildly. Again he settled it down.

Barnaby threw a punch at PJ, which landed on the point of her chin. PJ went limp.

Now Kirk knew he was in a fix.

He kept turning his attention from the front, where he was flying, to the back, where he needed to defend himself.

But Barnaby avoided him. She moved to the far seat, climbing clumsily over the unconscious body of PJ.

Suddenly she lunged over the copilot's seat and grasped the cyclic with both hands. She was going to sacrifice them all—the ultimate patriotism. She was bent on taking everybody.

The Kiowa's nose flew up and the craft climbed wildly, threatening to fly over on its back.

Kirk shoved forward, but she had all the leverage.

So he swung the back of his left fist and smashed her nose. The blow snapped her head back, but Barnaby held on, blood gushing from her nose and mouth. She even began choking on the blood, but her death grip was taking them all into an impossible flight attitude, from which the Kiowa could never recover.

So Kirk smashed her again. This time, she let go and dropped into the back.

Kirk dropped the nose and regained control. He saw he had been in a sharp turn and had spun around to fly back over the mountain.

He started a turn to the west and dropped the collective so they could be in a descent if Barnaby tried another of her stunts. He kept looking back so she would not jump him or try hitting him in the head.

But when she came, it was back over the copilot's seat. Kirk was ready, both hands gripping the cyclic.

It was wasted effort.

She grabbed the research log and remote firing device. He lunged at her, yanking the cyclic over, but she was out of reach, spitting blood and curses.

She stumbled over PJ's body again and moved behind him.

He was flying crazily, trying to aim a blow or raise an elbow in defense for when her attack came.

But there was no attack.

She gave him a vicious, bloody, broken-toothed smile, her eyes burning with hatred and triumph.

She flipped a switch on the detonator. Then she mashed a pair of buttons on the remote control.

Her wild eyes lit up with the white flash that came from below.

Kirk looked down. The top of the mountain already had started to slide away, illuminated by fires and secondary explosions.

The mountain shuddered with more explosions. Fire escaped from cracks in the night below, and the buildings were burning and continuing to explode, even as they became part of the avalanche. Utter destruction had been the aim of so many charges—once again The Corporation had been thorough. He wondered how many people down there had known they were working atop a bomb.

He heard a shriek.

Gail screamed some obscenity at him. If she tried to push PJ . . .

But Gail made no such threat. She glowered at him, her face contorted with rage and hatred.

God, he'd once thought she was so beauti—

Then, a final obscenity bubbling out of her bleeding mouth, she threw herself and the research log out into the night. The chilly air-blast was brief—the wind shut the door again and held it, lightly flapping an inch or two on its hinges.

A stunned Kirk looked down at the fire below and saw a glimpse of her body falling toward the fiery avalanche.

Whether she'd done it out of loyalty to The Corporation or simply to spite him, Kirk did not know.

But she had done it.

And now he knew the true meaning of ruthless.

EPILOGUE

1

He landed back at the warm spring-fed pond to tend to PJ. The horseman and his wife had been out trying to catch a glimpse of the distant fire and explosions on Judith Peak. They invited the pilot and his bleeding companion in. They seemed eager to ask questions, but they did not.

Kirk tended PJ until she protested almost angrily.

She was deeply troubled, even after he called Washington and awakened his friend in the Senate. The senator told him he would want to have the whole story again—in writing—after Kirk turned himself in to the FBI. The senator would guarantee their safe passage to D.C. After that, only truth would be a defense for all the intrigue Kirk had been accused of.

Kirk had agreed. He promised a detailed story that could be corroborated by events. Reluctantly he promised to tell the story in secret session rather than to the press.

But PJ didn't seem salved by that marginally good news.

"What's wrong?" he asked.

"That monster," she said.

He gulped hard. He didn't want to talk about it. He knew what she was going to say. He had put together the facts in his own mind.

But she spoke anyhow—in a low voice to be sure, but firmly, with conviction.

"The one with the hole in the ear. It was Mark. I saw it in the gray eyes. They were his eyes. That's why he tried to save us from . . ."

"PJ. Never. Don't say it." Even as he spoke, he knew he could not deny that the first beast he had killed had the same blue eyes he'd seen in the photo of Bertrand.

"No, I know it. His ear was shot through by Beard. He suffered so much because he'd been mutating inside . . . they altered his body chemistry somehow . . . until . . . like some . . . werewolf or something . . . he . . ." She broke and cried.

He tried to comfort her, the only woman who'd ever heard him say he loved her—although he'd said it flippantly. She was now crying over the man she really loved.

And she would not be comforted. She began repeating herself.

"The drugs they gave him . . . first the blackouts . . . the headaches . . . then a metamorphosis into one of those . . ."

"It couldn't be," he said without conviction, adding in a hopeful whisper, "it just couldn't be." But Kirk knew. He remembered the basic-training photo. The blue eyes of Bertrand. That beast. The white-haired soldier in the photo. The albino beast. E. Gardner Jacobs had been in Payne's platoon too. Jacobs the soldier. Jacobs the cop-killer. And Jacobs the beast? Could it be?

He shook his head to erase the horror of those thoughts.

"PJ, we'll get even. For Mark's sake . . . and Ken's . . . and all the others. We'll bring the rest of those

guys down. We'll destroy this . . . this damned Corporation. Together. We can do it if we stick it out. The
two of us. For Mark."

She sniffed and raised her chin to show some of the
defiance he'd seen on Judith Peak.

"You'll help? You'd do that?"

He hugged her gently, and she nuzzled into his arms
for a second, seeking comfort. The she remembered
something and pulled away.

"For Mark," she said.

He nodded. "I promise."

She began weeping softly.

Suddenly Kirk needed fresh air.

2

Gates sat boldly at Gerlach's desk. He pushed his
spectacles up on his nose. On one side of the desk he'd
stacked the destruction certificates for eleven research
logs. The twelfth he didn't know about. He hoped it
had been destroyed in the fire and explosions atop
Judith Peak.

But on his left rested copy number eight of the log.

He'd kept it, faking a destruction certificate for
Gerlach's peace of mind. He'd read it. He liked it. This
genetic research had possibilities. Military applica-
tions.

He'd gotten orders from very high up. The word
was already out in the Senate that there'd be secret
hearings. Which meant as good as public hearings.

There'd be no successor appointed for Gerlach.

Gerlach would take the blame for everything. And

he, Gates, was to dismantle The Corporation. He'd see people reassigned, and files destroyed—the incinerators and shredders had been going full-time for days now.

When the mantle of secrecy lifted, the investigators would find a house swept clean.

Eventually, even the small staff of Gates would be reassigned, and he'd be left alone, maybe even out of a job.

Unless.

Unless he could parlay this genetic research into something in the two or three years it might take to dismantle The Corporation.

Maybe he could leverage this monster stuff into something useful.

Imagine.

Drugs that progressively changed the genetic makeup of a man until the changes reached a sort of critical mass, until in the space of a couple of days the body convulsed, metamorphosing into one of those . . . beasts.

How could that sort of power be harnessed? How could this black science be used in warfare? What could armies do when such technology was refined?

Time.

All he needed was a little time.

3

In the years since the 1960s, clandestine domestic drug tests have stopped—but periodically there have been reports of manlike beasts in the great forests of the South and of the Northwest.

The reports persist to this day.

The reports have given names to these beasts.

They are called Bigfoot . . . Sasquatch.

And they *are* beasts.

But they were not always.

In the beginning, God created man.
Now man has created
the ultimate living horror!